Quest of Hope

THE JOURNEY OF SOULS

SERIES

Quest of Hope

C.D. BAKER

RIVEROAK®
Good News in Fiction

COOK COMMUNICATIONS MINISTRIES
Colorado Springs, Colorado • Paris, Ontario
KINGSWAY COMMUNICATIONS LTD
Eastbourne, England

RiverOak® is an imprint of
Cook Communications Ministries, Colorado Springs, CO 80918
Cook Communications, Paris, Ontario
Kingsway Communications, Eastbourne, England

QUEST OF HOPE
© 2005 by C. D. Baker

First Printing, 2005
Printed in the United States of America
1 2 3 4 5 6 7 8 9 10 Printing/Year 09 08 07 06 05

**Published in association with the literary agency of
Alive Communications, 7680 Goddard Street, Ste. 200,
Colorado Springs, CO 80920**

ISBN: 1-589190114

*To those humbled souls seeking grace
to endure the pursuit of Truth*

*Editor's note: please find at the back of this book
powerful discussion questions for group or personal
study (Readers' Guide, p. 479), as well as a helpful
Glossary (p. 491) for clarification of terminology and
historical information.*

ACKNOWLEDGMENTS

I am happy to express my gratitude to my wife, Susan, and the wide circle of family and friends who have offered supportive criticism and encouragement. The tale that follows would be very different without their good sense! I would like to thank my agent, Lee Hough, and my skilled editor, Craig Bubeck, as well as the many other enthusiastic professionals at RiverOak who have given life to this project. My heartfelt appreciation is extended to those whose unselfish support made my work more fruitful and enjoyable: my dear friends and distant cousins in Weyer, Germany; my old friend, Henk Haak of the Netherlands, who was a great help in Stedingerland; Father Vincenzo Zinno of *S. Maria in Domnica* Church and Mr. Constante Bucci, the curator of the *Sancta Sanctorum,* in Rome for their patience and generous hospitality; Joseph and Elisabeth Christ who labored over difficult translations; draft-copy critics such as my son David, my father and stepmother Charles and Elizabeth; and friends Mrs. Karen Buck, the Rev. Matthew Colflesh, and Mr. Edward Englert. Finally, let me thank Dr. Stephen Meidahl, Mr. David McCarty, and the Rev. Dr. Rock Schuler who, among others, contributed a wealth of spiritual wisdom, without which this story would be meaningless.

INTRODUCTION

*T*he hushed forests of Northern Europe stood like whispering sentinels keeping watch over the fog that shrouded the folk of legends and dreams until the legions of Rome climbed the Alps and nibbled at the edges of *Germania*. In due time the armies of the caesars subdued the clans of fair-skinned migrants dwelling there and seized what treasures they could find. As with all great empires, however, the Romans did more than just take for themselves. They blessed these lands with law, language, systems of administration, and means of commerce. And when the glory of Rome was laid to ruin, these gifts were left behind as a monument to her might.

Then, beginning in the fifth century A.D., another army eyed the lands of Europe. Traveling the very roads the Romans built, a small but brave band of light-bearers brought hope to a continent now covered in darkness. These determined soldiers were the spiritual descendants of St. Patrick and bore names like Columcille, Brendan the Navigator, and Columbanus. Called the "White Martyrs," they sailed from the rugged shores of Celtic lands to bring the Gospel of Christ to the peoples of Europe.

The lasting influence of these Irish missionaries is immeasurable, for the peoples of Europe quickly cast aside their pagan gods and with them the terrors and bondage these gods imposed. No longer fearful of the earth, they plunged wheeled ploughs deep into the soil and built villages within the comforting shadow of stone monasteries. During this time of dramatic change, Christianity remained the common bond that connected the new order to the virtues of chivalry, courage, sacrifice, and loyalty. Submissive to the sovereigns of the land, devout men and women of sincere faith committed their lives to serving the needs of body and soul. It was the time known as the "Low Middle Ages."

Cultures, like individuals, are inherently sown with the seeds of their own change. Each system of man's genius is sprinkled with just enough flaws to germinate imperfection and, subsequently, discontent. It is no surprise, therefore, that a revolution of immense proportion occurred during the late eleventh and early twelfth centuries. Known as the Papal Revolution of Pope Gregory VII, it began with the twenty-seven theses of the *Dictatus Papae* issued in 1075. In political terms, the Revolution established the pope's absolute supremacy over temporal rulers. In so doing, he inadvertently created a new realm known as "Christendom." Under threat of eternal damnation, the rulers of Europe's many kingdoms submitted their autonomy to the Church and, in so doing, yielded their armies as vassals of the pope.

With the knights of Christendom now at his disposal, the pope could strike a meaningful blow against the expanding Islamic empire. In 1095 Pope Urban called for the First Crusade, and over the next century subsequent popes and their subservient kings waged a violent defense of Christendom. The consequential influence of the Crusades requires volumes. Suffice it to say that seeds of change in Europe were well watered by the blood of Christian and Moslem alike. Transportation improved and commerce was enlivened. Fairs and huge markets for trade were created, as were systems of credit, banking, and insurance. New agricultural methods so significantly impacted harvest yields that the population surged.

It is these "High Middle Ages" that is the setting for the following story. It was an amazing time, for it was then that modern languages began to take their shape and when music began to move away from monophonic chants to take polyphonic form. Epic poetry, such as the *Song of Roland*, was written, and Bernard de Ventador touched hearts with his romance literature. Architecture began to reflect the spirit of the changing culture as well. Churches were no longer built with the squat, fortress-like characteristics of the Romanesque style, but rather in the triumphal confidence of the Gothic as expressed in Notre Dame and the Canterbury Cathedral.

Unfortunately, it was also an age that was in dire need of further rescue. Life was unspeakably hard. Pestilence, hunger, and violence were a part of everyday life. The lowly serfs suffered the most. They could not marry without consent, own land, freely leave the manor to which they were bound, nor avoid the confusing and weighty obligation of taxes, tithes, duties, and fines that maintained their poverty. Lacking liberty, health, and learning, this great host of souls languished through short, miserable lives in timid expectation of God's imminent Judgment. Life was viewed as little more than preparation for death.

This story is a tale of common life in the Middle Ages. These ordinary events and seasons in the tiny village of Weyer, located in the very heart of Christendom,

embrace dyers and millers, reeves and yeomen, house-
wives and witches. It was these simple folk who served
their lords as the muscle and sinew of Western Civiliza-
tion. So, though you shall encounter knights and lords,
monks and merchants, it is the simple *Volk* with whom
you shall break bread.

Under the guiding light of Truth, history is one of our
greatest teachers. From the past we can learn much
about hatred, vengeance, and loss; and much about
love, forgiveness, and grace. It is wisdom that is the great
gift of history, and what wisdom teaches us is that Hope
is our faithful companion—even in the village of Weyer.

Veritas Regnare

The Order prowls the darkness, pressed and shadowed
By the millstone of its own craft,
And the groaning turn of seasons add but weight.
The lances of the stubborn sun are poised and sure,
But few precious beams do split the shadows.
And midst the chaff and dust and seeds a caterpillar
crawls ...
But butterflies fear to rise between the coils and clouds of
smoke.

The breeze turns tempest and roars against the smoke;
Its source and purpose fixed.
The faithful sun sows golden seeds upon an anxious heart.
And color, that most wondrous fruit of light,
Does claim its place of sacred blessing.
And midst new air a butterfly lifts from the grinder's floor,
If but to later pause within a somewhat brighter haze.

Book 1

Die Ordnung
(The Order)
1174 – 1206

Chapter 1

THE CODE

Brave Heinrich stood in the first line, nervous and unsure. He breathed quickly and gripped his weapon with fists squeezed white with fear. Behind him and to each side crowded the woollen horde of angry peasants. They chanted and cursed and raised their spears and axes in defiance of the ordered ranks of knights preparing to charge them once again. A long trumpet blasted and the earth began to shake.

Heinrich licked his dry lips and closed his eyes. A warm wind blew through his curly hair, and it felt good as it brushed across his stubbled face. Yearning only for peace, the simple man seemed always beset by strife and disharmony. He had spent his life offered to the bondage of things familiar, yet he was ever pursued by the disrupting purposes of something greater than himself. Persistent, patient, and persevering, Truth had labored to stir and prod, to urge and teach until, at last, the poor wretch might be freed to lift his eyes toward the light beyond his own dark world. Now he had been placed in the center of the greatest paradox of all his troubled years.

The mighty warhorses raged closer and closer like a furious tempest bearing down upon a helpless village. The thundering hooves filled Heinrich's ears with dread, but the man held shoulder to shoulder with his stouthearted comrades. Steely-eyed and bearing all the confidence of their *station, the knights crashed into the stubborn line of these lesser men.*

With a shout and a lunge, Heinrich entered the whirlwind. All around him swirled the blurred images of horse and knight, the flash of swords and the splatters of blood. The stench of butchered men and slaughtered beasts filled his nose and choked his lungs; his ears were crowded with the thuds and clangs of hammers and steel, the cries of men and the whinnies of stallions lurching about the mêlée. Heinrich jabbed his glaive this way and that, impaling whom he could and dodging others. The man fought well.

But somewhere in the fury Heinrich's world fell silent. He dropped to the ground gently and closed his eyes as if to sleep. It was then, it seemed, his spirit was lifted like a hawk on the wind far above the bloody plain. Higher and higher he climbed until he felt he was soaring and drifting in the sun's kind currents. There he sailed and fluttered free, like a butterfly on a summer's day. His weary heart was glad, and he sang with joy as the warmth of the merciful sun bathed his wounded soul. Calmed and steadied, he was touched by hope and returned to his struggle in the world of time.

ॐ

In the tiny village of Weyer, a young peasant woman gave birth to a son on the nineteenth day of January, in the Year of Grace 1174. The event was not uncommon, of course, and only a few bothered to give it the slightest pause, but the story of a life had begun, and it, like that of every other life, would not be common at all.

Two days later the mother carried her child out of the cold shadows of Weyer's dark stone church. The woman was pretty, though haggard, having the sunken eyes of one already wearied by life. As baby Heinrich turned his squinted face toward the warm rays of the winter's sun, she quickly raised her thin hand to shield the infant's eyes from the light.

"Too much sun 'tis never good for young eyes," grumbled the priest.

Berta nodded solemnly and drew her cloak around her newborn's chin. Her husband, Kurt, leaned close to his

Frau and wrapped a thick arm around her shoulders. They both thought this to be a good day, for a dip into icy water and the mumbled words of an old priest had pronounced their newborn's soul safe from the fires of hell.

Now certain of their child's eternal safety, Kurt and Berta could turn their hopes toward the lad's survival of things temporal. They could only wonder what events might shape Heinrich in the time he would be granted. In the two days since Berta's painful delivery both parents had surely grown close to the little one, and Kurt, of course, was quick to boast of his manhood in the siring of a son. Yet, they knew it would be wise to hold loosely to their affections, for bundlings were so very often laid to rest in sad, tiny graves. For this reason, the young mother, though content to lean against the solid frame of her broad-chested husband, now found deeper comfort in the Church's sure embrace.

Berta turned and addressed the priest dutifully. "You'd be welcome to our home by sext for a bit of mush and mead, father."

The old priest thought only of spending the remainder of this cold Sabbath day sleeping in front of his own good fire. There he'd be chewing salted-pork and white rolls, not grinding dark rye between his few remaining teeth or sucking mush from his fingers. "Nay, methinks m'old bones needs stay here on the hill. But blessings for the asking and God's best to your family."

Berta then spoke to her father-in-law who had just reached her side. "You'd still be coming for a bite?"

Jost, little Heinrich's wiry, outspoken, and overbearing grandfather, spread his arms wide and draped them around the shoulders of Kurt and Berta. "Aye! But of course, m'lady! Y've beer or mead on hand ... or a keg of cider perhaps?"

Berta's face darkened slightly. She did not approve of excess on the Sabbath, particularly excess in drink, and most especially if Kurt's family would be doing the drinking.

"*Ja, ja,*" interrupted Kurt. "We've no cider, but we've plenty of beer and mead for drinking!" He laughed. The eldest of four, he had long since learned that it was helpful to laugh when caught between his father and another.

Jost's leathered skin wrinkled with a smile. "Good, we'd be by at the bells ... ach, but now I've needs tend to some business."

Kurt watched his coarse, aging father bluster his way down the steps and then turned to his wife and gave her a wink. He knew that Berta was not pleased to host his family, but he was relieved she had risen to duty. He was equally proud that she had consented to allow his brothers and sister to stand as godparents. Kurt had learned to love his wife and was now happier than ever that his father had chosen her rather than that awful girl from the neighboring village of Oberbrechen. Berta was pleasing to his eye. He liked to tangle his fingers in her thick, cherry-red hair. He thought her eyes to be as blue as a sunny summer sky and her curves to be just ample enough to please. Her complexion was clear and she smelled better than most.

Berta pulled her hood close against her head and clutched it beneath her chin with one hand. "I do so try to give you a proper household, husband, one beyond gossip and pleasing to God. I needs keep us safe from evil."

Kurt shrugged, a bit annoyed by his wife's perpetual fears, then gently took her by the arm to descend the steps of the church hill. The pair followed the other peasants toward their simple hovels below until they all stopped to listen carefully to a faint but all too terrifying rumbling in the east. An eerie silence gripped the village and nothing could be heard other than the rush of wind—and the pounding of hooves! Then, as if commanded by a single voice, the peasants abruptly turned and surged back up the steps and toward the sanctuary of the church. Berta cried out and clutched her newborn tightly as her husband hurried them through a swarm of desperate neighbors.

Weyer's church had withstood the onslaught of both nature and man for nearly four hundred years. Men-at-arms might torch the thatch of a peasant's hovel and slay a child along a village path, but few would test grace by despoiling the house of God or spilling blood upon the glebe.

So, the poor *Volk* raced toward the arched doorway as

sounds of heavy horses thundered ever closer. The trusted bell, ever faithful to the sacred hours of each day, now clanged a frantic warning to urge the villagers on. The peasants poured through the low archway like an anxious funnel of tangled wool as their priest spread his hands over them. *"In nomine Patris, et Filii, et Spiritus Sancti ..."*

Kurt pressed his way into the straw-floored nave, secretly wishing for more than the Spirit's help, holy or not. "Come, Berta! Come by me!" He wished he might rather hear the sounds of their lord protector's knights galloping to their rescue than to have his ears filled with pleas to heaven. "Berta, here, by me ... come quick!"

Berta's eyes were round with fright; her brows arched high. "Nay ... husband, here!" she shouted. "We've needs to be by the holy altar ... here ... hurry!" Berta pushed through the crowd and crouched at the foot of Weyer's bronze-plated altar, clutching the earth with one hand and holding baby Heinrich tightly with the other. The earthen floor at the front of the nave had been sprinkled with sand from Palestine; sand that long ago had been soaked by the Savior's blood. It was a well-blessed place.

Kurt climbed through the mass of frightened serfs and wrapped his large body around his wife and child. The trio huddled together until the oak doors of the church were slammed shut and locked in place by a huge wooden cross-beam. The priest's tremulous voice seemed suddenly invigorated by the crisis, and its confident timbre quickly calmed the jittery throng. The thick walls of the damp church muffled the sound of the approaching horsemen, but watchmen at the small windows soon gave news of their arrival.

A column of armored knights had, indeed, entered the village by way of the road from Münster in the east and now paused at the base of the church hill. They milled about on steaming horses pawing impatiently at the frozen earth. Though dressed in chain mail and heavily armed, none seemed purposed toward pillage or rape. One watchman whispered that they seemed lost on their way to some other place. The priest was unsure; it was uncommon for knights

to be about their business in January. The harvest crops
were not stored in the villages except for what the peasants'
small barns might hold, and he was not aware of present
threats against the holdings of either the village's lord, the
abbot, or his hired protector and neighbor, Lord Hugo.

The priest opened the door slowly and stepped to the
edge of the churchyard wall to steal a peek. He stuck his
pointy nose into the cold air and studied the men carefully.
"Hmm. No torches, no drawn swords, no forays into the village. Would seem to be a pitiful lot of lost fools." He called
upon his instincts and stepped cautiously through the gate
to descend the hill. When he reached the bottom he ambled
to the nearest horseman and bowed. "Greetings! How may
I serve you?"

A red-faced knight leaned toward the priest and scowled.
His breath steamed into the cold air and he hissed impatiently through his frosted beard. "*Ja*, you can serve us!
We've been ordered to the keep at Betzdorf and methinks
m'sergeant's turned us wrong!"

The priest had no knowledge of Betzdorf and now oud
denly faced a dilemma. He could plainly see that the men
were agitated and he knew they could easily unleash their
frustrations on his flock. The anxious priest feared to
expose his ignorance, but also feared to point the soldiers
in the wrong direction. Confused and sweating, he whispered a desperate prayer and begged for a plain sign from
heaven. At that moment a black bird flew along the roadway in the direction of the village of Selters, to the south.
"Ah, yes, praise the Virgin," he muttered. He turned to the
knight. "Good soldier. Betzdorf be south by some distance.
Y'needs ride hard to this way," he pointed to his right, "first
westward through Oberbrechen, then south at the fork to
Selters and beyond. Methinks it to be a hard ride ... but my
prayers shall go with you."

The knight grumbled and swore an oath at his sergeant.
His horse snorted clouds of white vapor over the priest.
Spinning his mount, he hesitated for just a moment—a
long moment for the anxious cleric—then led his soldiers
quickly away.

The relieved priest fell to his knees and cried a prayer of thanksgiving for the sparing of his helpless sheep: *"Laudamus te, adoramus te, glorificamus te, gratias agimus tibi propter magnam gloriam tuam, Domine Deus!* We praise thee, we adore thee, we glorify thee, we give thee thanks for thy great glory, Lord God!"

The villagers crept out through the church door and descended the steps warily. Fearful eyes watched the road carefully and ears were yet cocked for the return of the warriors. But, before long, a nervous laughter broke the silence and, relieved, the families of Weyer hurried toward their smoky hearths. Kurt, Berta, and their round-faced child reached the bottom of the hill and crossed the road. Here they followed the well-worn footpath to their two-room hovel located near the village center.

Kurt's hut was little more than two years old and still smelled faintly of fresh thatch and clay. He boasted it would be a three-generation house, not merely serving one like so many others. "When our lad weds, it'll yet stand, and for his lads after that!" Instead of simply sinking posts into the earth, he had dug a deep foundation that he lined with large rocks. Posts were then stood every rod or so and tightly packed with stones and gravel.

The walls of the hut were not unlike the others of the village. They were covered inside and out with wattle and daub—woven wands of oak or willow smeared with a mixture of mud and straw. Kurt was pleased to have a two-room dwelling; a large common room about three rods square, and a smaller room for a private sleeping area. The roof was about two rods tall at the peak, sound and covered to a generous depth with good thatch. Built with a design becoming ever more popular, it rested on long, collared rafters instead of a clutter of interior posts.

In keeping with her duty and despite her soreness and fatigue, Berta began the preparation of the day's meal. She planned to surprise her guests with wheat rolls and beer that she had bartered with the monastery's kitchener. The expensive wheat had cost her a double quantity of her best rye loaves plus two ells of spun wool, but this was the day of

Heinrich's salvation, and she was pleased to pay the monk his due.

Kurt heaped a generous supply of wood onto the floor-hearth that was set in the exact center of the common room. He watched as sparks flew around the iron kettles suspended over the flames, and he followed their ascent to the small mouth of the smoke-hole. Suddenly, the door burst open and a cold blast of wind chased a loud tumble of homespun and fur into the room. Kurt laughed and turned to greet his family cheerfully. "*Ja, ja*, welcome! Now every-one, first to the fire and a tankard of beer! We've needs be glad-hearted for our good fortune this day. Ha! Let them burn Selters! We've no fires to quench and none to bury, no loss of barns or beasts!"

As the family crowded around the fire, Berta carefully ladled dark amber beer into the circle of wooden tankards now waving impatiently toward her. The first served was Jost, the patriarch. He, too, had been eighteen when his own firstborn, Kurt, was baptized. A steely, shrewd, vindic-tive man, Jost was more able than most to climb and claw his way about the world.

To Jost's right stood his second born, Baldric, his favored son and the pride of his life. Baldric was about a year younger than Kurt and very different from his brother, indeed. He was hard-hearted, blustery, and ambitious. A barrel-chested, brutish, heavy-limbed young man of seventeen, he swaggered about the village daring any to challenge him. He stood a head taller than most men and could crush the whole of a large apple in his hand. His brown hair curled atop a broad head, and his dark blue eyes were set narrowly, giving him the look of an angry bear.

To Jost's left stood Arnold, the third born. Almost two years younger than Kurt, he was broad-shouldered and lean, dark-eyed, and cunning. Though only sixteen, he suf-fered the weight of life like a cantankerous village elder. Brooding, covetous, and mean-spirited, Arnold spent each waking moment calculating a way out of his position as a cart-hauler for the monks. Most thought he should be grateful for his good fortune, but he was one who sought the greatest gain for the least possible effort. His ability to avoid the labor of the fields was renowned and some claimed they had never seen a single bead of sweat drip from his furrowed brow. The youth's chief pleasure was eavesdropping on the manor, for he had become a gatherer of whispers and a merchant of secrets.

"No spills," pleaded Berta. "Kurt worked a long day to buy this from the monks." She served the men, then turned to Sieghild, Jost's fourth born and Kurt's only sister. At fourteen, Sieghild was blonde and fair skinned, lanky and plain, a bit stubborn, like her father, but also compassionate like her deceased mother. Normally quiet and reserved, at times she was overcome by fits of fury that the village women murmured were nothing less than possessions by devils.

"You ... girl," grunted Jost. "You'll not be drinking more than a small share. We men 'ave claim to the next draught and we want plenty to go 'round." Jost looked with contempt at his daughter. "Nearly fifteen and no offers ... 'tis no wonder. Now, where's m'little Heinz? Let me give m'blessing to the little Christian!"

"Berta," warned Sieghild, "the last time he blessed an infant he passed wind in the poor girl's cradle!"

Berta immediately stepped between her father-in-law and the helpless infant sleeping peacefully in the straw-filled cradle. "Perhaps it'd be best that you be sticking only your face in there!"

The hovel roared with laughter.

"Well said!" boomed Baldric.

Jost shrugged innocently. "Ach, I was only about to put some good sense into the boy."

Berta grumbled beneath her breath and turned toward one of the iron kettles filled with steaming water and a basket of mixed grain. She began preparing her *Mus*—a porridge-like mush—by adding several fists of grain to the water along with a few pinches of precious salt. For the next quarter hour she stirred the thickening staple with a long, wooden spoon while the household chattered quietly.

Finally she handed the spoon to Sieghild and lifted her crying son from his cradle. "Kurt?" she called. "The blessing
for Heinrich?"

Kurt was bristling at some remark of Baldric when he
heard his wife's words. He nodded and took his son awkwardly into his calloused hands. "Aye," he answered. The
young father cleared his throat and took a deep breath. He
let it out slowly as the circle quieted. He held the suddenly
quiet, wide-eyed infant at arms' length. "Heinz—" Kurt
looked at his wife and remembered her dislike of nick-
names. "Heinrich of Weyer." He paused as he struggled to
remember the words he had rehearsed for weeks. Finally
he began. "Ah, *ja*. I've a good blessing for you, lad." He
cleared his throat, looked deeply into baby Heinrich's eyes,
and spoke clearly.

For this circle of kin I vow
To stand by you and humbly bow
To God above and blood below,
To join our hands against all foes.

I pray you courage and arms as steel,
A mind of wisdom, a heart that feels.
Though battles may find you, may each one be won,
Your eyes turned toward heaven and lit by the sun.

The room was silent. Kurt was not known for using words
well and the blessing had the ring of a poet. Baldric belched
and wiped a woollen sleeve across his face. "Ha! What kind
of talk was that?" He turned toward Arnold and guffawed,
"Sounds like the ramblings of a mad monk!"

Kurt handed Heinrich to Sieghild. "Just because you'd
be the family fool ..."

Baldric leapt to his feet and swung at Kurt, landing his
monstrous fist squarely on the young man's chin. Kurt
collapsed atop a mound of straw against the far wall.
Then, amidst the approving cheers and roars of Jost and
Arnold, Kurt climbed to his feet and charged Baldric, bellowing like a raging bull. Baldric was the size of a seasoned knight and tossed his older brother aside with

ease. Kurt, no easy prey for most, crashed against the trestle table, upsetting Berta's wheat rolls and honey. Baldric seized Kurt by the throat as he raised his hands for quarter. Baldric had won every boyhood brawl, and this day would be no exception.

Berta shook her head as Sieghild tilted the table back to its legs and gathered the precious buns into the basket. She stared into the pot and grumbled a few oaths, then asked Sieghild to fetch more water from the nearby village well. A good mush was bubbling, and two scrawny chickens were waiting to be boiled in another pot, now steaming. The woman looked wearily around the room and, content all was now restored to calm, turned toward her husband. "You might reach out the door for a bit of snow and put it on that swelling face of yours." Kurt grumbled and nodded but was soon laughing again with his brothers.

For the next hour the two women huddled together in conversation, stirring the mush and sinking the chickens, trying their best to ignore the men. So, despite the blustery, cold winds of January that bent the smoky columns atop Weyer's rooftops, the house of Kurt was returned to proper order.

By the bells of nones the household had sucked the last bit of meat from both birds and fingered the mush bowl clean. It was a good mush, a stout and hearty blend of boiled barley and rye. The wheat rolls had brought a roar of approval from all gathered, and the taste of sweet honey on that bitter day was likened to a gift from the Holy Virgin herself.

Outside, the sky was a heavy gray and darkening as the day aged. Inside, Kurt kept the fire blazing and now cradled his newborn in his strong arms. Berta sat with Sieghild on one side of the hearth while the men lounged about the straw-strewn floor atop their woollen cloaks and furs.

At last, Jost stood to his feet and stretched. After shaking the straw from his hood he ceremoniously reached into his leather satchel hanging on a peg and withdrew a mysterious parchment scroll. "Afore I present this, I've needs to speak of some things." Jost the Shepherd was not a tall man, nor strong-built, but his resonant voice and imposing eyes commanded the unwavering attention of all. He looked into each face carefully and then began to speak.

"All here be kin. I've a half-hide of land, as y'know. Now, a half-hide's not enough to earn a man's freedom, but 'tis more than the cotters can claim and more than what I had when I was but a shepherd." He paused a moment, suddenly picturing in his mind's eye his late wife and their difficult years spent in drafty, one-room huts on the outskirts of nearby Villmar. He could see himself walking over the endless pastures of the Lahn valley as the monks' shepherd. He remembered the few pennies they had always kept in a wooden bowl, never as many as a shilling at a time and barely enough to pay the taxes they owed.

Jost returned from his musings and continued. "Hear my wheezing chest? Not the sounds of a man likely to see Lammas. Methinks I am near m'grave. No matter. It is time to leave behind what I can; a few thoughts and a promise. Lads, look to me hard in the eyes! There'd be two things not to forget once I'm gone and you needs teach the little one. Your lives need rest on these two things and these alone: the code and the cause.

"First, cursed be any who shames this family by breaking the code of m'father, Thonges. I've taught you the way before, but I say it again, plainly: hate sloth, steal naught, keep a pledge. 'Tis simple enough."

Jost stopped to let his words settle and took a long draught of beer. Baldric nodded to his father. He liked to work and had no urge to scrump; he had made no vows. He was suddenly relieved, as are all who imagine the way of salvation so well within their gifts.

Sieghild offered timidly, "*Vater*, the priest says some different."

Kurt groaned, but he recognized the courage in his sister's challenge—for true valor is in proportion to fear, and the poor girl was terrified.

Jost's face tightened like wet deerskin in the summer's sun but he allowed her to speak.

Sieghild began. "The father says we've to keep the rules of the Holy Church. He says the Church has its place, the men-of-arms have theirs, and we have ours. We needs keep the order of things right. Our place is to be kept without questions and other contempts. We ought 'seek truth only through the Holy Church and protection but through our rightful lords.' He says the end of the world is at hand, that Judgment is close and the world needs to be fit and ready. He says we've a code of ten commandments to live by ... not three." Her voice faded to a fearful whisper.

Jost bristled but found himself on precarious ground. He, too, feared the Judgment to come so he thought carefully before he answered. "*Ja, ja,* follow the bells and chants, heed the mumbles of the churchmen as y'wish, but never, never stray from the family code. Ach, I know The Commandments, but they are ten ways to say the same as what we say in three! Now, enough of this."

Sieghild took her seat and the circle grew quiet once more. Jost took Heinrich from his mother and held him at arm's length. "You've a good code to follow, boy, and also a worthy cause."

Berta moved to protest, but Kurt silenced her with a stare.

"It is our duty to avenge the wrongs we have suffered at the hand of Gunnar's kin." Jost looked hard at the child. "This next generation shall not fail its duty. The day my mother was savaged by Gunnar of Arfurt we were bound to her revenge as sure as our ancestors bound us to these lands. That ancient oath of vengeance still stands, as does ours!

"The whole realm knows Gunnar kin to be thieves of sheep and cattle, witches and worshipers of the old gods. They cast spells and hexes and dance naked in the night ... I've seen these things. For their crimes they've lost little more than a barn of grain, a hut or two, and but one small child. Our cause is this: we live to avenge, without quarter and without fear."

Jost paused. Satisfied his point had been made, he relaxed and a smile lifted the corners of his lips. "Now, one

more thing 'fore I leave for m'bed! Hear me, 'tis important."
He turned to Arnold. "You, boy, have y'not wondered why
you are spared the plough?"

Arnold shrugged nonchalantly.

"And you, Baldric, why is it you are the woodward's
helper? When I was your age I was shearing wool and
tending the demesne on boon-labors! You! Ach ... you
spend your summers in the shade of tall oak whilst others
sweat.

"Not a single one of you half-wits has thought to ask why
I am now a carpenter's helper instead of a miserable shepherd like my father. Well, 'tis a reason for these things. It is
enough to say that a few years back I caught the abbey's
prior and Runkel's steward cheating with the tax scales. I
made short work of them! I found a good monk to be my witness, then I marched to the abbot. Well, you should've seen
the two squirm. In an hour I had a pledge to buy m'silence,
but I was not bought cheaply!

"The abbot thought it best to muzzle me with some
sweets. Kurt and I were released from duties as shepherds
to earn a better wage with the carpenters, and I was given
land that I can pass to the next. 'Tis how we've our half-
hide."

"*Ja?* You say 'our' half-hide but it will pass to Kurt,"
griped Baldric.

"The new way is for the eldest to get all and I so pledged.
But 'tis Kurt, not you, who ploughs, scythes, and threshes,
and he'll pay the tax. There'll be no more talk of it."

Jost laid his hand on Baldric's shoulder. "But hear me,
lad. This is the way that I saved you from the sheep herds
and set you into the forest that you love. And when the old
woodward is dead you are to be the next." He turned to
Arnold. "And you shall be forester in time!"

Arnold smirked and nudged Baldric. The two, in alliance, could work the trees to give them more than shade.

Jost raised the parchment high. "The abbot vowed
another thing and sealed it under God on this scroll. He
pledged that my eldest son's grandsons would be instructed in the abbey school. This means if Heinrich sires

sons they shall sit under the monks' lindens and learn of things that might yet set their families free!" He handed the parchment over to Kurt who stared at it in disbelief.

Ignoring the shadowed scowls of his brothers he embraced his father and exclaimed, "Such a miracle does bring hope to life!"

The hovel became quiet. Arnold and Baldric settled in a corner grumbling and whispering together. Soon enough, the family tired. The night had grown long and it was time to bid farewell. Jost and Sieghild left first with a few words of thanks. Baldric and Arnold hung their hooded, fur cloaks atop their shoulders, and when the door shut and Jost was beyond hearing, Baldric turned toward Kurt. Speaking from the dark recesses of his hood he said, "M'thanks for the meal, brother. Good fortune with little Heinz and his special gift." He pulled Kurt close to his face and then growled, "You and your brood are favored, 'tis surely unjust!"

Wisely, Kurt said nothing. Arnold flung open the door and a blast of frigid air rushed in, sweeping sparks and glowing ashes across the straw floor. With a few grunts and angry growls the unhappy guests stepped into a fresh falling snow and hurried away along the footpaths of Weyer.

Chapter 2

SAINTS AND SINNERS

he patient village bore the cold of yet another winter upon its snow-laden shoulders. Ever faithful to the sure and steady passage of time, it served with other things certain: the sun, the moon and stars, the labors of the wind, the habits of beasts, and the ways of men. The land lay silent beneath the snow, awaiting the appointed time to once again yield its fertile bosom to the plough and pick of weary, calloused hands.

Weyer was an ancient community, settled in the shadows of the distant past by wandering Celts and Frankish tribesmen. Lubentius of Trier, a faithful monk who brought the first light of Christianity to the smoky village, had long since chased its pagan gods into the dark forests. Then, in the Year of Grace 790, Charlemagne granted the monks of distant Prüm a large, triangular manor of land marked at its easternmost point by the tiny village. Those monks soon established a new cloister to shepherd the land and its peasant folk.

A soaring hawk would see the haphazard collection of cottages, sheds, barns, and workshops that lay in a narrow flat of land between a stream to the southeast and a slope to the northwest. A clear-flowing stream, the Laubusbach, ambled past Weyer and the nearby village of Oberbrechen, eventually joining the Lahn River at the opposite boundary of the monks' manorlands. The opposing slope rose rather steeply to form a long ridge, broken by a protruding knoll, atop of which stood the church.

The main road led into the village from the southwest and forked at the base of the church hill. One side bent to the right around the village and led eastward away from the monks' lands into another lord's manor and the village of Münster. The other bent left and headed northwest, over the ridge and through the heart of the abbey's lands to a monastery alongside the village of Villmar.

Little more than an hour's tramp from Weyer, Villmar was equally ancient and sat peacefully along the northern boundary of the abbey's manorlands. A small cloister of Prüm's monks settled there, but soon the see of Mainz took control. In 1165, with additional grants of land from Emperor Friederich Barbarossa, the Benedictine monastery became residence to an abbot, making it the Abbey of Villmar—a fledgling manor of some thirteen thousand hectares and eight villages, including Weyer, with approximately three thousand land-bound residents and a handful of free yeomen.

Wise to the ways of a dangerous world, the Archbishop of Mainz had insisted that his abbot in Villmar negotiate an alliance with the lord of the nearby castle of Runkel. For generations, Runkel's lords ruled vast holdings of lands adjoining Villmar's manor and maintained alliances with others. The decision to hire them as the abbey's protectors had proven to be a shrewd choice.

Forested with beech and oak, pungent spruce and pine, sweet linden and ash, the soil of the abbey's manor yielded generously, though stubbornly, to the plough, and its virile streams could turn the abbot's new mills with ease. The region quickly became known as the "Golden Ground," for it was rich and ripe and profitable. The simple villagers of these manorlands served dutifully, submitting to the seasons and the order of things as they supplied stores of wool, mutton, hides, timber, slate, fruits, grains, and pork to the abbot who ruled them for the good of all.

Perhaps this ground was golden for some, but it was not easy land for the folk born and bound to it. It seemed oft to yield as much stone as grain, and while stone might make a fitting church, it weighs heavily upon the faith of the ploughman. And such labors were not all that bore upon these simple folk. Beset by storm and famine, pestilence and plague, the quick-forgotten souls who filled the abbey's villages had little choice but to yield themselves to their pitiful place and time. For them the world was but shadows and eventide. And they, like their sluggish oxen, dared not turn against the yoke. Most of these poor and weary wretches spent their days with faces bent toward the earth, ever pressing their aching legs against hard-won furrows. Fenced by fear of both life and death, they dared hope for little else than a secure soul and a few moments of joy before they were returned to darkness just beneath the very earth they sweated and bled upon.

⁊

The despair of winter had taken full hold of Weyer by late February of 1174. Baldric blustered about the forests as the woodward's helper, seeing to the foresters' harvest of winter timber, keeping a close watch on crews of charcoalers, and giving special heed to poachers culling deer and wolf and fox from his master's lands.

In this frozen month Baldric was to be wed to a young woman named Hildrun whom his father Jost had chosen a year earlier in exchange for the forgiveness of a debt. Baldric reluctantly pledged her a fair dowry of two shillings, a small gold broach, two rams, and six ewes. Should Baldric die, it would secure her until another husband could be found.

Weyer's priest had urged Jost to delay the wedding. After all, it was the Season of Lent and the carnal pleasures of marriage were thought unseemly for this time of denial. But Jost, conscious of his own mortality and not wanting to lose his bargain through delay, ignored the priest's counsel. So, on a cold winter's morning in late February, Baldric of Weyer and Hildrun of Villmar were wed within a circle of their kin in the snow by the village well. Given the priest's objections, none dared stand in the doorway of the church according to the new custom. In fact, the priest was asked not to attend and he was happy to oblige. Instead, as in former times, Jost and Hildrun's father heard the vows and pronounced the matrimony. Baldric then tread his foot upon his bride's and the deed was done—for better or for worse.

Baldric spent little time with his new wife. She was hard-eyed and stiff. He complained her face was too bony, and he cared little for her black hair. She suffered skin-scales and sores, her hips were narrow, and he doubted her ease of birthing.

For Baldric and Hildrun and all the folk of the manor, the labors of winter dragged on through the tedious days of March. Time was spent spinning wool and repairing barns, carving spoons and plaiting baskets. Willow and ash were purchased from the village forester for shaping into harrow teeth, and the smith forged spades and ploughshares. Early lambs were tendered to the sheepfold where ewes suckled them with care. The stores of harvest-time were dwindling, and all eagerly awaited the mercy of spring.

The joys of Easter came early, on the twenty-fourth day of March, and the village was soon busy wedding more of its vital youth. Among the betrothed was Arnold, recently contracted by Jost to Gisela, the daughter of a servile merchant from the free-town of Limburg-by-the-Lahn. She was known for her beauty and high spirit. Although pleased by her appearance, Arnold was yet tremulous at heart.

Spring labors passed quickly—as did summer's, and by mid-September Kurt had paid his penny for time on the thresher's floor where he pounded his flail late into the darkness. The sanguine joys of long, warm days and the feasts of Lammas and the Assumption were soon but pleasant memories. Kurt worked long hours with the sickle as well as shouldering carpenters' beams.

It was on a rainy evening in late September when Kurt's door was thrown open by his brothers and a stranger. The trio stared mutely until Baldric crossed the common room and laid a heavy hand on Kurt's shoulder. "Kurt, Leo's come to take us to father. He … he was found in the millstream with his head split apart. Leo thinks a mason's foot nudged loose a rock on the scaffold. Father was below."

Berta lovingly wrapped hers arms about her husband's shoulders and wept for him as tears rolled down his ruddy cheeks. Kurt said nothing but leaned into his wife's embrace like a small boy.

Arnold stood in front of the floor hearth and stared into its small fire. He was weary from months of hauling harvest goods over rutted roads. His father had kept order to their crowded hut and he knew things would now be different. He'd have to face his nagging Gisela without help and deal with Baldric's wife, Hildrun, as well. Hildrun was with child and growing more unbearable every day. He groaned and wished both mother and infant might soon join Jost.

Jost was buried in Weyer's churchyard on a warm afternoon. His life had been better than that of other shepherds. He had lived to dream more than many and had achieved more than most. His shrewdness had shaped a legacy that would reach beyond his own time, and, after all, what is ever left behind other than one's effect? Jost had often dreamt of his descendants toasting his good name, and he had spent his last days believing himself a good and worthy man.

The bereaved family huddled by the open grave. Their common sorrow found comfort in its sharing, and the grief of the circle was a healing balm. Kurt sighed and stroked Heinrich's ginger-colored hair. The little one was plump and pink, oblivious to the cause of tears on his father's face. Finally, Berta took her husband's hand and the family slowly turned away, leaving Jost behind.

October brought both beauty and additional melancholy. Sieghild moved into Kurt's hovel to escape the miseries of life with her other brothers. Then, as the oaks turned crimson and the beech released their golden leaves, part of Arnold's cursed wish bore true, for poor Hildrun woke one night in terror to find her newborn gasping for air. Less than a fortnight old, little Ida had been early and jaundiced. It was a long night of suffering and no finger-tastes of thyme could spell her coughs, nor sage-balm ease her fever. On All Hallows' morn Baldric watered the earth with a tear of his own. The tiny infant was washed and wrapped in a little shroud, then laid beside her grandfather in the shadow of the church.

౭

On the morning after All Souls' Day, just past the bells of terce, the monks in Villmar's abbey set their tasks aside and were gathering to pray. A black-hooded stranger peered through the cloister's jarred gate into the abbey grounds and waited impatiently for prayers to end. At his side stood a weary donkey laden with a humble assortment of baggage. Atop the haphazard collection of satchels and rolled blankets were tied a crude, three-legged stool, a well-wrapped table of some sort, and an iron candle stand.

The man was a wandering monk in desperate search of a community that might feed and house him, or even welcome him into their fellowship. Many such monks drifted the countryside and were usually viewed with suspicion if not contempt. These *gyrovoagi* were seen as an ever-increasing menace, gluttonous parasites consuming the good will and hospitality of their charitable brethren. In his day, St. Benedict viewed them with particular fury and prescribed a remedy in his Rule. This monk was not unaware of his likely predicament, but he hoped the parchment held tightly in his grip might open both gate and hearts.

Beside the brother and his exhausted beast stood a young woman and her infant of one year. Despite her fatigue and the dampness of the cold November morning, the woman smiled cheerfully and caressed the wisps of white hair blowing from under her baby's wrap. She wore a dark, hooded peasants' cloak that fell a bit short of her ankle-length gown, exposing a pair of good, black shoes. She turned her face toward the sun to feel its warmth against her round, pink cheeks. "Ah, and you, my precious Ingelbert, can you see the blue? Does the sun not touch your tender skin?" She hugged the little one. "Brother, you do have the letter?"

The man nodded.

"And you'd be sure they'd be a willing host?"

The man shrugged.

" 'Tis a good day for m'son and me."

The monk nodded.

"But I do hope they shall honor the archbishop's request. He made no demands for this and—"

"Oh ye of little faith."

"Ah, well there's oft truth in that for me. Methinks little Ingelbert is a good reminder of that." She sighed.

"Those who plough evil and those who sow trouble reap it." The monk stared at her with a quality of scorn that would bend most others' eyes to the ground.

Instead of cowering however, the stout woman turned her warm brown eyes directly into his. "Aye, 'tis so, indeed, Brother Martin, and it was so very kind of you to remind me."

Martin studied the woman. He noticed that her dress was common, but her face belied a quality of intelligence that had made him suspicious since they met in Mainz two days before. Brother Martin had been told nothing of her past, of her status, or of what purpose she now stood at this gate. He held his tongue and turned his back.

The greeter, a fresh-faced novice, opened the gate and welcomed the three. "*Deo gratias*, thanks be to God. Blessings, *frater*. How might I serve you?"

Martin stared at the boy and held a scroll just beyond the novice's reach. He remained mute and waited for the lad to calculate his duty. *Dolt*, he thought.

The nervous boy brightened. "Ah, you must be bound under a vow ... is it for silence?" he asked.

Martin rolled his eyes. *Pathetic fool!*

"Oh, what an unwise and sinful question!" the novice stammered. "Had you answered, I'd be guilty of your sin and I'd be an accessory to temptation!" He fell on his knees.

The woman chuckled. "Ah, good lad. Stand to your feet! Ha, ha! You've brought me a good laugh and y'needs never repent of that! What'd your name be?"

"Brother Oskar."

"Well, little brother, perhaps you ought fetch the porter."

The boy stood up and rushed away. In a few minutes he

returned, blushing and stuttering. Brother Egidius, the abbey's porter, was a bit shamefaced himself. The rule of his order required the porter to be a sensible man, not given to wanderings from his post. He thought a quick trot to the latrine after prayers would go unnoticed. "Thanks be to God, Brother. I'm told you'd be bound to a vow of silence?"

Martin shook his head. "I must speak only the words of Scripture or those of saints."

"Ah, I see," answered Egidius. "Perhaps I ought fetch the guest-master."

Martin shook his head again. "Many seek an audience with a ruler." He stared intently as if to drive some point into the man's mind. Egidius and Oskar looked at each other and scratched their heads.

"Forgive me, brothers," interjected the woman. "I am Emma of Quedlinburg and this is my son, Ingelbert. The archbishop's clerk sent this shaveling as my escort from Mainz with a message for your abbot. Methinks him a bit tiresome, but—"

"A fool's mouth is his undoing!" scolded Martin.

Egidius grunted and sent Oskar to find the prior. "Brother, remain outside the gate while I find you both a cool drink. I shan't be more than a moment." The porter lifted his habit and ran to the nearby kitchen. He rushed back with two tankards of beer.

"Let us be thankful, and so worship God," offered Martin.

"Aye, to Him all praises we give," muttered Egidius.

As the monks prayed, Emma drained her tankard and then graciously offered her thanks.

The porter smiled and set a tender hand on the infant. "Your child has no father?"

"Every child has a father," answered Emma.

"Ah, well said! I should have asked if he has a father to care for him."

Emma thought for a moment before answering. "None with the liberty to enjoy the lad's happy laughter, nor one free to hold him when he cries."

Egidius lifted the boy from his mother's arms and looked at him carefully. The baby's eyes were deep-set and blue, close together and not in proportion to one another nor rightly aligned along his little nose. The monk tilted the boy's face upward and took note of the child's chin. It was far too short, leaving the upper lip protruding severely over the lower. The boy's large ears sprouted unevenly from a sloping head and were bent forward toward his face. The monk said nothing but gently blew the boy's ghost-white hair and brushed the lad's pale white skin with a calloused finger. "Ah, a fine boy, Frau Emma, fine, indeed."

"Scrawny, very ugly, and lean," blurted Martin.

Egidius leaned close to the stranger and growled, "I don't like you, Brother Martin, and I think your vow is suspicious. You should know that I've done penance twice for beating the brethren!"

The prior appeared and interrupted the porter with his greeting. "Thanks be to God."

Egidius bowed to his superior. "Prior Paulus, we've a visiting brother with a letter from Mainz and a woman with some business as well."

Emma bowed. "The paper is about my business. This wanderer is but my poor escort, assigned to me by a well-meaning clerk."

Prior Paulus looked at the woman and her child and took the string-tied scroll from Martin's hand. He cracked open the wax seal and unrolled it. It contained a message from the archbishop regarding the year's plantings, taxes owed to Lord Hugo the protector, and the apportionment of the glebe harvest to the priests of the villages. He read further to find a list of repairs, tithes, dues, and hospitalities that the abbey might expect in the coming year. Toward the bottom a reference was made to the threats of a western lord and the likely gathering of Knights Templar to oppose him. At the very end was a brief statement regarding Emma: "Without known reason I am asked by your protector, Lord Hugo of Runkel, to provide this whore and her ill-formed bastard a shelter fit a woman of virtuous repute. She seems of high birth and I suspect her to be a despoiled nun. Receive her, but her cursed son is not to be an oblate; he is to suckle at the sinner's breast and bear the weight of his mother's scourge without benefit of alms."

Paulus rolled the yellowed scroll and turned to Martin. "Brother, I see nothing of regard to you."

Brother Martin folded his hands and kneeled. "When did we see you hungry and feed you, or thirsty and givest you something to drink? When did we see you a stranger and invite you in?"

Paulus was not impressed. "*Gyrovoagi*," he muttered. Yet charity was a virtue he had vowed and it could not be ignored. "Brother, we may either feed you and send you on your way, or offer you our fellowship as brethren. Your wish?"

"I wish to join you as your brother."

Paulus's face darkened. "I see. Then you must abide the difficult rules of joining our community. In keeping with the Rules of St. Benedict, you must remain outside of this gate for five days. At the ringing of each bell you shall entreat the porter for entry. You, Brother Egidius, must refuse him at each request."

"Aye. 'I rejoice in following thy statutes,'" the porter smirked.

"Then at compline of the fifth day you shall be allowed in, and you shall be brought to a novice's cell as a postulant, and there you shall dwell for one year. After this time has passed, you shall stand before the community in the oratory and take a vow of stability promising us your faithful presence until the Lord takes your soul. You shall vow obedience to our rule and prostrate yourself to each brother in turn. Then, Brother Martin, perhaps we may serve one another."

Martin said nothing but left his knees and bowed. Prior Paulus turned to Emma and her son. "My child. Come, enter in and let us show you to your quarters until we've settled you in one of our villages."

"Grace to you, Prior Paulus," she answered. "And thanks be to God. But as you consider our prospect, might I humbly ask to be housed near water? 'Tis somewhat soothing by its sound and—"

"Considering your sins, methinks you to have little to say

in this matter!" scolded Paulus. He paused, then softened his voice. "We've the village of Villmar, here, by the Lahn River, and we own some four villages by millstreams." He looked at Ingelbert and his eyes saddened. "You have naught to fear, daughter. Your sins are at your breast each day; you have no need of an increase in your misery." The prior paused for a moment. "I believe our village of Weyer to be a good place for you. It has a good stream, thick woods, *Volk* with no thought to idle time. *Ja*, Weyer shall be your home."

And so it was by the late days of November in the year of our Lord 1174, Emma of Quedlinburg became Emma of Weyer. She was housed in a hastily repaired cottage at the village edge and—to the young woman's great joy—by the pleasant waters of the Laubusbach.

⁊

Spring came early in the year 1175 and brought life and new hope to the village. Arnold and his wife welcomed their firstborn, Richard, on the fourteenth day of March. By April, Kurt and Berta were busy planning the season's labors. Berta was large and cumbersome, her second child expected to be born in June. Since Easter would be late she counted the days and prayed the child might be born on Pentecost. Heinrich's birth had missed the Epiphany by nearly a fortnight, and Berta still worried that good fortune was forever denied the child.

Meanwhile, Kurt had added another member to the household. Besides sheltering his sister, he rented space on the straw-strewn floor of the common room to a young man named Herwin, a distant cousin on Berta's side. Herwin earned only a few pennies a week as the thatcher's helper, so he offered Kurt a little cash as well as labor in Kurt's fields. Herwin was sixteen and bright, gentle, and rather timid, given more to dreams than to the coarse ways of the sons of Jost. But Kurt thought him trustworthy and hardworking; virtues his father had taught him to honor.

Days passed quickly and without excitement until Kurt announced the betrothal of Sieghild. After shocking the girl with the unexpected news he gave her instructions.

"Sieghild, you are to ride with Arnold on the morn to the Lahn. He's to deliver a cart to Lord Hugo's clerk in Runkel, then take you to meet your betrothed and his father by mid-day's meal."

Sieghild trembled. Kurt had negotiated with the father of a ploughman who lived in a border settlement along the Lahn River near Lord Hugo's castle. Kurt had met the young man's father while working with the carpenters. Sieghild did her best to hold back her tears, but her face revealed her fear.

Kurt looked at this sister with compassion but without mercy. "You shan't be a spinster under my roof. You'd be sixteen, girl. 'Tis time for you to marry. I was able to bargain nearly a shilling for your dowry. Father told me you would not be easy to barter and I think I've done well."

At that moment Herwin came through the door, his woollens covered with thatch from a hard day's work atop the roofs of Oberbrechen. The look on Sieghild's tortured face stopped him in his tracks. "Sieghild?"

"Sieghild is to meet with her family-to-be on the morrow. The wedding's in June 'fore Midsummer's and she has yet much to accomplish," answered Kurt.

The next morning Sieghild trudged slowly to Baldric's hovel. Though Jost had passed his land to Kurt, he had given Baldric his hut and its gardens, and had given Arnold two shillings of pennies. Sieghild hesitated to enter. She paused for a long moment and finally took a deep breath and called for Arnold. Within the hour she was bouncing through the byways of Weyer.

అ

Somewhere on the road to Runkel five men charged from the wood and intercepted Arnold's cart. "Ha!" boomed one as he grabbed the horse's bridle. "You'd be comin' with us, son of Jost!"

Cursing, Arnold stood on his wagon and snapped his whip at the man. "Off with you! Get off, now!" He swung his whip over and over again, drawing blood and oaths. More hands grasped at the panicked beast and at Arnold and his shrieking sister.

Arnold quickly reached under his seat and yanked out a stout stick with a rock lashed to one end. He roared and flung his weapon in all directions, pounding at the heads and shoulders of the gang of men now clambering into his cart. It wasn't long, however, before Arnold was knocked to the ground where four of the rogues kicked him and beat him furiously until he went limp in the dust.

Meanwhile, a fifth man held Sieghild by her hair as his fellows rummaged through the cart. Like ignorant apes at the fairs of Champagne, they poked and sniffed a satchel of spices destined for Lord Hugo's kitchen and some herbs intended for his physician. One squeezed warm cider from a wineskin into Arnold's face. "Look at me, son of Jost! You and your kin needs pay for yer sins."

"Aye, you'd all be in needs of a lesson, methinks," snarled another.

Arnold struggled to open his blood-matted eyes. He peered through a red haze at the filth before him. Toothless, and smelling worse than most peasants before their spring baths, they reeked of garlic and field scallions; their leggings were threadbare and crusted by years of neglect.

"Rot in hell," muttered Arnold.

With that, poor Sieghild was thrown to the ground. Arnold struggled to his feet, only to be hammered in the belly. He collapsed, gasping and cursing. The writhing girl's gown and under-gown were yanked from her shins and bunched above her hips. Sieghild's face was pummelled mercilessly by heavy fists while her wrists and ankles were pinned tightly to the ground.

It was not long before her screams and pleadings faded into wounded whimpers as one by one each attacker took a turn. At long last the five stood shoulder to shoulder spitting upon both Arnold and poor Sieghild. They laughed and mocked the girl, adding vulgarities to their blasphemy, then crowded into Arnold's cart. With a slap of the whip they disappeared into the darkening wood.

Arnold groaned and covered his trembling sister. Stunned and ashamed, Sieghild stared vacantly from behind haunted eyes, then turned her face away.

❧

The next day, little Heinrich awakened just before dawn. He cried for his mother and, while Berta attended his needs, Kurt stood in his doorway, anxious and suddenly filled with dread. Sieghild had not yet returned from her journey, and the man sensed something was wrong. He stepped lightly past his trestle table and raised the hardwood latch of his door. The village was dark and smoky, the air heavy and clinging. He hurried to Baldric's hoping for news, but, having none, he could do little else but report to his duties with the carpenters working in the nearby village of Oberbrechen.

By the bells of nones, Kurt returned to Weyer and inquired again, only to learn nothing. Gravely concerned, he reluctantly marched to his fields that lay just north of the village. He arrived and stared mutely at the large stones that marked his strips. With a deep breath Kurt forced his attention to the fertile ground and calculated his hopes for the growing season ahead. Of his half-hide, half were in fallow and the rest would yield barely enough for a profit. He needed to keep about one third of the harvest for the next planting's seed, another third for taxes, and only the last third would be his own. That final third needed to feed his family and leave enough to be sold for profit.

Herwin, Kurt's tenant, was clever and insisted that more manure would increase the yield. Unfortunately, Kurt owned no sheep or cows and would have to purchase it. Kurt preferred to argue, "the best fertilizer is the farmer's foot." He knew his land, he said, and somehow that would have to be good enough.

For the remainder of the day he labored behind his rented oxen, but Kurt's thoughts were never far from Sieghild. Twilight finally urged him to follow other weary silhouettes toward the village. He was hungry and his legs ached. His mind pictured Berta's bubbling mush and Heinrich's laughing face.

Kurt made his way to Baldric's hut once more—only now he arrived to find a scene of horror. Baldric's face was purpled in a rage that Kurt had never seen. Arnold's wife was holding Sieghild dutifully and turned cold eyes toward Kurt. "Your brother's half-dead from a Gunnar beating and this one's been used—by more than one—and she's in need of a midwife."

Kurt paled. A shiver chilled his back and anger coursed through his body. He looked at Sieghild with a devastating pity. He reached for her but she pulled away and turned her face in shame.

Baldric roared, "By God, Jesus, by Odin and thunder; by the wind I do swear this night that blood will spill!"

Kurt nodded and turned toward Arnold who was slouched and unattended in a corner. The badly beaten young man looked up from swollen eyes. His nose was broken and he was bent in two with pain.

"I ... I am sorry, brother," Arnold wheezed and coughed. "There was five, methinks. I—"

"Hush, Arnold," snapped Kurt. "There'd be no shame for you in this."

Baldric crouched by his younger brother and Arnold grabbed his shoulder. "Vow this: vow you'd not be seeking Gunnar kin without me. I ... I needs time for strength, but by God, I must make them pay with m'own hand."

Baldric hesitated. He wanted to strike that very night. He stood and paced the room like a wounded bear. His narrow eyes flickered and flamed. With a howl and an anguished cry he smashed a stool with the edge of his huge fist. He hesitated, then relented. "Aye, brother, I so vow."

The next morning Berta reluctantly held a cup of the midwife's infusion to Sieghild's lips while her sisters-in-law stood grimly in the corner. Berta was told the drink might keep God's judgment from the girl's womb by sparing her the consequence of her attackers. "A blend of secret herbs and steeped in water hexed years ago by a passing Syrian," the midwife said.

Berta was not unkind, nor without compassion, but she wanted no part of this uncleanness. She had worked too hard at her own perfection to be soiled by this woman's indignity. Her pity was blended with disgust. "Touched and handled by so many," she whined. "Methinks some spirit within her must have drawn them ... talk's always been of such."

Hildrun nodded. "Despoiled, I say, and none will want her now. What Christian man would?"

Gisela agreed. "I've always thought her to have demons hovering about."

Poor Sieghild had said not one word since the attack and had done little more than stare and groan in pain. Though mute, she was not deaf, however, and had the other women bothered to look, they would have surely seen the unspoken anguish flooding the young woman's eyes. Evil men had plundered her body, but it was her own kin who now ravaged her soul. A wicked tongue and haughty heart are surely among the most ruthless of evil's weapons, and in the blackness of the night, poor Sieghild could bear the eyes of shame no longer. Slipping out of Baldric's hovel and across the Laubusbach, she wandered past the boundary poles of her manor and was gone.

Chapter 3

THE FEUD

einrich had become a cheerful little lad. The child was strong and healthy, keen-eyed and happy. He laughed easily, always eager for the soft comfort of his mother's arms and the playful toss of his father's hands. The toddler spent his days trundling about the hovel, bouncing between the trestle table and the three-legged stool. He brought little trouble to his mother, though the same could not be said of his brother, Axel, now nearly one year old.

Kurt had long since given up his search for Sieghild and had sorrowfully turned his attention to his many duties. The first weeks of June were unusually eventful as Weyer and its neighboring villages had almost fallen prey to the rogue knights of a disenfranchised lord. Christendom's most admired defenders, the white-robed warrior-monks known as the Knights Templar, soundly defeated the insurgents. The victorious monks secured vast lands adjacent to the western border of the abbey's manor, and the folk of Weyer were delighted to be living under the watch of such valiant protectors.

Secretly, Berta was certain that the Templars had won the day because of her own precious relic that she kept hidden under her bed. The relic was a gift given by her father years before with a warning that she should show it to no churchman. It was a gold bezance, suspended by a silver chain, that had been minted in Barcelona nearly a century before. According to the peddler who had sold it to Berta's father, it had been carried by a French knight in the First Crusade. The knight had touched it to the Holy Sepulchre and had it blessed by the first Grand Master of the Knights Templar, Hughues de Payen. Upon hearing of the battle and the Templars' great victory, Berta had clutched the relic to her heart and wept for joy.

Within days Berta had another reason for joy as well. On the thirteenth of June she presented a third healthy child to her husband, a red-haired girl they baptized Effi. To the family's dismay, however, the colicky bundle did little other than keep everyone from a good night's rest!

One bright Sabbath after Midsummer's, Berta took the baby and her two boys for a morning walk near the bubbling Laubusbach. It wasn't long before they happened upon Emma and her son, Ingelbert. Berta turned quickly as if to leave, but Heinrich ran ahead to greet Emma's little lad. Heinrich grinned and reached out his hand to touch Ingelbert's white hair.

Ingelbert bore the unfortunate curse of being an outsider. He was the illegitimate son of a woman from an unknown place, of unknown blood, and odd ways. That would have been enough to cause suspicion and fear, but the little fellow's appearance added yet more to his troubles. Though only three years old, the boy already had the look of an old man. His nose was long and hooked, his thin, white hair wisped atop a sloped head. His front teeth protuded over a jaw that was so weak it virtually disappeared. Yet, for anyone daring enough to see beyond his imperfect shell, there awaited an eager smile, a longing to please, and a selfless heart bursting with kindness.

Heinrich was still blessed with the innocence of childhood. He saw only a happy face and an honest smile. Only six months younger than Ingelbert, Heinrich was still a bit clumsy on his feet and stumbled toward his new friend until he fell into him. They both tumbled to the ground, laughing and rolling like puppies in the soft grass.

"No more!" cried Berta nervously. She avoided the sad

and knowing eyes of Emma and whispered to herself, "No curses upon us."

Emma had kept a respectful distance but now took a slow step toward Berta and offered her a kind word. "Frau Berta? I pray you and your lovely children peace." She smiled kindly, then turned away from the startled woman and reached her hand toward Heinrich. The boy stood calmly, almost entranced, as Emma gently rolled her finger through a ginger-colored curl looped across his forehead. Heinrich giggled and Emma grinned, her round face lit by her twinkling eyes. "Frau Berta, methinks this boy of yours to be special. There's a ... a light of sorts within him, and a look of mercy ... and ... ah, well ..." With that, Berta shuddered and she quickly led her children away.

&

At dusk a few days later, Kurt was summoned to the council where the men of Weyer would review village business by torchlight on the roadway just below the church. About forty men gathered, women being strictly forbidden. The elected village chief, or reeve, was a mean-spirited, blustery yeoman named Lenard who proceeded to review a number of issues, including the village's constant plea for a wall and news of a grinding machine driven by wind. "A peddler told the monks of it and they've some interest. Seems a tower's been built in Normandy and atop it is some contraption of arms with windsails. It catches the wind and turns the grindstones below." Lenard paused as the men muttered in disbelief. After some debate, they finally decided harnessing the wind was too much of a risk.

The reeve then announced the appointment of a new hayward to oversee harvesting schedules, and he reviewed the status of the sheepfold, the swineherd, and the condition of the ox teams, as well as complaints of firewood allotments and sundry fees. "I'm told the mill fees may increase," he added bluntly.

An angry murmur rippled through the group.

"Aye, but the abbot says 'tis needed. Enough of it. I've other news as well. The abbey plans to build a larger bakery so you'll be needing to buy from them again, and only them.

When it's finished you'll be closing up the village oven and you're expected to eat less *Mus* and buy more bread."

"Nay!" shouted an angry voice, quickly followed by a chorus of protest. Bread was life itself and they surely preferred it to mush, but they feared the monks' prices.

"You've no choice. I should tell you now that you'll soon be buying their beer as well."

"Curse them, those—"

"Hold your tongue, man, or burn in the Pit!" Lenard was incensed. "I've two more things. There's talk of a witch with a babe in the east wood by Münster. Arnold's brought us news of bat's wings and heads of chickens. He's seen a lean-to of sticks and heard a baby's cry in the night. Is it not so, boy?"

Arnold stepped from the darkness. "*Ja,* I swear to these things. I've heard reports from pilgrims north of the Lahn as well."

"Men," continued Lenard, "we've all lived with witches and their spells, fairies, sprites, gnomes, and the like. We've a good, stout church here in the village. Keep your families true to the Holy Virgin. I don't want any of you seeking out this witch to help with harvesttime, planting, sickness, or troubles. We've no need of her spells and magic; they'll only bring us trouble to be sure."

The reeve looked hard at his men. "Now, one last thing. I've given thought to the strumpet Emma and her freak child. Methinks she's no witch, but strange to be sure and uncommon. I think she does not belong here but the monks say to leave her in peace."

The men laughed. "Have you seen that little beast of hers? Big nose, crooked eyes ..."

"Front teeth sticking out and ..."

"Aye, and ears too! Have you seen its ears? We could use them to catch the wind for that windgrinder!"

The group howled. Lenard, laughing with the others, settled them. "Well then, good men, tell your kin and householders to keep a safe distance but leave the two fools be. They seem content to watch the water."

ॐ

The harvest of 1177 had been poor and Kurt's household was worried. Adding to their misery were the unbearable moods of Baldric who had lost his wife to childbirth several months before. The angry bear now prowled about the forests and villages in search of a target for his fury.

Poor harvests were a particular problem for the abbey. Good stewardship required revenues be collected regardless of conditions. After all, the abbot owed considerable fees to the Lord of Runkel for protection and to the see of Mainz as well. Certain that an abbey bakery could turn a quick profit, the abbot insisted work continue on its construction in Villmar. He planned to eventually construct a bakery in each of the abbey's villages as well, and, in time, breweries. In addition, he had been entertaining new ideas on crop rotation and mining. Travelers had brought news of interesting techniques in France and England that were increasing harvest yields. The area was also rich in marble, silver, and shale—products not yet fully exploited. The business of shepherding souls, he sighed, required a clever mind and a resolute spirit.

Stewardship was a heavy responsibility not to be taken lightly. Business for some was a problem of revenue, for others, a question of expense. The abbot was determined to address both. He had lessened the pressure on his treasury by limiting the number of oblates and postulants. Novices, too, were a costly venture, he reasoned, always in need of new habits, eating more than their elders by twice or thrice—in spite of the Rule that demanded they eat less. They were famous for damaging tools, spilling inks, wasting dyes—the list of expenses was endless. So, when a wealthy merchant from nearby Limburg appeared at the monastery's gate with a young child in tow, the abbot was wary.

Corpulent and well dressed, the merchant strode with an arrogant swagger to the abbey gate. Egidius, the porter, bowed. "Thanks be to God."

The merchant grunted. Dragging a stout, young boy of about five years of age forward, he said, "Its mother's dead. I've no need of it."

The porter looked at the plump, pink-faced lad with sudden compassion. "Has he no kin, an aunt or ... ?"

"No. I've no one who wants the thing. I've a bag of coins that should keep it fed and in clothes, more coins than the thing's worth, to be sure."

Egidius had a strong urge to assault the man but obediently offered charity, instead. "Come this way," he growled.

The merchant followed the porter into the courtyard of the monastery and passed the kitchen. It was fortunate for the man that it was neither Wednesday nor Friday and the monks were not in fast. This assured him of a good meal, especially since it was just now midafternoon. The merchant wasn't certain, but he thought he smelled mutton stew and fresh bread. He licked his lips in anticipation.

The three soon passed the dining hall and crossed the inner courtyard to the abbot's chambers. The hooded monks scurrying to their meal did not speak to the stranger for their Rule prohibited it, but they did bow respectfully, as did Abbot Boniface upon the merchant's arrival at his door.

Boniface prayed and then greeted his visitor with a kiss of peace. He recited a few verses of the Holy Scriptures and then washed the merchant's hands and feet. As he dried his own hands he prayed again. "God, we have received thy mercy in the midst of thy temple." He motioned for a brother to fetch food for his guest and beckoned the man be seated.

"Now, how may I serve thee, good sir?"

"My name is Leopold of Limburg and I've needs to find a home for this." Leopold pushed his son to the fore.

"Ah. Good sir, and what of your wife?"

"I've no wife."

"Ah, she is dead?"

"I've had no wife. The thing's mother died of a fall a week back."

Boniface stroked his face and stared at the moneybag. "You are the child's father?"

Leopold grunted. "Yes. A momentary slip off the path, Father Abbot. I thought to make penance by offering a heavy price for its care."

Boniface sighed. He stared at the man with a mixture of

pity and contempt. *The man is indulgent. He is fat and soft like a November hog. Hmm. The otter hat, embroidered cloth-ing ... he obviously has wealth.* The abbot cleared his throat. "We've a need to better steward our finances. I pray God's wisdom for you as you seek elsewhere for the lad's care."

Leopold sat quietly, picking at the large mole on his left earlobe. "Nay, methinks you'll take it from me. Think of the thing like a little Christ child, and think of me as a Magi with silver a'plenty." He slammed his purse hard upon the abbot's desk. It was stuffed full and the abbot knew it to be worth about ten shillings—the rent of one full hide for two years. The two stared at each other for a long moment. But it was Leopold who erred. He, being less shrewd than old Boniface, spoke first. "It whines a little but comes of good stock."

The abbot nodded politely.

Leopold waited, then finally snatched two coins from a hidden pocket. "Ach, *mein Gott!* I'll add two gold pieces from Genoa!"

Boniface extended his arms toward the waiting child. "God's blessing for thy father's selfless and most generous gifts. Ah, a soul and a purse for us, oft traded for each other, are both now granted to our humble abbey."

Leopold released his son to the monk. "I'm in no further debt and owe no other penance?"

Boniface bowed. "Go in peace, my son, thy sin is forgiven. We shall raise the boy into a fine smith, perhaps a—"

Leopold looked suddenly solemn. "The thing's a bit lazy but methinks it shows cleverness at times. Swear to me, Abbot, that he'd be no workhand for the monks his whole life."

Boniface shrugged. "I know not God's will for him."

Leopold paused. "You see my clothing? My fine doublet? It took me near to a lifetime to get out of my short-slit tunic and the fields. I've no love for this ... nuisance, but I swore an oath that no issue of mine would ever wear a serf's tunic, nor a workman's apron. I'll not bear that shame no matter what I think of the thing. It's to be trained a merchant or a priest and wear linen and silk or the robes of a churchman. I want your vow on that!" The man pulled a purse from inside his silk sash. He lowered his voice and leaned close to Boniface. "The bag and the two coins are given to the Holy Church for its care. But this is for *your* pledge and for you alone."

The abbot smiled and tapped his fingers next to three gold coins stacked neatly before him. "Yes, my son. I believe the little fellow might make a good priest." Then, like a snake striking its prey, the gold was snatched away to a dark pocket within his simple robe.

Leopold nodded and smiled and cast a final look at his son before he turned away. As he followed the porter toward the courtyard he called to Boniface, "If any should ask, he was baptized Pious."

~

The hay harvest of the following spring was poor again. Kurt and his tenant, Herwin, labored for hours under the hot sun in order to fulfill the work requirements of the abbey. They swung their scythes over the monks' meadows by the Laubusbach but sheaved less than half a good year's yield. Thorny weeds seemed to always do best in hard times; it was as though they relished adding pain to misery. Kurt had pricked his hand on a thick thorn a week prior and the wound made his grasp of the scythe an agony.

Kurt's own fields were suffering badly in a second year of drought. The harvest would yield little more than his rent required, and as he worked he wondered how he would buy barley for the field now waiting in fallow. With the carpenters' guild now hiring laborers from Villmar, Kurt would have to rely on the harvest from his own small holding and the pittance Herwin paid in rents.

Most of the village men were working in the field that day. Each owed a fixed number of days in service to the monks in exchange for their protection. It was the ancient way. At the far end of the meadow worked the old men, most sitting in the shade with the village whetstones, sharpening dulled blades for the harvesters. The meadows were filled with scythe-swinging men, and behind them followed the women and children, including young Heinrich, raking and bundling the cut grass into sheaves for the carters to haul away. Berta, however, was home carding wool. She was due to deliver her fourth child and was suffering much discomfort.

At the bells of compline the weary peasants were dismissed from their tasks and most immediately plunged into the Laubusbach for a cool respite. A few splashes in the stream's waters did wonders to brighten spirits, and soon a column of peasants in dripping woollens began the short march from the meadows to the village, singing songs of spring.

Kurt and Herwin stumbled through the door in search of beer or cider, but came upon the midwife in the middle of her work. "Out! Out at once!" she shrieked. Men were strictly forbidden to be present at times like these. By the look on Berta's face Kurt knew something was not in order. He retreated through the doorway and sat against the wattled wall of his hovel where he winced and grimaced at the cries of his wife. Heinrich and Axel stared wide-eyed and sat close to their worried father.

At last there was silence. And then sobbing, followed by a curt reprimand. "Enough, woman. 'Tis as God wills it to be!" The midwife came through the doorway wiping her blood-stained hands on her apron. "Kurt, you've lost a son. He was born breathing so ye'd best call on Father Gregor and have him baptized straightaway."

"Kurt ... Kurt!" cried Berta from within. "Kurt, get the priest and quick, we've needs to catch his soul before it falls in the Pit!"

The man's face hardened in grief and he pushed his boys aside. He stepped into his hut and stared at his sobbing wife lying in the bedchamber. She was whimpering and holding her limp newborn tightly to her bared breast. He knelt by her dutifully and kissed her on the forehead.

By matins little Reinhard was baptized a Christian, bathed, and shrouded. He was buried in the morning, and before the bells of terce Kurt was scything hay once more.

≈

The harvest feast of Lammas, August the first, was only two weeks away, yet the village was still bustling with its summer labors. The hay had been gathered and carted to the abbey, the wool had been carded and bundled into bales for sale in Limburg. The parched grain fields stood ready for the scythes, while the fields in fallow were turned by sluggish oxen.

Kurt grew weaker as an infection spread from his hand through his forearm. Heinrich faithfully bathed his father's sweating brow through long nights of fever sweats, yet at each dawn the man rose to fight his way to dusk with a resolution that would have greatly pleased old Jost.

The summer had brought few changes, no season really ever varied much, but one addition to the village proved an annoyance to all. A stray mastiff had wandered into Weyer looking for food and attention. Reeve Lenard took ownership of the beast, hoping to train the dog to hunt.

Lenard's new dog proved to be playful and bright but preferred his own pleasures to those of his master. Each night, Lenard loudly commanded the animal to sit or lie down, roll or fetch a stick. The more the man commanded, however, the less the dog performed until, exasperated, the man beat and pounded the dog with a leather strap. "You shall yield to me, beast!" Lenard cried each night. Then, night after night, grumping and grousing and bellowing foul oaths, the defeated reeve collapsed into his straw bed.

Heinrich lay awake each of those nights teary-eyed and sobbing for the poor animal. By day, the four-year-old would sneak over to Lenard's cottage and play with the dog. Though the animal was twice the boy's size, he had no malice in his simple heart and gently rolled the little lad around the ground. The beast was kind and gentle, though strong; intelligent and tender of heart. Heinrich sat quietly by his side and stroked his dusty, red-brown fur, laughing at the drooping tongue of his panting kindred spirit.

Heinrich's affections had become quickly attached to the dog as they had to his best friend and cousin Richard, the son of Arnold. Blond and handsome, Richard was lean, strong, and quick of mind. Arnold swore he'd see the boy knighted in Runkel's castle someday—an ambitious dream for the son of a cart-hauler.

The mastiff and young Richard were not Heinrich's only friends, however. Emma's son, Ingelbert, was one whom the lad had oft wished he might see more often. Heinrich rarely saw Emma's son, save those times Ingelbert fetched water with his mother at the village well. Heinrich's own mother, as well as the other mothers of the village, had banned their children from speaking with Ingelbert, believing Emma and her misshapen child to bear a curse of some sort.

For her part, Emma persistently offered Berta kindness on every occasion. Heinrich had watched the lonely newcomer help his mother break the ice off the well one cold day in the winter just past. It was such kindness that had caught the child's attention quickly, and the selfless acts were beginning to calm Berta's fears.

It was July thirty-first, just before the feast of Lammas, when Baldric and Arnold arrived at Kurt's hovel. Exhausted from the day's toil, Kurt slowly opened the door and stepped out into the humid night air. After the brothers conversed in low, urgent tones for a few moments, Kurt finally nodded and returned to his wife, his face tight and flushed. "Wife, we've business to tend to this night and tomorrow we feast. Sleep well and mind the children. I shall return soon."

Berta felt a sudden chill. She sensed danger but dared not ask more. Holding her husband's palm against her cheek, Berta whispered a blessing to her man. With that, Kurt moved toward the door. He touched his boys' heads briefly. Weak with fever and favoring his badly infected right arm, he paused to retrieve a steel carving knife hidden beneath the table. He shoved it under his belt and stepped out into the dark village.

Arnold's labors as a cart-hauler earned him two pennies per day but also paid a hearty wage in information. A peddler told him of a distant shepherd's family swearing oaths against some folk in Weyer. He further learned that some shepherds of Runkel's lands were conspiring to "teach another lesson to Weyer" after they delivered bales of wool to nearby Arfurt, lying on the far bank of the Lahn.

Arnold and Baldric's closest friend, Dietrich, were waiting

on the road beneath the church with another man, Paul, the dyer for the monks. Paul had come from Mainz as a freeman in search of work. He had married a dyer's daughter from another village but moved to Weyer in hopes of establishing a shop in the growing village. He had made the unfortunate mistake of borrowing money from Baldric and now was required to pay his terms of interest.

Under the cloak of a new moon the five men whispered their plan. Arnold flashed a knife normally used to bleed swine and demanded the others show their weapons. Kurt yanked his blade from his belt and Dietrich revealed his own. Baldric preferred a mallet he had taken from an ironsmith in a wager. Paul shrugged timidly. "I've no weapon, I—"

Arnold snarled, "You of all of us ought have a sword or bow! Fool, dimwit!"

Indeed, serfs were not permitted to own weapons, but freemen were expected to keep a long sword or bow in case called upon to render military service.

Baldric growled. "Here, I've a blade in m'boot. Take it, y'dunce and use it well."

Paul took the short knife with a trembling hand. He touched its edge with his forefinger and closed his eyes.

It was soon after the bells of compline when the five men began their dark journey. They climbed the steep roadway leading them out of Weyer, paused briefly along the ridge-line, and then began to trot down the long slope toward the torches of distant Villmar. About halfway to the abbey's village they veered off the road and followed Arnold along a cartpath heading northeastward. They ran quietly under a star-sprinkled sky, and before long they could smell the wet mud and waters of the Lahn River.

The Lahn was fairly deep, hemmed by steep banks. It was a bowshot in breadth and sluggish, except in the spring thaw. The group paused at the bank for a moment and crouched in the night's mist now hanging about their knees. Then, without a sound, they slipped into the Lahn's warm waters and vanished in the fog. They swam awkwardly through the black water until they found themselves clawing their way up the slippery bank on the far side. The group was now across the border of the abbey's lands and was trespassing the lands of Lord Klothar, the new lord of Runkel.

As bound serfs, all but Paul could be severely punished for leaving the realm to which they were pledged. The oaths of their ancestors had shackled them to the land they were born upon and only escape to a free city for a year and a day or the purchase of manumission could set them free.

Lord Klothar's village of Arfurt was about the size of Weyer and was perched atop a high bank directly on the Lahn. The men had crossed the river upstream from the sleepy village and now sat in the low grass of a hayfield to catch their breath. Arnold gathered his comrades close. "We've another league to travel to Arfurt," he whispered. "The cart-way's fairly smooth but the dark will slow us some. We shall soon hear the bells at matins and that gives us just enough time to do our business and get back 'afore daybreak."

Baldric looked carefully about the circle. "None can fail, do y'hear me, Paul?"

The dyer nodded nervously.

"Humph!" groused Baldric. "You've thin arms and a soft way about you, dyer. And you'd best have clean hands. If you leave the color of dye behind you'll swing!"

Paul was sweating in the humid night air and his hands began to tremble. He wished he had never met Baldric nor ever borrowed a single penny from the man.

"Kurt, you're quiet," said Baldric.

"Aye, frightened, aren't you?" laughed Dietrich.

Kurt turned stiffly toward the miller. "Methinks you to be a fool ... and a cheat. Keep yerself away from me else I'll deal with you when this business is done!"

Dietrich pulled the knife from his belt. "Now, now you son of a har—"

Arnold held the man. "Save your rage, friend. Kurt's with fever, leave him be."

With a few more oaths the men stood and followed Arnold's lanky starlit silhouette like sheep trotting behind their bellwether. They slipped through the darkness, waist deep in mist, their thin, leather shoes padding lightly atop the wet grass. The bells of matins echoed through the Lahn valley from nameless village churches scattered about. The troop hunched and bobbed under the night's sky, each lost in his own thoughts until Arnold suddenly stopped. "Hold!" he hushed. The smell of burning wood wafted past his nose. Arnold crouched and whispered to Baldric. "There, about a bowshot, methinks."

Baldric assumed command. He huddled his men and spoke in low tones. "Now listen well. They've surely set a guard by the wool. He's the one to die first, then we take the others, but we must move slowly else the ox'll bellow a warning."

Kurt was trembling all over. Fever raged through his body and he thought he might faint, but he took a deep breath and crept forward with the others. The dew and heavy mist muffled their movements as they crawled to within a stone's throw of the Gunnars' camp. As Baldric had guessed, a sleepy watchman was leaning against the large wheel of a single-axle cart. The dim glow of the campfire lit the man's left side and Arnold studied it carefully "Baldric," he whispered, "no blade."

Baldric nodded and motioned for Kurt and Paul to advance. As the two moved forward, Baldric, Arnold, and Dietrich crept toward the guard. "Arnold," whispered Baldric, "you two, move in close and be ready." He pointed to the sleeping shepherds as he crept through the mist toward the sentry.

Paul and Kurt were now crouching within striking distance of the camp and waited nervously as Baldric stalked the guard. The ox suddenly raised his head and cocked his ears. He lifted his nose to scent the air. The men of Weyer froze. The beast snorted and grunted and the guard stood erect. "Huh?" he muttered as he stepped toward the animal. He set a hand atop the ox's broad back and stared out into the darkness. Seeing nothing, he turned back toward the wagon with a shrug but had barely taken a step before Baldric's mallet smashed hard into his face. The awful sound startled the ox, and the beast lurched forward, bawling loudly.

Five sleeping Gunnars were suddenly awake and on their feet, and Arnold and Dietrich sprang forward, Baldric close behind. Kurt was nauseous and dizzy. He stood and took a step, but fever blurred his eyes and he could barely feel the handle of the knife in his grip. He hesitated, but only for a moment. Anger for the shame of Sieghild suddenly pulsed through him, and it was as though he could feel his sister's suffering. He charged forward into the fray.

The Gunnars fought hard, like their Frankish fore-fathers. A mighty swipe of Baldric's mallet, however, dropped one, then two. Another wrestled Arnold to the ground but Baldric struck the shepherd on the spine as Arnold plunged his knife deep into the man's belly.

Dietrich was in trouble, however. He tripped and lay helpless on the grass as a Gunnar rushed toward him. Kurt turned to help the miller and crashed into Dietrich's foe. But as he did, the blow of a hammer glanced off his cheek. Stunned, he fell face first to the ground and the man quickly pounced upon him, plunging sharp shears over and over into Kurt's arching back.

Baldric rushed to Kurt's aid. With a vicious swipe of his mallet, Baldric crushed the head of the shear-wielding Gunnar. The man fell to his side with a whimper and lay openeyed and lifeless.

Baldric dropped to his brother's side. "Ach ... nay ... *Gott in Himmel!*" the man cried to the heavens. He clutched his brother's body in his arms. "Kurt!" he wailed.

Kurt felt a chill drift through his body. For a moment he felt a flutter. He heard distant voices calling him—familiar voices, perhaps Arnold's, perhaps his father's? He gasped for breath, then felt suddenly calm and the voices grew faint, finally fading away to utter silence.

The vanquished Gunnars lay strewn about their campsite, dead or dying. The survivors of Weyer stared disbelieving at their fallen comrade and said nothing as they carried his body to a dewy patch of unspoiled grass. They laid him down respectfully and the three of them knelt by his side.

The group was quiet and the air deadly calm. Paul the

dyer approached from the darkness and bowed his head in sorrow. Baldric was fighting a tear—a battle seldom engaged—as he turned his blood-splattered face to the quaking dyer. "You? You hid?"

"Y–Yes," answered Paul. "I've not the stomach for such—"

The gentle man never finished his sentence. Baldric snarled and swung his mallet into the man's thin frame, felling him to the earth like a broken willow. Paul collapsed with a gasp and his eyes rolled as his soul flew away.

Arnold and Dietrich grunted their assent to justice served and stood to finish the night's business. With a diabolical grin Dietrich set about the task of assuring the deaths of any Gunnar yet twitching on the ground while Arnold rifled through their purses to take whatever treasures he might find.

"Do we toss them in the river?" asked Arnold.

"Aye, fish food," answered Dietrich.

Baldric paused. "No, leave them for the birds so their kin finds them. They needs see the price they pay for Sieghild and their threats!"

Dietrich wasn't so sure. "Lord Klothar will learn of it and go to the abbot. Your feud is no secret."

"Ach! Let them accuse us. We've oath-helpers enough who'll swear by our innocence."

Arnold pointed to Kurt and Paul. "And these?" he asked anxiously.

Baldric thought for a moment. "Berta needs claim Kurt died of the fever. We'll shroud him quick and Father Gregor won't know. He's too fearful to ask questions of us anyway. We'll sink Paul in the river downstream."

"But Paul's wife will wonder," blurted Dietrich.

"Aye," answered Baldric. "I'll simply tell her the last I knew he'd been visiting the strumpets in Limburg."

ॐ

As the dawn of Lammas broke bright over Weyer, Baldric and Arnold bore the body of Kurt to his wife and three children. Berta collapsed onto the dirt floor of her hovel and wept inconsolably. Heinrich stood bravely at his father's side and stared into the lifeless face. The lad's lower lip quivered and tears rolled down his face. He had already been taught to hide such weakness, and he quickly wiped his tears away. He walked bravely toward his mother and offered her the comfort of a tender hug.

"Leave me be!" shrieked Berta. "Are you stupid, boy? Can y'not see I needs be alone?"

Shamefaced, the four-year-old ran from the hovel.

Baldric related the night's events to Berta and recited the story she must offer to Father Gregor.

"I ... I dare not lie to a priest! Are you mad, Baldric? I'll not put my soul in peril or that of little Axel here, or Effi! No, I'll not be telling your lies!"

"Then Arnold and I shall swing on Runkel's gallows and Kurt's land shall be taken in payment for the dead."

Arnold whispered to Baldric. "If she'll betray us, then she's to join him."

Baldric nodded. "Woman, listen and listen well. I am the elder of this household now. I'll speak to Gregor, you say nothing!"

Resigned, Berta nodded obediently. "Then hurry for him, Kurt's soul has need of the prayers!"

"Not before he's washed and shrouded!" barked Arnold.

Herwin, the tenant, was sitting in the corner, frightened and silent. Baldric turned to him. "You ... come here y'mouse. One word and you're dead. We've need of your rents else you'd already have your throat cut. Be off now to the well with a bucket. Arnold, get some linens from your wife. We shan't spend for deerskin and we've no time for a box."

Immediately the family was busy. Berta sewed her husband's wounds so no blood would stain the wraps while Herwin washed the body. Within the half hour they quickly shrouded the corpse.

Father Gregor had a fine Lammas day planned, one filled with good food and drink, village dances and games. He had fields of grain to bless and was not pleased to be bothered with Kurt's death. "He died of what cause?" he asked Baldric.

"Fever from a prick on the hand some weeks past."

"Ah, yes, I did notice it swelling. You have already prepared the body?"

"Aye, father, we thought with the feast day it would be good to hurry about it. The widow wants words for his soul, though, and quick."

Father Gregor sighed. "Aye, 'tis an hour yet to terce and I've much to do. By the saints, the gravediggers shan't be happy about this! Methinks he needs wait for burial till the morrow."

Arnold was standing next to Baldric and nudged him. Neither wanted any delay. The Gunnars would be discovered soon and Kurt needed to be in the ground. None would dare dig him out to check his body.

"The widow wants this done now. The diggers always have graves-in-waiting, put him in one of them." Baldric's eyes narrowed.

Gregor felt suddenly uneasy. "And what is the hurry, my sons?" Suspicion laced his tone.

Baldric answered straightaway. "No hurry, father, but Berta believes a feast day to be a more blessed day to bury."

Gregor shook his head. "Where such notions are born!"

Father Gregor greeted the family at the churchyard and prayed for the little cluster of kin gathered around. Throughout the brief burial service small Heinrich stood stone-faced and tearless. His mother had commanded him to be the son his father expected. But as soon as the priest finished, the young boy turned in hopes of flying to a safe place to shed his tears. Father Gregor snagged him by the arm. "Heinrich, now 'tis time for you to be a man. Know your place and forget it not. Learn the ways and serve well."

The young lad nodded soberly.

Chapter 4

MADONNA AND THE WITCH

Without a husband, life became unbearable for Berta, and she blamed everyone, including her eldest son, for her suffering. "Boy," she said flatly one night, "you understand it was for your honor that your father died?"

Heinrich stared at her in confusion.

"Aye? Your father had a code to keep."

The little boy didn't understand.

"There's an order to life, 'tis something you've needs learn now from Father Gregor. There is a proper way to follow and you must learn the code, like your father and grandfather. But you ought heed the priests' ways more than your father did. It would be your gift to me and I shall love you for it."

Berta was lonely and often desperate. One afternoon she led her children to the village well for a brief respite from the oppressive hovel. It was late and no one was near except for Emma, who usually came after the others had left. The outcast carried a wooden bucket in one hand and gently led her son with the other. Berta thought the woman to be odd but not as fearsome as some did, and on this summer's evening her loneliness was greater than her discomfort.

"Good evening," smiled Emma warmly.

"G–good evening to you, as well," Berta stammered.

Emma cautiously approached and spoke gently. "I was sorry to learn of your husband's death." The woman laid a tender hand on Berta's forearm. "I have not suffered that kind of loss, but I imagine you must be lonely and confused."

Unable to speak, Berta stared at the woman's hand on her sleeve and nodded. No one had bothered to comfort her in these past few weeks. Gisela didn't care, she had no true friends, and her cousins were indifferent.

"I've a beehive, you know," Emma continued. "Could you and your little ones come for a bit of bread and honey?"

Berta was shocked. "Honey?" Only the monks owned bee-hives and she feared it was poached.

"Oh no, good Berta," chuckled Emma. "'Tis honest honey. I bought the hive and paid the fine to have more. And I've a special place to show you!"

Heinrich was wide-eyed. He waited respectfully for his mother to answer, hoping with all his heart that she would say yes. He studied Emma carefully. He thought her to be softlooking and warm. She was shorter than his mother and plump and snugly. Her brown hair was braided and rolled neatly atop her head. Her brown eyes sparkled kindly from within a gentle, round face.

After a moment's hesitation, Berta wavered. She was not quite ready to receive the woman's kindness, though she wanted desperately to do so. At last she blurted, "Might we come on Sabbath afternoon?"

"Yes, of course." Emma masked her disappointment. "I shall look for you on the morrow."

The women smiled at each other and the boys bid each other a reluctant farewell. Emma reached out to lightly touch Heinrich on the head. It felt good to him, reassuring and loving. He sighed and stared at the kindly woman with happy eyes. He hated to leave.

The next day Heinrich could barely endure Mass and begged his mother to hurry. After a meal of mush and a Sun-day pottage, Berta asked Arnold's wife, Gisela, to mind Axel and Effi. Within a quarter hour, mother and son were walk-ing toward the village edge and were soon within sight of the pleasant waters of the Laubusbach.

They walked a little farther until, just ahead of them, Emma's cottage appeared. It stood alone beyond the footpaths of the village and near the water's edge. A squat, one-room hut surrounded by a woven fence, its roof was thatch, its walls well-mudded, and all in all very much like every other hovel in the village. Yet it was enchanting in some indescribable way.

Emma and Ingelbert saw their guests approaching and hurried to meet them. They welcomed them through the simple gate where Berta suddenly stopped and gaped. The edge of Emma's croft was lined with the most beautiful assortment of wildflowers she had ever seen. Every color of the rainbow was represented, forming a glorious collage that brought tears to Berta's eyes. She was drawn deeper into the flower garden and then gasped aloud, for atop the many blooms fluttered more butterflies than she could have ever imagined in the most wondrous of dreams!

"I ... I ... have never seen such a thing in all my days!" Berta finally choked. "Ah, Emma, 'tis a good thing you've done here."

Emma smiled. "God's hand is one of wonder and His eye is true." She turned her face to the sun now blazing high above. "The sun 'tis a warming glimpse of what's sure and always."

Heinrich tilted his head backward and smiled as the sun warmed his cheeks.

"So, my little Heinz—"

"Frau Emma, I prefer him be called by his baptized name—Heinrich." Berta was firm.

Emma smiled. "Ah, and what does he prefer?"

Berta darkened. "What does that matter?"

"I see," answered Emma slowly. She turned to the boy. "Heinrich, Ingelbert shall show you about whil'st I fix our honey."

As the two boys scampered off, Emma motioned for Berta to sit on a stump while she left to fetch the treat. Berta's eyes followed her hostess as she disappeared through the doorway, but curiosity tempted the woman beyond restraint and she quickly followed after her host. Stepping timidly across the threshold, she entered a neat, warm room furnished with two straw-mound beds, stools, a table, and a puzzling item covered by a large blanket. "Beggin' your pardon, Emma, but what is that?"

"Aye?" Startled, Emma whirled about. "'Tis nothing, only ..."

Berta was normally timid and reserved, but she walked boldly to the blanket and reached a hand for a corner. Her eyes searched through the shadows beneath the blanket as she lifted it away. "What is this? A ... a scribe's table?"

"Well ... yes," answered Emma nervously.

But Berta wanted more. She looked about the room and spotted some inkpots and colored powders tucked behind a broom. She squinted, puzzled and curious. She took a few steps toward another wall and studied a small grinder, a thick, iron-strapped chest, and a clay jar of honey, complete with a crowd of bees climbing over its stopper. Hanging on a peg was a wicker basket with several well-worn quills peeking over its edge, a few flat knives, and a stylus.

"So," sighed Emma. "You've uncovered m'secret."

Berta was confused. A breeze blew through the open doorway and toyed with her hair. "I ... I thought only the monks knew how to write ..."

"Times are changing."

Berta nodded. "You'd be a taught woman, with a ... a bastard child?"

Emma sighed, patiently. "'Tis true that I am somewhat learned and, yes, my good boy is a bastard. Methinks the two facts are opposed, for how learned could I be to have a predicament such as this?" She chuckled.

Berta became subdued and thoughtful. The two spoke in low tones until Heinrich and Ingelbert came tumbling through the doorway. "Ha, ha!" chortled Heinrich. "I like you, Ingly ... I—"

"Nay!" scolded Berta. "The boy's name is Ingelbert, not 'Ingly'!"

"Ah, Berta, 'tis alright. My son seems to like the sound of it," smiled Emma. "He's never felt the joy of a friendly name. Heinrich, you have my permission to call him as he likes."

Berta stiffened. She felt somehow insulted, and her mind quickly whispered reasons to reject her new friend. "Frau Emma, m'son needs learn the ways of right. Father Gregor thinks him already prideful, as do I, and I think it would be better he call your son as I say he should."

Emma gazed sadly at Heinrich. The boy was staring at his feet and waiting for the final pronouncement. "Good lad," began Emma. She bent down and laid a gentle finger under his chin. "Dear boy, look at me. 'Tis always good to honor your mother."

Heinrich nodded. His eyes brightened as they met the woman's and met with unspoken understanding.

"Thank you," interrupted Berta. "Things need remain as we know them to be. It is good to fix yourself to things right and true. Father Gregor says so."

Emma sighed. "Might I serve you some buns with your honey, and some cider?"

Berta paused. She struggled for a moment, surprised at the woman's charity. Berta was still drawn to the strange woman. "I ... I can stay for a short time, but needs return home soon."

Emma understood Berta's struggle—she had been witness to such hesitation before. Graciously she set a small table of rye rolls, cider, and a jar of precious honey. Then, having made her guest at better ease, she patiently listened to Berta's recitation of her many penances, her successes in fleeing temptation, and the wonders of the Virgin. But when Berta began to slander a neighbor, Emma interrupted. "Ah, 'tis a glorious day, is it not? Would you be pleased to walk in my gardens?"

Berta fell silent, then nodded. And, while the two boys played innocently by the Laubusbach, the two mothers were soon walking midst Emma's joy. The kitchen garden was filled with pungent herbs like rue, sage, and basil; also parsley, hyssop, parsnips, turnips, garlic, and chives. Berta was astonished at the abundance of green things lush and ready for the gardener's knife.

Emma's true treasure, however, was her garden of flowers. It was a masterpiece no painter could have ever captured, even on the canvas of a king. Emma led her guest to a plot of her favorites. "These are m'most precious ones. They are simple corn poppies, found wild in the grain fields. But I water them and sing to them, and they grow big and happy. Look how their red petals lift and open to the sun. See how their faces shine yellow with seed? Oh, I do love them so."

A soft breeze cooled Berta's skin, and she smiled as the kindly sun yielded its precious fruit of color. She picked a corn poppy and held it to her heart as she turned this way and that, marvelling at Emma's glorious garden. Her burdens and fears were quickly chased away by beauty as she sat down among blossoms of borage and marigold, langdebeef, heartsease and other sundry perfumed blooms. Berta's nose was bathed in heavenly perfume and, were that not joy enough, floating flocks of butterflies circled about her sunlit hair.

      🙠

Autumn labors proved difficult and strained Berta's household to its limit. Faithful Herwin worked the fields, harvesting the grain and threshing it late into the night. The hayward had ordered a rotation of barley for the coming year and the fields just harvested would be left fallow for a year's rest. Herwin thought there ought to be a better way of using the land. He had heard of other manors rotating their crops in a three-field system rather than the ancient two rotations the abbey still demanded. *Why do they fear change so? One year fallow, one year planting, by the saints, we lose profit! Why not one third fallow, one third a spring crop, and one third an autumn harvest?* he wondered to himself.

But there were other pressures on Berta and her three children. The Gunnars had come under cover of night and burned the hovel shared by her brothers-in-law. While Arnold's family found other residence, the bitter Baldric forced his way into Berta's home.

By the Epiphany a dark melancholy had overtaken the woman, and it had deepened like the snow blanketing the smoky village. Berta looked about her cottage and began to weep. Baldric's very presence had cast a fearful pall over everyone, but she could do little more than hang her head and yield to duty. Baldric was the brother of her husband and she, a mere widow with three children and a tenant. She was thankful the priest had not required they marry.

Winter now lay across the manor like a heavy white woollen. Biting cold, privation, darkness, and despair were the demons of the season and little could bring comfort. In this gloom even the beasts of the forests shivered and hid deep in their caves or far below the frozen sod. But despite the natural lethargy, there was much work to do. Baldric was particularly busy working long, cold days overseeing the sawing of timber in the forests, the making of charcoal in the wood near the Lahn, and the management of fences for the swine now foraging for mast in the great stands of oak. Herwin was commissioned to work at repairing the roof of the mill in Oberbrechen and the walls of Weyer's ewe-house. Arnold's cart was shed-bound by snow, but he was assigned the task of hauling bundles of chopped stubble and straw by sleigh.

Within each hovel the peasant women were hard at work as well. Some, like Arnold's wife, kept busy carving bowls and forks, platters and spoons, or pleating baskets with rushes gathered in the autumn. Berta spent much of her time spinning. This year she was skillfully turning coarse flax into good linen thread. The prior had ordered higher taxes to offset a poor grain harvest, and Berta's spinning helped provide for her obligations.

It was just two days past mid-March, less than two weeks before Easter, when Berta became ill. She had suffered aches and an unusual weakness in her legs through much of Lent, but she had attributed it to the added privations of the season as she readied her soul for Holy Week. For days Heinrich stood faithfully by his mother's bed, often dabbing her brow, so he was surprised when she silently slipped from her bed and out the door into the freezing rain, only to return a few hours later with a small satchel stuffed beneath her cloak. "Shhh," she whispered. "Ask nothing, boy, to bed with you."

Baldric rose just before prime of the next morning, and as he was tearing at some stale bread he heard Berta calling his name. "What is it, woman?"

"Baldric ... a word?"

Baldric ambled into the woman's room. Now a burly man

of nearly twenty-three, he filled the doorway. He stared at her
with his narrow-set eyes and picked at his brown beard. "So
what is it?"

"I am dying."

"Aye. And what of it?"

"You shall have charge of my children. The law shall let you
have the harvest until Heinrich is of proper age. Methinks a
half-hide's harvest a fair payment for their care till then."

"Humph!" scoffed Baldric. "You've three brats and I've no
wife to mind them." He leaned close to the woman. "Add your
dowry, then I shall agree."

Berta was too weak to argue and handed Baldric a box she
had set beside her. "The day I wed I was given two ewes and a
boar hog, three shillings and this table. The ewes have
dropped lambs and the shepherds say they now mark twelve
ewes and one ram for us. The boar yielded and we've credit
for ten pigs in the swineherd ... six due for taxes. Kurt added
a shilling for his work with the carpenters and from one good
harvest. Your father gave ten shillings, though Kurt spent
some on woollens, thatching, and some harvest tools. Here'd
be all the coins that are left, 'tis no more."

Baldric took the little chest and counted the silver. He
looked hard at Berta. He knew she feared for her soul and he
leaned close to her face. "So, on the Virgin you do swear this
to be all?"

Berta felt suddenly nauseous. She had no intention to give
Baldric all. That would mean she'd need to give him her
golden relic. Surely, she imagined, she would burn forever if
she gave it to the likes of Baldric! Yet, if she swore a lie on the
Virgin would she not also perish? Her mind and heart raced.
She closed her eyes.

Finally certain she was damned for either choice, Berta
chose the sin that did not advantage Baldric. "Aye, Baldric,
'tis all." She shuddered. All her life she had worked so very
hard to avoid the Pit, and in this one moment all had been
lost! She groaned.

The man smiled smugly, but before he could speak, Berta
hissed. "Hear me: the monks know all. Should you try to
cheat my children, they will serve you justice."

Baldric grinned. "There'd be one more thing."

Berta closed her eyes.

"I needs honor m'father's gift to Heinrich's sons-to-be. You remember—the parchment with the abbot's promise?"

Berta lay motionless. She said nothing for nearly a minute while Baldric waited. Then she slowly dug her hand deep into the recesses of her straw mattress and retrieved a flattened roll. She handed it to him without a word.

The gray sky hung heavy beneath the noon sun of the next day. Effi was playing with a ball of linen thread like a bored kitten and Axel was busy jabbing the hearth with a smoking stick. Berta called hoarsely for her eldest son. "Boy ... come here," she whispered.

Heinrich entered his mother's bedchamber. She nodded weakly and bade him sit by her side. "I needs speak of things. I've asked for Arnold to fetch the bailiff and Father Gregor. You must be here when they come. Now, hear me." The woman raised herself up on one elbow. "Honor the ways and make me proud. Make your father proud." She fell back. "Do you remember my story of the ox that coveted the saddle, and the horse the plough?"

Heinrich nodded solemnly.

"Good. Do not seek change, allow what is, to be." She sighed a little, then her tone changed. "Obey your uncle. I have given him charge over you all. Care for your sister ..."

Berta closed her eyes and listened to the wind now howling from the east. The door of the common room suddenly burst open and a chilly air blew through the hovel. Three men in heavy wraps tramped across the room and crowded into Berta's bedchamber.

Arnold pushed Heinrich aside and bent over the woman. She was now breathing quickly and her skin was pale. "Woman," he blurted. "Here's the bailiff and the priest. Now, what's this about?"

Berta peered through the room's gloom into the haunting dark eyes of Arnold. "My thanks," she whispered. The woman leaned upward on her elbow. "Can y'give me leave with these two?"

Arnold grumbled and left the room, leaving a perplexed Father Gregor and the stiff-eyed Bailiff Herold staring at the bed. Herold picked at his long nose and tapped his foot impatiently. The woman then reached beneath her and pulled a pouch from the straw. "Bailiff, thanks be to God you've come with the father. Listen, I beg you. I am about to die. M'papa taught me to keep things to good order." She paused. "I've needs to know m'sons and Effi shall be watched. And I needs to know that Heinrich's land will be safe for him as well as this house and—"

Herold cursed the woman. "You'd drag me through the mud and ice for this!"

"Hold, good sir," pleaded Berta. Her lips trembled. "There's more ... but please swear on the Virgin you'll tell no other." She held her hand open on her belly. Heinrich, wide-eyed and dumbstruck, leaned between the hips of Gregor and Herold as his mother whispered, "This ... this is a relic. 'Tis no common gold piece. I do swear on my soul this comes from Jerusalem. It was touched to the Holy Sepulchre by the Grand Master of the Templars."

Herold snatched the piece and held it to the dim light of the room's smoky candle. The priest gawked. "Relic? Hmm, look here, it's been bit! Have you ever heard of a relic that's been gnawed?"

The men laughed. Indeed, the gold coin bore a long dash and a short one—marks made from a good tooth next to a broken one. Heinrich squared his shoulders bravely. "If m'*Mutti* says it to be a relic, it is! She's never spoken a lie, she's—"

Herold cracked the five-year-old boy hard across the face. "Shut yer mouth, ye dim little fool!"

Father Gregor spoke firmly to Berta. "Woman, your soul is in peril of the Pit this day; you needs speak truth."

Berta's eyes fluttered. "What, what did you say, father?"

"You ought not be lying to your priest whil'st in death's valley!"

"Lying? Oh, I'm not lying, father. I prayed to it when the Templars came to save us, I ..."

"Enough, woman!"

Desperate tears fell from Berta's widened eyes. She spoke with hoarse urgency. "Father, I am not lying. I needs beg forgiveness for m'sin, I've ..."

Herold laughed out loud. "Woman, you're a fool!"

Young Heinrich had enough. He leapt from his corner with a shriek and swung his little fists at the bailiff's legs. Herold kicked the boy away and Father Gregor slapped him hard to the ground. "Lie there, Heinrich, and do not move! Do not look up, stare at the ground to which you shall someday be returned!"

This was all too much for poor Berta. She gave up her ghost while no one noticed.

ॐ

The household of Berta became the household of Baldric. Heinrich, Axel, Effi, and Herwin now spent each day in constant terror of the man who raged about his little empire like a tyrant. Void of affection, vacant of joy, filled only with heavy shadows and rage, the hovel that had once been full of love and warmth now did little more than shelter them from the harsh elements.

But for Baldric, life seemed suddenly improved. He now had charge of four lessers on whom he could vent his wrath. His position with the monks was envied, and his soul was about to be rescued by the coming of Easter. He had learned that Father Gregor had received an edict from the archbishop's nuncio ordering the priest to administer the sacrament of Eucharist to the folk of Weyer. The Eucharist was taken weekly, sometimes even daily, by the parish priests on behalf of their flock but was rarely offered directly to laymen. For those bearing the increasing weight of life's sins it would be a relief beyond measure. Baldric hid his torment well, but he suffered an increasing fear of the Judgment. The blood and flesh of Christ followed by an Easter penance would make him feel clean again.

The whole village was enlivened by the Easter Mass, and they looked toward spring with new hope. On May Day's dawn, Effi gathered dew on a bunch of wildflowers and wiped it on her brothers for good luck. Heinrich thanked her, then climbed the churchyard steps to sit by his mother's grave and mourn. It was a ritual he had followed each day since her death. From time to time he ambled to his father's grave and stared. He had never understood the mystery of his father's passing. Some, including his uncles and the priest, told him Kurt had died from infection, yet his mother had blamed him somehow. And so, with such heavy thoughts as these weighing on him, Heinrich considered his predicament and that of his siblings and he wept. After all, it was easy to reason that their current misery was on account of his failures as well.

May Day gave way to six weeks of hard labors before Midsummer's feast. And this particular year's feast presented the village with something of a surprise, for midst the afternoon's celebrations, Baldric reluctantly wed. In a ceremony that lasted less than a rich man's confession, the brute was married, ironically, to Hedda, the widow of Paul the dyer who was slain that awful night. Baldric was not particularly pleased with the choice, but he had been pressured to take her by the abbey's prior who had little patience for the problems of widows. After claiming her by ceremonially stomping on her foot, he introduced the limping bride to a circle of applauding witnesses.

Heinrich bowed politely and introduced himself to his stepmother. "I am Heinrich." He looked carefully at Hedda. The lad was insightful for a boy of five. He saw the brown-eyed woman as sympathetic and caring, but weary and withdrawn.

Hedda smiled and reached a hand toward the boy, but Baldric grabbed her by the wrist and twisted her arm cruelly. "Fetch me beer!" he growled.

Herwin shook his head as Baldric belched and turned away. "Children," Herwin whispered quickly, "follow me." He led the three through the footpaths of Weyer to the village well. There, to Heinrich's great joy, were Ingelbert and Emma. While the children played, Herwin entreated Emma to keep the boys and their sister overnight.

Herwin's request proved to be a wise one, for soon after the next day's dawn, Baldric was bellowing about the hovel like a madman. Poor Hedda had made a confession to her new husband. "I am barren and ... and cannot conceive," she wept. After three years of marriage to Paul she had not so much as a miscarriage. She had done penances and drunk infusions, worn amulets and even gone so far as to seek the witch near Münster, but nothing had eased her shame.

Upon hearing the pronouncement, Baldric beat her senseless and tossed her out his door. He then punched his fists through the walls of his hovel and smashed a stool atop the coal-red hearth. Cursing the prior for his trickery, he grabbed the morning's kettle, steaming with heated water and charged outside to douse his bride when Reeve Lenard intervened, backing him against the wall with the points of a hay fork. Other men rushed to the cottage and circled the raging man as Hedda was taken away.

Heinrich, Effi, Axel, Ingelbert, and Emma were blissfully unaware of the morning's turmoil. They had spent a wonderful night sleeping under the stars in Emma's butterfly garden and laughing at the wondrous stories good Emma could tell. In the morning they begged for more. "Well, my children," laughed Emma, "have I told you of the *Nixie* of the Rhine?"

The spellbound children leaned forward, gaping and wide-eyed.

"Ha, ha!" chuckled the sparkling-eyed woman. "She lives with other *Nickers* by the water's edge and spends her days combing her golden hair under a magic sun!

"On Midsummer's she and her *Nixie* friends dance with their male friends, the *Nixes*, and in their secret palace below the water they sing and feast until the moon is high above.

"They are good, you know. They dance upon the water when a man is about to drown. They say it is a call for help."

"Nay." Heinrich was suddenly gloomy. "Methinks they'd be happy for death."

"Ah, now Heinrich, why do you speak so?" asked Emma. She looked at him with worried eyes.

The boy shrugged. At the tender age of five, he had more reasons than he ought to think as he did.

～

It was a wondrous afternoon on the second Sabbath of July. A happy breeze toyed with the fields of thigh-high grain, bending them like folds of soft satin. The sky was blue, even bluer than the laughing eyes of young Heinrich as he dashed up the slope behind his good friend and cousin, Richard. The two reached the summit of the high ridge that overlooked Weyer from the east and waited impatiently for Ingelbert and Emma who were lagging behind.

Emma, panting and sweating, collapsed next to the boys and laughed. "By all the saints! I am getting a bit old for this." She pulled a clay jug of last year's cider from her satchel and smiled as the boys squealed in delight. Each took a swig and gathered close to the woman. She sat quietly for a few moments, enjoying the company of her son and his young friends. She reached deep into her satchel again and withdrew some rye and cheese. Soon the four were gnawing on dark bread and sharing the cider jug as the woman told tales of artful dwarves and cunning gnomes, the Knight of the Swan and the Dragon-rock.

The soft melodic voice of Emma lulled all to sleep beneath the golden sun; their backs nestled in thick, soft grass, their tender faces turned toward the warm light of the ever-constant sun. And while the foursome slept, the sun's caring visage arced in an ever-certain path, its very sureness offering hope to the shadowed order grinding far below.

A hurried breeze awakened Emma from her sleep and she sighed contentedly. She lay quietly in the green grass and thought of her life, of hard times and good. She recalled her childhood and thought of the mother she had never known. *Would she be pleased her life was forfeited for the likes of me?* she wondered. She then remembered her father, a wealthy lord, surrounded by the best physicians and moaning in fevered agony. Her memory took her to his solemn burial, and then to the long journey to the nunnery in Quedlinburg. As it often did, her mind quickly flew to the man she did yet love and the season of confusion in the orchards near the convent. A tug on her shoulder gave her a start.

"Frau Emma," insisted Richard. "Are you awake?"

"Ah, good lad," answered Emma. "*Ja,* I am indeed! And methinks it a good time to look to the sky!" She stroked Richard's hair and marveled at the lad's handsome features. *Hardly the son of Arnold!* chuckled Emma to herself. And when her own son tumbled next to Richard she fought back tears. For there sat one boy pleasing to all and the other doomed to contempt. She cupped Ingelbert's homely face in her hands and kissed him. "Now, children. Lie on your backs and look up. Always be looking up! The light comes from above. The sun and the moon are like the eyes of truth; sunshine is hope, and moonlight is mercy. Heinrich, can you remember this?"

The boy nodded.

"Now, lads, watch the clouds and tell me what you see."

A few moments passed. Finally Richard laughed. "I see Father Gregor's face!"

The others squealed. Indeed, a thin, white cloud with a large nose was drifting by. "Ha, ha! Richard. Good one!" chortled Heinrich.

Ingelbert pointed to a round, puffy cloud. "*Mutti!*"

Richard giggled.

"*Wunderbar!* Wonderful, Ingly! Ha, ha, 'tis fat like me!" Emma beamed.

The four laughed and tumbled, wrestling like pups with a playful mother. They rested in the grass and pointed to the sky once again where they discovered rabbits and cows, a hog's face and a monk's hood. "Can you see how the wind brings change? The sky is ever changing as the sun stays on its path. 'Tis wondrous."

The boys were puzzled by the woman's reflections, but there seemed to be something right and true in the words she spoke. They gathered close and felt joy in her presence.

೫

It was a gray, foreboding morning as the bells of Weyer's church rang prime on the day of the Epiphany in the year 1180. From the sunny spires of Constantinople to the rain-soaked chapels of soggy Ireland, the faithful of all Christendom gathered to celebrate this high day, this Feast of the Three Kings. The abbot of Villmar was pleased to know that the subjects of his manor were winding their way to the village churches, all worshiping God in service to their earthly masters.

But as the column of peasants climbed the steep steps of Weyer's dark-stoned church, they stopped as one, held for a moment by a shrieking cry from a clearing on the ridge above the Laubusbach on the opposite side of the village. All eyes turned to see the outstretched arms of a woman shouting and screaming at them with a small, white-haired child by her side. "A curse!" the woman screeched across the rooftops. "I cast a curse upon each soul. I throw a spell on all:

May fever, sores, King's Evil gasps, come to whom it may,
St. Vitus's Dance and pox and grippe befall this place this
　　day!
All grain to dust, all swine to fits, all sheep to wolves, I
　　pray,
All thatch to flames, all wells to bane, and Satan stain your
　　way!"

Heinrich stood speechless and cold, unnerved and fearful. He, like the others, had heard of her, and some were reported to have secretly counseled with her in the dark forests. But none had been hexed before, nor had any heard of a whole village being cursed. Father Gregor paled and leaned, faint-hearted, against the stone wall of the churchyard. He raised the silver crucifix hanging round his neck and offered a pitiful prayer in response. His timid, quivering voice was impotent and weak, and few thought the legions of heaven would rally to his cause. "*Jesu Christe*, have mercy."

Heinrich followed his poor fellows as they raced up the steps and huddled in the damp church; a gray bundle of tattered wool and matted hair, tightened faces, and tongues tied in terror. Father Gregor watched the witch throw a handful of ash into the sky and dance wildly. She joined hands with her little one and the two circled one another, faster and faster until the child stumbled. Then, with a final cackle and crow, the black-clad sorceress waved her open-palmed hands over the earth as if to summon the demons of Satan's Pit to her side. Gregor was certain she had.

Chapter 5

COURAGE AND GRACE

The Sabbath following the Epiphany was known as the Baptism of our Lord, but for the terrified folk of Weyer there was little joy in the celebration. Few had dared venture from their homes since the fearful hex of the woodland witch. Rumors abounded of hairless swine found tied in the trees and of infants suffocated in the night. Finally, Father Gregor convinced a reluctant Arnold to escort him to Villmar where he entreated the abbot to rise in defense of the village. After exchanging messages with the archbishop, the worried abbot decided to invite the Templars, holy monks themselves, to help Runkel's men-at-arms scour the forests in search of the witch. He wanted her captured and brought to trial in the church court at Mainz.

Gregor returned from Villmar with Father Johannes, a younger priest just sent from Mainz to assist the aging man. Father Gregor was nearly fifty and had endured his tenure in the service of a damp and gloomy parish church. The appointment of an assistant made for a bittersweet gift. The old priest was pleased to have the younger man's companionship, but his very presence was an unpleasant reminder of his own mortality.

Father Johannes had been raised as an oblate in the pink-stoned cloister at Maria Laach and, though his heart was sincere, he had been granted just enough education to cause harm. For all his lack of learning, however, the thin man was sincere and eager to do God's work. He imagined himself a guardian of the Virgin, and his piety and zeal were evident to all. As he followed Arnold and Father Gregor down the hill into Weyer's hollow, the young priest wept aloud for joy. "Ah, thanks be to God for this place! It is my place and I shall guard it well!"

No sooner had the clerics entered the village before a group of peasants crept from their hovels and scurried to the safety of the priests' shadows. One desperate woman held out her sick child for help. "Fathers, in the name of Blessed Mary can y'not help us? The witch's hex has taken one of m'children and now this one is sick with the King's Evil, just as she said!"

Others crowded around, including Heinrich. The sun disappeared behind a thick cloud and a sudden gust of snow showered the village. "My children," began Father Gregor slowly. "The brothers in Villmar are fasting for you now, this very day. They fast and they are doing penances for what wrongs you have brought upon yourselves. And God has sent us Father Johannes in our hour of need. He, too, shall pray for you and fast with me for thy safety."

"My child's eyes are failing and she lies sweated with fever," shrieked a woman. "I've spent all I have for bilberry but it is for naught. The witch is taking her sight!"

"Enough, woman!" answered Father Johannes sternly. He walked toward her purposefully and beckoned all to listen. Heinrich pressed close.

"The Savior healed the blind; 'tis blindness that be our foe! Seek not herbs to save your child's sight! 'Tis faith that is the balm, faith I say for all to hear. Woman, all of you, vow to me this very day that none shall put their trust in herbs or cantations, remedies or cures! Vow to fast and yield yourselves to the prayers of God's men.

"From here to the end of the curse any who would use a potion or an infusion or chant shall bear the wrath of the Holy Church. It is your lack of faith that has brought the curse, and by your faith restored the curse shall fail! Now on the morning Mass I shall grant absolution for all confessed sins. Your souls will be forgiven in heaven, but I cannot grant plenary indulgence for the temporal penalty still due until you perform penance for your weakness.

"So hear me: none are to eat honey, all must swear to charity; you needs pay another tithe by Sabbath day. One of each family must walk the village paths barefoot and without a cloak. By these penances we shall begin to overcome."

The folk were desperate and the young priest's confidence gave them hope. At the bells of nones groups of penitent villagers hurried toward the roadway. Among them were Baldric's bruised wife, Hedda, as well as Reeve Lenard with his huge dog in tow. Heinrich took his sister by the hand, and the two walked to the end of the frozen footpath to stare at the huddled column trudging obediently round the village like the Hebrews circling Jericho. But in Weyer there were no trumpets and there was no victory; only shivering peasants tramping barefoot through the snow.

≈

By Holy Week much had changed in Weyer. The child with failing sight was now completely blind, and nearly two dozen others had entered their graves. Most had died obediently—dutifully refusing to use the herbs offered by a kind Creation. The swineherd was decimated as well as the sheepfold, more from neglect than by the curse.

Among those lost to that terrible season was Father Gregor. He had fallen ill with the grippe just two days after the village penance had begun. Some said he ought not have walked barefoot with the others. But he was anxious to prove his mettle in the presence of a rival, and he led his little flock like the good shepherd he claimed to be. He had taken no herbs to ease his distress, though he was sorely tempted. "To whom much is given, much is required," had scolded Johannes. Gregor agreed and had poured his cup of coltsfoot upon the floor. So the man died faithful to the notions of Johannes—if not to the voice of Wisdom.

To the great joy of Baldric, another taken by the scourge was the woodward. For him, the witch's hex seemed a blessing for he was quickly appointed to the dead man's position and would now rule all the forests of Villmar's lands. Another was lost as well. Abbot Boniface had become ill, stricken with a cramping colic and consumption. Overcome with pain, he lost all enthusiasm for the ban on remedies. An oblate—a lad named Pious—had smuggled jugs of barley water and raspberry vinegar from the infirmer for the abbot's relief. Upon Boniface's death the lad confessed to all, and the disappointed brothers were sure the hand of God had stricken the hapless abbot for his unfaithfulness.

In his place came Brother Malchus. The monk had taken his vows in Lorch, the home of Emperor Barbarossa. Malchus had been a knight by another name in the service of the emperor and had lost his left ear in a battle in Palestine. Believing himself spared to serve God in new ways, he had joined the monastery in Lorch where the novice-master gave him his name. There he proved himself to be a man of wisdom, true humility, and deeply committed to the Rule of Benedict. He secretly resented the control the Archbishop of Mainz exercised over the abbey at Villmar, especially since most abbots now answered directly to papal legates. It would be his hope to bring the liberation of the abbey.

Malchus arrived on Holy Thursday and immediately summoned Prior Paulus to review the spiritual and temporal condition of his new stewardship. Before long he imposed stricter fasts on his brethren and ordered new aggressive plans for village bakeries, breweries, and mills. "And more," he said. "We've must look to a new system of planting like we've done in Swabia. Gather the village reeves and haywards and we'll set upon the task."

≈

The summer proved to be a grave disappointment for the new abbot. The harvest was a disaster and morale of the monks was low. Worse yet, the abbey's treasury had been pilfered. Since the fiscal year of Christendom began and ended on Michaelmas—the twenty-fifth of September—the treasury had held nearly a year's worth of revenues. Of course, the abbot dared not let the villagers know of the violation lest they lose heart. After all, the monastery was their final redoubt from Satan's evils. If God's fortress could be penetrated so easily, what hope would they have for themselves?

The abbot was frustrated by the theft but also extremely agitated by the parish priests' continuing ban on remedies for sickness. Since the village priests answered to their bishop and not to him, he sent messengers to the archbishop in Mainz begging him to correct the foolishness. Mercifully, the archbishop agreed and dispatched a simple message to his priests: "Encourage your flocks to trust God by trusting in God's people and in the tools of God's creation."

Immediately, Abbot Malchus summoned an herbalist skilled in modern techniques and, on a warm day in mid-October, Lukas of Saxony appeared at the abbey's gate. Lukas was of medium height, with dark brown eyes and hair. A young, eager, and good-natured monk, he had gentle, pleasing features, was quick of wit and wise beyond his years. Lukas had been schooled at the Abbey of St. Gall and had taken a special interest in medicines and herbs. The monk had a love for life that gave joy to many, and he knew no better way to serve than to probe the wonderful mysteries of God's good earth.

But more troubles soon loomed over the manors of the abbey. Just two days after Lukas's arrival, the abbot received a messenger from the Archbishop of Mainz warning of danger. Apparently, the lord of nearby Mensfelden had revoked his loyalty to Emperor Barbarossa and pledged himself to a prince of Saxony who was building a treasonous alliance. Barbarossa learned of the betrayal and immediately stripped the defector of all his lands, granting them to another. The Abbey of Villmar was under the protection of the Lord of Runkel, himself a loyal subject of the emperor. It was now feared that the disenfranchised Lord of Mensfelden might send his knights into the abbey's lands to exact revenge.

The days of October became days of vigilance and fear. The men and women of Weyer regularly soaked their roofs with buckets of water and filled the church with what stores their scanty harvest had yielded. At night they lay awake in their beds, imagining what horrors might await them by the following day.

Six-year-old Heinrich lay upon his straw mound wide-eyed and restless. He stared at the dark thatch glowing ominously in the failing light of the hearth and could not sleep. The village was nervous but quiet, until Reeve Lenard began to ease his nerves by beating his hapless dog. Heinrich squeezed his fists and pleaded with God to strike Lenard dead if the soldiers came.

"You, boy!" Baldric stormed from his bedchamber. "You are not to speak at night! Now stand where you be!"

Heinrich climbed to his feet. He knew what was coming and he gritted his teeth. Effi began to sob.

"And you, little brat! If I hear one sound, I'll strap you too!"

Herwin rose to intervene, only to be knocked to the ground atop Axel. Baldric snatched Heinrich by the elbow and slammed him against the wall. He bent over and hissed in the boy's ear. "You worthless scrap of dung. You've no value to me, so cause me more trouble and you'll not live to see the morrow. Now take this strap like a man. If you cry out, I'll hit you all the more!"

The man whipped the boy three times, then four, five, and six. By seven lashes, Baldric's brave wife ran from her room and fell to her knees between her husband and the stone-faced boy. "Please, I beg you to stop. I—"

Her compassion earned her a stripe of her own, then another. She whimpered and stretched her arms toward Heinrich. The boy mouthed a polite "thank-you" and stood ready for more.

When it was over, Heinrich lay awake all night. He remembered the voice of Emma on the hilltop that wondrous summer day and wished to feel the sunshine warm his face again. He longed to press his bare feet against a soft carpet of tender grass and lift a butterfly to flight. If only he could fly away from Baldric.

To the relief of all, the pillaging knights did not come, and the days passed with the gentle rhythm of the season. The village men labored behind their oxen in the fields, while the women gathered reeds and willow wands, chopped cabbage for the brine, and picked apples and pears from the abbey's orchards by the stream. Given the poor yield of flax, many of the women were busy wandering the forests in search of nettles for thread making.

Emma rose with Ingelbert early one misty morning and they walked together to the common well before the others would be about. The pair shuffled through the smoky village footpaths, crunching lightly on the leaves now lying thick beneath their feet. Emma was content, as was her usual state, though saddened as she surveyed the poverty all about her. Even in the blue haze of dawn her eyes could see the pall that hung atop the damp huts scattered about her. The loud crow of a cockbird startled her and Ingly giggled.

No sooner had the woman snuggled the little six-year-old to her side when Lenard's dog began to bark loudly. Emma groaned. "Ah, Ingly, it seems we've wakened the poor beast." In a moment, the reeve could be heard shouting and cursing at the howling dog. No amount of beating would silence the animal. But then Emma heard what the dog had heard. She stood perfectly still and closed her eyes. "Dear God!" She grabbed her son by the arm and raced for Heinrich's hut, shouting the alarm. "Riders, riders!" she cried.

Baldric leapt to his feet and flung open his door only to see Emma and her son racing toward him.

"Run! Riders are coming!"

At that moment Reeve Lenard began blowing his ox-horn, warning the village of imminent danger. Herwin bolted from his bed and joined Baldric in the doorway while Hedda gathered the frightened children to her side.

Suddenly four riders rounded the bend of the Münster road and pounded up the road. The peasants emerging from their huts panicked and scattered. Emma urged Hedda to escape across the Laubusbach. "Come, Hedda! Run!"

Baldric pushed her aside. "Go, woman! Take your freak and begone! I'll tend m'own household!"

The soldiers reined in their mounts and stopped to laugh at the chaos in the terrified village. Clad in leather vests and armed with long swords and bows, none wore helmets but each wore a mail hood. Small, triangular shields hung on their forearms, and each fist was set securely in a plate-armored glove. None knew if these were knights, sergeants, squires, or highwaymen, and none cared, for bloodlust was in their eyes.

Again Emma pleaded with Hedda and reached for Heinrich. Baldric's heavy hand fell hard across Emma's face and sent her sprawling into the crush of frantic peasants.

With kicks of their spurs and a loud shout the mounted men charged into the heart of the smoky village. The terrified folk scattered before them like dried leaves driven by a gust of wind. The rogue knights lifted their swords and sped after the fleeing peasants. First one, then another fell to the razor-sharp edges of the four flashing blades. Poor Otto, a neighbor to Arnold, fell first, his shoulder split to the center of his chest; then Elsbeth, the kindly wife of a ploughman and Werner the shepherd with his little infant, Ruthard. Others fell atop each other, bellies opened, limbs hacked, faces punctured.

While the soldiers continued their attack, the house-holds of Baldric and Arnold hastened toward the Laubus-bach and the safety of the far wood. Baldric paused a moment and turned an angry eye back toward the carnage. There, at the rear of the throng he saw his good friend, Dietrich the miller, stumbling along and holding his infant daughter, Meta. Behind him followed his wife, Gudrun, with the forearms of young twins Sigmund and Marta grasped tightly in her hands. Baldric gasped as Dietrich tripped, spilling baby Meta to the ground. Gudrun let go of her twins and lunged for Meta as Dietrich dodged a blade. An arrow struck the mother's chest and before Dietrich's eyes his wife toppled to the ground, baby Meta tumbling beneath the grinding hoofs of the archer's horse.

Baldric had seen enough. He bellowed for Arnold and grabbed a threshing flail. He tossed Arnold a fodder fork and the two pressed against the swarming tide of wool. Herwin, seeing the men turn, grabbed an axe and joined them. Inspired by the courage of these three, Reeve Lenard,

Gunter Ploughman, Edwin the thatcher, and others turned to fight as well.

Dietrich rolled into the safety of an open doorway and tossed his twins deep inside the hovel. Seeing Baldric and his comrades storming toward the horsemen, he leapt from his cover and picked up a hog mallet.

Baldric struck first. He swung his hinged flail squarely into the face of one surprised rider, dropping the man to the ground where two others smashed his head with heavy rocks. Arnold deftly feigned a thrust with his fork at another soldier's side, then rammed the iron points through the sweated horse's ribs. The animal buckled and collapsed on its side, spilling its rider into the grasping hands of the raging peasants.

Arnold took the fallen man's sword and turned against the remaining two, who, shocked by the serfs' resistance, reined their horses hard. Herwin grabbed one horse's bridle and held fast against the beast's urge to rear. In that moment Dietrich leapt onto the horse's rump and swept the rider to his death. The final soldier threw his sword upon the ground and raised his hands in surrender to the crowd of gray-brown tunics now encircling him. "No quarter!" roared Baldric as he pressed between the shoulders of his fellows. "No quarter!"

With that, he swung a woodsman's axe into the man's belly, folding the murderous rake like a stalk of barley struck by a dull sickle. The man gasped as Baldric pulled him to the ground where he crushed his skull.

Weyer fell as silent as a winter's night. Slowly, those in hiding crept from sanctuary, and those who had fled to the forest returned to join the others in the village center. Emma clutched Ingelbert to her breast and searched the crowd until her eyes fell on Heinrich. Relieved to find him safe, she wept. Wide-eyed and speechless, Heinrich, Richard, and their siblings stared mutely at the scene.

≈

In late March of 1181 the winter wheat sprouted green atop the frosty hills, and the bells of nones tolled loudly above the churchyard where the village council was preparing to conduct business. The men of Weyer sat in a large circle atop pine boughs and bark and waited for Reeve Lenard to begin. Meanwhile, Heinrich and Richard crouched behind some bushes at the far edge of the churchyard. For boys of seven and six this was an adventure indeed. If they'd be caught they would surely feel the hard slap of a willow wand!

The business of the day began, dealing mostly with issues of the fields, taxes, encroaching fences, petty thefts, allotments of firewood, and the like. Dietrich the miller, with the influential support of his friends Baldric and Arnold, was elected as a village elder and had much to say about grain fees and thefts of flour. Little else of any account was discussed, and Heinrich and Richard grew weary and cold.

After a few yawns by those gathered, Reeve Lenard moved on to other matters. A man had been accused of robbing a grave but was judged innocent on the word of three oath-helpers who had sworn, under risk of God's wrath, to his innocence. A discussion was entertained on the constant problem of firewood and two neighbors disputed a fence. At long last Reeve Lenard came to the final issue. "You've heard it said that we've had rumors about this woman, Emma. Bring her here."

Heinrich and Richard jerked to attention and peered from their cover as Emma was pulled out from the church doorway. Her hands were bound and little Ingelbert clung to her side in terror. The tattered woollen cloak Emma wore seemed little defense against the stiff wind, yet she walked upright and proud into the center of the circle.

"Woman, this is no trial. There is none with proof to accuse but we needs ask you things." Reeve Lenard sounded reasonable in his tone, though Heinrich did not trust any man who would beat a defenseless dog. "It has been said that your spirit flies by night to scrump. Swear by the Virgin it is not so."

Frau Emma looked about the village men and sighed. A breeze pulled her scarf from her head and wisps of brown hair fell into her eyes. She faced the reeve submissively but answered with a hint of sarcasm. "Good Reeve. Neither me nor my ghost has stolen anything."

"Do you so swear?"

"My answer is enough."

"But do you swear it?"

"My 'aye' is 'aye.'"

The reeve began to pace. "Are you a witch?"

"No."

"Are you heathen?"

"No."

"You seem ... odd. And your freak child bears the mark of evil."

Emma flushed and her temples pulsed. "With respect, Reeve Lenard, are you a Christian man?"

Lenard was dumfounded. "What? Of course I am a Christian man!" He turned to Father Johannes who nodded, approvingly. His confidence assured, he pressed on. "From whence come you?"

"Quedlinburg."

"And ..."

"And what?"

"And why are you in Weyer?"

"It has a nice stream."

The villagers chuckled. Lenard was now impatient. "And tell us of the shadows on All-Souls Eve!"

The men grew suddenly quiet and leaned forward. All had heard rumors of strange things around the woman's hut on that dreaded night, but none had dared venture near. None, that is, save Arnold. The woman was visibly startled by the question. She drew a deep breath and smiled wryly. "I bar m'door well at night. If I be on the inside, I dare say I'd have no idea what those without do see."

She had barely finished when the men began to grumble. "Nay, 'tis no answer!" groused one. Another rose with a pointing finger. "You'd be lyin'! You've visits from the Devil on the deads' day ... and y've this monster as our proof!"

The men approved as the accuser went on. "Y'needs confess to us now, strumpet. Tell us of your harlotry and blasphemes! You're in league with the witch, as well! Since y've come we've naught but bad ways and plagues, swords and famine. Methinks y'needs be put out, else flogged for what heresies must go on behind your walls!"

Midst the uproar of the men, poor Emma stood still and silent. Finally, a chunk of muddy snow was hurled at the woman and struck her on the face. The men laughed. Brave Emma held her son under her bound arms as the melting ice slid slowly down her face. The council grew quiet until another ball of snow was thrown, then another. The woman bent over her son and sheltered him as best she could from the ensuing storm of ice and mud until a shrill voice was heard above the din. It was Heinrich.

The boy charged from his cover, his brave cousin at his side. They threw rocks, not snow, into the council, earning a roar of disapproval. They kicked and clawed their way to Emma's side and stood by her, screaming and cursing at the men now laughing all about them. Father Johannes tripped his way through the jeering crowd and cracked the two atop their heads. He then turned and whispered to Lenard. "You've proof of naught. Methinks that if she's guilty she's been frightened to stop, if not, 'tis not pleasing to heaven to do more."

Reeve Lenard raised his hands and declared the council ended.

&

The mid-August feast of the Assumption of the Virgin was glorious. Baldric had been granted a bonus by the bailiff, and Arnold, in turn, was granted a shilling extra for his exceptional care of the forests around Weyer. The fields were yielding more grain than could be remembered in recent years and the villagers rejoiced in plenty. For Baldric's unfortunate wife, Hedda, however, the feast was not glorious at all. She had lain on her bed for nearly a month, sickened with milk-leg and scabs. Baldric refused her any remedy and commanded her to rely solely on her faith.

Early in the morning of the feast day Heinrich slipped the suffering Hedda an herbal infusion. Despite the lifting of the prior ban, the lad had hesitated, less out of fear for

Baldric than for fear of God's judgment. When he had seen the poor woman's pleading eyes, however, he sighed and scurried to do the deed, hoping all the while that God would forgive him of his sin and that Baldric would never know.

With the deed done, the young boy drove away his guilt by joining Richard in a race along the village footpaths. The morning was bright and warm, and the village was filled with tables of early fruits, honey cakes, and boiled mutton. The pair danced and sang with others and played hard at village games. It was about an hour past noon when the two finally made their way to Emma's hut. The day was awash in the sunlight and birdsongs of the season, and the flowers in Emma's gardens were vigorous and bright. Butterflies of amber and black, orange, yellow, and blue floated in happy flocks above and between tall, bloom-heavy stems. In the center of her garden, waist deep in a rainbow of blossoms, stood Emma, smiling and singing for all heaven to hear.

As the boys approached they paused to marvel. Emma's round, rosy face seemed to glow in the sunlight of midday. The bundle of brown hair knotted atop her head shined like polished satin. Her brown eyes twinkled and sparkled as she laughed and danced between the slender stalks of her blessed flowers. Heinrich whispered in wonder, "Richard, even the butterflies dance with her. I've a new name for her! She shall be the 'Butterfly Frau'!"

Richard squealed with delight. "*Ja! Ja!* 'Tis good, Heinrich ... a good name."

"Welcome! Welcome!" the woman cried as she spotted the two.

"Yes, Frau Emma!" cried Richard as the pair sprinted toward her. "Heinrich has a new name for you!"

Heinrich blushed.

"A new name? Wonderful, I love new names! What is it?"

Heinrich fumbled, not sure whether she would be pleased. "Well ..."

"Ach, 'tis fine, boy. Speak it."

"Butterfly Frau." Heinrich held his breath.

"Butterfly Frau? Hmm. Butterfly Frau ... Butterfly Frau!" A slow smile spread across the woman's face. "Heinrich, I

love it! I shall be now and forevermore, Butterfly Frau!"
Emma laughed and gave Heinrich a hug.

"I knew she would love it!" cried Richard.

Emma reached to embrace him and he quickly retreated.
Heinrich laughed.

At that moment Ingelbert scampered out of the forest.
His face brightened when he saw his two friends. "Ingly!"
called Richard. "Ingly, let's play."

Ingelbert laughed and pointed. "See there!" he cried.

Heinrich and Richard turned to see a reluctant but curious group of village children approaching. Behind them
stood a group of wary mothers, arms folded and watching
from afar. The children were partly frightened and partly
intrigued. Emma had invited them earlier with a promise of
beeswax and berries. She hoped to win their affections for
her son and thought time spent together might make a
good beginning. Emma drew a deep breath as the five new-
comers approached. One already was pointing at her son
and the others were giggling.

"Welcome, children," smiled Emma, nervously. The
children arrived, carefully studying the woman and her
mysterious home. "Come in," Emma offered. Heinrich and
Richard scowled a bit. They hadn't known of this little plan
and weren't the least bit pleased. The Butterfly Frau was
theirs—and not to be shared, especially with the likes of
these! In the fore stood Ludwig, the son of Mattias the yeoman. The lad was free and, though only seven, he already
knew his place to be above the others. Next to him stood
Anka. She was ten and a bully of girl, demanding and
stubborn. At her side stood six-year-old Marta, the pretty
and petite daughter of Dietrich the miller. Marta scowled
and whined at Ingly who was making strange faces at her.
Behind were Edda, daughter of the new dyer, and hard-
eyed Baldwin, the young son of Reeve Lenard.

The occasion was already proving to be awkward at best.
Emma sat the children in a circle and bade Ingelbert to
greet each one. Heinrich thought Ingly's face to have more
color at that moment than he had ever seen! The hostess
then beckoned her timid son to fetch a bowl of blackberries

they had picked early that very morning, and the lad quickly passed the bowl around the room.

"And what of the beeswax?" groused Ludwig. "You said we'd have beeswax in honey."

Anka raised her nose indignantly. "You've lied to us like m'*Mutti* said you would," she whined.

"Oh, no children!" answered Emma. "I thought we might play a game first, then Ingly will serve us his honey."

"*His* honey?" challenged Baldwin. "How is it his honey and not the abbey's?"

Emma smiled. "A very good question, good lad. The monks let me buy a hive when I moved here and—"

"And that's the end of your stupid questions!" blurted Richard.

The two boys stood nose to nose and readied for blows when Emma calmed the room. "Ah, lads 'tis time for our game!"

The perspiring woman gathered the children in a circle and stood in the center to explain her contest. "We shall all make the sound of an animal. It can be a bird or a beast, matters not. The best shall take a honeycomb home!"

The prize met with a round of approval and the children began to tease one another. Ingelbert sat anxiously on his haunches, nervously awaiting his chance to whistle like a thrush. Heinrich beamed in anticipation. He knew he could imitate the priest's donkey well enough to turn the father's head.

Richard rose first and snorted and grunted, barked and squealed like the maddest swine in all the herd. The circle of children roared their approval and the boy sat down proudly. Edda followed with a well-tuned "hoo-ooo-oot" of an owl. In order then came Anka the ox, Baldwin the wolf, Ludwig the ram, and Ingly, the most excellent fluting thrush.

The group paused after Ingelbert's impressive perform-ance and, to Emma's hopeful eye, a seed of respect sprouted. The last to challenge were Marta and Heinrich. Heinrich bowed and let the fair Marta go first—after all, chivalry was the duty of every man. Besides, he knew he would surely win.

Marta came to the center of the ring, nervous and self-conscious. She was a pretty little girl, blonde and fair, even-featured, and void of scabs. Though bright and clever, she oft seemed troubled and fearful. Her eyes betrayed an unhappiness buried deep within. The girl closed her eyes and announced, "I shall crow like a rooster." With that she lifted back her head and wheezed a most wretched "caw-aw-a-oodle-eww." At first, the circle was quiet, but a slow titter soon began to ripple round and round, and it quickly grew louder and louder until the whole hovel echoed with belly-shaking howls! At first the poor girl stood helpless and humiliated. She faced her mockers slack-jawed and wide-eyed. Then, able to bear it no longer, she sprinted to a corner in tears.

Heinrich and Ingelbert did not laugh. Ingly walked to the girl's side and laid a gentle hand atop her shoulder. With a whine she swatted him away, and the good and gentle boy retreated with a kindly nod. Emma quieted the room with a fierce, scolding look and bade Heinrich take his turn.

Heinrich was now troubled. He cast a quick glance at the sobbing girl and drew a deep breath to think about the moment. "I ... I shall do a ... a duck."

"What?" cried Richard. "A duck!"

Emma scowled at the laughing children, but Heinrich sighed. He then contorted his face in a most horrid way and began to squeak and honk a painful cacophony of distortion that none could bear! His ridiculous performance drew to him the humiliation that had been so amply heaped on Marta, and the room of children laughed and mocked, jeered and taunted the boy without quarter. All that is, save faithful Richard and also Ingelbert, who quickly understood the purpose of Heinrich's sacrifice. Heinrich had intended mercy but when his eyes fell on Marta's mocking sneers, he knew his compassion had been spent on one who knew little of such things—and it hurt.

Emma wiped a tear on her rough sleeve and hugged little Heinrich as she called for the vote. Anka cried out, "We cannot vote for Ingelbert, he is too ugly! I vote for Ludwig." Most others agreed, though some began to quarrel while Emma closed her eyes and simply wished the day to end. In a few moments, over some loud objections from Baldwin, Ludwig received his prize, and all were fed the promised honey. Then, with nary a thanks, the visitors scampered out of the cottage.

As quiet filled the room once more, an exhausted Emma sat sadly atop a stool and stroked Ingelbert's quivering face. She smiled at Richard. She had seen him slap Anka hard for the insult and felt a secret satisfaction. She drew a deep breath and paused to look at her young companions' waiting faces. Nestled at her side was her innocent son and within her reach sat both the stouthearted Richard and the merciful Heinrich. Her joy was quickly restored.

Chapter 6

THE VOW OF THE WORM

So, lads." Emma smiled. "The others are gone but we've still some sunshine left. What say we play?"

For all children such an opportunity io a gift! Unhappiness forgotten, the three boys scampered through the door and dashed across the meadow that bordered the cheerful Laubusbach. They tossed pebbles into the stream, turned rocks over in search of snails and frogs, and soon decided to explore the forest upstream.

"*Mutti*," begged Ingelbert. "Can y'come with us in the wood?"

"Of course I can, and thank you for asking!" answered Emma.

So, as the sun arched slowly toward the west, the four began a journey along a deer path on the far side of the Laubusbach. They walked through tall, heavy spruce and smelled the pungent needles that shaded and cooled them. Emma told tales of woodland fairies and sprites, frog kingdoms, and the terror of the wandering knight.

The group followed the stream until it led them into a large clearing rich with blackberries and plums, thick-trunked birch and majestic oaks. The children paused to play as Emma surveyed her location. She offered a gentle warning: "Somewhere ahead is the boundary pole. We ought not venture beyond it."

Richard turned a keen eye into the forest. "Can we not go a

little more, just a few steps past the pole?" he begged.

Emma smiled at the row of bright eyes waiting expectantly. She lovingly squeezed Heinrich's round cheeks. "And
you, young squire? Would you like to cross over?"

"Aye!" the boy answered without hesitation.

Emma paused for a moment of contemplation. There
was something special about the lad, and she was sure he
was touched by destiny for something uncommon and
good. An orange butterfly danced at the boy's elbow, and
the woman held a long-stemmed flower toward it. With one
eye on the butterfly and the other on Heinrich she sang:

Oh, wondrous new creature, break from your cocoon
And stretch your fresh wings upon these tender blooms.
Come flutter 'tween flowers, and sail o'er the trees,
Or light on m'finger and dance in the breeze.

Since change is your birthright, fly free and be bold
And fear not the tempest, the darkness, or cold.
Press on to new places, seek color and light,
Find smiles and laughter and joy on your flight.

For though you see dimly; your certainties few,
Your Maker stands steady and constant and true.
He guards you and guides you till travelin's done,
His breath moves the breezes; His heart warms the sun.

Her song finished, Emma raised her brows and winked
slyly. "Well then, follow me!" The happy column pranced
through waist-high ferns, whispering and tittering to
each other until Emma suddenly stopped and hushed the
children.

"Sshh ... look." She pointed anxiously to a dark figure
bending at the dark edge of the forest wall. The group quickly
crouched low in the ferns as Emma studied the man carefully. He was moving slowly and appeared to be gathering
things into a large satchel hanging at his side. Curiosity
nudged Emma forward. "Quietly, children. Follow quietly,"
she whispered.

The excitement was too much for Ingelbert and he giggled
out loud. The man stood suddenly upright and turned

toward the clearing. "Who goes there?" he called.

Emma quickly threw herself in the grass and pulled the boys down beside her. "Sshh! Ingly ... sshh!"

Poor Ingelbert thought the moment to be a wonderful game, and he lay in the grass wide-eyed and chortling, two hands clamped firmly over his mouth. Richard punched him on the shoulder but it made the scene that much funnier to the good-natured boy.

Cautiously, Emma moved to see where the man might be. The bun atop her head rose above the grass and the man laughed. "Ha, ha! Is that a bird's nest I see?"

The woman drew a deep breath and stood up, shamefaced and nervous. She brushed the brambles and chaff off her woollen. As the man came closer, Emma smiled. With some relief, she turned to the boys. "A monk! He's a monk!"

The young brother smiled and waved. "You've naught to fear, sister."

Emma smiled timidly and waited respectfully. She watched the bearded man as he approached and judged him to be around twenty. As he came closer she noticed his gait to be strong and nimble, his features amiable and pleasing.

"Good day, sister. God's blessing on you and your lads."

"And to you, brother. I am Emma of Weyer. This is m'son, Ingelbert, and m'good friends, Heinrich and Richard."

"And I am Lukas, the herbalist of Villmar."

Emma nodded but was puzzled. The monks rarely left their cloister. It was usually forbidden for them to engage the world beyond the monastery walls, and this brother was at the farthest edge of the manor. Her confusion was evident.

"And you wonder why I am wandering the forest? Why am I not tucked away behind the walls, bound by the Rule? And, what of the prayers of nones on this holy day?" The monk smiled mischievously.

Emma knew the angels had blessed her with a new friend. She smiled and her dancing eyes told the man he was in sympathetic company. "'Tis true," laughed Emma. "I do wonder some."

"And I, as well!" Lukas chuckled. "The abbot demands

more order to his Order, but I reason that I vowed my poverty, obedience, and charity to God—not an abbot, archbishop, or pope! Methinks the whole of the world is His monastery. So, I'm apt to wander a bit. I believe it is the better way to serve."

Emma smiled.

"Ah, but forgive me, sister. I ought not bore you and these *Kinder* with such talk. I am collecting wild herbs and nuts for the new herbarium the abbot is building. I could use a few good hands!"

The foursome quickly volunteered, and before the bells of vespers tolled, the five had filled the monk's satchel with chamomile, dandelion, thimble, yarrow, hollyhock, and thistle; snips of coltsfoot, careful grasps of burning nettles, and strips of wild cherry bark. Their wanderings drew them far along the winding Laubusbach as it bubbled and frolicked through its deep-wood channel.

Lukas stood to stretch his back and laughed loudly. "Look, there." He pointed to three huge trees gathered in a cluster along the stream's bank at its eastward bend. He hurried through the ferns toward the giant trunks and smiled broadly. One was an old sycamore, another a towering ash, and the final a massive, ancient oak. Their trunks had grown close together, leaving only enough room for three grown men to stand between them. They towered into the sky where their heavy branches tangled into a marvelous canopy.

"Three kings! They look like three kings!" exclaimed Heinrich.

"Yes!" clapped Emma. "Like the Magi."

Heinrich chirped, "The Magi of the Laubusbach!"

"Indeed," cried Emma, "that's to be their name!"

Ingelbert squealed with delight and pointed to the old oak's trunk. The others looked and laughed, for there, about the same height as a mounted knight, was a large knot protruding from the trunk in the shape of a face.

"It has eyes, a nose, and mouth!" exclaimed Richard.

The five laughed and bowed respectfully to the Wise Ones. They climbed within the confines of their new, columned fortress, shielded from all danger. They loved their newfound place and vowed to tell no other.

A pleasant evening's breeze comforted the friends as they rested by the rooty feet of the Magi. Relaxed and happy, Lukas shared stories of life in the abbey; the boys of life in the village. "And m'uncle Baldric," murmured Heinrich, "says Hedda ought have no fix for her troubles. He says she needs show faith, like what Father Johannes said about the hex. And what of the blind girl?"

"What blind girl?"

" 'Twas a girl losing her sight ... Father Johannes forbade her ... bil ..."

"Bilberry?"

"*Ja.*"

Lukas darkened. "Heinrich, the foolish ban has been ended. Now hear me. You seem to be a clever lad, bright beyond your learning. Beware of religious men. They destroy all that is within their grasp."

The boy did not understand. He shrugged. "But, Brother Lukas, Father Johannes said God would punish us if we did not obey."

"Ach! Boy, hear the words of the Holy Scripture: 'Avoid those with the form of godliness but without its substance!' Methinks your priest is a dolt!"

Emma was surprised, but secretly delighted. *Who is this man?* she wondered. *May God keep him near us.*

~

Nearly one year later it was Arnold that brought news to Father Johannes. Baldric's long-suffering second wife, Hedda, had died. Baldric was working in the heavy wood near the village of Emmerich and was not expected to return for two days. The woman's body lay white-faced and cold upon her bed with scarcely a visitor save her nephews and niece who had gathered about her quietly. Heinrich stared at the corpse with cold shivers of dread climbing over his skin. He was sure God had punished Hedda because of the herbs he had given her, and a weight of guilt knotted his belly.

Effi thought it would be kind to gather wildflowers to scatter within the woman's shroud so, in the middle of a sunny afternoon in May, the three children of Kurt stooped and bent through the meadow grasses of the Laubusbach plucking white *Maiglücken* and violets, dandelion and pungent blue velchin. Hedda had been little more than an anguished maid trapped in the wretched grasp of a monster, but the three children had soft hearts for her. So when Father Johannes blessed her grave, each child shed a tear.

Baldric returned the next afternoon and flung himself atop his empty bed. He slept for hours, rising only to gulp down a few swallows of cider. He awoke to return to his duties without one word of his wife's passing, save a few complaints of the death tax he owed.

ॐ

"Baldric," said Arnold in the cold twilight of November the first.

"What?"

"'Tis All Souls' Eve."

"Aye ... and what of it?"

"You said we ought spy Emma's house for the shadow that comes each year."

Baldric felt suddenly uneasy. "It is only a legend, brother ..."

"No! Y'dolt! I've seen it m'self."

"Then why have y'not taken hold of it? Are you afraid?"

Arnold grumbled. "Methinks it better when there's two. It may be a demon ... a ghost? But methinks we've need both go."

Baldric was anxious. He had suffered nightmares nearly every night for many months in which he saw the face of Paul the dyer staring at him from beneath the waters of the Lahn. And lately he was certain he could hear Hedda's voice cursing him in the dark. "What of it?" he answered. "The harvest was good this year, the best any can remember. The hex is gone and methinks it best to leave well enough alone."

"What if it be just a man ... a secret lover. Secrets are worth money!"

Baldric shrugged. "I'll ... I'll go with you this once and we'll have a look, but I make you no vow. If 'tis a spirit I come home!"

Arnold laughed. "You're the biggest man in the whole of

the manor and you'd be afraid! We needs be there by matins' bell."

It was soon after compline when Baldric ordered his household to bed. He then climbed into his bed where he lay restlessly waiting for the next few hours to pass. In the common room lay Herwin, exhausted and snoring. Along the outer walls slept Heinrich, Axel, and Effi, each burrowed deep into their straw.

But none would sleep long, for Reeve Lenard's dog was whining again. The village groaned and muttered in the night's darkness, cursing and wishing the reeve would silence the beast once and for all. Lenard shouted and then could be heard swearing by the darkest places. Within moments the poor beast's whines turned to yelps.

Heinrich lay in the nightglow of his hovel and wept for the dog. The animal was a clumsy, oafish thing, perhaps a bit stubborn, but sincere and eager. When Baldric had beaten Heinrich at Hallowmas just passed, it was Lenard's tender-hearted creature that licked the lad's bleeding face. The boy sat up. For a moment he imagined sneaking over to Lenard's hut and releasing the dog, and his heart began to race. *But it would be stealing … I'd be a thief!* he worried. He argued with himself. *Aye … but is it better to leave the animal with that madman?*

Heinrich was suddenly paralyzed. He had woven a web and ensnared himself, for his conscience had trapped him into inevitable disobedience to *something*. He lay back and stared into the red-hued underside of thatch.

In the bedchamber Baldric was troubled too. He dared not close his eyes for fear of hearing Hedda, yet he could not keep them open for fear of seeing Paul's ghost. Mercifully, his brother finally entered the hut and strode into his room.

"We've needs go," said Arnold.

Baldric rose quickly and pulled a fur cloak over his shoulders as he stepped past the hearth and out his door. The autumn night was damper than usual, and a heavy fog had settled on the village. "Remember, I've only agreed to watch."

The two walked quietly through the sleeping village, past coughs and snores, a cackle from some fowl, and the soft cries of hungry infants. They approached Emma's hovel cautiously. It was beyond the end of the path, standing quite alone near the Laubusbach. The moon was new and the mist-shrouded stars barely cast enough silvery light to see the blurred silhouette of the hut and its fences. The men crouched and hurried to the cover of a thick-trunked tree.

For a time, the brothers could hear only the sounds of their own breathing. Then the church bell rang and they jumped with a start. "Ach!" groused Baldric. "Johannes ought let his novice sleep!"

"Shh!" whispered Arnold. "It should appear now."

He had no sooner uttered the words when heavy padding could be heard approaching Emma's hut. It sounded like soft leather on matted sod. The two froze and strained to see a shadow moving past the fence. "Baldric," whispered Arnold, "we needs move closer."

Baldric swallowed hard; his mouth was dry and his hands trembled. "N-n-not too close. It moves like a spirit."

Arnold crept from behind his cover, his older brother in tow. They each stayed low to the ground and stepped lightly until Baldric's heel squashed a walnut. The two froze, certain the ghost had heard the crack. Fearful to move, each held his breath.

The shadow stood still. The path was dead silent. Baldric closed his eyes and fought the urge to run. He was certain Hedda's awful whispers would break the horrid silence, and he began to sweat. Arnold was now frightened as well. Suddenly, a giant creature crashed through the underbrush behind the startled brothers and roared past them in the mist. The two cried out and fled in terror.

🙠

Heinrich lay wide-eyed and trembling as a chilly, breezy dawn welcomed Weyer. It was November the second, All Souls' Day—the day that warned of the coming Judgment Seat where Christ would judge all souls. The boy was aware he had sinned grievously the previous night, and he wondered how he might construct a confession specific enough for eternal absolution, while vague enough to avoid a beating. He further struggled over what secret penance he might do to secure his temporal forgiveness. Of course, he then wondered if secret penance was penance at all? He had been well instructed on the sufferings of Purgatory, and the lad feared what horrors his unremitted sins might earn him after death. He shuddered and began to sweat.

Reeve Lenard's voice roared with the first light of dawn. "Where's my dog? Someone's cut the rope! We've a thief!" The man stormed along the empty footpaths as sleepy villagers poked their heads out-of-doors. "'Ave you scrumped m'dog?" Lenard blustered at one flustered neighbor. "Nay? And what of you?" he shouted as he turned to another.

Heinrich paled in his bed. Effi looked at him, suspiciously. She leaned close to his ear and whispered, "Did you?"

Heinrich opened his mouth, then shut it again. If he told her yes, she'd likely be punished for not telling Baldric. If he told her no, he'd be lying—another sin to be set to his account.

Effi persisted. "Did you loose his dog?"

Heinrich set his jaw and closed his eyes. "Just hush!"

Baldric stormed to the door. "What's the noise out there?" He turned to the children now sitting straight-backed and fearful against the cold wall. "Something's afoot! I can smell it. You, Herwin, what's about?"

Herwin answered slowly as the church bells rang prime. He poked at the hearth coals. "Methinks Lenard's dog's been scrumped." He cast an unwise glance at Heinrich. The glance did not go unnoticed.

Baldric came across the room in two bounding strides and grabbed the boy by the throat. "What can y'tell me of this?"

Terrified, Heinrich fought tears. *Dare I lie?* His mind raced.

"Well, boy? Have y'no tongue?"

"I ... well—"

"*Mein Gott!* Y'little bastard whelp! Y'son of demons! Thief! If your grandpapa could know this he'd die again." Baldric lifted Heinrich off the floor and tossed him across the room. He charged at the frightened lad and slapped him about the face and head, screaming oaths and cursing until Herwin grabbed the man's shoulder. At the touch, Baldric slammed his fist into Herwin's face, knocking the thin young man backward and onto the floor. Effi cried and bravely stood between her brother and uncle. But, with a quick swat of the back of his huge hand, the little girl went toppling across the room and fell onto little brother Axel cowering against the wall.

Heinrich, now bloodied and shaking, crouched with his arms protecting his head. Baldric grabbed the lad by his hair. "Come with me!" he roared. "We've needs see the reeve!"

Heinrich yelped as Baldric dragged him out of the hut and across the footpaths to Lenard's hovel. When they arrived, Baldric lifted the boy's face close to his own. "You have shamed me! You have broke the code; you've shamed yourself and your kin. You are dung to me now, can y'hear me? Dung!"

Heinrich wanted to vomit. The man's heated breath was foul and his words were worse. The only comfort the poor boy had was the memory of Lenard's grateful dog bolting down the village path.

"Lenard! Here's your thief. Take the little bastard and do as y'will."

Lenard turned purple with rage. "You? What sort of low and worthless bit of swine *Scheisse* are you? I've a mind to beat you senseless, you—"

A tap on the arm from his wife interrupted him. She leaned her face upward and whispered to him. "Aye," grumbled Lenard. He took Heinrich by an ear and gave it a good twist. The boy howled. "I ought whip where y'stand, thief! Ach, m'Frau says we ought call the priest so's we not sin in this." He pointed to the circle of villagers now staring at him. "You … aye, you, fetch Father Johannes. The rest of you take a good look at the village thief! He sneaked into m'house whilst I slept and cut loose m'dog!"

Heinrich was humiliated as the village scoffed and mocked him. Little did he know how grateful many secretly were! A few suddenly accused him of other larcenies and losses, some throwing clumps of mud and small stones at the boy.

Heinrich hid his face behind his arms and peeked fearfully between them at the taunting faces until his eyes fell upon good Emma and faithful Ingelbert, brave Richard and little Effi. Each of these pleaded with the others for mercy. At last, they elbowed their way to the lad's side and stood with Heinrich until Father Johannes arrived with his newly assigned novice, Pious.

The priest huddled with Baldric and Lenard while the hayward dispersed the crowd to the fields. As the men discussed the boy's fate, Heinrich stared at the novice who was glaring at him suspiciously. *Humph!* thought Heinrich. *He's certainly a well-fed little priestling!* Indeed, young Pious was ample at the girth, puffed in the cheeks, and stood stoutly upon thick legs that swelled against the straining line of his outgrown robe. He sneered at Heinrich with a pompous pride that chased the shame from the lad and filled him with fury. Heinrich fixed a hard eye on the novice until the cutting words of Father Johannes turned his head.

"Thief!" scolded the priest with a slap across the boy's head. "Bend your knee and hear me. God's judgment is upon you this wicked morn. Your name is 'Scrump Worm' to your God, to your household, to your village, and to yourself. Dost thou hear me? Scump Worm!

"Yet in your thievery lies an even greater sin, 'tis pride, the greatest of all sins. In your pride you have claimed the right to steal. In your pride, you have thought yourself above God's Law. Woe to you, boy. Woe I say!"

The priest drew a deep breath and received an affirming nod from Lenard. He then softened his tone and bent toward the kneeling, stiff-jawed lad. "Though you have brought shame upon us all, your sins can be forgiven and the final purge lessened through your penance."

Heinrich's mouth went dry and his breath quickened.

"First, you must confess thy sin to me in the church for absolution by God's grace. Next, thy good uncle shall pay fair restitution to Lenard for his loss and you shall settle with him for that. Then, hear this: You shall receive eight stripes with a willow wand for your theft. Do you know why eight?"

Heinrich shook his head and fixed his eyes on Emma's.

"It is the eighth commandment which you have broken first. You have also violated the fifth commandment, so you shall receive five more strikes for dishonoring your uncle.

"Finally, and listen well boy, thy pride must be reckoned. The good monks in Villmar do keep their eyes to the ground lest any think themselves more than they are. Neither shall you seek a lofty vision of thine own, for vainglory is a great tempter and an evil thing. Therefore, I demand, this day, your vow to the Virgin Mother and the host of saints above, that you shall *never* lift your eyes higher than the spires of whatever holy church is in thy view. Do you so vow?"

Heinrich was nervous and confused. A mere boy, he lived in terror of the order around him and the eternal one to come. His eyes were wide and darted to and fro until they fell upon Emma's once again. The blessed Frau looked at him tenderly and her own eyes begged him to refuse. She then shook her head vigorously. "No Heinrich ... no ..." she mouthed.

Heinrich hesitated until Baldric slapped him on the side of his face. "Answer the priest, worm!" he boomed. "Take the vow!"

Emma could contain herself no longer. She cried out, "No! 'Tis an evil, wicked thing they demand of you!" She clenched her fists and turned on the priest with righteous outrage. "Black-heart! Serpent! Do not bind the boy to such a horrid, unholy vow!"

"Silence, woman!" shouted the priest. "How dare you speak! Take her away!"

Arnold stepped forward and fixed a tight grip on Emma's elbow. He hissed into her ear, "Go witch, go with your freak child, else you'll both have a high price to pay." He squeezed her arm until she cried out in pain, and he dragged her away.

Father Johannes turned an icy glare on Heinrich. "Boy, you've a choice before you. You have broken the code of heaven and the code of thine own kin. Hearken my words and take the vow, else your rebellious soul shall face the Judgment in grave peril. And more! Your penalties will be passed to your brother and sister, and family to come!"

Heinrich, ashamed, confused, filled with terror and with

dread, hesitated. He knew what he was condemned to do. No longer could he lie in the grass and find pictures in the clouds. No more might he follow birds across the blue sky, nor feel the noontime sun upon his chin. Yet he felt he must obey. He believed with all his tender heart that he had placed himself and those whom he loved in grave jeopardy. With a sad, tearful sigh, he nodded. "I ... I do so vow."

ༀ

Martinmas passed with little notice, celebrated only by a liturgy none could understand. It was now mid-November and Weyer was busy with the slaughter. The abbey's lay-bailiff, Herold, was about the villages insisting that the blood month yield well for the abbot. After all, though the monks were sworn to eat little meat, they needed to pay their tithe to Mainz with carts of salted, smoked, or pickled pork and pound upon pound of mutton. "So," he proclaimed to the village men, "round up your swine and be clever with the slaughter, we needs use everything but the squeal!"

The villagers did as they were told—they nearly always did. The swine herdsmen marked the hogs with dyes as to their rightful owners and gathered them in the village pens. The best sows and boars were separated and saved for breeding; the rest were herded to meet the men who stunned them with heavy mallets. Once unconscious, the hogs' rear legs were tied and hoisted upward while the slitters, including Heinrich and Richard, cut the throats for bleeding. The blood was drained into buckets and carried to cauldrons where women stirred in fat to make bloodwurst. Once drained of blood, the carcasses were scalded with boiling water, the hair scraped, and skins preserved. Once the slaughter was complete, every spare part would be put to good use.

Others worked at culling the herd in the sheepfolds. The youngest ewes were saved for springtime lambing and next year's shearing. The older ones, however, were chased into pens where they were bled, skinned, and carved into sheepskins and meat, ground bone and fat.

At the end of several weeks, the villagers proudly loaded carts filled with the fruits of their labor. The products filling these barrels, kegs, bundles, and sacks would help pay the fines, taxes, tithes, rents, and fees still owed after shipping the abbey a full third of the grain crop just two months before.

The final days of November passed quickly, and just before Advent a cart bearing two strangers rolled slowly into Weyer from the Villmar road. The few villagers who saw them turned away, for outsiders were seldom welcomed. Heinrich, however, had just descended from the fields where he was helping plough a fallow strip and, in his exhaustion, nearly walked directly into the cart's path. A man cried out in a foreign tongue and the startled boy jumped back. "I-I am sorry, sir, I did not see you."

The man kept a tight rein on his ox and turned to the boy. "Reeve—?" he asked carefully.

"You needs see the reeve?" asked Heinrich.

The man nodded. The woman sitting next to him smiled.

Heinrich stared with amazement at the stranger. He was the largest man the boy had ever seen. The giant pointed to himself. "Telek," he said, then turned and gestured toward the woman. "Varina."

Heinrich barely heard the man. His gaze was fixed on the six fingers that hung on each of the man's hands. He dropped his eyes to the man's bare feet and the boy gasped. "And six toes on each foot!"

The woman chuckled. She spoke in heavily accented German. "*Junge* ... I am Varina and this is my brother, Telek. The monks in Villmar named him 'Goliath' ... after a character in the Scriptures. They wish us to call him that, though he is not happy about it." She smiled affectionately at the man.

Herwin caught up to Heinrich. "Greetings, friends," he offered with a sincere smile.

"And greetings to you. I am Varina ... this is my brother, Telek. We are Slavs, captured by Christian knights and bound to Lord Klothar of Runkel. We converted and have lived in Runkel for nearly two years. Now we are sent by the abbot to serve in this village. We are to find your reeve. 'Tis all we know."

Heinrich listened intently. His eyes fell upon the woman's swollen belly.

"*Ja.* I am with child."

Herwin stared at Varina. Though she was rather plain, he felt strangely drawn to her. She was blonde and blue-eyed with fair skin. Despite her advanced pregnancy, she was thin-framed, but had a broad, open face.

"They are looking for Lenard," said Heinrich.

"Yes, boy, so I heard." He motioned to Varina, "Follow me."

As Herwin led Klothar's slaves to Lenard's hovel, Heinrich entered his own. It was past nones and there was only one hour of daylight left. Baldric had returned early and was furious to see the boy. "You've come home early while work can yet be done?" he shouted.

"Nay, Uncle. We needed return Gunter's oxen ... one's foot-sore and we daresn't keep it on the plough." Heinrich knew Baldric had been drinking and he was frightened.

Baldric shoved the boy to the wall. "Thief! You listen to me, Scrump Worm. You'd steal a man's dog and you'd steal a man's time! You needs labor till dusk, any less is sloth—another sin. By God, y'damnable, wretched waif, were y'not the son of m'brother I'd throw you to the dogs. I work this manor hard both day and night. I put food enough into yer worthless belly and y've good wool on your miserable back. You repay me by shaming the good name of your grandpapa to the whole village! Now you come home sneaking to rest! By the saints! No more! By God in heaven, 'tis enough. Y'd be in forfeit!"

Heinrich leaned against a far wall, trembling. He set an eye for a quick escape. Then he wondered aloud, "Forfeit ... ?"

Baldric grabbed Heinrich by an ear and dragged him into the rear bedchamber. He tossed the boy to the ground and fumbled for a box beneath a candlestand. He threw up the lid and grasped a folded parchment scroll that he held in front of the boy's face. "Here, little man. Here is the birthright your grandpapa passed to you for *your* own lads should you 'ave any. 'Tis a promise for your sons to be taught in the abbey school ... a vow from an abbot to a shepherd! Of course, I've no such gift for me! Seems m'blood was never as good as yer father's. No matter, you've shamed our ways and have lost the right of blessing ... you'd not be fit for it, you've broke the code again. Now watch, thief, slug-gard. Watch it burn away!"

Heinrich stared openmouthed and confused. He knew lit-tle of the birthright but it hardly mattered now. Baldric stormed to the common room hearth and held the parch-ment to its flames. He smiled coldly in the failing light as the dry parchment smoked and flickered, then floated into noth-ingness out the smoke hole above. He dropped the final ashes to the straw-strewn floor and ground them with his heel. "It is done. Now things are set to right."

Chapter 7

A SECRET REVEALED

It snowed lightly on the first Sunday after Advent in the Year of Grace 1182. Richard walked with Heinrich and pointed to the sky. "Look at the clouds. Methinks a storm is coming."

Heinrich shook his head. "I cannot look up."

Richard shrugged. "Ach, Heinrich. No one is here to tell."

Heinrich was sorely tempted, but refused. And when he refused he felt suddenly good and clean, as if his shame were redeemed, if only for a moment. His eye suddenly caught a glimpse of a satchel lying half-buried in the snow by the side of the road. "Look, Richard. I've found something!" Indeed, the lad had found a set of quills, some sharp knives, and ampoules. "We needs take this to Father Johannes," said Heinrich.

"Johannes? Nay, Heinrich, are y'dim? We should give them to Frau Emma. I've seen inks in her hut."

"But she'll want to find the rightful owner."

Richard paused. "Hmm. Then we tell her ... we tell her a peddler lost them to us in a wager!"

"A wager! She'll scold us for wagering, and besides, what would we have wagered?"

"You think too much. She'll never ask such a thing."

"And if she does?"

"Then I'll have an answer."

Heinrich wasn't so sure. "Richard, methinks we're about to lie again ... more sin."

Richard thought for a moment. "Then let me talk."

Heinrich shrugged, and the two turned and ran toward the smoking thatched roof of the Butterfly Frau. They arrived to a warm welcome. "Ah, my boys!" exclaimed Emma. She smiled and held each one under her thick arms. "You've been growing again!"

"Frau Emma," blurted Richard, "I ... we've something for you."

The woman sat down and wiped a wisp of long hair from her forehead. Taking the satchel from Richard's outstretched hands she opened it carefully and her eyes widened. "Boys, where on this earth did you find these? They are marvelous! Look, here, goose quills, the very best! And they come from the right wing ... most unusual. Hmm, and they are well dried and sharpened. Here, a burnishing knife, a leaf-knife, and ... and gold powder! And here, too, good gall ink! Boys, you've quite a find. Someone's suffered a loss, indeed."

Richard cleared his throat. "Nay, Frau Emma. Heinrich and I won this for you in a wager."

"A wager!" Emma's face darkened. "You boys ought not be wagering, and what on earth could you offer in exchange?"

Heinrich knew she'd ask that! The worst always happened. Richard set a steady gaze at the woman, his eyes betraying an active imagination. "Now, Frau Emma. Do not be angry. The man was a thief by his own word, and not a thief like Heinrich. I mean a *real* thief."

"Enough, boy. 'Tis quite enough. I cannot accept this ... this *gift* from you. What do you think, Heinrich?"

Heinrich was speechless. He stared at Richard and stammered, "I ... I ... methinks you ought keep it, Frau. We've no idea where ..."

"And are Richard's words true?"

Heinrich turned white. "I must not lie again! But if I say that it is not so, then I betray my kin as a liar ... another sin, methinks." He turned to Emma and answered, "I did not hear Richard talk with ... the thief, so I ... I cannot say in truth."

Emma paused. She looked at smiling Ingelbert and tapped her finger on her chin. "And what use have I of these things?"

Richard shrugged. "Methinks Ingly has said something about you writing."

Emma took a deep breath. "I see. Well, I shall keep this for a season and I shall listen for any talk of it. If it is not claimed after a reasonable time, I suppose it might be God's will for me to keep." She winked.

Richard cheered loudly and joyful voices filled the room as all began talking at once—all, that is, except solemn Heinrich.

"Heinrich," Emma said. "You seem a little sad."

The boy nodded.

"Is it shame you feel?"

He nodded again.

"I hope you know how proud I am that you loosed that poor beast!"

Heinrich brightened somewhat. "You are? But I stole a man's property and was prideful."

Emma sighed. "There is also the law of love. Methinks you loved that animal."

"But I stole it."

"Perhaps it was the only way to obey the highest law."

Heinrich sat by the woman. "I am told I am swine dung... that I have shamed myself and my kin."

"Good lad, none of us are perfect!" Emma chuckled.

"I wish to face the sun."

Emma stiffened. She desperately wanted to point the lad to wisdom without breaking him of faith. She was angry that the priest had set the two virtues in opposition. "Heinrich, the Holy Church calls us to seek truth, but to find it I fear we must sometimes look higher than its spires."

Heinrich seemed confused. "But there is more. Sometimes I feel good when I keep this vow I hate."

Emma slowly released an understanding sigh.

"And Baldric hates me and he burned a parchment," the eight-year-old suddenly blurted.

Emma's face tightened and she flushed red-hot with anger. She closed her eyes for a moment, then held the boy tightly. "Heinrich, my son, I fear you've much to learn and shall suffer much to learn it. You've been shackled sooner than most. For now, hear this one thing: knowing who hates you can teach you much about yourself."

༈

The years turned and crept, dragged and weathered their way along for the weary, ever-somber village. To be sure, the loving sun urged some days of temperate warmth, and the promise of the seasons' feasts bore brief and cheery respite. But for the simple peasants of Weyer, life was defined by the dreary rhythm of dull constancy and dread.

In the larger world, in 1183 Emperor Frederick Barbarossa had made his peace in Lombardy where he had been waging war against stubborn foes. With his southern lands in order he had recently returned to his wife, Beatrix, and had begun a tour of feasts throughout his realm.

In the spring of 1184, a courier advised Abbot Malchus that the emperor's entourage had chosen to spread their great tents on the banks of the Lahn between Villmar and the castle of Runkel. Here they planned to lounge for three days in June. Barbarossa would be traveling north from his wondrous castle on the high summit of Hohenstaufen. It was rumored that he had spent many a night in the arms of a washwoman from nearby Lorch Castle, the sandstone residence of his own Staufen ancestors. So smitten was his heart, it was whispered, that he recently bequeathed the ancient home to the same mysterious woman. For the folk of Villmar's manors, however, the pending arrival of Red Beard brought hope, if only for three days.

On a comfortable June day word quickly spread amongst the villagers that the Emperor was bathing in the Lahn— *their* Lahn! And more; he was traveling with a company of Norman knights who bore the bones of St. Aurelius of Rome. Beheaded by Nero centuries before, the saint was now believed to heal all manner of afflictions. One needed only to touch a bone of the relic upon one's body, or touch one who had touched a bone, or touch a cloth that had been touched by one who had touched a bone. Such was the hope that suddenly cheered the abbot's dreary land.

As throngs of peasants pressed the margins of the emperor's camp, Arnold begged a priest to let him touch the saint. His scabbed and itchy skin had tormented him both day and night for years and he was, in that moment, willing to bow and scrape like the others of his kind. But the size of the crowds was great, and few were permitted entrance to the canvas shrine. For his part, the emperor took pity on the peasants waiting on bended knees and, against the pleadings of the papal legate, instructed the imperial guard to carry the relic through the growing mob. So, St. Aurelius was held high above the straining fingers of the clamoring serfs. Unable to touch the bones themselves, the crowd was content to reach for the patient soldiers whose shoulders bore the bier.

Unfortunately for Arnold, he had touched neither the bones, nor another who had touched the bones, nor one who had touched someone who had touched the bones. He returned to Weyer more miserable than when he had left. But ten-year-old Heinrich had climbed amongst the legs of his fellows and managed to thrust a hand between some knees to touch the boot of a soldier whose shoulder had brushed the bronze litter bearing the holy relic. It was good enough, the boy was certain, to claim power from the saint, and he was happy.

Heinrich had other reasons for joy, as well. His friend and secret counselor at the Magi, Brother Lukas, had urged the prior to consider the lad for the position of baker's apprentice. To everyone's surprise, the repentant "Scrump Worm" was accepted to the abbey's bakery and began his career amid the scoffs and envy of his peers.

Under orders from the abbot, Prior Paulus had demanded the villages buy their bread from the monks and from the monks alone. He had unwisely closed the communal ovens that had served the villages so very well for generations. Now, each morning, bread was carted to the villages with their day's allotment. Paulus argued that this control would pro-vide needed revenues to the abbey and "protect our good people from the risks of the 'corn witch,' the cheats of the millers, and the poisons of ergot."

While Heinrich enjoyed his good fortune, his brother Axel soon enjoyed his own. Baldric, now a village elder, was eager to make room for cash-paying tenants in his hovel. He was paid well as the overseer of the manor's hunting, fencing, timbering, and assarting, but was eager for more silver. While the hovel was yet his own, he was determined to squeeze every penny he could from within its walls. Since blood kin paid no rents, it would serve Baldric well to make room for those who would. So, after a brief visit with a hired carpenter from Limburg and with the reluctant approval of the prior, Baldric arranged for young Axel to join the crafts-man's household as his apprentice. Axel, for his part, was happy to leave the labors of the fields to Heinrich.

It was Herwin, good and faithful Herwin, who still remained to shelter Effi and Heinrich from their uncle. But he would no longer stand guard alone, for to his great joy he had married the Slav, Varina. Considering the immediate increase in rents, Baldric was a willing creditor and loaned the happy man what pennies were required to pay the merchet. And so, into the household of Baldric moved Herwin's new wife, her baby son, Wulf, and her twelve-fingered, twelve-toed, giant of a brother, Telek. The marriage proved fruitful, for in another year Varina bore Herwin a child of his own, a daughter, baptized Irma.

Meanwhile Emma, the Butterfly Frau, had aged with grace. She did her best to offer patient kindness to the village women who seemed ever disposed to disparage and deride her. Perhaps it was her very grace that earned her scorn and such contempt. Or, perhaps it was the unfortunate appearance of poor Ingelbert. Many, it seemed, remained convinced the woman was somehow connected to the witch of Münster's forest. After all, she had come from another land with the freak child, she lived apart in her cottage by the stream, and she seemed to be of mysterious means. But more than all of these, rumors now abounded that she was visited each All Souls' Eve by fearful shadows in the night.

For Lukas these years had proven difficult. His herbarium was grand, airy, and large, and his gardens had been fruitful in each season. Yet his heart was heavy and his mind oft troubled. It was his joy to serve his fellow man, like in the healing of little Alwin—the orphaned Gunnar oblate with fever, or even Pious—the pompous novice at Weyer. Many of his brothers in the abbey, to whom he brought infusions and balms, tinctures and ointments, thrilled at his duties, for he was skilled in the gifts of Creation and tender of spirit. But despite his competence, the man was often angry with his masters and sometimes doubtful of his faith. The man saw more than most and dared heed the call to brighter light.

ॐ

On February the tenth in the Year of Grace 1186, Abbot Malchus yielded his body to plague and his spirit to the Almighty. It was fitting that he should die on the first day of Lent; his tenure had been characterized by self-denial and all within his shadow had been denied things temporal. Nevertheless, he had served his chapter vigorously and was mourned by most. The abbey's priest blessed his soul and his remains were laid to rest in the monks' graveyard to await the Resurrection.

The abbey had grown and prospered in Malchus's final years. He had built a small scriptorium, complete with its own separate cloister, and he had been quite pleased with its construction. He had added storehouses and granaries to the perimeter walls; a herbarium, chapter house, and stable were built, as well as a dormitory for the men-at-arms that were occasionally quartered as guests. His only failure was that of not wresting the abbey from control of the archbishop.

After Malchus's death, Pope Urban III, near death himself and railing against Emperor Barbarossa, sent his legate to Mainz recommending a friend, Stephen of Ghent, as a candidate for Villmar's growing abbey. Stephen had a worthy pedigree, himself once a lord in Flanders. He had earned a fortune shipping textiles down the Skelt River and just four years prior had been feasting in the huge hall of Count Phillip's castle.

Stephen had set aside his earthly treasures and took the vows of St. Benedict in order to serve as a brother in the vast French complex of Cluny. It seemed an odd decision at first, at least to his fellows. Many lords left their fortunes in old age to join a monastery, but it was clear they were simply guarding their souls as they faced death. Stephen, however, was not an old lord. He had just seen his thirty-third year, and some wondered what crime he was evading. "Christ," he claimed, "gave His life at precisely this same age," and Stephen chose to follow in kind.

The new abbot had learned the Rule quickly and rose in stature among his humble brethren—a paradox that earned the cynical eye of his superiors. However, as his peers feared, it seemed his former life had, indeed, reflected advantage into his new one, and he had been sent first to St. Bertin as prior, and now to Villmar as abbot.

Abbot Stephen addressed his brethren with grave humility and serious deportment. His reputation had preceded his arrival on Holy Saturday, the twenty-eighth of March, 1186, and the sixty monks and twelve novices gathered on the gradines of their new chapter house listened with respect. He instructed them on the virtues of the Rule, of the need for discipline, of the virtue of prudence, the necessity of industry, the vice of sloth, and the wrath of God. When he had finished he washed their feet, prayed over each head, and blessed every soul with a psalm.

On the Monday following, the new abbot invited Prior Paulus to his ample table. As he spread honey on fresh-baked wheat bread, Stephen shared God's will for the aging prior. "Good Paulus," he began, "you have served Almighty God humbly and with great effect."

Paulus bowed, outwardly modest, but secretly pleased.

"I am told by the archbishop that you have filled the treasury of God's kingdom here in Villmar."

Again, Paulus bowed.

"It is my wish, good brother, that you shall serve us yet."

Paulus smiled, relieved and encouraged.

Stephen paused. He leaned into his chair comfortably and stroked his beard. "Brother ... might I ask your age?"

Paulus was suddenly uneasy. "Though I am uncertain, brother Stephen, I do believe I am near to fifty and five."

"Hmm. And what of your health?"

Paulus became nervous. "I ... I am fit of mind and body ... if I may say so humbly." The man bowed his head.

"Brother, I have taken you before God's throne and have asked His wisdom for thy welfare." Stephen laid a hand firmly on the prior's shoulder. "And He has spoken."

Paulus waited, now anxious. He closed his eyes.

"You can, this very day, rejoice! You shall retire thyself to the dormitory for our blessed aged ones. Go with God's blessing, my brother."

&

Early April was soggy and muddy as usual. The footpaths of the damp village were rutted and puddled, the road to Villmar riddled with washouts and trenches. The sky sccmed eternally gray and the barren trees were still stripped of life, save the stubborn buds now swelling on their dreary branches.

In Weyer, the foretokens of spring had not yet nudged the folk to joy. Though the thrush had begun to sing in the wood and swallows danced along the wind, the peasants of the village were huddled in fear. It was not because the neighboring borders of Mensfelden had been granted to Tomas of Goslar. None knew of this vassal and none cared, so long as he had no lust for the abbey's land. Indeed, the leagues and alliances of lords and kings meant little unless they brought the sword.

Instead, the simple people of the village trembled in dread of a plague that had swept upon them in the weeks of Lent. Many now suffered with fever, racking coughs, and horrible eruptions of the skin. Dozens had died despite the heroic efforts of Brother Lukas. The monk was, himself, under the weight of reprimand, for his superior had forbidden him to serve beyond the monastery's walls. Nevertheless, the man had been determined to suffer what penance would be later required in order to give what comfort he could to body and to soul. "Scrofula," he muttered in a quaking prayer. "May God have mercy on us all."

The households of Arnold and Baldric were spared the plague—or at least the agonies it savaged upon others. Though none of them were bedbound, each was required to shoulder the burden of their village fellows and perform both their own labors as well as those of the stricken. Herwin and Telek spent long, difficult days ploughing the stubborn earth and sowing the precious seed.

The women also strained beneath the additional burden. Gisela and Varina spent their days bent in half, planting demesne peas with sharp sticks, churning sheep milk for cheese, or carding wool. At day's end they hoed, manured, and planted their own gardens; and as charity demanded, they did the same for the gardens of their neighbors. The reward would be green rows of peas and beans, garlic, leeks, lentils, cabbage, onions, and the like—all desperately needed food in the months to come.

For his part, twelve-year-old Heinrich rose at matins each day and rode to Villmar with the brewer to begin his work in the bakery. Then, before the bells of prime, he returned to Weyer with the peasants' bread that he sold in the commons for pennies, or for eggs, fowl, or herbs. By terce, with three hours of sunlight already gone, he presented the fees to Reeve Lenard who, in turn, held them safe until the next morning's ride to the abbey. Then, though having already worked nine hours, the lad joined Herwin and Telek in the fields.

By the end of April the barley and oats were sown, the fallow fields turned and fertilized, and peasants' crofts planted and waiting on the faithful sun of May. Baldric's friend Dietrich was now the monks' miller for Weyer, and their mill, located along the Laubusbach at the village edge, was in desperate need of attention. So, in addition to all other tasks, all able-bodied men and boys were forced to work on repairing the mill, for in a few short months its service would give purpose to all the labors of spring.

❧

At twelve and a half, Heinrich was beginning to take the shape of a man. His growth lagged behind others of his age, though his shoulders were beginning to broaden. Most thought he resembled his round-faced father, Kurt, though the boy had not yet gained his father's burly bulk. His hair was now reddish brown—some might call it auburn. It curled and looped and shone in the sun. His manner reminded some of his mother's father, for he was calm and gentle, sensitive to the suffering of others, and friendly to all. Yet the lad could be angered and stubborn, and was given to hiding his feelings. He spent much time in melancholy and reflection, and suffered the superstitious fears of his mother. He gave great weight to things of heaven and hell and was given to night torments and dreams. Baldric boasted the boy was finally "well-shamed," and, indeed, the lad had grown to be ever more bound and fettered by the demands and expectations of others. Little did he know how his world was shaping him for things to come.

On a Sabbath in June, Heinrich raced from Mass with cousin Richard toward the beloved gardens of Frau Emma and her son. Ingly worked long days with the cotters in the monks' demesne—ploughing, sowing, harrowing, weeding, and serving at whatever task the season called him to perform. He was gentle, still slow of mind, but grand of heart. He bore the jeers and taunts of others with a grace he learned from his mother's godly ways and offered kindness for insult at every turn.

The boys charged to the woman's wattled fence and leapt over it like happy deer. Forgetting their manners, they burst through her door without warning and stumbled across her earthen floor. Emma screamed with a start. "Ach! Boys! Can y'not knock on m'door!"

The two stood perfectly still, embarrassed and surprised by her anger. Richard spoke first. "Beggin' pardon, Frau Emma. We'd no right to rush in like that." His eyes moved away from her and fell upon what appeared to be a parchment setting atop her scribe's table.

Emma gathered her wits and drew a deep breath. Her heart slowed to its normal pace and she spoke more gently. "You nearly frightened me to death! It is better for you to knock … but, no harm done."

Both boys now stared at her table. The woman sighed.

She had many secrets and had learned it was sometimes wiser to preserve them. She was about to speak when a familiar voice was heard at her door. The woman closed her eyes and sighed again.

"Frau Emma?"

"*Ja.* Come." The woman wiped her hands on her apron and smiled halfheartedly as Brother Lukas stooped through her door and stepped into her room.

"Peace to you, sister," he said.

"And peace to you, my friend," answered Emma.

The monk surveyed the room and nodded a greeting to the boys. "I heard a scream and thought there might be trouble."

"Ah," chuckled Emma, "no trouble here. The boys put a scare in me and I'm sorry for your bother. Now if y'needs get back to your—"

"Oh! And what have we here?" The monk joined the boys at Emma's table.

Emma shook her head and closed her door. She walked over to the group huddling over her parchment and bit her lip. "Ah, yes ... this," she answered slowly. "I had no thoughts of others coming today."

"It is marvelous! Beautiful! It is ... heavenly!" Lukas was amazed.

Heinrich, Richard, and Ingly stood quietly. The man bowed his head low to the table and stroked his short beard with delight. The table was positioned near the window of the hovel and the late morning sun was casting a pleasant light atop it. "Emma, you've a gift from God, but I must confess I am very confused. In my days I have ne'er heard of any woman, and surely no peasant woman, set to this task! Ach! By God the abbot would have you flogged! You can let none know!" He turned to the boys and laid a stern eye on them. "You lads! You must keep the secret of this good woman—"

"Aye! And so we shall," boasted Richard.

Heinrich nodded. "We'd known her to have quills before ... but we only ever saw her doodlings."

"Think no more of it, boy, put it out of your mind, for one

slip might cost her plenty. The abbot wants the scriptorium to be a profitable commerce. He contracts his scribes to make Scriptures, Books of Hours, and Psalms for Mainz and for lords in the realm. He needs no secret competitor under his nose! And, Emma, you must know that all income is subject to tax and tithe. You'd be punished for a hidden work—I fear you'd be punished harshly."

Lukas turned to the boys. "Lads, if you love this woman you shall ne'er speak of what you see."

Heinrich stepped forward. "Brother, we would die before we'd see her harmed. We shall say nothing of it ... but ... what is this?"

Lukas had forgotten that the uneducated peasant boys had never seen such a thing. To them it was a wonder, and they were drawn to it like bees to blooms. The monk looked at Emma and she smiled. *It would be good for them,* she thought; *it would be good for them to know of things beyond their world.*

Emma laid a hand on Heinrich's shoulder and led him to her table. Richard crowded close and Ingly looked on while Lukas kept a nervous watch at the door. "As a young girl, boys, I was privileged to learn a trade from an aged monk in Quedlinburg. Some said he had lost his mind, others that he had an untoward eye for the sisters! But I thought him to be the kindest, most caring man I had ever known. He grumbled that the scribes ought not be the keepers of color. He thought color to be the gift of God for it is the product of light. Do you understand?"

The boys shrugged. Lukas moved closer. She continued. "Color, lads, is only present when there is light—it is the sun's fruit. That is why I love my flowers and my butterflies as I do. When there is no light, there are but shades of gray." She looked into Lukas's face. "And many would deny us even that! They would that you see only the black of the letter or the white of the page. They would deny you both color and shade, for in their own blindness they would keep you from the light."

Lukas nodded, for he understood of what she spoke.

"Boys," she continued, "listen well and remember this: there is blackness and there is white, but there are also shades and more. When truth is present, light is present, and when light shines, shades and color are born. Live your life in truth, look always for the light—it is the source of hope! Live in color! Dance waist deep in flowers, lads, and let butterflies float above your heads; let sweet aromas fill your nose, and turn your face toward the sun like the tender buds of spring." She looked sadly at Heinrich. *That cursed vow*, she thought, *that vow from the Pit!*

The room was quiet and Emma looked at the faces staring at her. "So, enough of m'thoughts; you've more interest in that." She pointed to her work. "I was secretly trained by Brother Vigilius in the arts of the scribe, beginning with stretching and scraping the skins. He preferred to use the skins of calves, though this one is from a piebald goat ... can you see the brown shades?"

The boys nodded, spellbound and excited.

Emma continued. "Calves and some goats yield a finer skin, called vellum, but skins from sheep make what we know as parchment. He then showed me how to stitch the 'quires,' or the gatherings of folded pages that are later sewn together for the final book. Of course, this was a bit tricky, for he insisted the parchment be folded and stitched so that the hair-sides always face each other, and flesh faces flesh.

"Then came a most important part. I was taught how to rule the pages with a stylus and was beaten each time I cut through the parchment! Now I use a lead stick to make the lines. I needed to learn to make them straight and to draw a grid of proper proportion so the letters would be even and pleasing to the eye."

Richard was bored. "So what of this one?"

Emma chuckled. "Ah, good lad, patience! I then needed to learn of inkmaking and pens! Vigilius said the best quills were from the goose, though I have used the feathers of crows and ravens. It is the left wing of the bird that offers the quill bending to the right and this is what is best for right-handed scribes. I—being under some curse

I am told—am left-handed, which is why, dear Richard, your wager proved so timely for me. The quills you ... won ... were from the right wing of the bird, a most unusual find!"

Lukas started. The abbey's left-handed scribe had commissioned quills some years back—quills that had never arrived.

Emma continued her lesson. "I take my quill and dip it into my inkhorn. The black ink I have is good, gall ink, and is made from copperas, which comes from the earth, and gums and oak apples. Heinrich, you've helped me pick oak apples before. They are the tumors the wasps make in oak buds. I also have red ink, which is made from vermilion mixed with egg whites, or with certain woods and urine. But my joy, dear friends, is in the illumination!"

Lukas marveled. "I was amazed that you were a scribe, but now you say you are an illuminator?"

Emma blushed.

"By the saints!" Lukas exclaimed. "This is wonderful. A peasant woman illuminating psalms and prayer books for the unsuspecting! Boys, see the large letter at the start of the page?"

Richard pointed to the tall, ornate figure. "That? That is a letter?"

"Aye," answered Lukas. "It begins the word *Pater*. She is writing the '*Pater Noster*.'" He turned to Emma. "This is a prayer book ... for a lord?"

She shrugged. "I don't know."

"May I ask who gives you work?"

Emma stiffened slightly. "Perhaps another time."

The monk nodded, respectfully, and turned again to the boys. "See, lads, see how she creates the letter ... with red and black, green inks and even blue! And see the gold! Ah, it is the gold that shimmers in the light of the sun, 'tis why the craft is called illumination."

Emma showed her friends the gold leaf hidden in the floor, her rare inks and powders, her pumice, knives, grinder, and the honey used to grind both gold and silver. "And all, good friends, done for the glory of God."

≈

It was a warm summer morning, a few days past Mid-summer's, when Heinrich heard the hue and cry. He had just sold the last of the abbey's bread to a grumbling *Hausfrau* when the trumpeting blasts of Reeve Lenard's horn echoed through Weyer. Following the tribal tradition of his forefathers, Heinrich immediately joined the men of the village streaming from the fields toward the village common.

Lenard stood atop the stone wall of Weyer's well and called all to silence. "Listen … listen! A shepherd's been found murdered along the Emsbach in Selters—on abbey soil. His throat was cut clean through and his hands taken off. Arnold saw a man running this direction through the wood by Oberbrechen. Methinks he's headed toward the heavy wood by Münster and we've been given permission to give chase across the border. Now, go in tithings according to your elder. Dietrich—take your men over the stream and up the ridge."

"In the new lord's lands?" asked the nervous miller.

"*Ju!* And be quick about it y'dolt All of you listen, spread yerselves, each man within a bowshot of the next. Go two leagues and circle back."

Dietrich had been hard at work grinding flour and was covered with dust. Heinrich and Richard laughed out loud, thinking he looked like a ghost! Dietrich's pretty daughter, Marta, however, captured the boys' attention as she ran from her hut and handed her father a draught of beer. The girl smiled at the boys flirtatiously and then tossed her head with a disdainful look. Heinrich grunted, "Her!" and followed Dietrich's group of ten toward the stream.

The men were panting when they reached the top of the ridge overlooking the village from across the stream to the southeast. Heinrich put his hands on his knees and sucked hard for air. He stood between Richard and Dietrich's son, Sigmund, while he waited for Dietrich's orders. None could believe Sigmund was the twin of Marta. From the day of their birth it seemed the one had been blessed and the other cursed. As beautiful as Marta was, Sigmund was ugly. His face was knotted in lumps and blemished with scabs, and though just twelve, he had the disposition of a crotchety old man.

Dietrich organized his group carefully. He spread the three lads among the older men. Each of his tithing was positioned about one hundred fifty paces apart, and was ordered to make a quick but wary advance eastward. They were to comb the forest carefully, looking for the fugitive behind the thick-trunked oaks and within the cover of ferns and thickets.

For Heinrich, his first hue and cry was a great adventure. He felt like a man grown, an equal of the others and an important part of his world. He pressed through tangles and briars, his woollen leggings snagging and catching on pickers and thorns. Leafy branches scratched his face and his hands became sticky with pine sap. From time to time he spotted a deer darting from cover or a fox sliding through distant shadows. He was sure he felt the eyes of a wolf staring at him from the heavy shade, and hoped no wild boars were about; it was not uncommon for one to kill a man.

About five furlongs away, Richard picked his way through deep ferns. They were waist deep and growing in the dark shade of ancient spruce. He had lost sight of his fellows, though occasionally he heard a call or a snapping branch. The boy carried a stout stick in his left hand and a small rock in his right. He prowled the forest like a well-bred predator. Tall, thin, agile, and handsome, he resembled the yellow-haired warriors of ancient times. Suddenly, he heard a loud snap ahead of him. He held his breath and stopped. He focused both eyes and ears and crouched shoulder deep in ferns.

The lad heard another crack and a crunch not more than fifty paces in front of him. He wondered silently, *Is it a deer? A wolf? ... A ...* The back of a man's head suddenly popped out of the ferns. Richard's eyes widened. The man's head began to turn. Richard squatted deeper. The man then stood slowly and began to move toward the boy. Richard's heart pounded as he came within twenty paces, then ten ... then five ... then ...

Richard jumped from his cover with a loud shriek and

heaved his rock with all his might. He struck the startled man in the center of his belly, driving the wind from his lungs. The boy then charged with a yell and pounded the fugitive squarely on the head with his stick. The man stood stunned and glassy-eyed before Richard struck him again and again. He then fell backward in the ferns, bloodied and unconscious. The breathless boy cried loudly for the others, and in a matter of moments Richard and his prize were encircled by the cheering men of Weyer.

Chapter 8

TRIALS, DREAMS, AND FEAR

he cycle of seasons turned again until once more the land was warmed by the kind sun of springtime. But by the days of Pentecost in 1188, troubling news had found its way through the gentle valleys of Villmar's manors. Jerusalem had fallen to the armies of Saladin; some said on a night the witch was heard cackling in the wood. It was a terrible blow to all.

Heinrich, now fourteen, had become broad-shouldered and strong. His skin was dry from the flour dust of the bakery, but his eyes were clear and his mind was keen. He had kept his vow and had faced neither the sun nor the stars since that awful day nearly six years before. Instead, the lad had learned to draw a curious comfort from keeping the cursed pledge. But, as with all who suffer self-deception, to embrace the darkness the boy needed to deny the light, and to Emma's great despair Heinrich had grown ever more introverted and melancholy. She could only hope that seeds planted early in the boy's tender heart might someday turn the lad toward better things.

November brought news of tragedy for Lord Tomas of Mensfelden, the ruler of the manors bordering Weyer to the south and east. The lord's son was named Silvester and was known to spend his days in the deep wood with his falcons or his bow. He was considered an odd youth, however, given to solitary, midnight bonfires and moonlight rituals.

Most thought him to be drawn to the witch's daughter. It was rumored that the young girl was a rare beauty—tall and willowy, white-haired and fair. Yet, given her owl-like screeches and spine-tingling howls, she had become known as "Wilda the Wild."

Early on Martinmas, it was poor Ingelbert who found Silvester's body. The simple lad had spent a quiet dawn at the Magi when he thought he heard a whisper beckoning him toward the deeper wood. The young man followed trance-like until he was knee-deep in wilted ferns, giving no heed to the boundary pole he passed. He sang and danced in the early light of the gray day, but as he skipped his way through the forest, he suddenly came upon the base of a short cliff. He stopped for a moment, sensing something amiss. He raised his eyes to the top of the rock wall, then let them drift slowly down the sharp contours of the cliff's face until they reached the bottom. The young man gasped. For there lay the broken, battered body of Silvester.

The bountiful feast of Christ's Mass was now of little interest to Heinrich and of less to poor Emma. Her beloved son had been shackled to the cold walls of Lord Tomas's castle dungeon for more than a month, accused of illegal trespass and of Silvester's murder. She was forbidden to leave Weyer to see him, and no oath-helpers were permitted to testify on the lad's behalf. In truth, only Heinrich and Richard had even offered to speak, and much of the village would have been happy to witness *against* the poor boy. Lukas—who was not allowed to leave the cloister due to his latest infraction—sent messages of encouragement to Emma via Heinrich and spent hours begging God's mercy for the boy.

Ingelbert was slow of mind but not numb to pain. Bound to the damp, plastered walls of the dark dungeon, Ingly wept inconsolably for his mother and longed for the warmth and solace of her hearth. He could not understand the charges against him but was familiar with the jeers and taunts of the jailers who mocked his odd and disquieting form. Ingly's trial was set for the thirtieth day of December, and Lord Tomas planned to personally judge his case. The narrow-faced, bitter lord was determined on vengeance.

As having assisted in the hue and cry, Reeve Lenard, Arnold, Dietrich, and Baldric were granted permission to represent Weyer at the captured man's trial at Mensfelden's castle. The night before, the four men were delighted to find themselves sitting at the edges of Lord Tomas's great hall, gulping great draughts of beer and reaching for scraps of meat and cheese. They toasted and laughed, bellowed and belched late into the night, feasting on salted pork and venison, boiled rabbit, and roasted duck. Joining them were a dozen or so sergeants-at-arms and two bored knights, as well as a few ladies of Limburg who seemed to have more than a passing familiarity with their hosts. Finally, the overstuffed, indulged visitors collapsed against the castle's cool walls and slept until nudged awake by the morning bells of Mensfelden.

Dawn broke and the captured fugitive from the hue and cry could be heard moaning from deep within the hole where he had been confined for many months. It was a narrow, lightless shaft dug into the castle floor about two rods deep and one pace in width. Atop was an iron grid where passersby paused to relieve themselves. About an hour after dawn a trumpet sounded, and the dung-covered, wet man was hauled into the frigid air where the crowd assaulted him with oaths and blasphemies. He fell cursing to the snow-covered earth. A mounted soldier tied a long rope to the man's wrists and dragged him to the outdoor court.

Lord Tomas's bailiff sat as judge. A gallows was hastily set in place as the prisoner was delivered to him. The bailiff looked indifferently at the man and ordered him tied to a wall while other matters were tended.

The first business was that of a boundary dispute; the second a charge of premarital relations against a tavern wench of Mensfelden; the next, a claim by a village reeve that his neighbor had diverted water. After an hour's deliberation the court turned to a complaint against a baker stealing dough from his neighbors. It seems the

clever fellow hid a child beneath the table where his cus-
tomers set their doughs for measuring. Once the dough
was set on the table, the child removed a wooden plug
from beneath and dug out fingers' full! At the baker's
signal, the imp would quickly replace the plug and wait
for the next. The scheme earned the baker a good flogging
and a severe penance from the priest.

The judge moved on to other business, including that of a
frustrated yeoman and his strident wife. The plaintiff was
convinced that his wife and a tinker were conspiring
against him, and he proceeded to explain a confusing plot.
His wife interrupted him time and time again with oaths
and loud belches, eventually heaving a handful of pebbles
at the man and then more at the court. That poorly aimed
insult earned her an immediate flogging!

Finally, the judge turned his attention to more important
matters. He quickly found the man captured by Richard
and the men from Weyer guilty of murder and hung on the
spot. He had been tried by ordeal; a method which yielded
to God's omniscience. The man had been bound and cast
into the moat. If he floated he was to be judged guilty, if he
sank, innocent. Sadly for the accused, he failed to drown.

It was shortly after the bells of sext when the drunken
crowd was dispersed for the midday meal. The four men of
Weyer sauntered off for a bite of bread, a fist of smoked
pork, and a two-handed flagon of ale. They soon found
themselves squatting by the warmth of a small bonfire
where they chatted with the subjects of Lord Tomas and
waited for Ingelbert's trial to begin.

They did not need to wait long, for the agitated lord soon
stormed to his place in the fore of the court, quickly replac-
ing his bailiff as the judge. "Now," bellowed Tomas impatiently, "to the business at hand! Bring that demon freak!"
The crowd hurried to the courtyard and watched the lord
pace in his black mourning cloak. He peered angrily from
beneath a black, broad-rimmed hat with no mind for
mercy. Within moments, Ingelbert was dragged before him.

The lord circled the young man like a hawk menacing a
mouse. He mocked the lad's bowed back and spindly legs;

he slapped his sloping forehead and squeezed his retreating chin. Then, in a rage, he pounded his gloved fist into Ingly's protruding top teeth and drove the lad to the ground. He circled faster and faster, his eyes red with grief and with fury. He kicked Ingelbert viciously, over and over again and none dared stop him. None, that is, save one.

"My lord!" boomed a voice from the crowd. A tall, black-haired knight stepped forward with a hooded cleric at his side.

Lord Tomas stopped and stared. "Who dares interrupt? Who dares!?"

"I am Simon, knight of Lord Klothar in Runkel. This is m'priest."

Tomas turned from Ingelbert and strode through the hushed crowd. "And what business have you in my court?" he growled.

Simon set his fists upon his hips. "I am bored. You've little here to watch, save that monster you'd be kicking like a sack!" The knight threw back his head and laughed.

Lord Tomas relaxed and clasped hands with Simon. "*Ja!* 'Tis a curse on legs, methinks! Look at the wretch. He murdered my son!"

Simon nodded his head. "Hmm." He set a finger on his bearded chin and circled Ingelbert thoughtfully. "Was your son a slight lad? Young perhaps? A boy?"

"Nay! He was a strong lad ... skilled at arms and a falconer."

"Ah. And of what cause did he die?"

Tomas turned a hateful eye toward Ingelbert who lay still and whimpering on the ground. "My Silvester was found battered and crushed, his neck broken. It seems he was killed, then thrown from a high cliff to the rocks below."

"And you'd be certain a feebleminded willow like this could have bested him?"

Lord Tomas did not like the question. His face puffed and reddened. "Some say the freak has a demon; his mother's thought to be odd, perhaps a witch or sorceress."

Simon took the man by the shoulder and spoke in low tones. "You needs be sure you've the right man."

The hooded cleric shuffled forward and agreed. "Good

lord," he whispered, "if you have the wrong man, thy son's soul shall not be avenged. I think it best you be careful that God's will be done, else you shall never be at peace."

Lord Tomas pounded a fist into his hand. "Nay! This monster is the one!"

Simon nodded. "I see. Then forgive me, sire. But perhaps trial by ... combat would serve you best."

Lord Tomas was startled. He faced Ingelbert. "Combat? He could bear no sword unless he truly has a demon—but a Christian knight would overcome and ... Ah!" The man smiled wryly. "I understand. It shall be for our amusement."

Lord Tomas whispered with his priest, then addressed the court. He spoke loudly and sternly. "Hear me. In the matter of the prisoner of Weyer, graciously yielded to our justice by his master, Abbot Stephen of Villmar, I, under the authority granted by the emperor and in the name of our Lord Jesus Christ, do demand said accused to stand trial by combat."

Baldric's eyebrows arched. "Combat?" he whispered in astonishment. "'Tis an ancient way. I've not heard of it in my lifetime and ne'er for a peasant! Ha, the fool's to be cut in two!"

Lord Tomas continued. "In honor of God's will and perfect knowledge, I shall surrender my rights to the sword to my faithful proxy, Lord Hans of Saalfeld, a vassal in my lands of Thurungia." An impressive young knight bowed. Tomas sensed a rumbling among the spectators. He cleared his throat and continued. "This decision has been made with the counsel of the Church and is right and fair. But, in mercy, I do not require either man to take the life of the other. The verdict shall be plain when one is the better." His last words drew nods of approval, and Lord Tomas took his seat upon his high-backed, oak throne.

Ingelbert was lifted to his feet and his bonds were removed. He was given a long, two-handed sword with a chuckle from a guard. Tomas's priest prayed over Hans and moved slowly toward Ingelbert. As he lifted his arms above the baffled lad, Simon's voice suddenly bellowed through the crisp air of the castle yard.

"My lord, I declare my right to champion the accused."

Lord Tomas nearly fell from his chair. His eyes bulged and he jumped to his feet. "What! What sort of trickery is this? You ... you've no—"

"But I do! I have the right to stand in the man's stead and so I shall! If you refuse me, may the lad's blood be upon your soul at the Judgment." Simon's lips twitched with delight as Lord Tomas gawked incredulously.

The grinning knight and his black-robed cleric strode boldly into the open yard. The churchman winked at Ingelbert, and the lad's eyes brightened as he recognized the kind face of Brother Lukas peeking from within the shadow of his hood.

"You must think me a fool!" bellowed Lord Tomas. "How dare you come to my lands and make a mockery of this trial!"

Simon stood straight-backed and turned. "Think of me as a vassal of justice, sire." He smiled and the crowd began to applaud.

"Then so be it!" roared Tomas. "But now it shall be a test unto death!"

Hans turned nervously to his lord. "T–to the death?" Before he could speak another word the command of his master rang in his ears. "Serve me this day, man, or be stripped of all and shamed forever." Hans swallowed hard and beckoned his squire to his side.

Neither knight was dressed for combat. They wore no chain mail or heavy leather jerkins. Neither had a shield or armored glove, not even so much as a quilted vest. Instead they were each dressed for comfort, Simon wearing only a fur cloak, a long, woollen tunic, loose breeches, and high leather boots. His opponent was dressed in similar fashion, though he sported a beaver cap that was now removed.

Hans was younger than Simon and a bit shorter. He was of average build and graceful. Simon was lankier and better seasoned, though not as nimble or quick-of-foot. Simon had learned to calculate an opponent's strengths quickly, and he immediately recognized that Hans's youth and agility would give the younger man advantage if they fought with short swords.

Simon turned to Lord Tomas. "My lord," he offered shrewdly, "I carry only a short sword but it is one with which I have grown accustomed. I would prefer its use to the longer one you handed the simpleton."

Tomas was still furious with the man and was eager to penalize him. In his haste, the lord was snared again. "Nay! You shall use the swords of my choice. Each of you take the long-sword!"

Simon bowed, happy to submit. In short order, he and Hans faced one another with blades crossed. A castle priest prayed God's holy and perfect will be done, then blessed each man and backed away. Lord Tomas's heretofore silent lady angrily waved a yellow kerchief and the courtyard fell silent.

Simon had served the Holy Church in Palestine, warring against the infidels on the victorious plain of Ferbelet just six years prior. There, in the company of French knights, he had proven himself to be stouthearted and ruthless, skilled with the long-sword and axe. Restless with life in the quiet valleys of the Empire, the man was now preparing to join Barbarrosa's Third Crusade already underway. His hands were itching for a fight. Opposing him stood Hans, knighted only months before. He was uncertain and tentative, suddenly wishing he were still a squire.

After exchanging chivalrous bows, Simon circled his foe, studying his movements and judging his skill. It was easy to see the timidity in the young man's eyes. *He's ne'er drawn blood*, Simon thought. The knight knew the contest would be quick.

Hans gritted his teeth and bravely lunged toward Simon with a ferocious two-handed swipe. Simon deftly ducked and parried with a restrained thrust that drew a small stain of blood to the belly of the man's shirt.

"Yield now, son. 'Tis no shame in it." Lord Simon's words were fatherly and kind.

"Nay, Hans!" roared Tomas. "Kill him!"

The young knight licked his lips nervously and shook his

head. Again he charged his elder. Hans's blade sang through the cold air, missing its mark by a wide margin. This time Simon countered with a single, powerful thrust. His aim was true and his long sword plunged through Hans's chest and burst out the young man's back. The young knight stared at his better, helplessly impaled upon the steel blade. He coughed and his eyes rolled as Simon released his grip from the long hilt. Hans collapsed to his knees, then fell backward with a gasp.

The crowd in Mensfelden's castle was dumbstruck. Lord Tomas stood slack-jawed in disbelief. The woolly mob remained silent until their master spun on his heel and stormed away. Brother Lukas then flew to Ingelbert and embraced the simple lad in tears.

Staring in disbelief, the four men of Weyer huddled slurping their beer and cursing the fortune of dead Hans until Lord Simon suddenly strode toward them. Arms folded confidently, he stared at them from his dark-eyed, bearded face. "What's your complaint?"

Baldric bristled. He opened his mouth wide and he bellowed, "That freak'd be no business of yours!"

The knight winced at Baldric's singeing breath, then mocked the man. "You've but half your teeth, man, and what's left is black and bleeding. You'd be a pitiful sight, yourself."

Baldric promptly closed his mouth.

Simon looked at Dietrich. "And look at you; thick like a plug and short like a woman."

Dietrich cowered.

Lord Simon glared about the four and shook his head with disdain. He grunted. "Humph. I'm told one of you is the sire of the boy, Richard, who captured the hanged man."

Arnold stepped forward cautiously. "Aye, 'tis my lad."

The knight laid a gloved hand firmly atop Arnold's shoulder. "I am from lands by Arfurt, vassal to Lord Klothar of Runkel."

"I know who you are, sire," mumbled Arnold, "and I know of Arfurt."

"I am in need of a page. Mine was lost to fever in Saxony. I could make demands on the abbot and seize the boy, but I'd prefer a willing one. He's of servile birth, so he's not likely to be a squire, but a page oft becomes a sergeant and a sergeant's wage is a good one. He'd be well placed to keep you fit and fed in your old age."

Arnold had already reckoned that.

"So, it is settled. I shall pay the abbot for the lad's use."

Arnold had hoped to bargain. "Good sire, worthy knight ... I ... I need the boy to tend the fields. Our taxes are heavy and the new abbot demands much."

"Enough, fool!" barked Simon. "Do not dare to press me. I can have him taken or I can just as easily find another."

Arnold bowed while his mind raced.

"Surely," whispered Dietrich, "he will pay something for the lad, and the boy will learn of things in Klothar's lands ... secrets of the nobles."

Arnold's money pouch was filled with knowledge of what he called "penny sins," and he was certain the sins of knights and lords would be worth much more than those of mere villagers and monks. He smiled at Lord Simon. "Good sire, it would be my privilege to serve you in this way. Ah, but could not a token of Christian charity be given? I am a poor man and you'd be takin' a strong lad from m'fields."

Simon snarled. "Aye. You shall have a shilling and a palfrey. See that the boy is scrubbed, shorn proper, and delivered to the abbot."

～

The season of Lent began on the twenty-first day of February in the Year of Grace 1189. Fathers Johannes and Pious seemed quite zealous to honor this time of denial and repentance. For his part, the younger priest had taken it upon himself to wander the village footpaths in the dark of night in search of excess. Father Pious, though corpulent and obese, was eager to deny others the objects of his own desires.

Baldric, Arnold, and Dietrich snickered as Pious passed Baldric's barred door. They had indulged in two jugs of well-spirited cider and were the happier for it. The three lounged in the dim light of the hearth, sputtering and slopping their muddy drink midst foul stories and sundry blasphemies. Herwin and his family huddled against a far wall, feigning sleep, while Heinrich and Effi attempted the same. Unfortunately for Heinrich the ruse had little effect, for he was soon rousted from his straw-mound bed to fetch more mead.

"And hurry, Heinrich!" barked Baldric. "You've but sloth in your blood, y'worthless worm!" The man's eyes were blood red and hung heavy in their baggy sockets. His graying beard was matted and wet, the front of his tunic stiff with half-frozen cider.

The lad rose slowly. He dared not look into his uncle's face for fear of inciting his anger. The fifteen-year-old trembled and kept his eyes to the floor as he wrapped himself in a sheepskin cloak. Arnold belched and the sound drew Heinrich's head up involuntarily.

"Aye? And what would you be lookin' at?" growled Arnold.

"Nothing," answered Heinrich timidly.

Baldric stood to his feet. "'Tis your uncle, boy. You spoke with disrespect!"

With that, the man struck Heinrich across the face with his open palm. The slap stirred Herwin. "Now, boy," boomed Baldric, "have you nothing to say for yourself, y'worthless half-a-man, you coward?"

Heinrich held his arm over his face and peeked upward at his towering uncle. "I–I am sorry, sir. I was about to fetch your mead from Aunt Gisela and—"

"Sorry? You say you're sorry? Ha! 'Tis what you said when you scrumped Lenard's dog! 'Tis what you said when you threw rocks at m'friends at village council! 'Tis what you always say!" The man thumped the boy on the back and then again in the face. Poor Heinrich tumbled across Telek.

The giant stood to his feet. He had often been witness to Baldric's violence but now it was enough. The broad-headed Slav took Heinrich by the shoulder and escorted him out the door along with Effi. He then walked over to Varina and her children and led them out-of-doors as well.

With a grunt, Telek re-entered the hut and closed the door, barring it with the table.

The Slav grabbed the gaping Baldric by the throat and tossed him against the wall. Before the woodward could gather his wits, Telek seized the stunned man again and threw him over the hearth. Baldric crashed to the floor and then pulled himself to his feet. He pulled a knife from under his wolf-skin cloak and pointed it nervously at the giant. Telek held his ground and growled.

"Y–you, freak!" threatened Baldric. "You'll hang for this! You've attacked your master's man." Baldric turned to Herwin. "You—tenant! He'd be kin to you, y'fool. You shall pay a price as well!"

Herwin spoke bravely. "You ought not beat the lad so, or Effi."

"Find me one man who cares so little for his kin that he stays his hand!"

"Telek loves the boy, as do I. You beat him for hatred, not for care."

"You've bitten the hand that feeds you, fool. Now tell that monster of yours to back away, else I'll have you and your miserable litter bound in Runkel."

Herwin knew Baldric meant what he said and he needed to think—and quickly. "Telek was ... wrong to lay a hand on you. I should like to add it to my debt."

Baldric laid the edge of his blade against the Slav's throat. "I ought cut it," he threatened. "I'd be in my rights."

"You've no right to that dagger, friend," said Dietrich. "Methinks you'll be bringing more trouble than what we needs. Heed Herwin's words."

"*Ja*," added Arnold. "'Tis always better to build another's debt! And y'know what needs doing up by Arfurt."

Baldric licked his lips. "Aye, 'tis sure." He turned to Herwin. "You'll add no pennies to your debt but you'll pay this: we've business in Arfurt—business with Gunnar kin."

Herwin paled. "I've no part in your feud, I've—"

"You and him have a part indeed. 'Tis the debt you now owe!"

Herwin closed his eyes and nodded in resignation.

೭

It was the Sabbath before Easter when strangers arrived in Weyer. A freeman from Limburg had moved his family to the monks' manor in search of business as a mason. He had been promised work at the bakery now under construction at the north end of the village where Heinrich would soon serve. It seemed that the new prior, Mattias, had successfully influenced Abbot Stephen to return baking to the villages. It was a reasonable scheme, considering the gross inefficiency of carting dusty bread to each village every morning. He had argued it would also improve relations between the peasants and the brothers. Such consideration—and the profit attached—was a worthy advantage for all.

The traveling mason brought with him a household of six, as well as news of Axel. Heinrich eagerly questioned him about his younger brother and was pleased to learn that the apprentice was doing well at trade, as he was naturally adept at calculating distance and weight, and agile atop the scaffolds of Limburg. His master could be heavy-handed, but was known to be a good teacher.

As Heinrich bade the mason farewell, a young girl stepped from the man's modest quarters. The young man stopped and stared—captured by the girl's bright green eyes and smiling face. He tried to speak. "G–g–good day, s–strange ... good strange maiden ... I mean ..." The lad took a deep, rasping breath. "I mean, good day, stranger."

"And good day to you, sir." The lass smiled kindly.

Heinrich's heart soared. He studied the girl carefully and guessed her to be near his own age. She was willowy and had the soft curves of a young woman. Her hair was blonde, and her face strong, yet gentle. "My name is Heinrich and I live there." He pointed toward the village center. "I am a baker," he continued proudly, "and will be the village baker as soon as the building is done."

"Oh," she answered softly. "My name is Katharina, of Limburg. My father is the mason for your bake-house. He's worked on a bakery in Mainz and the ovens in Runkel."

But Heinrich was not listening. He could only hear his heart hammering hard within his heaving chest. *Ach!* he thought. *Could it be that I might claim her for a wife? She is quiet and lovely, well-shaped and clean-smelling.*

"Heinrich ... Heinr—"

"Oh ... yes?" the startled boy replied.

Katharina giggled. "For a moment I thought you were not listening."

"Oh, no! You said your papa is a brick layer from Mainz."

Katharina smiled and nodded. "He is. But, I—" She shrugged and winced as her mother barked her name. "I must go now, Heinrich, but perhaps I shall see you at your bakery. We shall speak again?"

Heinrich sighed and smiled. He turned and closed his eyes. *"My bakery" ... she said "my" bakery. Oh that it could be so!*

ॐ

"Frau Emma!" cried Heinrich. "Frau Emma?"

Ingelbert came racing from the wood. He was smiling, as usual, and Heinrich laughed as his friend drew near. *Poor creature*, he thought. *Now a man but, oh, what a sight.* Indeed, Ingelbert was nearly sixteen and able to be wed, but neither his mind nor his body would be anything but a burden for even the most tender of young women. His broken bones had healed from Lord Tomas's beating, but he was as thin and white as ever. Some imagined he was little more than a skeleton wrapped in parchment. His distorted features were more pronounced than ever, but a great heart still beat within his gangly frame.

Heinrich clasped hands with Ingly and followed him to his mother waiting patiently by the stream. "Good Sabbath afternoon, Frau Emma!"

"Ah, lad, and to you." The woman chuckled. She rubbed her round belly and laughed. "Well, we've eaten more mush than what's fitting, and we can barely wait for Easter feast next week. And you, boy, have you eaten?"

"Aye, we've mush as well, but Varina put some dried herb in it and it tasted better than before. I cannot remember its name."

"Hmm. Perhaps rosemary? Nay? Well, I needs ask her. She's a delight."

"Aye."

"And what brings you to us?"

"Ah, 'tis a good day for me and I thought I'd spend it with you and Ingly."

"Oh? And why such a good day?"

Heinrich blushed and looked at his feet.

"Come, boy! Y'needs tell me!"

"I ... I met a stranger in the village."

"Ah, the mason?"

Heinrich shrugged.

Emma put a finger under her chin and pretended to think hard. Her eyes then brightened. "And you've met his daughter, Katharina?"

Heinrich reddened and squirmed, delighted to be found out.

"Ah, good lad! I thought as much!" Emma laughed and gave the boy a hug. "She seems to be of good stock." She winked. "Wonderful! Well then, Ingly and I were about to sit by the Magi. We've been summoned there by Lukas. Might you join us?"

Heinrich eagerly agreed, and before long the three crossed a newly built bridge and were walking along the bubbling Laubusbach. The trees were bare but budded, the sky blue, and the sun warm.

The monk was waiting patiently at the three trees, casually plinking stones into the clear water rushing past. He turned and waved as his friends approached. "God's peace to you, sister and young lads!" he called.

"And to you!" panted Emma as she pulled herself over a fallen log. "How do you escape these days?"

"I bribe Egidius." Lukas grinned.

"Well, blessed brother," Emma chuckled, "I am just thankful to God for your company."

The four spread pine boughs across the ground and lounged about their oasis with no care in the world. The Laubusbach was dancing and sparkling in the bright light of midafternoon and a warm breeze moved softly through the trees. The three Magi towered high above the forest keeping a faithful vigil; their sturdy trunks stood straight and wide like the marble columns in the cathedral of Milan.

Neither Emma nor Lukas were much for frivolous speech, so, after a few pleasantries, Lukas came to the point of his meeting. "Emma, I do not yet know all your secrets, nor you mine, but I have seen your gifts in illuminating. That parchment I saw was among the finest I have ever seen."

Emma colored.

"Now hear me. I do not know by what means you pay your rents or fees, but I presume you must sell your work to someone?"

Emma did not answer.

"No matter, your work needs to be offered for God's glory. The abbot has filled his new scriptorium with idiots and trembling hands! I've seen their work; 'tis a pitiful sight, an abomination and insult to art! I've heard it whispered in the refectory that the Father Abbot is anxious over it. He fears his profits shall soon dwindle. So ... what if I proposed to Mattias that we hire you?"

"Me?" Emma laughed in disbelief. "He would never hire a peasant and surely not a woman!"

"Ah!" Lukas's eyes sparkled mischievously. "Scribes and illuminators are placed in the towns now, working for pay to do what only monks had done not so long ago. I could say I found a skilled person who wants to remain unnamed. Aye! A person who is modest and has vowed against pride so he wants none to know his identity!"

Heinrich interrupted. "It sounds like a deception."

Lukas sighed.

"She took no vow against pride, and she is no 'he.' "

Lukas mumbled under his breath. "Listen, lad. Frau Emma is in need and we can help her. Have you no charity?"

Heinrich was confused. He was Emma's faithful friend— he would do anything for her. But deceiving the Church seemed too much. He wanted a better way. "Can y'not help her without sin?"

"Perhaps not helping is the sin!" challenged the monk, impatiently.

Heinrich was not convinced. "Can y'not just say the person is modest and fears pride?"

Lukas thought for a moment, then sighed. "Ah, well said, lad. 'Tis much better, indeed. And you, sister, is this agreed?"

Emma smiled. "Yes! 'Tis good!"

"Then you shall be the illuminator for the abbey! Can you believe it? The odd woman of Weyer serving a chapter of shavelings? It is marvelous, sweet as honey! And the old fools shall never know!"

Lukas turned to Heinrich. "You've a tender conscience, lad, and that is a good thing. But heed my words: beware of virtues, for they easily become the objects of arrogance. 'Do not be overrighteous, lest you destroy yourself'—wise words from the Holy Scripture, lad. Heed them!"

Emma was still reflecting on her newfound opportunity. "Methinks you are God's most willing servant, brother. This is a great gift from a loving God. *Gloria Dei!*"

Heinrich's jaw dropped. "Y–you speak the language of heaven, Frau Emma?"

Emma grew quiet and nodded.

Lukas leaned toward the woman. "*Verba mea auribus percipe, Domine, intellege clamorem meum* ... Give thine ear, O Lord, to my words, understand my cry ..."

Emma finished the verse. "*Intende voci orationis meae, Rex meus et Deus meus.* Hearken to the voice of my prayer, O my King and my God."

Silence filled the chapel of the Magi. Emma's life contained a wealth of secrets, and for her it felt strangely comforting to release another.

Brother Lukas smiled at her and waited for a few moments. Ingelbert was content to toss pebbles in the stream, while Heinrich held his tongue.

With tears in her eyes, Emma decided to reveal more. "I was born of high birth," she began. "It is called 'high birth' for no proper reason, for my father was a knight who was wont to slaughter whom he willed. My mother was widowed when I was but two, and she chose retreat in the nunnery at Quedlinburg. Here she lived well, free from the 'burdens of beastly men' she would oft say. But she died of fever when I was nearly ten.

"To my great wonder, the abbess showed a special kindness to me and taught me with great patience. She led me through the Holy Scriptures and trained me in rhetoric and mathematics, philosophy, and, of course, the doctrines of the Holy Church. And, having noticed my keen eye for the gardens and the kitchen, she assigned me duties with our lay-cellarer and the kitchener. I learned to prepare meals for the abbess and her guests who ofttimes passed our way. I became familiar with saffron and spices from the east, with ginger and salts. I learned to roast pheasant and venison, duck and quail. I could stew cherries with wine and tempt the angels with honey cakes and cinnamon!

"She, too, loved the gardens and taught me of butterflies and flowers. I think my time with her there was my favorite, indeed. I remember one summer day after a brief rain shower we both looked up to marvel at a glorious rainbow arching over the whole world. I remember how she clapped and wept for joy. She said she could picture the Christ seated atop that rainbow while the saints and angels slid down both sides like happy children! Ah, dear woman, what a wondrous vision!

"But all too soon it all passed." Emma sighed. "I had not yet taken my vows when I … I strayed. It was then necessary for me to take my leave, and it was the archbishop, through a bequest from my superior, who found me this good home for which I am most thankful."

Lukas listened with amazement and laid a gentle hand on the woman's arm. He looked at Ingelbert but asked no more questions. With a sincere prayer of blessing for the woman and her son, the monk disappeared into the forest.

⁊

Heinrich returned home to find Effi waiting for him outside the hovel. Effi hushed him as he approached the door. "Shh." Effi was nearly thirteen and beginning to show the shape of a woman. In three years or certainly four, she would be married. Heinrich often groaned in pity for whichever poor village lad was so sentenced! She was spindly and full of "spit," as Aunt Gisela was apt to say. Her hair was long and fiery red, braided down the center of her back. "Those dung-heads are planning feud again!"

Heinrich stiffened. "Feud!" he groaned. An uncontrollable shiver passed through him.

Effi opened her mouth. "Heinrich ... they'll be taking you ... I heard them!"

The door of the hovel flew open and Baldric stumbled into the twilight. "Heinrich!" he belched. "Get in here. You, girl, get to Arnold's with Varina and the new brat ... and be quick about it. Tell the women to stir the mush; we'll be eating there in short."

Heinrich stepped into his hovel, trembling like a rabbit in the sight of a wolf. Against the far wall sat his uncle Arnold, Dietrich, Telek, and Herwin. Arnold's dark eyes flashed in the hearth's firelight. "We've good news for you, boy," he began. "Your father fought for his kin, now 'tis your time."

Heinrich licked his dry lips and cast a nervous glance at poor Herwin. The man stared at his feet; there was nothing he could do. Heinrich lifted his chin and choked his reply. "The feud is outlawed by the Holy Church. Father Johannes has said any who raise an arm against another Christian shall be exc ... exc ..."

"Excommunicated," answered Baldric. He was familiar with the term.

"Aye, sir. I do not wish any to burn and—"

"Enough! That dolt Johannes speaks out his arse! Someone ought tell him that lyin' earns a few years in the purge. The Book also says "an eye for an eye." Have you no heart for the memory of yer own father? And the aunt you never knew, good Sieghild, suffered at the hands of Gunnars as well. They've ne'er been avenged in full."

Heinrich thought of his father. He had been a small lad when Kurt died, but he remembered something about the man's laugh and the easy touch of his calloused hands. He nodded.

"Good," said Baldric. "Now all, listen well. The Gunnars bring their sheep to Arfurt in a fortnight."

Dietrich rose on his squat legs. "We needs not risk venturing over the Lahn again." He lowered his tone. "Would be better to draw them. Arnold, you've ways to spread a rumor?"

"Aye."

"Good. Make it known we've a mind to come for them. That ought draw the vermin to us like moths to a flame."

Baldric extended his hand for silence. He stared into the low fire of his hearth. Heinrich thought him to be an old man now, etched and shadowed by the firelight. "Aye. Methinks it to be a good plan. They would most likely set their strike on the night before Sabbath. The Lahn's high, so they shall cross into Villmar on the bridge. They'll skirt the abbey walls and go wide round Villmar village. Then they'll come upslope toward our ridge. We needs meet them at the crest ... we can take their bodies into the heavy wood in the east."

Chapter 9

GUILT AND MYSTERY

wo weeks later, at the bells of compline, Baldric, Arnold, Dietrich, Heinrich, Herwin, and Telek were lying prone in a wet ditch. Despite the April evening's rainstorm, they waited patiently, certain that their enemies would be moving that very night. Arnold had passed a false report to a peddler of when he and his kin would be crossing the Lahn to strike the Gunnars. It was surely hoped that the fools would take the bait and think themselves clever in striking the night before.

It was hard to see the wide, gentle valley that spread before them, for the setting sun was hidden by heavy, gray clouds and the rain was falling hard. Behind the six men the steep slope dropped into smoky Weyer. From time to time young Heinrich cast a woeful glance backward.

The lad was shivering and near tears; totally unprepared to fight. He now knew it was the Gunnars that had killed his father and raped his aunt, but he was told that his own kin had robbed, burned, and murdered Gunnars as well. Furthermore, Heinrich had met an oblate named Alwin who was the son of a Gunnar killed on the same night of Kurt's death. *Perhaps m'own father slayed his*, he thought. Heinrich knew Alwin to be a good lad. He did not seem like the demon-possessed monsters his kin were portrayed to be. Lying in the rain, he once more wondered if his family's cause was a righteous one. He wanted to turn and run, yet that would add to the shame already heavy on his heart, and he wanted desperately to be free from such misery. He could only hope the Gunnars never came.

As darkness fell the Weyer men began to worry. "They'd yet be coming," argued Dietrich. "We needs wait till matins. Arnold, be sure yer wagon's still tied tight."

"*Ja?* If by the bells they've not come, we're out of this cursed rain!" grumbled Arnold. He had no sooner spoken, however, when voices were heard on the roadway some thirty rods ahead. A small, swinging lantern illuminated a short column of men emerging from the cover of rain and mist.

Heinrich and his fellows nervously checked their weapons. Most had knives or hammers; Baldric a swine-mallet. The Weyer men quickly divided to cover both sides of the narrow road as the voices drew steadily closer. None knew yet if they were Gunnars or simple passersby.

Baldric and his company listened carefully. The rain slowed to a drizzle and the muffled voices grew louder. They were within five rods when one of them could be heard plainly. "We've eight to their three! Ha, 'tis time to avenge Cousin Manfred."

The Weyer men coiled their legs—it was nearly time. An agonizing moment passed, then another, and finally Baldric's cry pierced the night air. Shouting like mad hellions bursting from the confines of Hades, Baldric's men sprang forward at the unsuspecting Gunnars. With Arnold on one side and Herwin on the other, the woodward swung his mallet into two silhouettes. From the other ditch Dietrich led Telek and Heinrich into the mêlée.

Poor, confused Heinrich heeded Baldric's cry and sprinted toward his foes on legs leading where his heart could not. But something rose quickly within him; a sudden fury filled his chest and he rushed at a shadow like a boar barrelling toward its prey. Perhaps it was fifteen years of rage that now boiled over, or perhaps it was the blood of the ancient Celts and Franks that flowed in his veins. Whatever the cause, the lad fought like a man possessed. He stuck his first foe hard with a slaughter knife. The man cried out as Heinrich yanked free his short blade and swiped at another, then another. For a few moments the young man felt nothing but violent anger, then it was over.

None of the Gunnars escaped the ambush. They lay strewn about the muddy roadway, some groaning, others still and lifeless. "Ha!" boomed Baldric as he embraced his brother. "And you, Dietrich, good friend!" The three clasped hands and cheered their victory under sheets of rain. But Herwin was on his knees weeping and rocking atop the huge body of Telek. None had expected such a giant of a man to be felled, but the deep slash across his throat was more than any mortal could survive.

Baldric turned to Heinrich and laid his huge palm on the youth's shoulder. "You've made me proud this day, nephew. Proud, indeed! No more talk of 'Scrump Worm' for you!"

Heinrich stared vacantly in the darkness, suddenly empty of fury and void of all joy.

"Now, help me send these bleeders to hell." To Heinrich's horror, the man took his mallet and began smashing the heads of the wounded. The young man vomited.

Heinrich clenched his jaw as he helped drag the fallen to the hidden cart still harnessed to Arnold's horse. He felt dizzy and sick as each lifeless body was heaped atop the others. He trudged behind his comrades toward the deep forest with his mind's eye still seeing Baldric's hammer smashing the helpless wounded. A thought knifed through his heart and he groaned. *And now I am a murderer!*

The young man stumbled through that awful, wet night weeping. "Never again," he swore to himself, "never again shall I raise my arm for evil!" Then, in the inky blackness of predawn, eight faceless strangers and good Telek were dumped into a shallow pit in the forests of the Laubusbach.

೩

Nearly a year passed, and Heinrich remained burdened by the guilt of that terrible night on the Villmar road. Lord Klothar had raised quite a stir when his shepherds were "gone missing." He was certain they had escaped to Limburg en route to their freedom and he had sent Lord Simon, page Richard, and five sergeants to search the town. It had been over a decade since the Gunnar-Jost feud had boiled to the surface, and in that time the village had a new priest, the abbey a new abbot, and the lands of the Gunnars a new lord. Few even considered the notion of foul play, and except for the whispers in Weyer and the oaths in distant Gunnar hovels, the matter of feud went largely unnoticed.

Since the time of the killings most thought Baldric had mellowed. His blue eyes flashed with less fury than they had and his drunken stupors were now more pathetic than dangerous. The thirty-four-year-old had not laid a fist on Heinrich since that night, and to some it seemed he was treating the young man with a certain grudging respect. But vengeance only satisfies for a season, and his heart was still as black as his rotting gums.

Heinrich no longer needed the shame of Baldric to weigh on his weary heart, for he had learned to add his own. He now saw himself as a thief and a murderer, a liar and a coward. Despite the encouraging words of Emma, he further accused himself of sloth and—given his happiness at baking—pride. His only relief, it seemed, was his knowledge that he had, at the very least, remained true to his vow.

Yet, unlike so many whose troubles leave them hard and bitter, the young man was still soft and tender in spirit. He was quick to see the sadness in another's eye and suffer the sorrow of another's plight. Though few would do the same for him, he was apt to shed a tear for man or beast and offer mercy where none was deserved.

Heinrich, now sixteen by a month and a few days, was settled in Weyer's new bakery. Katharina's father had done a magnificent job overseeing its construction and on the tenth day of March, Father Pious had blessed the bricks and the baker. Bread, all had been reminded, was the source of life. "Each time bread is broken," whined Pious, "we must needs remember the Savior's goodness to us all. 'Tis He who provides, for He is 'the bread of life.' "

The words inspired Heinrich, as did those of the monks who had trained him. "Boy," said one, "it is you who brings purpose to the labors of the field! When the men sweat and grunt behind their plough, then weed and harrow, and harvest and flail, it is so you can turn their tasks to food fit to swallow!"

At the north end of the bakery, a stone wall housed two chimneys of equal size. They extended several feet into the bakery where a brick-domed oven was attached with a hood and proper vents. Access to the brick-lined oven floor was gained through a waist-high, arched opening that was closed by an iron door.

The open room itself was well ordered with proper racks and shelving. Long-handled wooden paddles stood by each oven and within convenient reach of two trestle tables and two dough-breakers. In the center of the room was a wooden dough trough for mixing, and on one end stood a rack of shelves for raising dough. Along another wall stood flour bins to hold the rye, barley, spelt, or wheat flours. On the same wall was placed a salt box, spice boxes for onions, caraway, rosemary and the like, as well as two lidded barrels for sourdough. Since flour was measured, not weighed, a variety of measuring bowls and baskets were set neatly on a shelf, along with stamps for various feast-days. A firewood room was attached to the outside of the bakery and joined by a door near the ovens.

The second story was accessed from the inside by a short flight of wide, oak steps. Outside, a large double door could be opened, and a pulley above was hung on an extended beam. This would serve to hoist sacks of flour from the miller's wagon for storage.

Heinrich strutted through his new bakery and his chest swelled with more pride than he later confessed to Father Johannes. He also felt some disappointment. He had secretly hoped for a bake-house separate from the ovens; it would be so much cooler in the heat of summer. However, Prior Mattias insisted a single, half-timber, two-story building was adequate to serve. Johannes would later assure him that the discomfort might keep pride at bay.

During Pious's blessing, Heinrich could not help but fix his eyes on Katharina. As heavy as his heart so often was, it was she that brought a flutter and a song. He thought her like a butterfly from Emma's garden, or a light-winged bird soaring within his soul. And when she smiled at him, her green eyes sparkled with the warmth and hope of a summer sun. "Katharina, I am so pleased you've come!"

The maiden smiled shyly.

"Your father did a good thing here. 'Tis the best bakery in all the realm!"

Katharina was pleased. "*Ja,* methinks so. He's a good papa, smart and hard-working." She looked about the room. "Seems there is much to do as a baker. Have you no helpers?"

Heinrich beamed. "Well, the monks send me workers from time to time, but we've no need for an apprentice as yet. Actually, 'tis important I watch all that happens here. You know, Katharina, bad things can happen if the bake is bad."

Katharina drew close.

"The monks warned me and Dietrich, our miller, of the poisons and hexes on the grains. It seems thousands in France were burned from the inside; their flesh pulled from their bones by an invisible fire! Some went mad, rolling about their huts. We needs watch for black or sweet-tasting grains, especially any with tiny drops that taste like honey. They say it is a fearsome temptation, like the forbidden fruit. They told me if bread is ever cut and 'tis black inside, though it may be sweet, 'tis surely cursed. Some think the witch or her daughter may try to hex our fields, so the priests bless each planting and harvest."

Katharina was spellbound, or at least appeared to be. She was happy to be near the young man. The two brushed hands as Heinrich led her to the door. Neither said a word, but for each the light touch was a gift from heaven.

⮿

Abbot Stephen ordered the villages to hold councils on the afternoon of the Ides of March, and Weyer's Reeve Lenard placed his elders in the fore of the crowd on the blustery, sunny day. Father Johannes and his assistant, Father Pious, shouted a blessing over the wind and maintained a visible presence in the center of the gathering. Of course, it was particularly difficult for Pious to be obscure no matter where he stood! The eighteen-year-old priest was a rolling mound of indulgence and gluttony. His face was puffed and doughy and his skin white as sun-bleached parchment.

Old Lenard motioned for silence and beckoned Baldric to his side. As woodward for the whole of the abbey's lands he was well versed in the issues at hand. "We've items of some importance this day," began Baldric. He was now com-pletely toothless and weatherworn. Heinrich thought him to look grizzled and mean, huge and foreboding, but also stiff-jointed and weary. "First order for a vote is for a new reeve."

Lenard stiffened and soured. He had not been warned of this! He opened his mouth to object, but a blazing glare from Baldric quieted him. In moments, Lenard was out and another was in. "We've more things," continued Baldric. "The bakery is at work each day, save the Sabbath. Any caught baking their own bread shall be fined. Any dough found in your huts gets you a fine and a flogging."

A grumble rolled through those gathered.

"Forester Arnold identified Rolf, son of Hugo, poaching deer in the beech near Oberbrechen. I had him bound and taken to the abbey where he is being held for trial by the bailiff. Listen to me, men. You may take no fish from the stream, no hares, no deer, no fox, bear, boars ... not even a squirrel! No acorns, beechnuts, hazelnuts, wild plums, berries ... nothing without the approval of Forester Arnold or me!

"Further, the new abbot wants care taken in the fields. Any caught moving a marker shall be whipped, fined, and subject to hard penance. At a second offense he shall forfeit land rights. None shall block drainage, deepen a furrow, dam a spring. None shall move a fence, cut an orchard limb, or take firewood without the permission of the reeve or hayward. None shall marry in secret, none shall bury in secret—the taxes shall be paid. None shall refuse a man-at-arms food or quarters as needed. Lord Klothar is now in alliance with the Templars to our west and is quartering their sergeants as required. Fathers Johannes and Pious shall be keeping watch over all."

Baldric scratched his head. He couldn't remember much else except the matter he had saved for last. "Now, to the main business. Hayward, step forward."

A young hayward had been elected last year, though none knew the manner of his thinking. He and Herwin often discussed better ways to plant and harvest. He ran to the fore of the assembly and began to speak in a hopeful tone. "I met with Prior Mattias, the steward, and the abbot, himself. We met together with other haywards and reeves from all the villages of the abbey and learned of some new ways."

Another grumble passed through the village men.

"Nay, nay, y'ought not fear. Firstly, let me remind all we needs sickle our crops no more than a palm height off the ground. Some are wasting thatch by cutting too high. 'Tis easier on the back to be sure, but we can ill afford the waste."

He swigged some ale and raised his hands over the murmuring crowd. "Now hear me. The old ways are not working. We divide our fields in two and of all the land we have, we only keep a sixth part for ourselves. In France and England, and even in parts of our own Holy Empire it is now being done a different way. Take your strips of land and mark them so that we have three parts, not two. One part is fallow, another planted with a spring seed and the third in an autumn seed. Each year the parts are changed about so the land does not weary." He paused.

Herwin called out. "*Ja!* Would mean two of three parts would be yielding, and the work is spread over more time."

Another objected. "Nay! The old ways be good enough. They are tested with time and serve us well."

The crowd grumbled questions and complaints until Baldric raised his hands. The men quieted. "Listen, men, and hear me. What the young hayward says is what is to be. I'll have not a single word against it." He set his jaw and stared at the villagers until there was absolute silence—and submission.

The men were quiet, confused, and fearful of the new way. But for Herwin and the hayward this day was one of great hope, for they had always believed what manors across Christendom were learning: the land was a sure and constant servant, yearning to yield and gifted with plenty— if only men had the courage to change.

~

News did not travel quickly unless it was of such gravity as that which weighed upon the subjects of Emperor Friederich Barbarossa in the late spring of 1190. The emperor had risen to rally the armies of the German states in a third crusade against the infidels who yet defiled Palestine. He had led a consecrated column of knights, priests, and footmen from their rendezvous in Ratisbon, through the lands of the Huns, the realm of the great lord of the East, Isaac Angelus, and finally into Asia Minor. But, while pausing to bathe in the icy waters of the Calycadnus River, the seventy-year-old guardian of the Germans drowned.

A pilgrim bore the sad news to Weyer on a summer's night. He and a small company were passing through the village on their way home to Cologne in the north. Most travelers hurried past the dreary village in hopes of finding comfort in the guesthouse of the abbey, but darkness had fallen and they sought shelter in Weyer's church.

Strangers were rarely welcomed, for they were generally feared. These pilgrims, however, walked with a large, wooden cross at the head of their short column and the symbol gave Weyer's peasants a sense of safety. So, before they settled into the sanctuary of the nave, the reeve begged their indulgence and invited them to address the village folk in the village common by the well.

Sitting beneath the linden, the pilgrims were served a gracious meal of boiled pork, some precious wheat rolls, a pottage of lentils, leeks, and dried peas, and a flask of mud-colored ale. Heinrich and the other village men sat round about, spellbound as the leader told tales of Palestine, crusaders, and the dark-eyed demons corrupting the holy places.

"My name, good people, was once Gerhard of Cologne. I

have taken the name of Balean, after Commander Balean of Ibelin." The man paused and licked pork fat off his fingers. He guzzled some ale and continued. "I left my city ten years prior as a man of means, a trader in cloth and furs, a freeman in a free city. But I was a man touched by the love of God in such a way that I thought my petty treasures to be vanity. I had lived a charitable life, was educated in the university, and became a man of letters. Ah, but I thought it to be of no end, 'a chasing after the wind.' "

Balean reached for a wheat roll and acknowledged the baker. Heinrich beamed. "Believing it would suit my soul, I began to wander the banks of the Rhine, and I recited the psalms to the squirrels and rabbits scampering about!"

The men laughed.

"Ha. I began to think of myself as a bit foolish until some aging monk surprised me from behind a tree. 'Well done!' he says. 'Your memory is far better than mine!' I stared at him in wonder, for he looked like no other churchman I had seen. 'What are you?' I asked. 'Ah,' answers he, 'I've oft wondered that m'self!' Well, I shan't forget the man. He was a bit reluctant to speak of himself, but it seems he was once a warrior, a priest, and a monk. He claimed to be a fellow priest, as it were, for he claims we Christian men to all be priests!"

The men of Weyer murmured, and Father Pious, sitting at the darkest edge of the ring, groused. "Fool! Heretic!"

Balean stared into the bowl of lentils cupped in his hands. He waited for a few moments, then continued. "Ah, father, I know less of these things than I once imagined, but whatever he was, he moved me closer to God."

Heinrich spoke from the shadows. "Have you his name?"

"His name? Nay, I shall sink in m'grave wishing I had thought to ask it. Nay, I've not his name but shall surely remember him. He was a bit vulgar, though his kindness and the twinkle in his eyes urged me somehow. He disappeared into the wood, but something of him remained within me. I bade my former life farewell and I vowed a pilgrimage to Jerusalem.

"My journey was joined by countless others: men,

women, and even a few children, and I found them full of piety, Christian charity, and a zeal I thought only could be found in the chambers of Rome. I had hoped to find passage from Genoa, but upon my arrival was told the seas were filled with pirates. Other pilgrims assured me it would be to my great gain to follow the steps of the first crusaders. Their sacred ghosts would lead me through the sunny cities of Greece, through the realm of the eastern Church, then across the sands of the Turks, past the citadels of Antioch and Acre, and finally into Christian Jerusalem.

"Ah, my new friends, it was a most wondrous penance. For my feet did bleed, like Christ's, and I thirsted as I had never thirsted before. I was naked and I was cold, I was hungry and in danger. I, like Christ, did suffer for sins and I paid for them. Then, when I saw the white walls of the Holy City, it was as though I were entering Zion!

"Here I dwelt near the Holy Sepulchre and I prayed at Golgotha. I served the Hospitallers in feeding the poor and tending the wounded. The infidel pressed against our lands all the while and we were in constant danger. Our young king, Baldwin, died of leprosy and we began to wonder if God's grace was about to be withdrawn. Many of us continued in fasting and prayer for many days when news came that Christian knights had plundered a caravan in which the mother of the great heathen sultan, Saladin, was a member.

"Saladin is a mighty warrior dressed in flowing white robes and a shining headdress. It is said he rallied legions to his side with but a nod. Somehow, I soon found myself a servant to both Templars and Hospitaller knights at the springs of Saffuria as they gathered for battle. I remember well the hard eyes of the Norman archers, the set jaws of the French and English axe-men, and the songs the mounted knights sang to their horses on the eve of that awful day."

Heinrich sat still as an owl in a summertime tree. He blinked his eyes in wonder and waited for more. His mind swirled and spun, and he only wished poor Ingly could grasp the magnificence of it all.

"We moved at dawn, hurrying toward Tiberius, where Saladin had gathered a great army. Our knights attacked the infidel with great courage, but a terrible slaughter ensued, and by evening we were driven back to Hittin, the place where Christ preached His Sermon on the Mount. The infidels charged our armies with their cursed light horses, dashing and darting about, weaving between our brave knights like a shuttle on a loom. In and out they came, forward and back, left and right, slashing and chopping away at our broken lines until the ground was littered with the bodies of our dead.

"When night came our conquered knights huddled in gallant expectation of their coming death. I was sent to water the wounded, and I spent the next hours of my life in some horrid level of hell. With my torch in hand, I stepped between the severed bodies, the split heads, the broken joints of men dead and dying. Our priests bobbed through the eerie light, bending on and off their knees, praying for the souls of their butchered sheep."

The man stopped and shuddered. The village was silent. "That night we servants were sent away so that we might find safety in Jerusalem. It was later said that our exhausted, outnumbered knights fought well, but in the end, they did yield. They submitted themselves nobly to the supposed mercies of Islam. Ha! They were beheaded by the thousands, and Rainald de Chatillon, the man who had captured Saladin's mother, was killed by the sultan himself. It is said that some forty-five thousand Christian warriors were lost in that awful place.

"Then it was not long before the armies of Islam were at our gates. We had learned of the fall of Tyre, Tripolis, and Antioch but we believed the Holy City would be held ... it must be held! Our city was bursting with refugees; families from fallen cities throughout Palestine had run to us for safety, each bringing terrible stories of the Turks and their cruel ways.

"Then the enemy came. First, they offered us peace. Indeed! They even offered us land in Syria if we would but give the Holy places up to them and their bloodstained hands. 'No!' we answered in one voice. 'We shall not yield this sacred city!' "

The men of Weyer cheered and clapped. Balean sighed. "Ah, 'tis surely how we were. Then to the fore came Balean of Ibelin! He was a brave and resolute knight, invincible it surely seemed. Our armies were weak and the city hard-pressed for food and water, but Jerusalem's walls, he said, would surely hold, 'for the angels fill the ramparts!' "

Again, the village roared.

"He took command and organized us well. And he armed each able-bodied man—servants, pages, groomsmen, it did not matter. Each Christian man held a sword!"

Weyer hushed. Heinrich was amazed and a chill tingled his back. His mind's eye pictured him taking up arms for his Holy Church and fighting for righteousness. *Imagine,* he thought, *me, a bound-man, armed in a just cause!*

Balean continued. "For fourteen days we fought well and we fought hard. But, alas, we soon learned that St. Stephan's gate was undermined by the demons."

An angry voice cried from the darkness, "It was them digging from hell!"

"Aye," answered Balean. "It seemed so when they climbed from their tunnels and spread across the city like a spreading shadow. Our brave commander led us into the churches where we prayed for God's protection. Alas, though our faith was brittle, God's mercy reigned. Saladin did the unexpected, he spared us, though Jerusalem was firmly in his grasp." The man drew a deep, woeful breath. "Now I've new troubles to tell you."

The villagers waited in trepidation.

"Our good emperor, Barbarossa, did in faith and humility leave on expedition to liberate Jerusalem once again; some of you have heard this. But, in the mysteries of God's ways, he did drown in a mountain stream."

The peasants gasped. Though the world of popes and emperors was often overshadowed by the daily needs of life, each knew this news would prompt ripples of change like the dropping of a rock into a pond.

Balean stood and raised his hands. "Good folk, fear not.

Heinrich the Sixth is now emperor and shall rule well. Meanwhile, the Duke of Swabia is asking the pope's permission to found an order of Germans to be named, the 'Order of Teutonic Knights of the House of St. Mary.' They will wear white robes with black crosses, and it is they who shall avenge Barbarossa and shall someday free the Holy City once again!"

The inspired villagers offered a hearty "hurrah" and filled the visitors' cups with cider and ale. The night then seemed to pass quickly, far too quickly for Heinrich and the others. They dismissed the bells of matins, aware that midnight was better spent in sleep, but keenly conscious that they might never learn of such things again. Balean spoke on and on of the great sea and its shimmering waters. "A place where the sun presses hope into the soul," the man said. The young baker closed his eyes and tried to imagine "blue water stretching as far as one might see." He opened his eyes but saw, instead, a wondrous black velvet sky sprinkled with shining, fiery lights, each twinkling like happy, playful eyes eagerly urging him to smile. For an instant Heinrich paused and delighted in the beautiful sight, then dropped his head and shuddered. He had violated his vow.

৯

By St. Michael's Day the village was busy with the last of the harvest and the final planting of the winter grains. The hayward had done a masterful job in reorganizing the fields and work schedules. Herwin was pleased with the changes, but unhappy at home. His wife, Varina, had barely spoken to him since Telek's death. She was certain her brother had not run away, as Baldric and Arnold insisted, and Herwin could do little but look away whenever she confronted him.

Heinrich did his best to avoid her, but sharing the same roof made his efforts difficult at best. He found himself facing her squarely one day as she asked her question directly. "Do you know what has become of my brother?"

Heinrich paled as Baldric emerged from the outer room. The young man looked Varina directly in the eyes and struggled for words. If he told her, Heinrich reasoned, he'd put everyone in jeopardy. If he lied, his soul would be in further peril. "Varina," he said flatly, "you'll needs ask another." Heinrich thought that was the clever answer of a shrewd man! He had avoided risk for everyone. But the wounded look in Varina's face turned the lad away in shame. He was, indeed, a coward.

Heinrich sighed and stepped toward the door when Baldric laid his hand on the young man's shoulder. "I've needs of a word with you out-of-doors."

Heinrich felt anxious as he stepped outside.

Baldric's tone was surprisingly easy. "You'd be sixteen and of age to receive your inheritance. Kurt left most to you and some for yer brother, Axel. I've been thinking it best to hold fast until Axel is of age. Then you can divide things in better order … and I hope you shan't forget my good care of what's yours."

Heinrich held his tongue. He hadn't forgotten the burned parchment and the promise that blew away in the ash. He knew nothing of matters of law, however, and it seemed right to wait until Axel's sixteenth birthday, only one year away. He nodded.

"Good. Then I've your pledge that I'm to act as your legal head until Axel's birthday?"

"Aye," answered Heinrich with an unconcerned shrug.

"You so swear on the Virgin?"

Heinrich should have been suspicious. "Yes!"

Baldric nodded, approvingly. "Then I've another matter. I've chosen you a wife."

Heinrich was stunned. He staggered a little and blurted, "W–what! You've not the right … I am of age to choose m'self and—"

"Hold your tongue!" boomed Baldric. "You've just agreed to hold your claims. As your keeper 'tis my duty to negotiate a dowry and make a pick fit for our kin. I've taken the matter to Father Pious and he is in agreement. You'll marry who the priest has approved and there shall be n'ere more talk of it! Refuse, and the girl shall be shamed and you shall be punished."

Heinrich was sweating and confused. "Uncle, I've need to make m'own choice in this. Can y'not hear me?"

Baldric grinned a toothless grin and laughed. His foul breath burned the boy's nostrils and Heinrich turned in disgust. "Speak, boy, who is the one you've such an eye for?"

Heinrich eyed the brute directly. "Katharina, the daughter of the mason."

"Ha! Ha, ha!" roared Baldric. "Katharina? That green-eyed wisp? Her? She's the daughter of a freeman, y'fool. The abbot forbids marriages 'tween bound and free."

"But what if I buy my freedom?"

"With what? Dolt!"

Heinrich lowered his head. Truly, the fee for freedom was high, far too high. His only other choices would be to escape to a free city and hide for a year and a day, or follow the colonists into the marshes of heathen Prussia—a bleak and dreary life for such as Katharina. "But what if she pledged her fealty to the abbot?"

Baldric shook his head. "I wonder what kind of man would ask such a thing!"

Heinrich was suddenly ashamed of himself. Indeed, what sort of man would ask a woman to surrender her freedom for his selfish desires? And what father would permit it? Heinrich yielded. His voice thickened and he asked his uncle the dreaded question. "S–so who have you chosen?"

Baldric grinned. "Marta, daughter of Dietrich."

Heinrich's legs wobbled. "Marta? Marta? That selfish, spoiled wench who ... who ... spends her days complaining and grousing ... and ..."

"Aye."

"Oh please, Uncle, not Marta. Give me ... give me Elke of the cotter, or Etta, or Maria of Tomas or—"

"It is done, boy. At least she's a pretty one, a bit small for my taste, but spirited."

"I'd rather marry a monkey!"

Baldric darkened and bent into the young man's flushed face. "But Dietrich's an old and loyal friend to us. He knows things 'bout us all. He's a miller, you're a baker; 'tis a fit match and 'tis done. The wedding shall be in two years or less. Dietrich needs her at the mill till Sigmund can be of some use. I've already pledged this, but you needs so swear to Dietrich and to the girl at the altar in the coming Lent.

"And I've pledged Axel to a carpenter's daughter from Emmerich. She is named Truda. Your brother's a good lad; he looks like Arnold but seems more like me."

Heinrich grunted. He was far too overcome by his own misery to care much about his brother's plight. *Marta!* echoed in his head. *My God, it cannot be!*

~

It was a miserable, damp morning on the first day of Lent when Heinrich and Marta faced each other to formally accept their betrothal. With a heavy heart, Heinrich stood beneath the low timbers of the manor's mill and stared vacantly at his bride-to-be. Marta, for her part, was not pleased with her father's selection either. She had little respect for this curly-headed baker with the melancholy eyes. But her desires were given no more heed than a groaning ewe, and she would submit to her father's decision void of joy.

Heinrich was sick of vows and weary of the expectations he labored to fulfill. He had paid a high price for a simple glance at the stars the year prior. For that he had been required to walk barefoot in the snow with a weight tied round his head that kept his neck bent toward the earth. And, at Christmas past, he had failed to mark the monks' bread with their dove stamps. For this he was called to publicly repent of sloth and carry firewood for Father Pious each day of Christmas's twelve.

Oddly, he still drew some pleasure from his sufferings, a sinister, captivating comfort that kept him chained beneath the millstones grinding at his soul. Perhaps his submission to the order granted him a greater comfort than did craning for the sun, and perhaps it was pride in penance that gave him pleasure in his pain. Either way, the young man had lost sight of most of Emma's dreams.

Heinrich and Marta stood stone-faced as Dietrich and Baldric clasped hands. For Dietrich, the gain was good, for his future son-in-law was a baker and would have the means to care for him should he ever lose the mill. Heinrich would also soon inherit his father's land, a half-hide of good yield, and he had coins as well.

It was formally agreed that the wedding would be delayed until Sigmund could be trusted to help with the affairs at the mill. Marta had kept the reckoning of measured grains and had quickly grasped the cunning ploys of the miller. Sigmund, on the other hand, was slow of mind and apt to err in the wrong favor. However, in the hopes of Sigmund's eventual success, Dietrich set the date for St. Michael's in the year following.

The matter settled, each turned away, save Marta's uncle Gunter who presented the girl a gift of a clay bowl he had fashioned for her with his own hands. Marta smiled halfheartedly, then cast an icy glare at Heinrich.

Heinrich returned to his bakery in a mood none had seen before. He kicked open the door, flung resting doughs against the walls, and broke his long paddle across the table. He tossed baskets in all directions and stomped the monks' stamps to pieces on the hard, clay floor. When his tantrum was over, the flour-caked baker collapsed into a corner and wept.

&

It was a warm day in May when Sigmund delivered the miller's heavy-laden donkey to the bakery. Heinrich greeted him with a grunt and pointed to the rope and pulley. Sigmund was one whose countenance was as horrid as his soul. His eyes were usually runny and yellow; his face covered with sores and pimples that crowded the bumps and scars of those that went before. None who knew him dared trust him with even a lentil. Sigmund grinned and motioned for the baker to come close. "I've something to tell you, Heinrich."

Heinrich sighed.

"Something you'll be wanting to know!" The man smiled and picked at the gaps in what few teeth remained.

Heinrich grimaced. "Well, go on."

"You know that mason's wench, Katharina?"

Heinrich tensed. He had just walked with her on the

Sabbath past. They had talked with Emma in her gardens and danced in the "ankleblooms" of the meadow. He remembered the shame he felt. "*Ja ...* what of her?"

"She's to be wed next year, like you." Sigmund grinned knowingly.

Heinrich felt sick. He turned his head. *No, it cannot be!* he groaned within himself. "To whom?"

Sigmund raised a brow. "She's been pledged to a free-man's son, Ludwig, son of dead Mattias the old forester."

"Ludwig!" exclaimed Heinrich. "B–but he's a brute. He has no heart ... he's—"

"He's to be her husband and you're not," laughed Sigmund.

Heinrich leaned against the bakery wall and shuddered in disbelief. The thought of Ludwig with his cherished Katharina was more than he could bear. The young man ran away, sprinting toward the comforting shade of his beloved Magi in the cool wood by the waters of the Laubusbach.

৵

It had been nearly two and one-half years since Ingelbert had suffered trial in the castle of Lord Tomas at Mensfelden. Since then, Tomas had become ever-more sullen and dark; he raged about his castle sending his knights after every peasant's rumor. It was an obsession that Arnold calculated could be of some advantage in solving another mystery—the shadows of All Souls' eve.

For years Arnold had hidden in wait, determined to snag the spirit that hovered by Emma's door at midnight, but in every case he was seized by fear, or chased by beasts, and was now banished from all dabbling in such things. "The shadows," claimed Father Pious, "may indeed be devils at her door, but to interfere risks hex and curse upon us all. Better to leave the woman be, and her monstrous son, else you risk your own soul." Arnold had heeded the priest's advice but with great frustration, for the man was drawn to secrets like a wasp to an eave. *Perhaps,* thought he, *Lord Tomas might press after Ingelbert once again, and why not on All Souls' eve, only two months hence?*

Lord Tomas, however, wanted no part of Ingelbert. His priests assured him that the combat was sanctified and God would surely be displeased if he ignored His just decree. But Arnold's whispers of spirits and forces in the forests played havoc with the man. Night after night he sat in his large hall facing the roaring hearth with sword in hand. He cursed the lifeless faces of quarry taken from his woodlands; bear and wolf, fox and deer, all prey once walking free amidst the timbers of his realm. The grieving man stared and drank his ale, railing against his priests and knights alike until late one September evening he stood and faced his vassals. "The witch! Of course, the witch!" he shouted. "Why have none of you accused the cursed witch?"

The courtiers grew nervous as the man began to grin. He wiped frothy ale off his brown beard and threw his wooden tankard across the straw-strewn floor. "She hexed him and hurled him off the cliff! I know it—I feel it! Rumors tell me my son did love the witch's daughter, Wilda. Ha! I'll ne'er believe it! But, I tell you this ... 'tis plain to me now ... the old one was jealous of his love and spied him out and killed him!"

Lord Tomas's knights became noticeably concerned. They whispered around the hall in anxious, hushed tones. His soldiers had no fear of combat; to face another knight across a field and rush toward him atop a snorting steed was their virtue and their joy. But to step lightly in the forest mists at dawn in search of witches was something else entirely.

"What is the morrow?" roared the lord.

"The first Sabbath of September," answered a clerk.

Tomas turned to his priest. "What say you, father, of witches? Have they the might to send a lad such as my Silvester to his death?"

The priest bowed his head. "*Ja,* my lord. From former times it is known that they've powers from Lucifer to incant and to enchant. 'Tis they, I have oft heard, who guide arrows into the joints of armor."

Tomas's knights leaned forward, listening in earnest to the priest's words.

"I've heard it said," he continued, "that they are some-times skilled in alchemy—a temptation of the Pit that draws others to them, but also provides them with means. For, it would seem, some do change acorns and beechnuts into gold, or even pebbles into silver pennies. Their witches' sabbaths spawn curses and hexes, blasphemies and plagues that do fill all hell with wretched souls.

"Beware, good lord and noble knights, beware! Even the mighty Karl the Great was beset by their powers."

Lord Tomas sat still, his eyes fixed on some unseen vision. He stood from his oak chair and raised his gloved hands defiantly into the air. His eyes burned hot with rage and his nostrils flared like a stallion readied for battle. "On the first dawn past Sabbath!" he bellowed. "We shall find these witches and send their souls to hell!"

ॐ

Hours before prime on Monday, Heinrich was sweating and shirtless in his bakery. He and his two assistants were preparing for the morning's onslaught of buyers. In good years the peasants would bring a penny for their bread; in difficult times they'd bring eggs or hands full of peas. In desperate years they'd not come at all, resigned to eating their mush. In this particular year the harvest had been good and the peasants were able to sell their excess for more than what the taxes required. Heinrich would be busy.

Each morning he took the night's rested doughs from their shelves. He and his helpers would knead them, pause for a short break, then shape them into loaves of various shapes and sizes. Afterward they were stamped, decorated, braided, or marked if necessary and as the season warranted. Otherwise, as on this day, they would be immediately placed deep into the hot, brick ovens.

Then, while the morning's bread was baking, the next day's yeasted doughs were prepared. Each day was the same: buckets of water were carried from the well to the barrels of the bakery, then the water was mixed with the flour taken from storage overhead, and then kneaded in long wooden troughs. When the first kneading was done, the heavy doughs were broken into lengths that draped across the baker's forearms and then set on shelves for the next day's bake.

The baking loaves were browned and sometimes blackened by the wood-fueled ovens and set into baskets where they waited for hungry *Hausfrauen* to appear. Usually about an hour before prime, a column of weary women began to snake its way toward the candlelit bake-house for the day's fare.

It was on this quite typical Monday dawn that Varina came for bread. By her side was Effi, Heinrich's sister of fifteen. Though younger than he by two years, Heinrich suddenly realized that she would need to be betrothed within a year. Given Baldric's eagerness to seal alliances and pay debts, Heinrich was puzzled why he had not yet bound her to someone. Heinrich loved his sister, though he rarely saw her. Her duties with Varina kept her in the fields, often sowing grains, pulling flax, and bundling willow wands as the seasons required. When she was not in the fields, she would be working with Varina at sewing or carding wool, spinning or managing the garden.

Effi had grown into a beautiful young woman; shapely and petite—a quality sought more by nobles than peasants. She was clearheaded and smart, and her hair was braided to the waist, though bright red—a color not pleasing to many. Her blue eyes were always kindled with a fire of spirit that kept many at some distance, but she was a hard worker and not lacking in mercy. She had been a good sister to Heinrich and one for whom he wished only blessing.

"Good morning, brother!" chirped Effi as she waited for her bread.

"Ah, and to you!" brightened Heinrich. "Have you punched or bitten anyone yet this morn?"

"Ha! You'd be the first!" With that the girl playfully struck her brother on the shoulder.

Heinrich feigned injury. "Save me, saints!" he cried. "I've been wounded by a ... a flea." He smiled.

"Humph!" Effi laughed.

"Enough! Can we not get some bread?" grumbled a voice

from the waiting line.

Effi winked and retreated for home to help Varina feed Baldric, Herwin, and a hut full of Varina's children. Baldric was in a particularly foul mood that morning. After storming about the dimly lit hovel, he finally bent his heavy head out the low doorway and disappeared into the gray light of the new September day. He had business along the borders by Weyer and had borrowed Arnold's pitiful horse. The day was young and cloudy, but warm. The forest's trees were a faded green, soon to begin their glorious conversion to the wondrous colors of autumn.

Baldric passed through the valley of the Laubusbach and kept a sharp eye for poachers rumored to be stealing the monks' deer from the heavy spruce just ahead. The widening valley was clean and green, pungent and pleasant, but the wood was thick and difficult to spy. Baldric followed the stream to an eastward bend where he paused not far from his nephew's Magi. He dismounted to cup some cool water and while he drank, he stared through the ferns carpeting the woodland. Something seemed amiss. As woodward, he had spent many long days beneath the canopy of the forest and his instincts were keen. He peered through the timbers, suddenly aware there was no sound—no birds, no rustle of squirrels—nothing. Even the wind was still.

The man walked carefully past the abbey's boundary poles onto Lord Tomas's land. He tied his horse, then moved deeper into the wood. Suddenly, he heard something—a crack, then another, and another. Baldric lowered himself into the ferns. For a long moment there was silence again. Then he heard loud snapping and a flurry of cracks and rushes. He lifted his head to see two women darting between the trees about a bowshot away. They were leaping and lunging like frightened doe and disappeared in the shade to his left.

Baldric followed them at a run but suddenly heard a loud noise to his right. He dodged behind a broad trunk and looked to see a long line of armed men trotting in his direction, presumably in search of the women in flight. Baldric's

mouth went dry and his heart began to race. He was trespassing.

Baldric, now in his midthirties, was not the youth he
once was. He found himself gasping for air and stumbling
over logs like a clumsy old man as he raced ahead of the soldiers. He crashed across the forest floor until he arrived at
his tethered horse and heaved himself upon its saddle with
the grunts and snorts of a stiff-jointed bear. With a jerk and
a whinny, the nag carried the man across the border to
safety.

Relieved to be on his own land, Baldric breathed more
easily. He drew another drink from the Laubusbach and
wiped the sweat off his face. Still curious, he turned his
horse northward along the narrow trail that followed the
abbey's eastern boundary. He trotted about a furlong
or two when he saw the two women once again. They
dashed across his path and disappeared into the stands of
spruce to his left. Now confident on his own lord's land,
Baldric kicked his horse forward.

The two fugitives had run into heavy brush and Baldric
was forced to dismount and follow them on foot. His track-
ing instincts were sharp, and in less than a quarter hour he
came upon their low, panting voices. The woodward
crouched and stepped lightly on the carpet of soft needles
until he spotted an outcropping of gray rocks. To one side
he spotted the ragged figures of two women talking in
urgent tones.

"Mother," urged the one, "we've needs go west." She
spoke with a strong, resolute voice.

"Aye," answered the elder woman. "But methinks it better to take different paths ... and quickly. You, head north
over the Lahn and into the beech groves near Arfurt ... and
I'll go west, across the Villmar road and into the forests of
the abbot. You go on now ... I shall hex this land 'fore I leave
... we needs call the grundlings and the sprites to build a
wall of shadows."

Baldric felt a chill. *My God, the witches of Münster!*

The old one continued. "I shall curse them with scabbies
and warts, fevers and blisters that shall bring tears to their

weeping eyes!" She cackled and wheezed, and strung a string of blasphemies that singed even Baldric's calloused ears.

As he listened, Baldric felt another unbidden chill tingle along his spine. *That voice … 'tis known to me …* He lifted his head for a moment and stared more intently at the two. Their clothes were little more than tattered robes, threadbare, and snagged with brambles, twigs, and pine needles. The old one's head was covered with stale gray hair, her hardened face worn and weathered like the pocked and broken face of a stony cliff. Baldric was certain she was mad. On the other hand, the young one was a striking beauty. Others had said as much. She wore her blonde hair knotted on either side of milk-smooth cheeks. Her body was lean and supple; she moved gracefully.

There remained something about the old one, however, that troubled Baldric. He studied her as she whispered with her daughter. Perhaps it was her tone, perhaps her gestures, he couldn't be sure. She haunted him, yet something drew him to her. And when the young beauty dashed away, it was the elder whom he resolved to capture.

Chapter 10

A VOW KEPT

aldric pressed himself into the earth as the witch passed near, then clambered to his feet. Leaving his horse behind, he jumped over a large rock and grunted his way through a short ravine only to realize that his quarry was no longer in sight. He stopped and peered into the wood but could only hear the heaving of his own chest. Then, to his rear, he heard a clang of metal and the snapping of wood. He whirled about and stared into the forest. Seeing nothing, Baldric hurried westward in the direction of the forests that lay just beyond the Villmar road. He had not traveled but a hundred paces, however, when the old woman suddenly appeared in front him, staring and pointing each of her forefingers toward the man's eyes.

Baldric gasped. He stood perfectly still and trembled as the witch inched her way toward him. Her mesmerizing gaze was fixed on his shifting eyes and she moved closer. The aged woman came within the smell of his breath and held her ground. Her arms dropped slowly to her side and she smiled a large, toothless smile. Her eyes flickered, fearless and cunning. She squinted, then leaned toward Baldric's sweating face. She nodded and set her jaw.

Baldric slowly relaxed. She had not struck him dead. He carefully turned his face squarely into hers. The witch said nothing, and the silence was more than Baldric could bear. "I ... I am Baldric, woodward of the abbey of Villmar."

"I know," she answered.

Baldric swallowed hard. "H–how do you know me?"

The witch moved closer again, staring silently.

Baldric shuffled his feet.

The woman said nothing for another long moment, then spoke in a low, commanding tone. "Look at me."

Baldric was confused but obediently bent a little closer and studied her carefully. He thought she seemed strangely familiar. Her features were plain, almost homely, her hair was gray, save the few stubborn strands of blonde not yet lost to time or sorrow. Her bony body was bent and awkward. She seemed hard and menacing, yet something in her blue eyes betrayed a hint of mercy that lingered despite what she had become. A blurred image slowly formed in his mind's eye. "No!" he gasped. "It cannot be! You cannot be! *Gott in Himmel …* !"

The witch spoke. Her tone was firm, sharp but not hateful. "Yes, brother Baldric, 'tis true. Look at me. I am Sieghild, your sister." Her voice became bitter.

Baldric was speechless. He stared at Sieghild with eyes that were as wide as one who has seen a ghost. She now stood before him as a broken woman—a tragic *melánge* of anger, relief, and loneliness that would have melted the heart of a gracious man. But Baldric could only gape.

The sounds of approaching men startled the two. They looked to their rear and saw movement. "You, Sieghild," said Baldric, "they're after you. Run—now!"

Somehow sadly disappointed with the overdue reunion, Sieghild nodded, and the two rushed together through the forest. Brother and sister ran side by side up the face of a long-sloped ridge and into a small clearing. Baldric knew it well and knew they were drawing close to the roadway where he was certain no foreign men-at-arms would dare venture.

"Hurry, Sieghild!" he cried. "Hurry!" Baldric cast a nervous glance behind and to his dismay, he saw a mounted man bearing down on them. "Oh God! Sieghild, to the road … faster … to the road … a rider … on my horse!"

The woman turned a half-glance and saw the rider

straining toward them on the frothing, winded nag. *Maybe*, she thought, *maybe all is not lost* ... She raced across the clearing and set her eyes on the thin wall of trees between herself and the busy road. Her light feet whisked her through knee-high weeds and she began to outdistance her heavy-legged brother. Sieghild's gray hair streamed behind as her chest heaved and her mouth sucked hard for air. She desperately searched her mind for an incantation to cry into the wind—one that might send both horse and rider into hell's fires.

Baldric bellowed as the knight flew past him. And he could do no more than watch helplessly as the soldier raised his long-sword in midair. He pressed his aching legs hard against the earth as the knight gained on his helpless sister, and he roared what blasphemies his failing breath could muster.

Sieghild turned her head toward the sound of hooves, but she saw only the flash of steel as it fell from the sky. The sharp edge of the sword sliced through her feeble body, cleaving her from the edge of her neck to the center of her belly. The hapless wretch fell apart like a brittle leaf in winter and crumpled lifeless to the ground.

The knight reined in Baldric's horse and circled his fallen prey with a satisfied smile.

Baldric, now raging like a bear gone mad, rushed toward the knight with a rock gripped tightly in his huge right hand. The soldier chuckled and nudged his heaving horse toward the charging woodward. Then he halted his mount and reached behind his back to grab hold of his crossbow. With a wry smile the knight loaded a well-sharpened bolt and took aim. He stood in his stirrups and calmly waited until he could hear Baldric's wheezing lungs and see the fury in the red-faced man's eyes. He pulled the trigger.

The hardwood dart flew hard and true and smashed into Baldric's chest with a bone-crushing thud. The woodward toppled to his back as if a mighty hand had driven him to the ground, and there he lay, open eyed and gasping. The dispassionate knight dismounted and stood over his fallen prey. He glanced around for a brief moment to be certain none was witness to his deed, then placed a heavy boot on the woodward and jerked the bloodied bolt from the man's punctured chest.

Foaming blood oozed pink and red from Baldric's mouth and nose, and his breaths were quick and shallow. His eyes rolled, then closed. He coughed, gasped, and gurgled, until, at last, he lay still and silent upon the ground.

෴

It was three days before Baldric's body was found. Bailiff Werner, the abbey's new lay law officer, was eager to show his mettle and quickly began an investigation. Indeed, the scene was a mystery. He had examined the man's wound but had found no killing instrument. He also discovered a curious pool of blood a dozen rods away from Baldric, but only a strip of tattered cloth lay where a body should have been.

On a cool September day Baldric was washed and shrouded and laid to his eternal rest near his father's grave in the churchyard of Weyer. Father Pious dutifully offered a final prayer, but none shed a single tear. Heinrich thought that to be the greatest tragedy of all. Baldric had lived his life deceived by the notion that reality lies only within the visible and hence, as do all men of vanity, he gave no thought to things of the invisible; things such as truth, kindness, hope, faith—or love. Void of these, he endured a meaningless life and suffered his death very much alone.

෴

At the request of Abbot Stephen, Lord Klothar of Runkel permitted Werner and a company of brown-habited Templar sergeants to search his lands for evidence in the mysterious death of Baldric—without success. Though Klothar preferred to use his own knights, the Templars were gradually increasing their influence over him and the lands he protected. It was the natural effect of borrowing money, and Lord Klothar had increased his debt to the wealthy Templars.

During the particularly cold winter, Heinrich had stayed warm within his bakery. The abbey's newly hired general counsel, Hagan, had affirmed the eighteen-year-old's inheritance. Kurt had possessed a half-hide—inheritable land the equivalent of about twenty-five hectares and twice the amount considered necessary to support an average peasant household. In ancient times inheritances had been partitioned among all the male heirs. However, the lords now worked hard to end this custom, for it had created havoc by dividing each holding into ever-smaller parcels.

So, it was Heinrich who received the greatest portion of his father's wealth, including his land, livestock, hovel, all chattels, and the garden plot. As a charitable young man, Heinrich was uncomfortable with his good fortune and gave his younger brother Axel a promise of a future sum of silver, and he began immediate plans to accumulate a small inheritance for Effi.

Finally free from Baldric's control, Heinrich paused to reflect on his new station. He had plans to build a coop for fowl and a pen for swine, had hopes to improve his land's yield, and dreamt of buying the bakery from the monks someday. He was now responsible to be a Christian land-lord to Herwin and the man's growing family. But most of all, Heinrich needed to consider his sister's future. She was nearly sixteen and Baldric had not bothered to find her a husband.

As head of his household, Heinrich now needed to relate to his Uncle Arnold as something of a peer. At thirty-five, Arnold's black hair had turned mostly gray and his lean frame had become bony and knotted. He was still cunning as ever and alert, but like his brother Baldric, his life was void of hope and he lived each day confined to the exploita-tion of the moment. Heinrich found every possible excuse to avoid the man.

With so much new responsibility, young Heinrich surely missed the company of his cousin Richard. Now seventeen and still serving Lord Klothar's vassal Simon, Richard had so impressed the knight that he was beginning to train with the squires. Simon thought Richard to be worthy of his freedom and had secretly considered offering manu-mission to the abbot once the lad's mettle was proven. It was a dream Heinrich wished for his friend.

ॐ

The summer passed with little note and autumn's brisk breezes soon blew fresh and clean across the village thatch. Emma, now a woman of maturing years bidding her youth a reluctant farewell, thought of this season as though it were her own. It was true, she was thirty-five, but she was still vigorous and keen. Her girth continued to broaden, as did her smile, and her creamy, pink face reflected the joy of a soul that danced to the music of songbirds. Her secret occupation, the illumination of parchment, filled her days with color, and her heart was ever warm with gratitude for her shrewd and kindly friend, Brother Lukas.

Lukas continued to charm the prior with the work of his "secret artisan." It was a subterfuge that delighted both Lukas and Emma and brought conspiratorial laughter beneath the sheltering boughs of the Magi. It was here, too, that the good friends shared matters of heart and mind safe from judgment or consequence. Each came with either remedy or need, enlightenment or confusion. Their chatter was sometimes of simple things and sometimes of things that plumbed the depths of Creation and Creator alike.

And so, while Emma harvested the last of her gardens, carded her wool, and worked at her table, the village labored long and hard at the tasks of the season. The recently harvested grain was now threshed with long-armed flails, winnowed, fanned, cast, and gathered into baskets. All was done under the watchful eye of the hayward and his deputies, and any caught sneaking the monks' grain into shoes, hats, or folds of clothing would be flailed themselves.

It was late on one busy day when a troop of mounted men-at-arms accompanied by the new bailiff loped into Weyer from the Villmar road. Atop the lead horse was Werner and behind him rode a youth and four Templars clothed in brown habits. These were sergeants—soldiers who had taken the Templar vows but were of lower birth and standing than the white-cloaked knights they served. Their waists were bound with cords to remind them of their vow of chastity and on their left breasts they, like all the

Templars, wore an embroidered red cross. The village knew these bearded, shorthaired monks to be allies of their lord abbot, but the folk watched them warily nonetheless. Men with swords were to be feared regardless of their affiliation.

Heinrich looked from his bakery door and watched the soldiers make their way closer and closer. The baker wiped his hands and waited. As he expected, the horsemen stopped and dismounted. He offered each a wheat roll.

"Many thanks," said the bailiff. "And sorrows for your uncle's death."

Heinrich nodded.

The youth stepped forward. "You are Heinrich?"

"Aye."

The boy smiled. "You do not remember me, but I was an oblate in the monastery."

Heinrich did remember him, for the lad was an orphan of the Gunnars—his father had been killed the night Heinrich's own father was slain. The baker felt suddenly uncomfortable and nervous. He licked his lips and nodded. "Aye. You are some bigger than I remember."

The blond lad smiled. "Yes, and I've needs to grow more if I shall take my sword as a Templar! I am Alwin, a novice page, son of a shepherd named Manfred of the Gunnars. I remember you oft came for bread when I was yet in Villmar."

Heinrich nodded. "'Tis so, I did."

"And you were kindly to me and the others. Remember when you would 'drop' loaves at the corner of the workshops for us?"

Heinrich blushed. He was never sure if that had been a sin or not but he always thought the oblates looked hungry. "I ... I do remember." Nausea rolled through Heinrich's gut. He nodded and looked away in shame, his thoughts on the awful night on the Villmar road. Before he could speak Werner interrupted.

"Have you heard anything 'bout Baldric's death?"

Heinrich shook his head.

"Might you know of one who'd likely have him slain, other than the Gunnars?"

Heinrich reddened and looked away from Alwin. "No,

sire, I've no thoughts on this. My uncle was quick to make enemies; it seemed in his nature."

The officer looked hard at the young man. "Was the man at odds with any in this village?"

"I think all hated him."

"Had he talked of poachers or highwaymen?"

Heinrich shrugged. "He oft spoke of such. He said he'd found deer bones in the forests and thought passers-through were poaching. Perhaps ..."

"Aye, Brother Lukas thinks his wound that of a puncture from a crossbow. A passing poacher is likely." Werner brightened. It was an obvious, simple solution that might just satisfy everyone. He wondered why he hadn't thought of it months before!

"I thought crossbows to be outlawed by the pope," challenged Heinrich.

The Templars laughed. "Aye, we're not to use them on Christians. You shall not see us with them, but few others care much about the pope on matters such as these."

Werner was relieved. He mounted his horse and said, "We've needs to press on, Heinrich. God's best to you, and on the wedding ... some three weeks yet?" Werner laughed.

Heinrich smiled halfheartedly as dread filled his belly. "And good day to you, bailiff, and to you, brothers ... and Alwin."

The troop nodded and turned their horses toward the mill. Heinrich watched them for long moment until they passed out of sight.

ॐ

The knight, Simon, was a vassal to Lord Klothar of Runkel, and his small manor lay within Runkel's vast estate just beyond the Lahn River, close to the village of Arfurt. Simon held three hundred hectares of fertile land and about five hundred hectares of forest, making his domain about half the size of the area surrounding Weyer. He had no village, but instead housed many of his five score servile subjects in a cluster of huts gathered near his manor house. Other peasants who were bound to him lived in Arfurt and walked each day to work in his fields. By the order of things, both he and they were also bound to Lord Klothar of Runkel, the greater overlord of many such manors north of the Lahn. Of course, Lord Klothar, in turn, was the pledged vassal to a greater lord and so forth, until the chain of command found its way to the emperor himself, now Heinrich VI.

Richard, Arnold's son, was gaining attention as Lord Simon's aspiring servant-on-loan. As a page, Richard had served the knight well, learning the arts of court life and combat. Richard no longer wore the gray woollen leggings and short homespun tunic of a peasant boy. He now dressed in linen hose, colorful shirts, and the long, sleeveless robe of the warring class. He sported narrow, leather belts, supple leather boots, and embroidered cloaks. Nearly eighteen, he was entering the peak of his vigor and manhood. Handsome, strong, forceful, and courageous, he had captured the attention of the court and the ladies. But he was far too old to be considered a page any longer, so he was introduced as a footman-in-training, a respected title for a peasant soldier.

It was the feast day of St. Michael's, and the serfs of Lord Simon had provided their lord with a plentiful harvest of food and beverages. Of course, Lord Simon had added plenty from his own surplus, and he offered the great hall and courtyard of his manor house for the celebration. Cartloads of cheese, bread, and vegetables were hurried toward large tables bowing from the bounty. Three oxen, two bullocks, five calves, seven sheep, and a dozen swine had been slaughtered the day before, and by the bells of prime they were roasting on spits or boiling in huge cauldrons.

The sun shone brilliantly and the air was cool as it should be in late September. In one corner of the courtyard, drunken peasants wagered hard-won pennies on cockfights, while others wrestled, played bladder-ball, or raced. All through the morning, children squealed and chased one another through rounds of blindman's bluff and prisoner's base. Indeed, it was a feast day not unlike others gone before!

For Simon and his squires, however, the day would be lost unless they had opportunity to display their skill at arms. The knight, having drunk more than prudence would advise, beckoned his fellows to gather in the court-yard while his subjects cleared the center. Simon's best friend and dearest comrade, Lord Wolfrum of Saxony, had also come to celebrate the feast day. He and Simon began a good-natured contest with long-swords and shields. The two circled round and round each other, their swords singing in the clear air. They laughed and roared as the razor-sharp blades breezed by their unprotected limbs. The two played like lion cubs in the sun until, at long last, they collapsed unharmed and exhausted on the grass. Several squires set straw targets by the granary wall and displayed their skill in archery as others lanced gourds from atop spirited steeds. A group of footmen tumbled about in a riotous wrestling match while Richard watched restlessly.

The young peasant from Weyer had spent time training with a battle-axe and was anxious to display his skill. He desperately wanted to have Lord Simon see his ability for—just perhaps—the knight might be moved to buy his freedom and offer him a knighthood of his own. Richard decided it was time. He searched about the tented court-yard until he finally found one man willing to engage his fancy.

With a reluctant nod from Simon, Richard and Squire Niklas soon faced one another in the center of the quieting courtyard. At the insistence of their lord, each donned an open-faced helmet and a mail shirt before choosing their weapons. It would be the object of the contest to disarm the opponent without causing mortal injury.

While Niklas surveyed a table of fearsome weapons, Richard laid hold of his battle-axe like a man claiming the love of his life. He gripped it tightly, but respectfully, and then turned his shoulders squarely toward his opponent.

Niklas was almost ready to be knighted. In fact, he had rehearsed his ceremony of homage just a fortnight before. He was the son of a noble in Oldenburg and a relative by blood to Lord Klothar. He was steadfast, devout, and confident of his place in Creation's Holy Chain.

The peasants gathered in a large ring around the combatants. They cheered most loudly for Richard, of course, since he was of lowly birth. The young man tied his long, blond hair in a knot behind his neck and crouched like a cat ready to strike. Niklas had chosen a fork as his weapon. It was a long-handled, three-pronged trident favored by the crusaders of Barbarossa for its ability to keep opponents at bay. Niklas reasoned he needed only to catch the handle of Richard's axe and twist it from his grip. The two combatants nodded as Simon's wife, the gracious Lady Irina, dropped a yellow kerchief to the ground. Surrounded by cheers and shouts, claps and whistles, the two circled each other slowly.

It was in that moment when Richard realized he was at a great disadvantage, for his axe was meant to be a rushing weapon, one used to charge a foe in an indelicate, crude assault. The trident was its perfect foil. "I should've chose the flail!" he muttered to himself.

Niklas thrust his fork forward, straight at Richard's face. The startled peasant turned his head and swung a blocking blow that swept through empty air. Niklas laughed and feigned another parry. Richard dodged, but had dodged nothing, earning jeers from the crowd. Embarrassed and humiliated, Richard then rushed his opponent with his axe held high overhead. Niklas stepped quickly to one side and flung his fork toward the ground in front of Richard's feet. The boy tripped and tumbled into the dust.

Now furious, Richard charged Niklas again. This time, Niklas deftly aimed his fork at Richard's falling axe and caught the handle in the crotch of his spikes. He then jerked and twisted the weapon in hopes of dislodging it from Richard's grip. But the peasant had learned well and held on tightly, lurching forward to absorb the squire's yank.

The two circled again and Richard wisely waited for his foe to thrust. *If my timing is good ...* thought the lad. He waited patiently, but the crowd was growing tired and loud, urging the two to get on with it. Richard looked sideways to see Lord Simon yawning and teasing with a maiden, and the lad knew he was not impressing anyone. He turned his eyes hard upon Niklas and varied his plan. He charged the squire with an ear-piercing yell.

Lord Simon turned his face to see young Richard's brave charge and stood to his feet in anticipation. The young man raised his axe high over his right shoulder and kept his eyes fixed on Niklas's fork as he stormed forward. Niklas stepped backward with rapid, short strides and kept his eyes fixed on Richard's axe as it fell toward him in a mighty swipe.

Niklas had been well trained, and he instantly lowered the angle of his fork to catch the axe's handle close to his opponent's hands. But he lowered his pole too far, puncturing Richard's right hand with one of the trident's spikes. With a scream of anguish, Richard fell sideways to the ground. The poor lad rolled in the dirt, then rose to his knees and held his bloodied hand with tears of agony streaming down his face. Three attendants raced to his side and wrapped his wound with Lady Irina's kerchief.

With words of comfort and encouragement they then carried Richard to a hastily cleared table in the great hall where the lord's surgeon attended him. The young man was held fast to the tabletop and cried out in agony as the surgeon did his best to stitch and splint the hand. Simon offered a few words of sympathy to the devastated youth and left him to rest; he knew Richard's hand would be forever lame.

ॐ

News of Richard's injury spread quickly to Weyer. Arnold was enraged and knew he had lost all hopes of a son well-placed in the warring class. Abbot Stephen was disgruntled as well, for he had loaned Lord Simon a healthy young body, only to have a disabled one returned. Indeed, Richard possessed qualities that were better suited for fields of battle than fields of grain.

Heinrich lamented his friend's misfortune, but he had troubles of his own. It was the eve of his wedding and he faced Brother Lukas with a quaking voice.

Lukas tried to comfort him. "Heinrich, the price of

joy is sorrow."

"Then I shall be a joyful man, indeed!" Heinrich moaned. "And what sort of comfort is that?"

Lukas shrugged. He was at a loss for words, and all Emma could suggest was that the baker renounce the betrothal. "Nay!" snapped the baker. "I cannot break the pledge!"

In another part of the village, Marta, too, bemoaned her fate. She had grown to be a beautiful young woman of seventeen. She was petite, perhaps too much so for the labors of a peasant woman. Her face was even and her skin soft and fresh; her hair thick and rich and braided neatly. She walked about with an air of confidence and had become ever more demanding and critical. She was often given to fits of temper—vices Emma said belied hidden terrors. Yet, beneath the tempest she sometimes showed a brief glimpse of mercy, at least for those at arms' length.

The wedding day of Heinrich and Marta was blustery and cold "like my bride!" complained the baker. Father Pious met the couple at Sunday's bells of prime to confirm each as a willing participant. Despite the customs of the folk, the Church had long despised marriages forced upon couples. In truth, Heinrich wanted nothing to do with this marriage, for his heart belonged to Katharina. But Katharina was beyond his reach and he had pledged himself to Marta. He felt bound under the oath by the code of his kin and the expectations of the Church. He suddenly realized, however, that he was facing another dilemma: he must either lie to a priest or break his pledge to Marta. He stared blankly at Father Pious.

"Heinrich, did you hear me? Do you come willingly?"

The baker hesitated.

"Your answer?"

Heinrich closed his eyes. "*Ja.* I come willingly, father." His heart sank. *Willingly?* he thought. He suddenly felt a great weight lifted from his shoulders. *Aye, I am willing, though not wanting. I did not lie.*

Marta both loved her father and feared him. Dietrich had been a demanding father but also indulgent. She did not dare break the vow he had bound her to. She stared at the auburn-haired baker with an acrimonious submission to her fate. So when Father Pious turned his puffed face toward her she nodded her assent with a snarl.

"And what of the dowry?" asked Pious. "Heinrich? Speak, my son."

Heinrich did not like Pious and did not like giving his hard-earned money to this woman for whom he had no affection. But he dutifully recounted the negotiation Baldric and Dietrich had arranged. "She's to have two shillings, a half-virgate of land, rights to ten ewes and their issue in per—"

"Perpetuity."

"And two sows with the same, rights of use in the bakery unless the prior takes it in my death ..."

"Which he surely would."

Heinrich scowled. "And I had to purchase three ells for her gown."

"Ah, indeed!" Pious looked at the pretty girl with a glint in his eye that Heinrich did not fail to notice. "Dear sister, you have a marvelous countenance this day! Thy beauty is only enhanced by thy gown."

Marta blushed. She wore a simple woollen homespun, but it was new and would serve her for many years to come.

"And, so, Heinrich, is that all?"

"Aye."

"Hmm. And the merchet has been paid, I am told."

"Aye."

"Hmm. Well, with assent from each and taxes paid, we are ready. We shall witness your vows at the church door before Mass."

With that, Heinrich turned away to spend the next hour waiting for the simple ceremony and the nuptial Mass that followed. He would have preferred the marriage to happen as in former times—a simple moment with a few by the village well. Or, better yet, he might have forgone all ceremony and simply live together with the shrew under the same roof; in that simple way God and man would so declare them wed, and he could have slipped into his noose more quietly. But the Church now demanded a public declaration with a priest at the church door. Heinrich spat on the ground. "Always under the eye of the pope," he grumbled. Irritated and miserable, he walked to his hovel, where he picked at Varina's meal of mush and boiled bacon. And when he finished, he collapsed into his private bedchamber a man still bound by the expectations of others and longing to be free.

ॐ

Heinrich arrived at the church door determined to face his future as a good and obedient servant. In the hour before, he had spilled what tears his broken heart had tendered, and in the wake of his grief he had felt shame. He had then sought out Father Johannes and repented of his rebellious and prideful spirit. On his knees he had clenched his fists and chased Katharina from his mind while he re-asserted his submission to the proper order of things. And when the moment passed he had become calm and oddly pleased with the strength of his resolve.

As others arrived, Heinrich found Emma and took her by the hand. "Listen, good Frau Emma!" he boasted. "I shall hold fast to this vow and to my other! For my spirit is strong and my soul is again secured, so Johannes has assured me!"

With those words it was Emma's time to turn and weep—and she did not weep for joy. She wept for her little butterfly that lay, once again, shackled and bound, consigned to darkness.

After the greetings and well-wishes of the gathering congregation, the couple faced one another. Father Pious offered a brief prayer and each was asked to state their vow. Heinrich set his jaw firmly and took a deep breath. "I, Heinrich of Weyer, son of Kurt of Weyer, do take this woman, Marta of Weyer, daughter of Dietrich of Weyer, to be my wife under God."

Marta stared steely-eyed and echoed, "I, Marta of Weyer, daughter of Dietrich of Weyer, do take this man, Heinrich of Weyer, son of Kurt of Weyer, to be my husband under God."

Heinrich dutifully placed a silver ring on Marta's third

finger, the finger said to carry the vein from a woman's heart, and then stepped lightly upon her foot as a symbol of his claim. Marta took her husband by the elbow and the two walked into the fore of the church where a holy blessing was offered.

The reluctant couple then descended the church steps to a lively village feast set beneath the linden tree in Weyer's center. Here, despite cool September winds, the village enjoyed special breads made by the groom, casks of ale purchased by the happy father-in-law, and sundry pottages and treats added by neighbors and kin. It was a time for others to be glad-hearted!

By the bells of vespers, the drunken villagers escorted the new couple to their home and all waited outside as the priests blessed the marriage bed. The crowd sang and danced, laughed and teased as the two then disappeared behind a closed door where they began their new life as one.

Chapter 11

A NEW FRIEND

It was midday on the eighteenth day of July when all within earshot cringed at the shrieks of Marta gripped in the pangs of childbirth. The midwife wiped the young mother's brow gently then smiled as she lifted a baby boy into the air.

"He's a fine one, Marta!" she laughed. "Red curls like his papa."

Marta, weary and soaked in sweat, reached for her little one. "We've needs call the priest for baptism."

"Yes, little mother. I shall fetch one and your husband as well!"

Heinrich was busy in his bakery when he heard the happy cries of the midwife approaching on the footpath. Frau Emma had been sure to tarry by the baker's door all morning in hopes of happy news, and when she saw the kind woman waving and laughing, she clapped and hugged the young father like she did when he was a little child playing in her flowers.

"You'd be a father! Heinrich … you'd be a father!"

Heinrich waited nervously for the midwife to announce the child's health and gender. *Oh, God, be it boy or girl, let it live long and well.*

The midwife stumbled into the bakery huffing and panting, red-faced and sweating. She took Heinrich's shoulders in her thick hands and wheezed, "A boy! 'Tis a boy! And all is well with both the lad and your wife."

Heinrich smiled and fought the tears welling in his eyes. "Thanks be to God," he whispered quietly. In the months since his wedding the young baker had graciously accepted his portion in life and had worked hard to serve his calling in a manner pleasing to all. He was a kindly man, good-hearted, dutiful, and selfless. He would be a good father. "Frau Emma. I ... I cannot speak ... I ..."

"Do not speak, lad! Run to your wife and see your son!"

Heinrich smiled and wiped his hands on his flour-powdered leggings. He hastily threw on a linen tunic and dashed for home.

Varina and her three children met the young baker at his door and congratulated him as he hurried past them toward the straw bed in the rear bedchamber. "Might I hold him?"

Marta scowled. "Nay, he needs to feed."

"But ... for but a moment?"

Marta's face darkened. "No! You've brought me enough pain this day. Now go to the church and wait for the priest with the others. Rosa shall bring the boy."

Heinrich took pity on the weary woman. *Indeed*, he thought, *I did bring her pain* .... He hid his disappointment with a kindly smile and answered softly, "Aye, perhaps later."

In an hour or so, soon before the bells of nones, Heinrich and some of his household stood at the door of Weyer's church and waited for Father Pious to arrive from his tasks in the glebe and for Rosa to bring the baby. The annoyed priest arrived on his donkey and dismounted with a grunt. He was sweating and dirty, covered with bits of grass from harrowing wheat. The churchman had grown ever fatter and ever more discontent. Pious wiped his beaded brow and stood in the summer sun impatiently. "Eh? Is someone going to offer me a tankard of ale or cider?"

One of Varina's children had thought to bring a jug of Herwin's warm ale. "Aye, thanks to you," Pious grumbled as he lifted the clay rim to his pouty lips. The household waited quietly as the priest finished guzzling. With a belch and a wipe of his sleeve, Father Pious was ready. "So, heaven's sent a new soul? The midwife did not christen it with some foul blessing?"

Heinrich answered. "Nay, father, and here she comes with the child."

As the midwife climbed up the church steps Herwin arrived from the monks' fields and greeted his landlord with a firm grasp on the shoulder. "Well done, good man!" he whispered.

Father Pious took the baby and held him against his own swollen belly. The infant cried and wriggled in the rough wool of the priest's black robes. Pious blessed the child, put salt in his mouth to ward away demons, and recited a psalm: "*Tu autem, Domine, ne longe facias miserationes tuas a me. Ad defensionem meam aspice. Erue a framea, Deus, animam meam.* But Thou, O Lord, be not far from me; look toward my defense. Deliver, O God, my soul from the sword."

"Now, Heinrich," continued Father Pious, "have you chosen a name?"

Heinrich smiled and winked at Emma. "Johann Lukas," he answered.

"And have you godparents?"

Heinrich hesitated. Marta wanted her cousin Johann, but he was unmarried, slothful, and often blasphemous. Heinrich's brother, Axel, was far away in the guilded halls of Limburg and too much like Baldric for Heinrich's comfort. His best friend and cousin, Richard, was despondent and miserable, wandering the woodland as the village's new forester in deep melancholy. He was viewed as promiscuous and unrepentant—a soul in peril. "My ... my ... tenant, Herwin, and his wife, Varina." Heinrich gulped. He should have talked about it more with Marta.

"Are they Christian man and wife?"

"*Ja.*"

"Are they in good stead and order with the rules of God and man?"

"*Ja.*"

"Then so it shall be witnessed. Follow me to the font."

As the group shuffled toward the baptismal of the simple church, Herwin and Varina exchanged nervous glances. Herwin leaned toward Heinrich and whispered, "Marta had oft spoke of her cousin. Methinks she'll be furious with us and ..."

Heinrich stopped and turned to Herwin with pleading eyes. "You've needs do this. None know of Johann's whereabouts and he's no wife to bring ... and Marta did not want this delayed on account of risk to the boy's soul. She thinks we've much sin under our roof and are in constant danger."

Herwin nodded.

Pious's voice echoed through the empty church. "Come, make ready!" With little ceremony he lifted the child over the tub and prayed, *"In nomine Patris, et Filii, et Spritus Sancti."* He immersed Johann Lukas. "Amen."

With that, the little Christian was lifted from the water by Pious and the gentle hands of Herwin, and finally placed in the longing arms of Heinrich. The man beamed with pride, a healthy and godly pride. He smiled as if all heaven's angels were gathered round, and he cuddled the baby's tiny face tenderly against his stubbled cheeks. After a precious few moments Heinrich turned to his witnesses and invited all to his house to savor a berry bread he had baked that very morning.

As the small group made their way toward the celebration Emma drew Heinrich to one side. She smiled and gave her good friend a hug. Heinrich laughed and he offered her a moment with his son. Emma took the baby gently and tickled his chin as the newborn cooed. "Ah, wonder of God's goodness ... live well and be happy." She softly kissed the little one upon his cheek and returned him to his father.

"Heinrich," Emma said with a tone of excitement. "Before you join the others I've something to give you." Her blue eyes twinkled as a huge grin stretched across the happy woman's face.

Heinrich stood quietly as Emma reached inside her dress and withdrew a rolled parchment. He stared at it as she handed it to him. "I ... I do not understand, I ..."

"'Tis a gift from your mother."

Heinrich held the scroll in hand and waited for more. By the puzzled look on his furrowed face Emma knew she would need to explain.

"You've heard of the old pledge between an abbot of Villmar and your grandfather, Jost?"

"Yes. I've heard bits of it over the years but I thought most to be wild tales. I was told my sons would be taught in the abbey school."

Emma beamed. "Aye! 'Tis true enough."

Heinrich was astonished. "How can this be?"

"Jost was shrewd enough to have it written, sealed, and witnessed on parchment so no abbot could ever deny it."

"But Baldric burned it. It would seem to be an empty hope."

"Well, young man, your mother was a bit timid, but she was no fool. She stumbled on m'quills and inks one summer afternoon and she put me in debt for her silence. Ha, the blessed woman had a good eye for a worthy scheme!" Emma chuckled. "Your *Mutti* brought me the abbot's scroll one night not long before she died. She had me vow on m'very soul to save this for you and present it at your first son's baptism. And she wanted me to make a forgery to leave for Baldric at her death. Your mother was wise to Baldric's black heart. So I did—and a good one at that!"

Heinrich was stunned. Tears of gratitude filled his eyes and he wrapped the woman's shoulders with his one free arm. He looked at his son. "You, lad, are heir to a promise! You shall sit under the lindens with the princelings and with what brothers may yet come! Ah, blessed Emma, my wonderful Butterfly Frau!"

Tears rolled down the joyful woman's face as she stood by the boy she had loved as her own now grown. She turned her face to heaven in thanksgiving for the glorious moment. "Ah, dear Heinrich," she said quietly, "things are not always as they seem … for sometimes they are so much better!"

≈

In the year of 1194 the feast of Lammas would be grand, or so it was hoped. The summer had been warm and dry, but not so in any extreme. The harvest was sure to be bountiful, for the green rye was chest high and the yellow barley was drooping heavy with seed-heads longing for the flail. The swineherds were healthy for once and the oxen void of footrot, lump jaw, scours, or bloat. The sheep had been profligate and the goats were yielding milk with ease. It seemed the witch's curse had finally lifted.

For Heinrich, Lammas was to be a great test of his skill. He had been told by the reeve that Lord Klothar would be enjoying the feast by the new mill pond in the company of the abbot, the prior, guests from lands afar, and a legate from Rome! It would be the duty of Weyer's baker to provide the loaves, the buns, the twists, and the dainties for all to enjoy.

Dietrich was flabbergasted that the monks chose him to grind their grain over the abbey's miller and began scrubbing his millstone of all residue of the inferior rye or barley chaff left behind from the villagers' last grind. However, he was as suspicious as he was flattered by the monks' decision and feared any error of his part. He wanted to give them no cause to take his mill away.

Dietrich was no saint. He knew of the conspiracies he and his son had plotted against their fellows and was in terror that God might now call him to account. He had insisted on a private confession of all sins and had further pleaded for Fathers Johannes and Pious to climb about the inner workings of his mighty, churning giant and bless each part with the sign of the cross. And when the weary priests had descended from the last oaken post, he begged them to offer one more blessing. "Please, good fathers," he lamented. "Please bless my ears that I may proper hear the stone sing the grind, and bless m'thumbs that I may proper feel the grist is good."

Heinrich was also anxious and his belly fluttered at every thought of the occasion. He did not fear what Dietrich feared. After all, he was no cheat; he had kept his vows, was not slothful at task, nor truant from Mass. In fact, he now attended three Sabbath services weekly as the priests urged of late. So, for the baker the day-at-hand was free of risk, other than to his reputation!

Lukas brought Heinrich rosemary, sage, a few pinches of thyme, and a bushel of onions. These were added to the bakery spice boxes along with some caraway and sundry herbs the baker had grown fond of. Sourdoughs were offered by the kitchener some fortnight before, and fresh salt had recently arrived from Ulm. The priests blessed the man's ovens and his water, his paddles and troughs, and the baker of Weyer was left to his business.

Several days prior he had finished baking the large squares of bread to be used atop wooden trenchers as edible bowls for the day's fare. These were best when hard and stale. Other breads were preferred soft and fresh, however, and their baking would keep him busy right to the time of the meal's blessing.

Early in the morning of Lammas Eve, Heinrich hurried the village bake and chased his faithful patrons out of his door with their day's bread. He turned to his helpers and barked orders to clean the shelves and ovens of "every bit of common rye dust." Shirtless and sweating, the men scoured the hot brick ovens, the troughs and paddles, and every other tool so that all would be ready for the precious wheat flour. Then they worked furiously to knead and rise, then knead the dough again for the ovens. Late in the night, the exhausted men set the formed, rising dough upon clean shelves for the next day.

Long before prime of Lammas, Heinrich finished shaping and stamping his loafs with doves for peace, lions for power, hearts for love, and boars for the fertility of the lord's household. He shaped thin dough for pretzels soon to be hard baked and heavily salted. Other breads he molded or etched with crosses; some were spiced with herbs and onions, others laced with honey.

The ovens burned hot through the early morning hours and rags of water were dragged across their steaming bricks to keep proper moisture in the air. Paddles flew from shelf to oven door as the heavy dough entered the heated chamber, only to be withdrawn as browned and airy mounds of wondrous bread. Bread! Bread, that simple sustainer of life for all time past and all time to come! Bread, the symbol of the body of Jesus and the offer of hope to all! For Heinrich, the baskets of hot, fluffy, blessed bread now filling his bakery were so much more than heaps of food, but rather symbols of all that was necessary and good.

As Heinrich labored in the stifling bake-house, the village prepared to host the grandest of picnics. The millpond had been dredged months before, and its banks were repaired and sodded with thick, sheep-shorn grass. Children had shovelled away all the manure, and the sheep were chased to distant hills, leaving a clean, green carpet atop the pond's wide banks.

The mill was located along the Laubusbach some distance north and slightly east from the village at a point where the monks thought the stream to be the most vigorous. Here a pond had been dug in hopes of using a dam to add force to the mill's great wheel during times of drought. A roadway had been opened from the Münster road, and its surface was now made even so the special guests could arrive with a minimum of discomfort. They were expected by midmorning, sometime near the bells of terce. The abbot had excused the village from all labors of the day. He had proclaimed, "You shall serve neither demesne lands nor croft, nor strips of your own, your hands shall serve only as hosts of our guest and neighbor, Lord Klothar of Runkel." And so the village prepared to celebrate in song and in dance, with games and sport.

Arnold, the abbey's new woodward, was authorized to have the monks' huntsmen provide deer and boar for the villagers as well as quarry for the guests of honor. Numbers of spits were arranged a proper distance from the mill pond so the smoke did not annoy, nor "burn the eyes of nobleman or cleric." Firewood was gathered, tables carried from the carts sent from Villmar, and, at last, the village women thrilled to the task of tying silk streamers and pennants atop trestle tables, canopies, and standards. The village was filled with the colors of the rainbow! Yellow, red, blue, orange, and purple tents and flags snapped and fluttered in a stiff summer breeze.

For Emma, it was as if her garden had spread its magic along the wondrous, happy stream. She lifted her feet like a young girl in springtime, prancing and dancing her way between her singing neighbors, adrift in the warmth and pleasure of the sun above. At the sounds of kettle drums arriving from Runkel, Ingelbert sprang from the ground with a smile across his face as big as all the world. His happy, little eyes sparkled blue and his white hair waved in the wind like the tops of dandelions in May. The simple man took his mother's hands in his own and the two danced in circles as flutes and horns and tambourines filled the air with joy.

Trumpets sounded and the villagers retreated to a respectful distance from the picnic grounds. From a vantage all along the roadway they marveled at the spectacle approaching them. In the fore of a long column rode Lord Klothar and his wife atop two beautiful chargers. Behind rumbled a gaily decorated horse-drawn wagon carrying the drably dressed abbot, his dour-faced prior, and several monks. The villagers strained to see the great Lord Protectors of their manor. It was they who defended them against their earthly foes and kept the Devil's minions at bay.

More horses soon trotted by the happy folk, horses mounted by the smiling knights and squires of Runkel. The men were not dressed for battle, but were graced in colorful robes, long and tailored. Alongside the soldiers trotted a horde of hounds from all parts of Christendom. These included wiry, gray wolfhounds from Ireland, smooth, honey-colored Danish hounds, mastiffs, and a variety of mixed breeds.

Behind this group rode another column of knights, the Knights Templar. These bearded, short-haired warrior-monks were dressed in their white robes emblazoned with red crosses on each left breast. Their standard bearer trotted by carrying the *Beausant*—their battle-flag of two vertical black and white panels—and the villagers grew hushed.

Next followed the ladies of Runkel's court. Adorned in all the colors of the rainbow, they were dressed in flowing silk over-gowns, rippling and folding gracefully to the ground at their dainty feet. Their hair was braided and bound by jeweled hairclasps. Most covered their heads with gauzy wimples; others with the hoods of their mantles. Atop their saddles lounged all manner of cats who glanced about the parade with aloof indifference.

About the ladies clambered the children. As with the villagers, these came in all sorts, but the children of this class were scrubbed and finely dressed. The girls were dressed as miniature women, complete with shiny accessories and jewels. The younger boys wore tunics to the ankles, more like the women, while the older boys wore them to the knees, where hose followed into leather shoes. Younger or older, the male children's hair was long, like their fathers, but neat and often capped by plumed hats.

Klothar arrived at the mill pond first and dismounted. Smiling, he stretched in the sun and embraced his courtiers as they arrived. The lord was then escorted to a place at the edge of the grass and from here he raised his arms and graced the awestruck villagers of Weyer with a smile.

The simple folk of that weary hamlet fell to their knees and bowed as the man acknowledged them. "Good people of Weyer!" he roared. "I am Klothar, Lord of Runkel, son of Hugo of Oldenburg, father of Heribert. God has willed our fortunes to be joined with your abbot, Stephen. May God's blessings be upon us all, this Lammas Day!"

With that, the village folk stood to their feet and cheered. With a brush of his hand and a condescending smile, Lord Klothar then dismissed them to their separate celebration as he turned to his own. A large, high-backed chair was set at the head of a long set of oak plank tables, each covered by colorful cloths and bending with the weight of the feast's bounty. Lord Klothar welcomed his wife, Mechtilde, to his side and seated her on a wooden chair not unlike his own. She was attractive, especially given her age. The daughter of Rolf, King of Saxony, she had borne her husband a healthy son, Heribert, the future lord of Runkel.

Along the sides of the tables were set benches where the guests of Villmar would be seated. To Klothar's right, the row began with the papal legate, followed by the abbot, the prior, and a long stream of merchants, lesser lords, and knights. To Klothar's left sat Hagan, various visiting guests, and finally Bailiff Werner and Woodward Arnold. With the slighted Father Pious scowling in the background, a priest of the abbey offered a blessing and a psalm.

Chefs from Runkel had worked hard to present a fine display, one fitting the guests and the season. They stood to one side as servants gathered in a long column from their cauldrons and pits, portable ovens, and mixing troughs. With great ceremony and the accompanying sounds of lutes and pipes, the parade of servers was quickly ordered toward the cheering entourage with a steaming, sloshing line of pots, trays, kettles, and platters.

Lord Klothar, his family, the abbot, and two or three esteemed lords were presented with their personal trenchers. The rest of the guests would share a platter with two or more of their fellows. Carvers scurried along the tables, deftly slicing slabs of meat and removing bones from juicy roasts. Other servants rushed to fill impatient tankards with wine from the sunny slopes of the empire's lands near Rome, or with Swabian beer, or local cider. And, while the lords and ladies plunged their fingers, spoons, and daggers into fatty meats and soft stews, their hearts were gladdened by the voices of minstrels, the strings of psalters, and the screeching reeds of *Düdelsacks.*

Scraps the peasants would have happily sucked or gnawed were tossed indifferently to the many pampered dogs which drooled overstuffed and haughty at their masters' feet. Heinrich stared from his appointed place and shook his head. *Those dogs,* he thought, *know their place and are fattened for it.* He turned to look at the gray horde of dim-eyed peasants gawking at their masters. *And we know ours but are the worse for it.* He studied the lords, then his fellows. A voice suddenly whispered in his ear and he turned to see Brother Lukas standing behind a nearby tree. Heinrich laughed. "You've escaped again!"

Lukas smiled. "Aye, I could not help but come ... it is all the talk of the cloister and I'd be in hopes of some food and drink that might be left."

"Humph, methinks the dogs are eating your share!"

"Ah, the dogs. I forgot about the dogs." Lukas watched the abbot toss a lunging mastiff a plate of scraps before he surveyed the gaunt faces of the peasants around him. "The lords of war and the lords of the Church; they rule the earth together and hoard its plenty. We have strayed, m'friend."

࿘

There never had been, nor would there ever be again a Lammas feast in Weyer like the one now passed. For Heinrich, it was a remarkable success, and his reputation as a skilled baker had quickly spread across the realm of the abbey and beyond. The man had other reasons for joy as well. His wife, Marta, was again heavy with child and Heinrich beamed with pride as he awaited the happy day.

News came just past the bells of nones on a hot afternoon on the tenth day of August. Heinrich had just finished wiping the ovens and was about to inspect the harvest with Herwin, when Irma, Herwin's eldest daughter, rushed down the path to beckon him home.

"Methinks there to be trouble!" squealed the girl.

Panicked and fearful, Heinrich charged ahead to arrive at the barred door of his hovel. Not permitted to enter, Heinrich paced the croft behind his hut. He stopped and listened to hear a faint whimper, then a scream—then the cry of a baby. The man smiled and raced to his door. "Hello?"

The midwife stepped out of the bedchamber and beckoned Heinrich to enter. "Marta is good, but weary. The child is crying but methinks it seems too blue and ... is ... odd to look upon."

"'Odd'? What do you mean, 'odd'?"

The woman shrugged as Heinrich brushed past her and hurried to Marta's side. Marta lay sobbing, holding the newborn with limp, disinterested arms. At the sight of her husband, Marta cried, "You! You cursed me and the child ... you ... some sin ... have you some secret sin?"

Heinrich stood openmouthed and speechless. *Sin?* he thought. "What sin? What—" He looked at his girl-child and his heart sank. She was of poor color and misshapen.

Varina's daughter had been summoned to fetch the priest but it seemed forever before Father Johannes appeared at the door. He was annoyed and sweating. He had been working with the harvesters as far south as the balk at the Oberbrechen border and was not pleased to trudge all the way to

Weyer on such a steamy day. As he entered the hovel he stomped the dirt clotted on his sandals and grunted. "Does the child yet live?"

Heinrich nodded.

"And where is it?"

Heinrich pointed toward his bedchamber.

The priest took the child from her mother's arms. He was in a hurry to return to his duties in the field. "The name?"

Marta answered clearly. "I wanted a girl-child to be Margaretha ... after my mother's mother, but—"

"Then so it is," interrupted Johannes.

Heinrich nodded.

"And the godparents?"

Marta scowled at Heinrich. She was not one to forget an offense. "I'll not burden my kin with this ... this cursed thing. Herwin and Varina shall be named again."

Varina looked sympathetically at Heinrich and the baby. She had long ago forgiven him the mystery of her brother and had grown to love him. Her heart now broke for him and the pitiful infant.

Heinrich nodded. Father Johannes hurried the sacrament. "We've no time for other things ... I've no salt and—"

"Father, I do!" exclaimed Heinrich. He was anxious that his daughter have every advantage against the wiles of the Evil One, and he withdrew a precious pinch from his apron.

Johannes touched a fingertip of salt to the child's mouth and poured water over her head. "*Et Filii ... in nomine Patris ... et Spiritus Sancti...*"

Wide-eyed and suddenly terrified, Marta shrieked. "Nay! Oh, blessed Virgin Mary! He spoke out of proper order ... the child's cursed and damned to be sure!"

Indeed, the aging priest had pronounced the baptism in error and the poor serfs were now in terror for the baby's soul. A great wail was raised to heaven.

"My God, father!" shrieked Heinrich, "You've sent my daughter's soul to hell!"

"It surely does not matter, my son. If it gives you peace I shall pronounce it again."

Marta screeched. "Not him! Get Pious!"

Confused and uncertain, Heinrich ordered the dumb-struck Johannes away and went to Margaretha's side to kiss her wet head. Then, angry and fearful, he stormed out-of-doors in search of Father Pious. In an hour he returned with Pious in tow. The corpulent priest was all too pleased to feign outrage for his superior's shortcoming and quickly rebaptized the infant. To the great relief of the household, he then assured all that he had salvaged her little soul from the ever-straining reach of Lucifer's evil grasp. "Pope Gregory had made it so very clear that all sacraments must be kept in perfect order. You were wise to call me."

Exhausted and grateful, Heinrich offered a half-shilling for the parish alms tin and a tankard of ale for the smiling priest.

The day quickly passed into night and sleep came easy to the weary baker. But sometime in the predawn darkness of the next day, baby Margaretha found her rest as well. Her teary-eyed father bathed and wrapped her in a tiny linen shroud and laid her in an infant's grave by the cold stone wall of Weyer's church.

ॐ

It was late September, a few days past St. Michael's Day, when Heinrich confirmed the betrothal of Effi to Jan, a merchant of Frankfurt who traveled the region each season. Jan was a freeman, a city dweller of good report. Two years older than Heinrich, he was twenty-two and a widower without children. Effi, it seems, had served him water from Weyer's well in the spring of the year prior and the two had met on several of his passings since that first meeting.

For his part, Jan was drawn to the little redhead's feisty spirit and twinkling eyes. He loved her banter and her barbs and saw the tender heart of mercy beneath the bluster. In fact, so great was his affection that he had reached far into his strong box to pay the manumission for her freedom. Prior Mattias had charged a heavy fee. "We need healthy women to bear us more good men for Weyer and we needs be paid well." He hoped to discourage others from snatching young wives from his village, though he was wondering if the villages were not beginning to become overcrowded.

Jan added a generous dowry to secure the woman's future. "Two pounds and a mark," he said, "are on deposit in the Templar's preceptory in nearby Lauken. Should I die, Effi may return here to claim it. Otherwise I shall surely provide for her as a Christian man ought."

Effi, weeping with joy, embraced the man as Heinrich offered his blessing on the two. To avoid much talk, the prior insisted the wedding be in Frankfurt. None of Effi's household would be permitted to attend—the risk of peasants leaving the manor was too great and the abbot thought it better to "spare them the sight of things they are not ordained to have."

The harvest season brought other news as well. Though the time for war and conquest most commonly occurred in spring, some lords had begun to realize that the time just after harvest was of some advantage; the knights would have their own fields scythed and their grains in storehouses, yet the weather would be suitable for travel. A quick conquest of nearby land could be accomplished before the Advent and winter would prevent a counterassault.

With this in mind, the abbot of Villmar was suddenly nervous about the plans of his southern neighbor, Lord Tomas. The ambitious lord was rumored to have an increasing appetite for an alliance with the abbey. By challenging and defeating Lord Klothar, the abbot's present protector, Tomas would be in a position to demand a contract of defense for himself.

In response to these rumors, Lord Klothar had presented his picnic on the border. But rather than dissuade Tomas, it was learned that the event had been seen as a provocation. Riders were now often spotted along the far banks of the Laubusbach. In fact, on one particular day a yeoman swore on the relics of his church that he had witnessed a company of armed men cross the stream at night and disappear into the forests toward Villmar. It was this testimony that prompted the prior to order Werner to begin leading scouting parties of his own.

The protection alliance between Villmar and Lord Klothar

of Runkel required the lord to furnish "whatever arms deemed right and necessary to provide order and safety to the lands, buildings, chattel, roadways, beasts, stores, and subjects of the manors of the Abbey of Villmar." Klothar, however, had problems of his own. Another alliance had drawn his soldiers into Saxony in support of imperial forces under assault. So Klothar was forced to do what he had hoped to avoid—hire the Templars to protect his contract with the abbot.

With certainty and precision, the Knights Templar had slowly developed their own lands into prosperous manors. Based to the west of Villmar's abbey, in Lauken, their borders extended from the Lahn at Limburg in nearly a straight line southeastward until it joined the Emsbach. From there it continued to a point just south of the village of Selters. Their entire manor was nearly twice the size of Villmar's lands and contained six villages. The Templars, however, had an appetite for more, including a contested wedge of land between themselves and the abbey's manor.

Lord Klothar feared the Templars. Many of these warrior-monks had been seasoned on the bloodied sands of Palestine and were nearly invincible in battle. Because of their vast network scattered across most of Christendom, they could summon companies of knights or sergeants in support from nearly every quarter. One could not offend a single knight-brother without risking the wrath of the others. Furthermore, they had become the single largest benefactor of dying lords whose last wish was to secure an eternal reward by granting large tracts of land and treasure to these devout warriors of the Cross. With such assets they had become the bankers of the Christian world and had the means to buy whatever supplies, mercenaries, or other advantages any situation might require.

It was early in October when Heinrich saw a group of four Templars and a squire enter Weyer on horseback. Three of the men were lesser brethren and wore their brown robes over chain mail. They each wore steel caps and carried long-swords and shields. With them was one of the knights, easily identified by his white, sleeveless gown draped over his mail. His left breast boasted an embroidered crimson cross, and atop his head was a steel helm. Heinrich stood in awe, for as the knight turned the baker saw a second red cross stitched on the knight's back—a sign he had served God in the great Crusades.

It was midday and the bells of sext rang out as the Templars approached the bakery. At the order of the knight, the group dismounted and aligned themselves into a perfect row, facing east. They bent on their knees and prayed, and when they were finished the knight led them to the bakery door. "God be with you, baker."

Heinrich bowed. "And to you, sir knight."

"Have you a bit of bread we might buy?"

"Of course, sire. But it would please the abbot, methinks, to grant our poor bread as a gift."

"With thanks, good man, but the abbot provides for us in other ways. Take this penny and we'd be forever in your debt."

Heinrich took the silver *Pfennig* and filled a basket with bread and two pretzels. "I ... I am so very sorry, brother, but I have naught but rye bread."

The knight grunted and stared at the dark rolls. "Rye," he sighed. "But, lad, it could be worse ... it could've been oats!" The man laughed and slapped Heinrich on the shoulder. "'Tis good, son, good enough."

Heinrich smiled and turned his eye to the squire who had finished hitching the horses to a nearby rail. It was Alwin, the Gunnar. Heinrich watched the lad as he recited words in Latin. Then, the novice began to walk about in a large circle, stopping to act out some strange movements. His odd behavior captured Heinrich's attention.

"He's doing a penance for losing a shoe," offered one of the brothers.

"But ... *what* is he doing?"

"Each day at the bells of sext he is required to act the fourteen Stations of the Cross. There ... he's at number seven, the second fall of the Savior. Next he shall bless the women of Jerusalem, then ... there ... he falls for the third time."

Heinrich watched, spellbound. The lad seemed to suffer the very emotions of Christ at each act. "The man is truly devout."

"Aye. There, he is dying on the Cross."

Alwin's face twisted as he stretched his arms wide. He groaned as if he felt the very anguish of Jesus, then turned his head upright toward heaven and cried, *"Eloi, Eloi, lama sabachthani!"* He fell to the ground, paused, then rolled to lie still as if shrouded in his tomb.

"There, the fourteenth station."

Heinrich was speechless, taken as much by Alwin's sincerity as he was by his precision and drama.

Finished, Alwin was summoned to greet Heinrich. "Good baker, this is Alwin, a squire-novice in training and soon to take his vows."

"Hello again, Heinrich." Alwin smiled and extended his hand.

Heinrich was uncomfortable. His own many hours of penance suddenly seemed pitifully lacking. He took the lad's hand and released it quickly. Heinrich ventured a quick look into the squire's face. *Touched by God,* he thought. Indeed, there was an intelligence and a charity in the lad's eyes that set him apart from others. He was about fifteen, Heinrich guessed. Five years younger than Heinrich, the young man was tall, strong, dark-eyed and blond. He was devoted to his faith and to his masters in the preceptory, and would, no doubt, take his vows soon. Eager and faithful, he was beloved by his brethren and the favored friend to all.

Alwin smiled. "We have not met since the bailiff was searching for your uncle's murderer."

"Aye."

"All agreed it was a poacher."

Heinrich shrugged and shuffled. He could not free himself from the images of the dead Gunnars dumped in that muddy grave. *His cousins ... perhaps uncles to him? A brother?* he wondered.

"Well, we needs be off. I hope to see you again."

Heinrich nodded.

"I hope we might be friends!"

The baker's mouth went dry.

Chapter 12

THE BROWN SERPENT

ather Pious warned Arnold to stay away from Emma's hovel on All-Saint's Day. He made it very clear that to interfere in the dark world of spirits and shadows would bring only trouble to Arnold and the entire village. Father Pious insisted that he would keep an eye on the woman and her unfortunate son, and his vigilance would be enough. Arnold mumbled a grudging assent and returned to his drunken brooding.

Richard was brooding as well. Since the injury to his hand he had not been the same man he once was. The kind words of Emma, the urgings of Brother Lukas, and the sympathies of Heinrich did little to encourage him. Even his new position as Weyer's forester did nothing to bring him out of his deep melancholy.

By nightfall of All-Saint's Day, Richard had left the hovel to go wandering in search of a willing maiden while his father staggered to the mill to find Dietrich. "F–friend, g–g–good and true friend," slurred Arnold. "We've needs to put something to r–rest this night."

"Ach, nay ... not the old woman!"

"Aye, so it is."

"Arnold, you put yer position with the monks at risk, methinks."

"*Ja?* Then so be it!"

"Hear me, y'drunken fool. I've no part in it. I'll not have

my mill taken in penalty for some hex you bring upon us all."

Insulted, Arnold pulled himself upright. "Then I shall settle the matter m'self, y'coward!" Arnold stumbled through the village but soon collapsed and fell asleep on the damp, cold ground about a quarter furlong from the village edge and within earshot of Emma's quiet hut.

The November night grew raw and a light drizzle of rain fell through the leafless branches of the trees lining the Laubusbach. A few hours later, Arnold awakened, disoriented, shivering, and wet. He wrapped his woollen wrap tightly around his shoulders and looked about. Remembering his mission, he hurried closer to Emma's hovel and positioned himself behind a tree trunk just fifteen paces from her door. Now he was certain he would learn the woman's secret of All Souls' Eve.

The dripping rain was the only sound to be heard as Arnold waited and waited, struggling aginst the effects of cold, hunger, and fear. Finally, he thought he heard a snap of twigs to his left. Arnold stiffened and tried to sharpen his senses. He trained his eyes on the muddy footpath leading to the woman's home and held his breath. He heard another snap, then a sloshing noise. His skin tingled with sudden fright. A large, hooded figure then appeared, stoop-shouldered and hurried. In a moment, the silhouette slouched through the low gate and was at the woman's door. In an instant it was ushered quickly within.

Arnold crept toward the fence edging the woman's croft. Certain he had just beheld an incarnate demon, his heart pounded. His shaking fingers plucked a dagger from within his cloak. *But is he made of flesh? Does a demon bleed? Indeed, can it even die?* A shiver ran through his body. Arnold stared transfixed on the cottage for nearly an hour before Emma's door creaked open. Arnold stood still as death as the figure filled the dimly lit doorway and lingered for a moment. The shadow turned and stepped toward the gate with a few long strides. Then, as it passed through the gate and onto the path, Arnold leapt from the darkness with a cry and a thrust of his blade.

The figure was quick to be sure, agile with catlike reflexes. It had sensed danger before Arnold had attacked and stepped deftly to one side. With a quick kick and grab the shadow felled Arnold into the mud.

"Aaahhh!" screamed Arnold. He begged and blubbered like a terrified child. "Please, demon ... please I—"

"What?" The figure remained motionless for a second and then demanded, "What be your name?"

Arnold lay quaking. The demon's voice sounded like that of a man. "I ... I ... it be Arnold of Weyer, sir."

"Ah, Arnold, your soul will be mine and now I can toy with it as my plaything for all eternity," hissed the figure.

"Nay ... oh, nay ... fearsome demon—"

"Shut your mouth, fool! Methinks your soul hardly worth the bother. Tell me why you are here."

"I ... I wanted to see about the woman's visitor."

The figure tightened his grip and Arnold writhed in pain.

"I shall release you on two conditions."

Arnold trembled. "Aye ... yes, of course, anything you ask ... anything at all."

"First, swear to me that you shall ne'er tell another of this night. Not of things you have seen or things you have heard."

Arnold nodded. "S–su–surely ... of course, aye, not a word, none, sir demon."

"I've heard of your bag of 'penny sins.'"

Arnold gulped. "Perhaps such a thing is pleasing to you?" he asked timidly.

The shadow paused. "Aye, as does all evil. Therefore ... your second condition is to leave your bag in the monks' herbarium by Martinmas."

Arnold was confused and suddenly not very pleased. "Sir demon, I do not understand, I ... I cannot ..."

"Then I shall take your soul this very night!" shouted the figure. He raised his arm high above his head. Arnold was sure he saw the glint of a devil's blade.

"Nay!" pleaded Arnold. "I shall do as you demand! Please spare me this night. I beg you release my soul!"

The figure jerked Arnold to his feet and peered at him

from deep within a dark hood. Arnold's legs bowed and shook; he clenched his hands at his breast and trembled as he heard the final words.

"Your soul is released upon news of the bag. First, swear your pledge to keep silence on these matters."

"I do so swear."

"Good. If you fail I shall steal your soul by night."

ॐ

Eleven days after Arnold's terror, Brother Lukas entered his herbarium to find a large, leather bag stuffed to near bursting with silver pennies. It was on Martinmas, the twelfth day of November, and Lukas thought the gesture most fitting. After all, St. Martin had given the cloak off his back to spare a freezing beggar. With winter coming, Lukas could now grant warmth and shelter to many.

A little more than two weeks passed and the season of Advent began. Father Pious insisted that the Sabbath before Christ's Mass be more solemn than in previous years. Therefore, the wool-clad folk rose well before prime and began the day in a long procession to the church where they crowded into the nave to stand upon the cold, straw-covered floor for a predawn homily. Then, dismissed until the bells of sext, the villagers returned to their green-bedecked homes and ate their mush, breads, boiled meats, and salted pork.

At the appointed time, the villagers returned to the church to hear prayers and to offer confession. Encouraged by the Archbishop of Mainz to press for the "greater redemption" of his flock, Pious demanded confession now be done at both Christmas and Easter, immediately after which his people would be offered the blood and body of Christ. Souls cleaned and spirits refreshed, the villagers were now free to celebrate the holy day and the three days of respite their masters granted.

Christmas was a time for the wealthy to help the less fortunate, and the abbot joined in the spirit of the season by delivering sundry tasties to his delighted villages. So, on Christmas morning the whole of Weyer gathered in the churchyard to enjoy large casks of cider, mead, ale, baskets of fresh-baked bread and preserves granted by their benevolent abbot. By midday of Christmas, the glebe was kindled with snapping fires and boiling pots.

Lord Klothar sent some musicians to add gladness to the celebration and the village sang and danced in the cold December air as though it were the early days of spring. Laughter echoed against the brown, stone walls of the silent church and on it went through Christmas and deep into the night of St. Stephan's.

Exhausted from the festivities, Heinrich stood off to the side watching the happy revelers at play. As he scanned the gathering, his eyes fell upon a slight form at the foot of the church's bell tower. It was a woman, alone and silhou-etted against the rooftops of the torch-lit village. He walked carefully through the darkness, beyond the stretched shadows of the feast straining his eyes to be certain it was she.

The night sky was moonless and overspread Weyer like a jeweled canopy. Heinrich walked slowly, placing each foot tentatively forward in the darkness. He came within a few yards of the woman when the front of the church was sud-denly awash in a brilliant white light. It was as if a thou-sand torches had burst into flame before him! There, wide-eyed and startled stood fair Katharina, bathed in a white light, smiling and staring at the sky.

"Look! A falling star … oh!" she cried.

Heinrich's eyes never left Katharina's delighted face, even as the illumination faded.

"Heinrich?" Her voice was tender and affectionate.

"*Ja*, Katharina, it is me."

"Did you see the star?"

"Nay, but … but I saw you and you looked like an angel."

If he could have seen her face he would have noticed the color fill her cheeks. Heinrich felt suddenly uncomfortable and a weight of guilt came over him. "I–I ought get back to the others. Methinks the round-dance shall start soon and Marta may want to …"

"*Ja*, and Ludwig shall be looking for me. But, first tell me, Heinrich, are you well?" Her voice was earnest, almost pleading.

The man wanted to weep, for he was surely not well. His heart had ached for Katharina since the day he first met her. "I am well. And you?"

Katharina's heart sank. She wanted to hear him say that he was miserable or angry, empty ... thinking of her each day. In the darkness she ran her fingers lightly over the bruises her husband had raised on her arm. "I? Yes, Heinrich, 'tis well with me."

The two paused for a brief moment and stared at each other in the blackness of the churchyard. Heinrich could hear her breathing and he closed his eyes. He could yet see the vision of her emblazoned by the star. A sound startled him and Heinrich's eyes opened. It was time to return to their worlds, apart and forever alone.

&

Heinrich could hardly bear Marta's touch as she grabbed his arm and scolded him. "You leave me with this brat! Where have you been?" Her voice was grating and harsh, like a blast of sleet.

Heinrich shrugged.

"Ha! Methinks you off with another! Listen to me, husband. If you stray I'll have you beaten by the bailiff and you'll be doing more of your pathetic penances for all the village to see!"

Heinrich sighed—he had much practice. "Give me m'son and go see your friend Anka."

Marta bristled and threw a tankard of warm ale into the man's face. He stiffened but stood quietly as others laughed, then wiped his sleeve across his face. He stared blankly at his wife as she disappeared into the torchlight, then picked up his crying son from the ground. Without a word he turned and walked away; he could no longer bear the joy of Christmas.

&

Lent was calculated to be forty days before Easter, Sabbaths not counted. Since Easter was to be on the second day of April, Lent would begin the fourteenth day of February in this most dreary and snowy winter of 1195. It was a reckoning that Father Pious dreaded, since the season of

Lent was his least favored time. While time still remained, the overstuffed churchman hastened to indulge himself in heavy breads, dark ales, and, according to the rumors, companionship unbecoming a man of the Church.

The priest's ambition would be also fattened, for Oberbrechen's priest had died a few weeks prior, and Father Pious had quickly petitioned his superior in Mainz. He hoped to be awarded that parish, including its prosperous glebe lands, as his own. Furthermore, Father Johannes was deteriorating and it would surprise none to find him cold and blue in his bed at any time, leaving Pious positioned to claim the parish of Weyer as well. Despite the looming severity of Lent, life for Pious was suddenly brimming with opportunity.

Life was not as happy for Richard. The young man was disgruntled and sullen, and his handsome face was beginning to show signs of the misery of his soul. He simply rose each day to go about his tasks despondently as a broken, woeful soul. To add to his miseries, Richard's father had pledged him to marry a woman the lad had never met. It was a profitable exchange for Arnold, negotiated in the quiet chambers of the abbot's residence and serving the secret purposes of many.

Heinrich nearly wept at his friend's wedding and thought Richard's fate to be as bad as his own. The couple had no feast, no merry-making, or the slightest pretense of joy. Richard had only met the girl one hour beforehand and was suddenly sure he would have been better off being chained to a mad cow. Brunhild was more attractive than most—thin, brown-haired, blue-eyed, and fair. But it took only a few moments to discern a heart hardened with anger. Heinrich was certain she must be blood-kin to his own Marta.

By mid-April the village was deluged with rains unlike anything seen before. Great sheets of water poured from heaven day and night and this, coupled with the melting snows, made life unbearable. The mud along the footpaths and roadways was shin deep in most places, knee deep in others. Several huts' roofs had collapsed and their occupants had little choice but to crowd into neighbors' hovels.

Rivulets poured from the high ground surrounding the village into the surging Laubusbach. Swollen with more water than it could contain, the faithful, cheerful Laubusbach had become uncharacteristically fearsome and untrustworthy. It quickly turned into a brown serpent, swirling and churning, swallowing great gulps of earth from the banks that were once its gentle shoulders. It bore atop its rolling back huge timbers and debris from places afar, and soon it carried death, as well, for drowned sheep from unknown pens began to tumble into its angry course.

Some thought the Easter confessions to be the cause; either they were lacking in truth, as some said, or were so forthright that God needed to exact a special penance of His own. But now, just two weeks later, it mattered little what the cause. The abbey's bailiff ordered Oberbrechen and Weyer to remove their residents to the safety of their churches' high ground.

The floodwaters brought more than mud, debris, and sheep carcasses into Weyer. When the rains finally stopped and the Laubusbach returned to its gentle course, a pestilence emerged from the many pools of stagnant water and spread its invisible terror from hut to hut. Many suffered and died, but to Heinrich's indescribable distress his good friend Ingelbert lay ravaged and tormented by fever.

Poor Emma sat by her beloved son's bed both day and night, refusing sleep and all but the most meager bits of bread for three days. Lukas often sat with her, pleading with all heaven to spare the simple-hearted lad. Ignoring the blistering complaints of his wife, Heinrich hurried about his tasks only to fly to Emma's badly damaged cottage where he kept vigil with his beloved friends and hoped for God's mercy. But, alas, it was not to be. On a sunny afternoon gently warmed by soft southern winds, Ingelbert left the embrace of those he loved to discover the wonders of a new world.

The death of a friend is a loss rarely recovered and those privileged to know and love Ingelbert recognized the beautiful soul contained by his imperfect vessel. Heinrich returned to his flood-damaged bakery deeply grieved, but determined to continue. The monks had sent extra flour from their granary but encouraged the bakers of each village to stretch their goods with sawdust and chaff—an act punishable by heavy fines or flogging at any other time. Those villagers who had secret handgrinders were granted pardon if they would give them to the bailiff or his deputies. Several surfaced in Weyer and these were put to quick use by the miller for grinding what grains had survived in the upper reaches of his storehouses.

The young Gunnar named Alwin had come to aid the village's recovery. Weeks before, Alwin had taken his vows as a Knight Templar. In so doing he asked for a new name to confirm his change in identity. He was to be called Brother Blasius, a name chosen by his marshal in memory of an Armenian martyr who had lived nearly nine hundred years earlier. Given his lowly birth, many were displeased when he was conferred as a full knight and not merely a sergeant. However, his piety and uncommon spiritual gifts had inspired his superiors to drape a white robe with the Order's distinctive red cross over his broad shoulders.

Blasius brought a quiet strength and calm to the distressed village. The sixteen-year-old spent hours each day on his knees weeping and praying for the folk, and his sincerity and devotion did not go unnoticed. As the peasants huddled for their portion of bread each morning, they found great comfort in his earnest prayers and kind words.

Another knight that caught Heinrich's attention was an elderly man in service to Lord Klothar. The man was heavily bearded, and his long, gray hair hung loose across his shoulders. He was broad-shouldered and tall, lean and strong, but had uncommonly sad and compassionate eyes.

"Good knight," apologized the baker one morning, "I've but a bit of barley bread for you."

"Aye, lad ... shall do well enough," he answered.

Heinrich hesitated. "I ... I am called Heinrich."

The man looked at the baker squarely. "Yes, so I have

been told. I am Gottwald, vassal to Klothar."

"You've lands by Runkel?"

The knight paused. "Nay, lad. M'lands lie elsewhere, but I journey to Runkel from time to time as duty requires."

Heinrich nodded. "Forgive me, sire, but I cannot help but wonder what interest brings you to our suffering village?"

Gottwald's face turned to stone. "I've interest in any who suffers plight!"

Heinrich knew the conversation had ended.

The warm sunshine of May gently coaxed green from the drying ruts of Weyer. Sprouts of grass quickly covered the village paths, and crofts now burst with springtime shoots and blooms. The fields surrounding the village were alive with grain and with workmen laboring to weed and harrow their precious furrows. Despite the land's return to life, Emma now found smiling more difficult, especially as she kneaded the earth to plant her flowers. Her hut had been repaired, but not her heart.

On Midsummer's morning, a happy Effi climbed into a horse-drawn cart to leave for her wedding in Frankfurt. Though she longed for life with her beloved merchant, it was a bittersweet farewell, indeed. As she hugged her brother tightly she cast one final look toward the distant, brown-stoned church of Weyer and the familiar comfort of her lifelong home. Heinrich wept openly and embraced his little sister. The ever-faithful Herwin and his household fol-lowed, in turn, until, at the bells of terce, the young woman finally turned her back on those she loved and faced her future in the bustling city by the Rhine.

Summer came and went and autumn leaves soon drifted atop the village thatch. It was the first day of October when Arnold, Richard, and Heinrich stood at eve-tide with hands wrapped round tankards of brown cider. Arnold had grown ever more fearful, traveling the woodland in terror of the demon with whom he had bargained for his soul. He had kept his vows: he had surrendered his penny bag to Brother Lukas and had breathed not one word of his encounter to a single soul. But the man was fearful, not repentant, and he was bitter as well. He remained certain that the Gunnars had murdered his brother Baldric and he lived day and night imagining how he might avenge the deed.

Richard suffered his own miseries as well. Life with his new bride was as unhappy as he had anticipated. Richard was his father's son, however, so rage became a balm to his fear. He spent his few idle hours conspiring with his father to make the world pay for their miseries.

Heinrich heard little of their plots and cared less. He had tasted vengeance and it was not sweet to him. He had sworn to himself that he'd never again take another's life in the cause of wrong. Besides, he had more pressing matters to consider—for his wife was in labor with another child.

Heinrich stood by his doorstep where he waited for the birth to be announced. A dog barked in the distant wood and Marta cried out in pain. He listened as the midwife calmed her, and then he waited some more. Heinrich grimaced as Marta screamed again, and then again. At long last, a baby's cry was heard and in moments the midwife came out of the doorway wiping her hands on a blood-stained apron. She was weary but relieved. "He'd be a strong-lookin' lad and has a good cry. All is well, Heinrich. He can wait till the morn for the baptism."

So, soon after the bells of prime, a beaming Heinrich and his household stood once again in Weyer's church as Father Pious claimed another soul for Christendom. The babe was baptized Johann Wilhelm.

࿔

Soon after the snowy days of the Epiphany in the year 1196, Heinrich's father-in-law, Dietrich the miller, was elected the reeve of Weyer. He had not particularly wanted the job but Arnold thought it would be of strategic value. Dietrich was not a popular candidate, and his election was secured only by the threats of Woodward Arnold. Dietrich's reputation for cunning and for deception was renown, and he was not the sort of man the monks wished to have in charge of one of their manors. But Villmar left such matters in the hands of their *Volk*; it was wise and prudent and helped keep the order of things despite the dubious tenure of any one man.

Dietrich's election cast a pall upon the village and scorn upon its elders. It was feared to be an omen of more troubles yet to come. So the coming of planting was greeted with a mixture of tension and hope. In such a state it was fear that always ruled the day, however. News of mad Lord Tomas's death added a portion of dread. He, of course, had held the lands along the abbey's eastern and southeastern borders. His heir was Conrad, Tomas's second-born son who resided at the family estate in Thurungia. The young knight was thought to be ambitious, and all eyes were turned eastward. The first aggressive act of the new lord was to arrest a roving clan of Lord Klothar's shepherds who had been caught stealing sheep near Kummenau along the Lahn. Lord Tomas had complained to Lord Klothar for years that his subjects were crossing the border to raid flocks, but his entreaties had fallen on disinterested ears. Young Conrad would have none of it. His soldiers snared their prey in early April, hanging nine men and capturing numbers of women and children who were sold into exile in the marshes of Poland.

For Arnold, the news was devastating. "Gunnars!" Indeed, it was so. The family for whom Arnold had borne such hatred was gone and with it all purpose for the woodward's miserable life.

"Audacious!" roared Klothar. "Conrad is as mad as his father. Next he'll encroach on Villmar's lands; I can smell it!"

It was true. The concerns of the abbey at Villmar and its ally in Runkel were not unfounded, though perhaps overstated. Nevertheless, the abbot and his prior spent urgent hours in council with Lord Klothar's steward and captains. A plan of defense was hastily drawn and Klothar was forced to hire mercenaries to support his knights in the expected attack. However, while they prepared themselves for Lord Conrad in the east, their allies in the west, the Templars, had plans of their own.

The preceptor of the Templars' holding in Lauken was Brother Phillipe de Blanqfort. He had received orders from his master in Paris to claim the manors that bordered the Emsbach, including the villages of Lindenholz and Eschoffen currently under control of the abbey. These lands, it was argued, had been the rightful, legal property of Emperor Heinrich IV many years prior and had been illegally seized by the Archbishop of Mainz. To further their claim, a papal legate presented the archbishop and the abbot in Villmar with a directive demanding the release of these manors to the Templars.

The news was a blow to the abbot. The contested wedge of land was blessed with rich soil and wide fields. It was part of the "Golden Ground" necessary to sustain the abbey, and its loss would reduce Villmar's income by at least fifteen percent, just at a time when the treasury was badly depleted by the flood. Abbot Stephen might be able to negotiate for lands elsewhere—his vision could not possibly be limited to the confines of a shrinking manor—but he would not yield this land easily. He dispatched his prior to Mainz with a biting letter of consent to be delivered to the papal legate. Then he turned to Klothar and reduced his pledged fees by twenty percent, "for it is likely you shall have less to protect and defend," he wrote.

The furious lord raged about his castle in Runkel and ordered the withdrawal of the mercenaries so recently sent to defend the abbey's lands in the east. "Less to protect and defend? You'd be right in those words!" So, by early June, Weyer and its neighbors along the Laubusbach were left with little more than a handful of grumbling sergeants, one knight of Runkel, and the watchful eyes of a few Templars.

News of the rift between Villmar and Runkel quickly found its way to the eager ears of Lord Conrad in residence at nearby Mensfelden. He called a council in the second week of June and organized a raid against the abbey's manor. "The time is right to strike! The abbot has lost his love for the Templars; he is in division with Klothar; he is ripe for picking! He shall beg to contract with us for protection.

"Now hear me, hear me well! Our purpose is to expose the weak arm of Klothar. We strike his men without quarter but do no harm to the villages."

It was two days before the Midsummer's Day feast when the Templars learned of Conrad's plans through a spy well placed in the young lord's court. Eager to thwart the ambitions of another rival, they sent messengers to both the abbot and Lord Klothar. By dusk the church bell in Weyer was ringing the alarm, and the distant gong of Villmar's new warning bell could be heard thudding faintly in the distance.

The Templars rushed a company of men-at-arms south to defend Selters from an attack from the corner nearest their own. Oberbrechen and Weyer were left to a reluctant Lord Klothar and his knights from Runkel. Though frustrated and angered by the recent amendments to his contract, Lord Klothar was a man of honor and dispatched a large company of soldiers into the abbey's land. Joining thirty mounted sergeants were seven knights, including Simon—the former liege of Richard—and Gottwald, the aging knight with whom Heinrich had spoken. Each of these two had insisted their swords be specifically used in defense of Weyer, and they separated from their larger company with a dozen seasoned sergeants.

Lord Conrad was young, but was no fool. He expected resistance but had no interest in quarrelling with the Templars. In fact, he had large sums of money held in Templar banks and thought it best to avoid any clash with the armed monks. When he learned of Templars riding in defense of Selters, he adjusted his plans. His forces quickly turned away from Selters and divided in the forests east of the Laubusbach. "You ... Roland, take a company to Weyer. I shall lead these against Oberbrechen. Godspeed!"

Roland, a robust knight of middle years, was savage and brutal. He was known for his cruelty throughout Palestine where he had slaughtered countless innocents in the mountain villages of that holy land. He was often drunk and boastful, frequently bragging of his butchery. Conrad was in fear of Roland and oft wished the rogue knight be slain. *Perhaps*, he thought, *this day shall yield profit in many ways.*

Roland led his men along the Laubusbach's high eastern

bank until the peak of Weyer's church could be seen below. He had heard the warning bells clanging all through the valley and knew there'd be no surprise, but surprise was not intended, for the purpose of the day was to engage the village's defenders. He urged his mount forward and stood in his stirrups to survey the scene below. His gaze scanned the empty footpaths and the vacant workshops of the abandoned village and could see no soul in either field or hovel. Nothing moved, save the smoke which curled perpetually from the thatch-covered huts. His eyes inched along the view until they fell upon a line of troops standing ready along the roadway at the base of the church. Roland smiled and waved his men forward.

Klothar's men had arrived in good time and they formed a formidable defense at the base of the church hill. Above, the churchyard was filled with anxious peasants crowding its stifling nave or peering over its chest-high stone wall. It was here that Heinrich stood between Emma and Richard, his family safely tucked within the sanctuary.

Lord Conrad's men were now visible, trotting casually along the ridge parallel to the stream until they disappeared into a tuck, only to reappear at the swine ford. They crossed the water carefully and angled toward the village center and the wall of stiff-faced soldiers waiting dutifully on the roadway.

"By the Virgin!" whispered Richard. "The fight's to be just beneath us!"

Heinrich nodded and begged Emma to find cover in the churchyard. "Nay," she answered. "I've naught to fear. Notice, lads, the enemy bears no torches, they pay no heed to the village. Methinks we are not their quarry." She began to perspire and breathe shallow breaths as she clutched her hands to her breast.

Emma had barely finished speaking when Roland raised his gloved fist and set order to his troops. With a few barks and gestures, his mail-clad warriors tightened into a knot of horse, steel, and leather. *They are impressive,* thought Heinrich, *disciplined, well-armed, and confident.* Roland ordered his company to advance.

A mere twenty rods away, Klothar's knights countered. They tightened their line and looked to their commander, Lord Gottwald. The gray-haired knight stood in his saddle and snarled. Then, with a wave of his hand a sudden flock of arrows was launched from a low hedge edging the glebe to one side. As the shafts whistled their descent at the surprised invaders, Gottwald pointed his sword and led his company in a charge.

Above, the peasants cheered, cried, and yelled as they watched the battle erupt below. Steel flashed and men screamed, horses whinnied and toppled. Archers hurried close to pinpoint their targets and shot their longbows with keen, passionless eyes. The grunts of men and clang of steel tumbled together in a horrid *mêlée* of severed flesh and crunching bone. Oaths and curses, cries and pleadings flew from desperate lips. And in moments it was over.

Roland lay dead; a lance had pierced his heart before his horse crushed his head. His soldiers lay strewn about, dead or dying, save one knight and a few wounded others who tripped through the village, across the Laubusbach and to the safety of the forest.

Lord Klothar's men had suffered loss as well and the villagers now scrambled from their safe perch to give what comfort they might. Two knights lay dead, one dying. Three sergeants and eight footmen were dead, several others wounded. It had been a brief but costly engagement, but for none was it more costly than to Frau Emma. She scuttled from the churchyard sobbing and groaning until she fell across the still breast of Gottwald. The broken woman wailed and raised her tearing eyes to a silent heaven. Confused, Heinrich wrapped a loving arm around her.

"Shhh ... good Emma. Shhh. All shall be well."

The woman struggled to her knees and embraced the young baker as she sobbed uncontrollably. Heinrich held her tight and wondered why.

"H–he was ... the love of my life," whispered the woman. "And ... and the father of Ingelbert ..." Her voice trembled and faded away.

Heinrich stared silently at the dead man's face. He held Emma tightly until Lord Simon touched his shoulder.

"You there, move off. We've needs bear our comrade home."

Heinrich nodded and Emma laid a tender hand across Gottwald's whitened face. She paused for a lingering moment, then turned away to spare the man scandal in death. The knight looked suspiciously at Emma but Heinrich quickly blurted, "She served his family as a child, sire, and ... grew to love him from afar."

Lord Simon shrugged and ordered four men to lift the corpse into a waiting cart. Emma collapsed when she heard Gottwald's body drop heavy and hard atop the oak planks.

"I should have kept my distance, Heinrich," Emma stammered. "In my love I risked shame for him ... a shame we hid for so very long!" The woman released a trembling breath.

Heinrich helped her to her feet and walked her slowly home where the two sat quietly in the grass of Emma's gardens until the woman was content to speak. "We loved in sin when we were young, Heinrich. I was near to taking vows in Quedlinburg and he was a squire like none has ever been. I saw him ride his stallion in the joust ... ah ... a sight to steal a young maid's heart, for sure! His white hair was like flowing snow upon his strong shoulders, and his smile lit the world for me.

"He loved his God and felt only shame when sin bound us together. He swore to marry me, but I loved him too much to bring trouble to his family." Emma paused to wipe her nose and eyes. The two rose to walk about the woman's flowers. "He had been pledged to another ... an alliance of families that would keep the peace for many. I dared not undo the wisdom of that betrothal.

"But he felt both duty and love toward me and used his influence to find me a place to raise our Ingly ... and found me quills and the like ... he loved my work."

Heinrich was spellbound. "And ... what of the mystery of All Souls' Eve? Has he to do with that?"

Emma sat atop a log at her garden's edge. She looked carefully at the young man. "I trust you, Heinrich, like no other. I've spoken no word of this to any. But secrets weigh heavy and I've become old and frail. It suits me now to share the burden.

"To answer you straightaway, aye ... it has been Gottwald who once pledged to come each All Souls' Eve, or send a trusted servant, with some silver for our care or a commission for my work. He would play an hour or so with Ingly ... I told the dear boy that the man was a caring friend who lived afar ... and we read a psalm and prayed." Emma looked at the sky above and her chin trembled. "Ah, dear Gottwald." She turned to Heinrich and took his hand. "There was no more sinning, lad, none. But there surely was love."

Chapter 13

THE GRINDSTONE AND A GIFT

he summer brought no rain upon the "Golden Ground." In fact, throughout Christendom the skies were cloudless and bright for week after thirsty week. The monks in the cloister fasted more than their Rule demanded in hopes of ushering in an army of rain-heavy clouds.

Without rain, the harvest withered. By Lammas there was little left in the fields except stiff stalks of hard and stunted grains. The meadows and pastures had become brown, and their parched grasses cracked and crunched beneath the hard hooves of thin sheep. So it was with the hay, the flax, the orchard fruit, and garden crops. For the peasants of Weyer, fear loomed dark and heavy despite the sunny skies above.

All-Saint's Day brought no feast, and All Soul's Eve brought added misery to poor Emma. She sat alone in her hovel and wept as she stared at the door in hopes of its midnight opening. Heinrich did not fail her, and soon after the bells of matins the kind man rapped gently on the woman's door. The Butterfly Frau rose slowly from her oak stool and shuffled to the door. She was nearly forty now but the sadness of the recent past had stolen years from her. Many of her age had long since passed to their reward but, like a few others, she had been gifted with a constitution that might have carried her for many years to come. Heinrich appeared in the soft light of her beeswax candles. "Ah ... good baker!" Emma smiled and embraced the man.

"I could not sleep, Emma. I could only think of you and how you must feel."

The woman nodded and her chin quivered. "Ah ... yes ... 'tis a pain I cannot describe. But God has been good to me. Ingly is surely dancing with his *Vati* in heaven's valley of flowers. It is a picture in m'mind that gives me hope, dear lad, hope indeed. So I look to the sun and know that its Maker is what is constant and sure. He is surely where I find m'hope ... not here, amongst our shadows and black robes." She took Heinrich's hand. "You needs lift your face to the sun, lad."

The young man hesitated. "Aye ... but I've m'vow ... and your sun has parched the land. What hope is that?"

Emma smiled, patiently. "'Tis true enough. We've a need to have eyes that seek far beyond it, for the sun is but a sign, like its sister, the moon. They both urge us to look past our world to the sure things above."

Heinrich nodded, then mumbled, "But ... I've m'vow ..."

The woman sighed and thanked him for loving her. "Now, good fellow, you'd best return to your two children and that wife of yours. She's to bear you another quite soon! Now go. I am content with my memories and my hopes ... and you've reminded me that I am not so very alone."

So Heinrich returned to the village. Despite the earth's struggle to bear fruit, the folk continued in nature's ways of both good times and suffering. Arnold's wife, Gisela, died from burns received at her own hearth. It seemed to most, however, that Arnold grieved less for her than for the loss of some silver in a recent theft. Richard's wife, Brunhild, bore a son named Georg, and on the thirteenth day of November, Marta gave birth to another boy. Certain the name "Johann" assured greater blessing, she insisted the lad be baptized Johann Gerberg.

Heinrich was now the proud father of three: Johann Lukas, three years old, Johann Wilhelm, one, and Johann Gerberg. He cherished the lads but often found his way to

Margaretha's little grave where his tender heart would sag heavy deep within his chest.

～

Pentecost was on May twenty-fifth in the year 1197. Brother Martin, Emma's old nemesis from the day she had first arrived at the abbey gate, had fallen ill with whitlow and the man was presented to the infirmer for treatment. The infirmer, in turn, sought Brother Lukas's advice on an herbal compress. Lukas found Martin to be the most pompous of all the brethren. The man would only speak in Scripture—a ploy, believed Lukas, to present a piety that could not be found in his heart. Lukas also thought the man to be a petty thief, a cheat, and one to "share the failures of others" with the superiors. *As with all things*, thought Lukas, *God has provided a means of justice!*

The monk recommended an infusion rather than a balm. "Odd," responded the infirmer, "the man suffers boils not cramps."

"Aye," answered Lukas, "but the boils come from poisons in his blood."

So Brother Martin obediently drank Lukas's concoction—a blend of stinging nettles and dandelion that left the poor man groaning for hours in the latrine, smitten with a condition that drew loud and earthy complaints from his offended brethren! Lukas was heard laughing loudly in his herbarium, and the smirk on his face when the prior confronted him only served to doom him to hours of penance with the latrine shovel. At thirty-five, the monk should be of a more "calm and serene demeanor," he was told, and needed to stop "acting as an unbridled novice!"

Lukas laughed loudly in Emma's garden as he told his story of sweet revenge, and Emma and Heinrich howled. It was a good Sabbath afternoon, one filled with sunshine and pleasant memories. Heinrich bounced young Johann Lukas on his knee and handed him to his namesake. The monk smiled and lifted the child, now nearly four, toward the sky. "Ah, good little Lukas: love God, love man, love joy!"

The monk laughed as little Wilhelm toppled into Emma's flowers. The child scowled and groused at the stiff plants scratching against his soft skin. "He's to be a strong one, Heinrich ... y'can see it in his eyes, they burn with fire!"

Indeed, the little boy, now a year and a half old, was headstrong and keen. His eyes were sky blue and his young features were even and pleasing. But his white hair stood up straight, like a field of wheat, and brought a hearty laugh to many.

"Now, Heinrich," began Lukas, "a peddler came by the cloister at midweek. He brought news for me to give you, good news!"

Heinrich and Emma leaned forward expectantly. "Yes, yes, go on!"

Lukas smiled. "Effi's had a boy-child and they've named him Heinrich!"

The baker smiled. "Ah, good Effi! Is she well, and the child?"

"The message is that all is well."

"God be praised," chimed a beaming Emma.

"Indeed!"

Lukas continued. "Ah, but there's sad news as well. Your brother Axel had a stillborn."

Heinrich nodded as Lukas went on.

"The famine's hard in Limburg and all the world beyond. 'Tis said even the wolves are seizing travelers in the great mountains to the south. What wolves don't get, robbers do. The merchants stay in long caravans, oft joined by pilgrims and men-at-arms. The weak ones are picked off at the rear. There's no rain to be found, the winter's snow passed us by. It seems all the empire is in great danger."

≈

The harvest of this present year had been so very sparse that the following winter claimed more lives than any had remembered. Many children had been abandoned to the monks in hopes of God's protection, one infant being found nearly frozen at the rear of the cloister's shearing shed. He was a black-haired baby boy and the monks baptized him Tomas.

In the May of 1198 spring sowing enjoyed a more proper

balance of sunlight and clouds, but, hope notwithstanding, the peasants of the abbey's lands had other reasons to despair. Emperor Heinrich VI had died suddenly and his realm was now plunged into a civil war between three rivals. To prepare for the troubles that were certain to come, taxes and fines were immediately increased. The demands pushed even Heinrich to near rebellion. For him and the other peasants of Weyer, even a better harvest would yield no gain.

Despite the pressures, the feast of Lammas was ultimately enjoyed with a modicum of gratitude. Weyer had not forgotten the hauntings of the past winter's famine: the sunken, gray faces of the dead, frozen skin stretched tightly over protruding bones, the swollen bellies of blue-faced infants. By contrast, the vigorous fields of grain waving in the warm winds of August now brought tears of relief.

Heinrich and his household were survivors. The children were thin but not sickly, and Herwin, Varina, Marta, and the baker were, indeed, grateful for the advantages Heinrich's position offered. Now, as a new harvest began, they bent their knees willingly as their priests prayed over both them and their crops-in-waiting.

Marta was in her eighth month of another pregnancy and the heat of the summer was becoming difficult for her to bear. She could not abide a cluttered house so spent most of her days chasing her three young sons out-of-doors, along with Varina's brood. "Everything and everyone in its proper place!" she shouted.

It was on one such day in the first week of August when Marta chased her five-year-old, Lukas, her almost four-year-old, Wilhelm, and her toddler, Gerberg, out the door and into the busy village to play. "We've all work but you three! Lukas, you're old enough to lend a hand, so you're to keep a careful eye on the imps, and keep out from under m'feet!"

Lukas smiled and waved as he led his two brothers along the village footpaths toward the bakery. The village was bustling with carts and oxen, women carrying buckets toward the fields, and old men sharpening sickle blades on their treadle-stones. The day was bright and blue; a gentle breeze blew from the west. Young Lukas was mischievous like his namesake. Cheerful and round-faced, the lad was soft-hearted and quick to laugh. His younger brother, Wilhelm, was game for any dare. Though still a child, Arnold claimed he had the "heart of a lion!" He, too, showed signs of tenderness but seemed to be the happiest when brawling with his brothers or throwing stones at passing little girls.

"*Ach, mein Kinder!*" laughed Heinrich as his boys tumbled into his bakery. "You'd be hungry?"

Three dirty little faces smiled and nodded. The baker glanced about to be sure no one was watching and handed his tikes a pretzel. "So, all of us be working hard except you three!"

"*Mutti* says m'work is to watch these two."

Heinrich smiled.

"And what shall you be doing?"

Lukas shrugged. "Grandpapa says come watch the mill grind the first rye."

"Hmm," answered Heinrich. "Could be worth a watch. But first, give *Vati* a hug!" With that, each laughing child jumped into the man's arms. He then gave them each a playful swat on the bottom as they charged out his door, and he smiled as they disappeared down the path toward the mill.

The first grind was truly "worth a watch." It was prayed over by Father Pious, now the only surviving priest in Weyer. With Johannes now in his grave, Pious covetously held a fist of grain in one hand and repeated his prayer of Lammas dedication, the *Immaculatum Cor Mariae*. Having so honored the Holy Mother, he raised his hands and cried to the Lord, "Restore us, O God our savior, and turn Your anger from us, so You wilt not be angry with us forever nor extend Your wrath from generation to generation."

The miller then poured the first basket of flailed grain into his funnel. Everyone watched as the brown seed spread atop the grindstone to be squashed to powder by the slow-moving wheel. It would be only one basket this day, for the harvest had just begun, but the ceremony was of great importance to all, and word was spread throughout the fields that Weyer's harvest had been properly blessed.

The deed done, the miller bade all farewell and then eyed his grandsons spying from behind a wide post. "Ha! Get in here, y'devils!" he cried. Dietrich smiled a huge, toothless smile and pretended to be a giant stalking his prey. The little ones scampered in all directions, shrieking with delight as their grandfather growled and pawed at the air.

Little Gerberg giggled his way to the ground where he was snatched by Dietrich and held under one thick arm. Wilhelm gleefully darted like a frightened hare, finding refuge inside an empty grain bin. Dietrich put a finger on his chin and peered about the shadows of his dark mill. His grandsons were quiet and well hidden. The man set Gerberg atop a stool and pat him on the head. "Good lad," he whispered, "shhh ... I shall find the others!"

Dietrich stepped lightly across the dusty planks and pecked behind crates and baskets, gears and posts. At last, he heard a muffled sneeze from inside a bin. The old man smiled and flung open the lid. Wil squealed and laughed as his grandfather tickled his belly. Dietrich then turned to find Lukas. "Where do y'think him to be?" he whispered to Wil.

Dietrich raised his brow and asked again. Wil giggled. A glance to the beams some twenty feet above gave his secret away. "Ah ..." Dietrich winked and slowly turned. "Hmm," he said loudly. "It wonders me where the lad could be." He took a few steps around his grindstone, then moved slowly toward the ladder leading to the crossbeams and the gear-works above. "Hmm ... methinks I needs have a look from up there."

With that he began his ascent toward the ceiling. From high above young Lukas was so excited that he could barely keep silent. He licked his lips and his heart pounded. He cast his eyes from side to side, looking for a place to shuffle.

Grandpapa climbed slowly, adding drama to the boy's game. Lukas was determined not to be seen, but smiled at his two brothers' upturned faces and ventured a wave.

With that he lost his balance for just a moment and his belly fluttered. He quickly grasped both hands upon the beam and looked for his grandfather, now nearly at the top of the ladder. *I must hurry!* he thought.

Lukas spotted a knot of gears and crossbeams directly over the grindstone and decided it would be a good place to hide. His five-year-old body was nimble and sprite and the lad deftly scurried across the beam like a hurried mouse. Dietrich, however, was neither nimble nor sprite. His old joints were stiff and weary. He saw the lad quick-stepping down the beam and he took a determined breath. For all his many vices the man was a good grandfather and he stayed in the game.

Dietrich had not been to the top of the mill for many years. After all, he was forty-three years old! The sport of chasing his grandson through the forest of posts and beams now invigorated him, and he smiled as his knees ached their way along the rough-hewn timber.

Little Lukas paused above the mill's mighty gears to glance back. Seeing his grandfather's slow approach, he grinned and looked for a place below to hide. He stared into the gears, the teeth, and the sprockets of the millworks and thought them to look like the inward parts of a sleeping giant. The brakes had been set so nothing turned, but the little lad could hear the water of the Laubusbach just beyond the walls. He looked once more across the dim-lit heights of the mill and saw the gray head of his grandfather coming slowly closer. He laughed, set his little hands timidly against a rough post, and stretched a curling leg forward in hopes of shimmying down.

Dietrich looked forward and with a start called to the boy. "No! No, no, Lukas … you mustn't climb—"

The man's echoing voice surprised the boy and he lost his balance, falling forward against the wide post. His little hands were too small to grasp the heavy timber and his young legs too weak to slow his fall. In a moment, with an anguished gasp of a grandpapa, the lad crashed atop the grindstone.

આ

The death of a young child was not uncommon, for disease and accident, foul play or war took young souls each day across all Christendom. But for the household of Heinrich it mattered little what was common for others. They lay about their smoky hovel in the heat of that August afternoon, weeping and angry. Lukas was dearly known to them—he had been cared for in sickness, laughed with at feast days, played with in springtime meadows, and romped with under the summer's sun. "He was yet a tender bloom," wept Emma, "bursting with life, full of good things." Indeed, and so he was.

For his part, Dietrich bore his own shame and carried it poorly. He cursed his mill and cursed his priest. The man sought comfort in excess of any ready vice and was quickly given over to the painless stupor of muddy ale.

Marta was utterly embittered by the loss. For days she would speak to neither her husband nor her father. For her, blame was a balm for pain and her long-suffering husband was willing to bear her wrath if it gave her comfort. For such strength he paid a withering price.

Heinrich often walked the footpaths of Weyer alone for nights on end. He could not express his brokenness in words, nor in actions, nor in thoughts or fits of fury. He could but trudge the nights in a vacant melancholy in hopes that time might finally soothe his heartache. One comfort did pursue him, however, and only one. Old Emma offered an ever-tender shoulder and a gentle touch. She could of course, because she knew.

ॐ

In the season of Advent Marta delivered the family a son whose gentle disposition proffered little comfort to those yet suffering their loss. He was immersed in icy water on the twenty-first of December and blessed and salted by Father Pious. His mother dispassionately named him Johann Karl. The child was round-faced and ruddy, winsome and bright. Sadly, he was born to a household that was heartbroken, making his arrival bittersweet.

The gray weeks of another winter dragged on until more sad fortune visited the baker's family. Two-year-old Gerberg

had suffered winter fever and quinsy. Though Brother
Lukas had supplied both fervent prayer and barley water,
the young soul departed to his Savior's bosom on a bitterly
cold early morning in March.

Heinrich said little and Marta even less as Father Pious
prayed for Gerberg's soul. The parents were reminded of
the hope of baptism as the tot's shroud was laid in a tiny
grave in the churchyard's frozen earth. Heinrich stood over
the dark hole and trembled with his faithful Butterfly Frau
dutifully at his side. Then, when the last hard clod of dirt
was dropped on the brown, frosty mound, the heavy-
hearted folk turned away.

For nights to come Heinrich stared about his hovel at the
haunted faces peering sadly into the ghostly light of his
hearth fire. *Herwin is aging,* he thought, *and Varina too.*
Their children were growing; the eldest now being fourteen.

Somewhere in her bedchamber lay Marta, angry and bitter and quite alone. She now banished Heinrich from her
affections, swearing he carried a curse into her womb.
"You'll father no more," she hissed from her bed, "y'hexed
and black-touched monster. You've unconfessed sin …
You've secrets that your children pay!"

Heinrich hung his head. This was not the life he had
dreamt of in Emma's garden so very long ago.

ह‍

Despite rumors of warfare in nearby manors, October was
a peaceful month. The harvest was ample, and calm ruled
the rhythm of the village. Effi had sent warm wishes with a
passing peddler. She and her family were happy and
healthy in the city of Frankfurt.

As the brown leaves of autumn once more fell along the
footpaths of Weyer, Heinrich was invited by Emma to spend
a Sabbath hour at her door. The baker accepted gladly and
brought his sons, Wil and Karl, with him. Little Karl, now
nearly one, was still a happy child. His head was covered in
tight, red curls, and his round face was rose-red like the
happy faces of heaven's cherubs. He chortled and giggled
and his presence made others feel warm and joyful. Young
Wil was keen and bright as ever. Healthy and playful, the

four-year-old raced about Emma's fading garden sword-playing with woody stalks and boxing against the air.

Emma dearly loved the boys—and their father. "Dear Heinrich, 'tis so good you've come! And look there, scratching bark from my walnut. 'Tis Brother Lukas. Look at him, aging, yet mischievous like a pup. Brother!" she called.

The monk waved and smiled and lifted his black robes as he trotted toward them. As he approached, he paused to dance and wrestle with Wil, then lifted little Karl up toward the sun. "Ha, a fine fat little fellow!" He walked toward Emma and Heinrich panting and smiling. "Peace be to you!"

"And to you!" chuckled Heinrich.

Emma laughed and handed the monk a flask of mead as Wil begged all to go to the stream.

"Should we?" asked Emma.

Lukas swallowed a long draught and wiped his mouth. "Aye! Of course," he roared. "Let's be off to the Magi!"

The sun was kind for October and filled the blue sky above with bright and brilliant warmth such as few had remembered on an autumn's day. The group walked through the quiet forest and soon came to their favorite place where, before long, Wil and Karl fell fast asleep atop the limp ferns beneath the outstretched limbs of the Magi.

Lukas enjoyed being the abbey's herbalist, but his strange brews and concoctions had some wondering about his sanity. He turned toward Heinrich and took the young man gently by the wrists. He pushed the baker's sleeves toward his elbows. "Hmm. You suffer affliction of the skin similar to your uncle Arnold, only not so severe."

Heinrich nodded. "Some days 'tis worse than others."

"Yes, 'tis the flours and yeasts you work with. I've told y'before y'needs wash your skin morning and night. Here, I've a good balm of marigold. Keep it on whilst you sleep, and you'll smell the better for it too!" Lukas paused and looked into Heinrich's eyes. "Hard times can bring the itch as well. Have you hard times, lad?"

Heinrich shrugged. "No more than another man. I've much on m'mind with the bakery and m'land, rents and taxes, and the like."

"And your wife?"

The baker grew silent.

Lukas narrowed his gaze. "And your wife?" he repeated.

"She means to do well for all, and she wants the best for her household. She's got a gift in charcoaling the likeness of faces and ..."

"And have you peace?" asked Emma.

Heinrich thought for a moment, then answered. "No more nor less than any other. Methinks I am doing well. I serve m'wife faithfully, feed my young ones, keep my vows, avoid sloth. I steal nothing. *Ja*, I'd say I am at peace."

Emma and Lukas exchanged troubled glances. Emma set her hand lightly on Heinrich's shoulder. "I almost never see you laugh," she said softy.

"Laugh? Ah, Frau Emma. Who laughs?" Heinrich tossed a pebble into the stream.

Lukas nodded and poked Emma with a stick. "Aye, sister. Who laughs in this place but you and I?" chortled the monk. "And they all think us mad!"

Emma chuckled. "So it is! I beg your pardon, Heinrich, it seems you are not mad yet. But if I could, I'd make you so!"

Lukas scratched his beard and turned to the baker. "So, friend, you say you'd be at peace?"

"Aye."

"Why?"

"Well, I ... I do as I am required, I—"

"Then why do you never laugh?"

Heinrich darkened. "I've little enough to laugh about! My eyes burn at night, m'wife's quick to find my faults, I wheeze in my bed, m'body aches for all its labors ... I worry 'bout the tax ... I've buried three ... death and suffering are all around! Unlike some, I've no cloister to hide in!"

Lukas's eyes twinkled. "Ah, so you'd be angry as well? Seems odd for a peaceful man."

Heinrich bristled. "What's your game? Methinks you've had too much mead."

"Game? I've no game, good fellow. I think you fail to see yourself, 'tis all. And that, my good friend, is an ailment common to most." Lukas picked at a dry leaf. "To be at peace one must be free, and you, my friend, are hardly free."

"Who is free? The yeomen? They are slaves to taxes. And even you are bound to a vow." Heinrich's voice was tight. "I ... I do not fight against the way of things ... I leave the world as it is and hope it does the same for me; that is the peace I have."

Lukas nodded and said nothing for a moment. "Little room for dreams in such a life. Perhaps this is why you cling to your foolish vow. You have given others power to bind you, and they have darkened your eyes. I do confess, dear friend, I cannot understand how a man banished from the view of heaven's hope can claim to be at peace."

The baker was uncomfortable. He stood and heaved a stone across the stream. "I think my penance and vows, my faithful labors must please God. I keep my face toward the earth in humility ... like you ought! When I hold to such things I feel right and good within m'self and it gives me hope enough."

Lukas cast a sad eye at Emma who was seated on a mossy rock. She smiled kindly at the two men and gathered a cluster of wildflowers in her hand. "Dear Heinrich. We do not mean to anger you, but please consider this: God's gifts are for those humble enough to abandon themselves." She paused to smell her bouquet and lifted her face to the sun. "True humility draws your face upward, not downward. 'Tis a glorious mystery." Emma continued softly. "Oh, my dear, dear boy, I long for you to face the sun and dance like a child again midst the flowers and butterflies."

The baker listened halfheartedly. He stared at the stream with a mix of emotions. A tone of condescension braced his voice. "There are times I wish I could laugh. I wish I could feel the sunlight on my face, but I believe it is better for all of us to serve the order of things. We are called to serve in a hard world soon to be destroyed by the Judgment. Let m'lads dance in the flowers while they can, but such foolishness is no fit call for a man." He flashed a hard eye at

Lukas with his last remark.

Emma sighed a little. Her eyes lost their glint and swelled, red and wet. She stood and gave the young man a tender embrace. "I do love you, Heinrich, and those lads of yours. Someday, when your strength wanes and your virtues fail, when you long for hope once more, turn your eyes upward and find another way." Emma was wise. She knew that conversations, like life, had seasons, and it was time to speak of other things. Wil crawled to her side and he rested his head atop her lap. "Heinrich, now I've needs tell you of something else."

Heinrich groaned.

She stroked Wil's hair and cast a loving glance toward Karl still sleeping soundly in the ferns. "First, Lukas tells me that Abbot Stephen shall honor the cloister's covenant with your grandfather Jost."

Lukas nodded.

"What a wonderful thing! I have other good tidings for you as well. By my best reckoning I am now some forty-two years on this earth and have enjoyed a wonderful life. Yet a feeling is coming over me that my time is short."

The tension left Heinrich's face and he stared at Emma suddenly anxious.

"At night, when all is quiet, it is as if a voice whispers my name. And sometimes I feel a squeeze about m'heart; a heaviness in my chest that sends some pain into my arms and a tingle to my fingers. I pray a few psalms and ask the angels to wait a bit longer.

"Heinrich, know that I love you and shall always love you as m'son. You have been a kind and faithful friend. Always a helper, always a listener, you've loved me and have brought me great joy. You loved my Ingly too. And," she smiled and her eyes twinkled, "I've always known it was you who stole wood from the village for my fire those many years ago. You and that devilish Richard!"

Heinrich grimaced. "We were but boys and—"

"But you knew better!" mocked Lukas with a grin.

Heinrich shrugged. "Aye, but Emma's woodpile had been scrumped by another … and it seemed fair justice."

"And whose did you scrump?"

Heinrich fought a smirk. "Dietrich's."

"Dietrich? Your wife's father?" roared Lukas with approval.

Heinrich nodded.

"Ha! Well done, lad! How many penances for you and your friend?"

Heinrich shrugged. "I made m'self do a hundred '*Ave Marias*' and a few psalms. But I think none for Richard … he saw no wrong in it!"

"Scoundrel!" laughed Emma. "He was always such a rogue. I loved him too, and I miss him."

"And me as well," answered Heinrich. "He's not been the same since … since things changed in his life. He wanders the forest sullen and sickly."

The group became quiet and remembered Richard as he was, a devilish young boy romping through these same trees, laughing and bold, stouthearted and spirited. Now, it was feared, his heart had been extinguished by disappointment and pain.

Emma beckoned Heinrich to sit close by her side. She took one of his hands in her own and began again. "I've told you of Lord Gottwald. He was the love of my heart, and I think I was his … though he ne'er spoke of our love from the day he was wed. Nor did he betray his good wife with me … nay … not once. Our love was spring love, the love of early things, things young and tender, bright and earnest. And unwise, it ought be added, as spring love so often is. Nor was it ordained by heaven.

"When I was found with child my superior was merciful and kind and used her influence to help me. To my great relief, Gottwald proved to be a man of honor. He had his ways to see that his child and I would be kept proper and safe. It was he that had whispered to the chambers of Mainz to find me a good place to raise his son. He had told me that he had confessed our sin to a trusted priest, who, in turn, had worked as his emissary to those above … those who never need learn of our shame.

"I am told that Gottwald lived his life as a knight of the Cross ought—courageous, loyal, faithful to his lords and to his God. And he was known as a humble man, a friend to the poor and charitable to any in need. Methinks it was Ingly who softened his heart toward the misfits and the unfortunate, for I am told he built a special home for those who wandered his realm in search of shelter and goodness. So, Heinrich, know that he was neither perfect nor without blemish, but he surely was a Christian man if ever one lived!

"Now, listen well. Lukas has informed me that Gottwald bequeathed a holding of land to me. It is said there was a titter in the audience as his will was read, but that his wife had agreed without complaint. It seems the man's conscience had caused him to confide in her many years before. God bless the woman, for she both forgave her man and me." Emma's voice trembled and a tear ran down each cheek.

"The land is five hides, a token of his affection and a kind gift, indeed. And it was partitioned with great effort. It lies on a fertile plain near Oldenburg where he held several manors. It seems the silver he would oft bring me on All Souls' Eve was rents from this good ground."

Heinrich listened intently, but suddenly bristled. "Five hides are a fortune for a peasant, but it seems a paltry grant from a wealthy lord to the mother of his child!"

Lukas interrupted. "It might seem so, but few would honor a bastard child under such circumstances and even less the child's mother. The man was faithful to his duty all these years and never once sought favors from Emma."

The woman nodded. "Now, Heinrich, we've not yet felt the war but surely we shall. Our protectors in Runkel are in alliance with the pope's choice, Lord Otto of Brunswick, as are the counts in Oldenburg who shelter Gottwald's lands. It seems the lands are safe enough, but protected by the counts or not, the land could be lost to the war or to others.

"Heinrich, I speak of this for a reason. As I have said, I do not expect to see many more years. Soon I shall be dancing with Ingly in God's valley of flowers and it brings gladness to my heart to think of it. It also brings me joy to tell you this: that I have sworn a will and you shall inherit my land."

Before the dumfounded baker could respond, Lukas interrupted, "Be warned. I would not boast or tell of this to others, nor tell your children until they are of age. There are those who would now profit from your death or those of your heirs; it is the dark side of wealth. I have told only Blasius, the Templar, so you have a witness. The lad is devout and has sworn his silence. He shall act as your emissary in matters of rents and receipts and shall keep your money in the treasury at the preceptory. Heinrich, when the time is right, you might have enough to buy the freedom of yourself and your children!"

The baker was silent. He was overwhelmed and suddenly overjoyed at his good fortune. This land, added to his half-hide in Weyer, would multiply his holdings beyond anything he had ever imagined possible. Yet he dared not feel the pleasure in it, for his gain would only come with the loss of that person whom he loved. "I ... I have no words, I ..."

"And none are needed," Emma said smiling.

Chapter 14

THE GARDEN POEM

Another year passed and the dawn of a new century spread slowly across Weyer's rounded hills. The *Volk* gave the moment little heed and simply plodded through their dreary days hard at task, bound to a monotony that had dulled their spirits and numbed them to the shifts of the troubling winds blowing through the realm. They wanted no part of the civil war now ravaging the empire and sought only the comforts of good thatch, a hearty mush, the simple pleasures of the village feasts, and the deep contentment of Sabbath rest.

On the nineteenth day of April, just ten days past Easter, news of Lord Klothar's death reached nearby Villmar Abbey. The monks climbed the ridge rimming their village to see black pennants hanging despondently from the ramparts of Runkel's nearby castle.

Two weeks later the abbot invited his subjects to gather on the grounds just beyond the abbey walls to witness the reception of Runkel's new lord. Pressed and packed closely together, nearly two thousand peasants anxiously faced their new protector, Prince Heribert, son of Klothar. The young man stood upon a silk-draped stage and faced the gray and woolly host in all his finery. He smiled and waved and received the blessings of the abbey priests. Some thought him to be a bit thin, yet his face was ruggedly handsome and firmly anchored by dark brown eyes that gave him a noble strength. The twenty-year-old was the son of Klothar, to be sure, but he was also the grandson of King Rolf of Saxony.

The throng grew quiet and some began to kneel, first here, then there. The young lord smiled and squared his shoulders. He beckoned his betrothed to his side. The fair Christine came forward and took his hand, bowing before the assembly as though she were a queen. Astonished whispers passed through the multitude, for the maiden was a striking beauty. Her hair was a deep-hued chestnut and shimmered in the sunshine like fine silk.

The abbot smiled outwardly, though the young lord's influence on the humble peasants was making him uncomfortable. Prior Mattias sensed his superior's worry and whispered quiet assurance: "He offers them protection, Father Abbot. He gives them peace of mind."

Abbot Stephen grumbled. "We guard their souls, he their flesh; I oft wonder which they treasure most."

Prince Heribert spoke a few words of promise and of pledge. He bade the peasants work hard at task; that they give their due for the abbot's good and faithful care. He embraced the preceptor of the Templar's house, Brother Phillipe de Blanqfort, and the two white-robed knights at his side. The act was witness to their continued alliance in the defense of the abbey and of Runkel. When the presentation was over, most hearts were steadied, willing and happy to return to their villages with a measure of hope.

৵

It was inevitable that the effects of the empire's war would ripple across the lands of Villmar. No blood had yet been spilled directly upon its ground, though some of Heribert's knights had been slain in distant combat. But fees for protection were raised in the face of dwindling revenues. The archbishop in Mainz was feeling the pressure as well and now demanded more from the abbot, adding greater friction to their already strained relationship. So the peasants' taxes, rents, and fees were increased yet again. The merchet was doubled, the heriot increased by half, and the charge for grinding flour was raised so much that the village millers were in fear for their very lives.

For Father Pious, these hard times presented new opportunities. With ambition consuming his soul, he sought every occasion to earn the notice of his superiors in Mainz. He had already proven his skill at serving both Oberbrechen and Weyer—a double duty that had relieved the diocese of a considerable expense. And he had managed the glebes well, squeezing a profit through both fair times and drought. Pious, knowing that the abbey had fallen behind in its tithes due the archbishop, now eyed the bakery in Weyer as a possible means of collection. Of course, the addition of the bakery as a direct asset of the archbishop would be one more success the priest could add to his credit. His shrewd dealings, however, had done more than gain the attention of the councils of Mainz, for they had also served to secure his reputation in the abbey as a greedy man of pompous self-importance.

The troubles of the realm touched other lives in ways not so opportune. Axel, Heinrich's brother, was sent home to Weyer, for the mayor of Limburg was no longer able to afford workers from the abbey. The unemployed carpenter was now married and the father of two boys, Arnwolf, age eight, and Thom, age seven. As the four hungry, homeless peasants stood at Heinrich's door, the baker knew he had no choice but to help.

Marta, of course, found this new condition intolerable. She had banished Heinrich from her affection long ago but now ordered him from their bedchamber altogether. Heinrich, tormented by the woman long enough finally took his stand. "You! You Housedragon! *Nörglerin!*"

Marta responded with a fist into the man's face.

To escape the cramped and unhappy conditions of the hovel, Herwin and his household moved. They found a gracious welcome from an old spinster who was happy to rent space in her run-down hut at the south end of the village. Herwin's departure was heart-wrenching for both him and Heinrich. The kindly tenant had slept under that thatch roof for twenty-five years, pouring out his life in service to the family of Kurt.

Heinrich embraced Herwin, Varina, and their children. "I ... I cannot bear to see you leave us."

Herwin wept and nodded. "And you, young man. You have been like a son to me. I ... I should like to stay in your hire to work your land?"

"Of course! I would have it no other way."

The two looked at each other for a long, heartbreaking moment. A breeze rustled through their hair and they turned to go their separate ways.

The year dragged on. The increase in taxes, fines, and rents kept laughter and good cheer in check, even at the May Day feast. By Midsummer's, thefts were increasing, and the abbot sent strong words of warning to each village reeve. The pope's armies continued to support Otto the Welf, as did Prince Heribert, but the armies of Otto's two rivals were vigorous. Heribert's treasury was badly depleted and the Templars suffered as well. So when the abbot demanded help in keeping order in his manors, the men-at-arms were neither patient, merciful, or kind. Crimes and offenses were met with the most severe penalties and administered without compassion.

By St. Michael's Day, Richard was the father of a daughter. Heinrich rarely saw his old friend, for the man still spent his days either deep in Weyer's woodlands or in a drunken stupor with his father. Richard had lost all hope, and what spark of life remained was shadowed by shame or buried in bitterness. Though always willing to yield a grunt and a wave to Heinrich, Richard was a man bent inward on himself.

It was a Sabbath afternoon in late October when Heinrich took his boys to walk again in Emma's fading garden. The lads had spent many a summer's day chasing butterflies and napping in the fragrance of her hollyhocks and lace. They loved the garden in any season, even when the herbs were picked and dry and the flowers brown and stiff. Young Wil and Karl especially loved Sabbath days, for these were when their father might join them, playing bladder-ball or sparring with maces made of weedy sticks; it was this gift of time they treasured most.

Heinrich sat with his Butterfly Frau and smiled as she hummed a familiar rhyme:

Oh, wondrous new creature break from your cocoon
And stretch your fresh wings upon these tender blooms.
Come flutter 'tween flowers and sail o'er the trees,
Or light on m'finger, and dance in the breeze.

Since change is your birthright, fly free and be bold
And fear not the tempest, the darkness, or cold.
Press on to new places, seek color and light,
Find smiles and laughter and joy on your flight.

For though you see dimly; your certainties few,
Your Maker stands steady and constant and true.
He guards you and guides you till travelin's done,
His breath moves the breezes; His heart warms the sun.

"Ah, my dear Heinrich. The song was once for you and for Ingly. Now it is for you and your boys. I am sure Ingly is far beyond the sun, dancing in the Maker's garden." She wiped a tear and sighed. "And, as I said before, I shall soon be joining him."

Heinrich protested. "Nay, good Frau Emma! It shan't be so ... I ..."

"Ah, enough." said Emma. "I am ready to go. I have no fear, though I admit to some pain. My belly's oft tender and m'back aches all the night. I feel sweats in m'sleep and sometimes my hands quiver."

Heinrich sat quietly and looked away. He took the woman by the hand and squeezed it lightly. The happy company then spent much of the day in Emma's croft, all content to ignore the bells. Heinrich sighed. "I've been to Mass at prime. Pious insists we now come for all his three services but I'd rather be here."

Emma chuckled. "You're a naughty lad! And what are you teaching the boys?"

"Hmm. Methinks I'm teaching them where love is found."

Emma brightened. A sparkle filled her eye as she watched the baker's sons wrestling in the grass. *Perhaps a little light is dawning after all!* she thought.

A while later, the two were still sitting quietly when Heinrich thought he saw someone pass quickly between some trees by the stream. He looked carefully. "Frau Emma ... methinks I've needs check on something by the water. I beg your leave. Please keep a sharp eye on the lads."

Heinrich moved cautiously from tree to tree, grimacing as his thin-soled shoes crunched the brittle leaves beneath them. He peered into the lengthening shadows of the wood until he spotted the silhouette of a slight form hesitating behind a thin veil of brush. "You! Hold fast!"

The woman stood motionless, like a fawn scented by a wolf.

The baker stepped boldly from his cover and strode toward the timid shape. "Name yourself!" he bellowed. As he approached, the woman stepped sheepishly from her screen. She stood submissively, her arms hanging limply by her side and her face turned toward the ground. "K–Katharina?" stammered Heinrich.

The woman nodded and lifted her green eyes toward the man. "I am sorry, Heinrich. I had no wish to take you from your boys and—"

"Ach, 'tis good to see you! I ... I just thought there might be some mischief in the wood." The man's heart was soaring. A long silence followed before he spoke again. "And how are things with you?"

Katharina smiled shyly. "All is well." Her eyes filled with pain and she looked toward the stream. "Might we walk, just for a while?"

Heinrich's belly tingled and he wanted to shout. He shrugged, feeling strangely guilty. "Oh, of course, but just for a bit. I must get back to the boys and Emma and, well, I ..."

"Just for a moment, then." Katharina smiled sadly. The two walked slowly toward the Laubusbach. Katharina spoke first. "I don't come to the bakery because Ludwig sends our tenant and makes me fetch the wood at each day's prime."

Heinrich nodded. "And y've spinning and little Erika and the like ... I understand. Marta makes others do her chores when she can. She says she's oft sick and ought rest more. But she does keep the hovel in good order. Everything in its place, all swept and ... and she likes to work at art. She makes a good likeness with charcoal and ..." Heinrich wondered why he was speaking of Marta.

Katharina listened respectfully and said little until they were standing by the water's edge. The two stared into the lively stream and were drawn, almost magically, into its cheerful, sun-tipped joy. The water danced and bubbled clean and bright like liquid crystal over smooth gemstones. "It wonders me some, Heinrich, if heaven shall have its own Laubusbach."

Heinrich smiled. *She is so very gentle,* he thought. Her voice was calming, like the waters at his feet. Her flaxen hair was neatly braided and laid along the nape of her slender neck. He wanted for all the world to touch it, but his wife's face suddenly filled his mind's eye and he felt fresh guilt wash over him. *Marta,* he thought. *So unhappy and hard.* He stared at the lapping stream. *Not wicked, just tiresome ... but oh, such a heavy burden.* A lump filled his throat and he turned toward Katharina. "I needs take m'leave." His voice betrayed a despair that drew tears to Katharina's eyes.

She smiled and nodded. "I think I shall stay a while longer. Ludwig thinks me gathering walnuts so I must fill this basket and be off ... else—"

"Else what?"

Katharina said nothing.

Heinrich nodded and slowly turned away.

෨

Two more years passed. Now twenty-eight, Heinrich was aging beyond the prime of his life. Many of his peers had already been laid in their graves; most from sickness, some by accidents or calamity.

Heinrich kept his curly hair short, as peasants ought,

and obliged the new abbot's command that servile men now be clean-shaven. He had more teeth than many and more silver than most. His fields were still well managed by Herwin and often yielded more than others. He had acquired a small piece of land adjacent to his hovel and fenced it for use as a larger kitchen garden. The baker had built a fowl coop as well. "I want eggs for the poor," Heinrich said, and, indeed, the man was generous to those in need.

The abbot now ruling the manor was Udo of Brandenburg, a benevolent though stern monk who had every intention of wresting the abbey from the control of the archbishop and submitting it, instead, to the Holy See in Rome. Abbot Stephen had been sent to a larger abbey in the south of France. He had done well to advance the small abbey in the midst of trying times and had proven great skill in his stewardship. It was good fortune that had helped him finally pay the tardy tithe, however, for new rents now flowed to Villmar from lands gifted by the will of Lord Gottwald; lands near Oldenburg that surrounded Emma's inheritance.

There were seventy-five brethren who received Abbot Udo in Villmar's growing cloister. The abbey grounds had recently been enlarged with new granaries and workshops, and work had begun on a new chapel and a novice cloister. Udo was delighted to leave his duties in the larger abbey at St. Gall, for he thought in ways that often earned trouble in more prestigious places. He was convinced that his Benedictines, despite the letter of his Rule, ought mingle and minister, talk and weep with the people they served. His ideas were, it seemed, far ahead of their time, though none in Villmar chose to challenge him.

The day of Udo's endowment was a fine and glorious Sabbath in June. At terce, the black-robed abbot raised a gracious hand over his brethren as they sang to him their psalms and prayers with comforting humility. The cloister's priests then prayed loudly and with vigor, charging all to "keep God's holy ways, stray not toward paths of sin, and honor the Virgin in each word and every deed."

෨

The feast of Lammas was met with dread as the harvest failed once again. The hay crop was poor and the blood-month of November would need to cull a larger number of stock than any wished. The grain fields were dry from drought; they would yield but a fraction of their potential at planting.

Herwin shook his head and groused, "My son and I sweat upon the fields Heinrich, but once more we've little to show for our labors! I shall never earn enough to buy even a vir-gate of m'own!" Indeed, the man's words were true and they stabbed at Heinrich's heart. Herwin was more deserving than most. He was hard-working, charitable, kind, and faithful. "He has never once scrumped even a fistful of grain for himself," grumbled Heinrich. "He ought have better."

In the larger world, the three-way contest for the empire's crown continued. Pope Innocent III maintained his support for Otto the Welf, but rumors abounded that he was beginning to speak with some sympathy of Duke Philip's cause. Some said he was even tempted to support Friederich's claim due to recent doubts of Otto's loyalty. The confusing matters of Church and empire went largely unnoticed by the peasants, however, except to the extent they raised taxes or hardened the hand of the abbey's bailiff.

Old Bailiff Werner raged about the abbey's manors with surly men-at-arms in tow. In years past, his title ranked him just beneath the abbot in matters of administration. To his dismay, however, the new abbot had granted more and more powers over legal and financial matters to the lay counsel hired from Runkel, even recently conferring the title of "steward" on the man.

Werner's duties now were more like a constable's—keeping the peace, collecting taxes, arresting criminals, and the like. Given the perpetual threat of invasion he was instructed to maintain order at any cost to life, limb, or property. And so he did.

On a warm night a few days after the Assumption of the Virgin, the men of Weyer were summoned together by Reeve Dietrich. "I've news from Werner," he began. "Seems the new abbot is severely troubled by all the scrumping. I've had grain stolen from the mill barns just this past week. Others have lost pennies here and there. Yeoman Gottshalk had near to a mark taken from his bed ... behind a barred door! The church in Emmerich was pilfered of a relic! Abbot Udo says the Devil's afoot again and needs be stopped.

"He's begged more Templars' help in keeping good order. He's garrisoned more of their mercenaries in the cloister and Heribert's men are roving about. Now here's why you'd be called: Lord Heribert's knights caught a young lad of Niederbrechen thieving the Templars' strongbox in the abbey. Some say he's filled with a demon."

"How old?" came a voice from the crowd.

"Methinks he's six or so."

A rumble stirred through the men. "And what of it? Why needs we stand here?"

"Aye ... here's the rub for us. We've been ordered at the morrow's eve-tide to witness the boy's penalty, we and every boy of the village over three years."

A loud protest rose from the men. "We'd be in harvest time! They drive us like oxen from light to light and now want us to walk hours for some waif from Nieder-brechen?!"

"Aye, 'tis the command."

"But why?" shouted another.

"Seems the abbot is weary of the troubles. 'Tis as simple as that."

The men cursed and swore, groused, grumbled, and kicked the dust, but by the bells of vespers on the next day they were descending the winding road to Villmar.

Heinrich thought the evening to be eerie and filled with haunts. He and his sons followed his fellows through the waning light into Villmar village where he was led to a flat field adjacent to the abbey's walls. Here the men and boys of the abbot's manor crowded into a murmuring mass of some thousand souls—a legion of weary, wool-clad peas-ants sweating and cursing in the humid summer's night. The men of Weyer found their place before a large square lined by torches and edged with well-armed footmen. The sight gave pause to all.

Heinrich held one son in each hand. The boys were crushed and pressed on all sides by the hips and elbows of those squeezed against them. *"Vati!"* cried Karl.

"Aye, little lad," answered Heinrich, "let me lift you here." The man hoisted his frightened redhead atop his broad shoulders and held one leg tightly. The boy grasped hold of his father's head and stared at the torches lighting the square. He was a happy child and one apt to giggle before he'd cry. But on this night the weight of dread gave the lad a chill.

Heinrich noticed a column of mounted soldiers with torches snaking their way through the crowd. A wagon was in the center of the procession and it bore a wooden cage. Wil could only hear the comments of those taller than he, so, against his father's command, the boy forced his way through the crowd and toward the square. He pushed and grunted, squatted and crawled his way to the front and finally found himself peering into the center of the field through the thighs of a wide-legged soldier. His gaze fell upon a platform and on the platform, two posts and a beam.

The wagon and the horsemen slowly made their way to the base of the stage and a company of footmen formed an impenetrable fence between the crowd and the gallows. Wil felt suddenly nervous and imagined the firelight was surely drawn from the furnaces of hell. The almost seven-year-old wished he had not left his father's side.

A priest, none knew whom, stepped first upon the platform. Behind him followed Werner accompanied by two knights of Runkel and the executioner. The hangman was bare-chested and his head draped in a black woollen hood. At the sight of him the crowd began to murmur. The cart stopped at the steps leading to the gallows and Wil spotted a small, skeletal lad shaking and crying within the cage. Wil had learned to hide his heart but he surely had one, and the sight of the helpless boy released a flood of tears.

"In nomine Paris, et Filii, et Spiritus Sancti," the priest

began. "Our God deliver us. We adore Thee, O Christ, and we bless Thee."

Bailiff Werner stepped forward and handed a parchment to a knight of Heribert. The man raised a hand and read: "*Gloria Patri, et Filio, et Spiritui Sancto.* Hear me, subjects of Abbot Udo, the most high Pope Innocent III, and Emperor Otto of our Holy Empire. All order is from the Most High God. His name shall not be blasphemed nor His ways offended. By right of Word and by command of the rightful Protector of this land, Lord Heribert of Runkel, it is so ordered that Albert of Niederbrechen, third living son of Hinrik the cotter also of Niederbrechen is accused and found guilty of stealing bread and cheese from the Templars' refectory in the abbey at Villmar."

A rumble rustled through the crowd. The knight lifted his face and scowled. Werner raised his hands and shouted, "Silence! Silence!"

After a brief pause, the knight read on: "As this is his third offense and no penance nor penalty has proven remedy for his unholy ways, it is the sad but just duty of the court of Runkel, under the authority granted by the abbot, to impose sentence worthy of his sins and crimes. Let God have mercy on his soul. Amen."

Wil and the crowd of his fellows fell silent. The hanging of a peasant boy was rare, though not unheard of, and most thought cruel. As little Albert was dragged from his cage a few voices cried out in protest and a rumble was heard on the far side of the square. A figure suddenly emerged from the dark mass, pointing his fist and shouting. "By all that is right and good, release this poor wretch!" the man cried.

Werner scowled. Elbowing his way to the fore was a Templar. The soldier climbed the steps of the platform and fell to his knees. "Free him! I beseech you, good bailiff, release this boy. Look at him! He is but bones; he is starving in these times! My God, have mercy on him." It was Blasius.

One of Heribert's knights pushed the young Templar with his boot, knocking him on his side. Blasius climbed bravely to his feet and faced the man squarely. "Have you no charity?"

"Do not interfere, Templar! 'Tis no business of yours."

"I say it is my business! A helpless child is to be hanged and you say it is not my business! Are you mad?"

Other soldiers quickly filled the platform and a scuffle began. A group of Templars stood by Blasius and railed against the soldiers of Runkel. To Runkel's aid came more of their knights and an angry company of footmen. Soon the stage was overflowing with brawling men, some falling to the ground, others drawing swords.

Then from below bellowed a voice like none had ever heard. *"Mon frères, suffisament!"* The Templars turned and faced their master, Brother Phillipe de Blanqfort. He stared at them firmly, then grabbed a torch and climbed the steps. The men parted before him like the sea before Moses. The veteran of Palestine shouldered his way toward Blasius, and the two faced each other for a long moment. The whole of the square held its breath.

"Never," began Phillipe, "never lose your heart of mercy."

Blasius bowed.

"But, my brother, it is not for you to tread where God does not call you. So, according to your vow ..."

"No!" protested Blasius. "No, I shall not ..."

"You shall obey me!" roared Phillipe.

Blasius shuddered and bowed his head.

Phillipe peered at the young knight's earnest face. Blasius's eyes were red and tearing as he turned toward the poor lad staring wide-eyed and frightened.

"Brother Blasius, leave this place. Let justice be served."

Blasius closed his eyes and yielded. Weeping, the warrior-monk descended the steps and walked stiffly away.

Wil was troubled and angry. He had not heard Blasius's pleas, though he could see Albert being led to the rope. But while the poor wretch received his final prayer, Wil's ears cocked to reports of the Templar's protest. The news raced through the woollen horde in a rising rush that suddenly surged like a stormy tide at full moon. The gathered peasants began to shout, "Mercy, mercy!" Wil jumped to his feet and joined his little voice to all the others. "Mercy ... mercy!" he shrieked.

But, despite the cries of the angry folk, the sentence was quickly executed. Little Albert was hoisted four feet off the ground where he flailed on the end of the rope for nearly a quarter of an hour. Little by little the throng of peasants fell silent and stood stupefied until, at long last, the boy hung limp and lifeless.

As Albert's body was lowered into a waiting cart, the disgusted crowd began to grumble, then to shout. They shook their fists impotently against the dark sky and cursed the order before them. Indeed, something good had happened in that awful place: mercy had been awakened in the hearts of the simple folk. And more, they had learned how much greater mercy was than justice—if only they would remember.

಄

Visions of the hanging kept Wil awake at night for months. The boy tossed and turned and whimpered in the darkness. Heinrich lay by his side through the blackest hours of those nights and gently rubbed his forearms, stroked his hair, or hummed a gentle rhyme.

Karl was spared the trauma of the hanging, as Heinrich had wisely hidden the boy's eyes from the horror of the sight. He was ever cheerful and chattered about each bright imagination that filled his happy mind at any given moment. The boy was endearing to all and eager to win the approval of anyone within sight of his smiling face. He was a blessed gift in a dreary place.

In the passing seasons Marta grew more distant, ever more miserable, and unbearably demanding. Her children were all that was dear to her, though she was often impatient with their troubles and annoyed with their unordered ways. Nevertheless, she wanted to receive their love and affection and she longed for their companionship. It was the weight of her expectations, however, that so often snuffed out the natural warmth the young hearts yearned to tender. So, unable or unwilling to see her own failings, the woman exacted penalties of increasing proportion. Fearful of God, disappointed in her world, and ashamed of herself, the poor woman hardened with every new sorrow that life delivered to her door.

"Wife," offered Heinrich one autumn evening, "you seem so unhappy. You ..."

"'Tis you! 'Tis you and the children, you are making me mad! Methinks I shall surely lose m'mind!" Marta glared at Heinrich with scalding eyes.

The man detected more pain than evil and his heart grew sad at her suffering. "I ... I wish y'to be more at peace, more—"

"You've brought naught but ruin to me. You'd not be the man I thought you to be; the children are not what they ought. None thinks of me and m'work. You never please me. And you'd be no man of business as is m'father ... nay ... not at all. If I could manage that bakery I'd show all how it's better done! You've no ambition. Y'spend your time in thinking and daydreaming with that old hag." Marta laughed a sneering, wicked laugh, and put her finger in her husband's face. "And I know you've secret sins ... 'tis why we've buried three!"

Her words found their mark and Heinrich stood mute and ashamed. Indeed, he thought, he was a sinner to be sure. Marta was right, he did harbor secret sins. How often had he wished his wife would die? What about the Gunnar blood he spilt that horrid night? Were they not two charges of murder? How he coveted the bakery for his own. And his dreams of Katharina, another's wife, were images that accused his pricked and knotted conscience. But more than all these, he knew his heart was filled with a secret hate for those who had bound his eyes to the ground. Oh, how he longed to break his vow and face the sun—a temptation that twisted through him on every blue-skied day. Yet his hatred for the vow and the God he thought demanded it filled him with guilt all the more, and in despair he nearly wept aloud. He closed his eyes. *I am a wicked man!* he thought. *I am a coward as well, for I will not confess these to any. My heart is filled with murder, hatred, idolatry, adultery, covetousness, theft, envy, and pride. I shall surely burn—and these others with me as well.*

Heinrich stared blankly at Marta's back as she stormed away. She, a woman bound in fear, and he, a man bound in shame. Together they suffered the firstfruits of Adam's fall.

The weary man turned and faced the gaze of his two sons sitting cross-legged by the hearth. He sighed and sat beside them, poking mindlessly at the fire.

"Father," said Wil, "I fear to sleep again. I fear I shall dream of poor Albert on the rope."

Heinrich put his finger under the lad's chin. He looked at Wil for a moment. *Handsome,* he thought. *Strong features like his mother. Melancholy and troubled like both his mother and m'self.* The man smiled kindly at his son. "Ah, lad, dreams are often what we make them to be. When you dream this night, dream of Blasius with his long, yellow hair. Dream that you are he. Then mount a big-chested steed and gallop from the darkness toward the torches. Then, as you come by Albert, swing your sword with all your might and cut that cursed rope! Ha ... won't that anger the bailiff! Then catch the lad and set him behind you on your horse. With a yell turn and charge toward your brother and me. We shall open a path midst your fellows and off you shall ride to a place far away and safe!"

Wil brightened. "*Ja,* I shall save him! And then I shall save others!"

Heinrich nodded and lifted Wil high toward the smoke hole in the ceiling. "Fly, lad, fly like the embers, far, far away ... and be free!"

Chapter 15

LOSSES

ince Gottwald's death Heinrich had spent each All Souls' Eve with Emma. The night was one of great sadness for the woman and she treasured the company of her friend. As Heinrich walked to her home on this particular November night, he sensed her time was short. Emma had battled her illness bravely and without complaint for the past several years. In the summer just past she was barely fit enough to walk in the garden and had spent only a few precious hours at the Magi with Heinrich and his boys. Of late she had become bedridden, ashen, and pale. No potion helped, though Brother Lukas tried many.

"Greetings!" Heinrich offered as he closed the door behind himself. A lump filled his throat as he tried to smile. His Butterfly Frau was lying atop her straw mattress with her head resting on a goose feather pillow. Lukas sat quietly by her side. He had arrived at Emma's cottage just after vespers with a flask of chicken broth smuggled from the refectory. The two friends had spent a quiet hour together before Heinrich joined them.

Above Emma's head hung a season's worth of dried flowers and herbs that filled her home with a musky scent more potent than the sweet smoke of her spruce-log hearth. She breathed lightly and was half-asleep but smiled as Heinrich came to her side.

"Ah, good and dear friend," she said slowly, "I am so ... so very thankful to God that you have come to see me on this night."

Heinrich knelt by her. "Dear Emma. I am thankful to be here."

Lukas wiped her head with a scented napkin. "Rosemary and flower of thistle."

"What does that do?" asked Heinrich.

Lukas shrugged. "I don't really know, but I like the sound of it."

Emma laughed weakly until her eyes watered. "Ach, Lukas! Do not ever change!"

The monk grinned. "Now, sister. It is you who taught we must *always* change!"

Emma coughed and chuckled. "Ah, and so I did, so I did." Her voice faded a little. "Heinrich, all is in order with your land. I've received the rents and I've given them to Blasius, that wondrous Templar." She grimaced and clutched her chest. The pain passed quickly and she went on. "The prior is furious ... I must confess, I like that somewhat." She smiled. "He wants your land very badly. It seems Gottwald ..." Another pain gripped her and this time she cried out.

Heinrich backed away and let Lukas comfort the woman. The monk held her to his chest and entreated God's mercy with a desperate prayer. The two were still for a few moments until the pain eased, and the woman wiped the tears off the brother's kind face. She smiled at him and turned to Heinrich once more. "Gottwald granted your land in the very center of what he gave to the abbey! He was an old fox, ha! An old, gray fox indeed. He knew the abbey would offer a heavy price for it."

"But Emma, I want it to be *your* land, always. I ..."

"Ah, dear boy. You know that cannot be. I am ready to die, quite ready, indeed. Brother Lukas brought a priest from the abbey for my final confession just an hour before you came. I think he was angry I did not die right away; he thinks he wasted a trip!" She chuckled, then paused. "I told him the suffering of Christ was the only penance I need look to. I told him the perfection of Christ was all the goodness I might claim. He said I was strident." The woman sighed peacefully, then closed her eyes in sleep.

The monk and the baker sat quietly alongside Emma's bed for an hour or so, when a sudden pain awakened her. She grimaced. Lukas bathed her head and prayed with her. She then fixed a glassy stare on Heinrich. "Hear me, lad, m'precious little Heinz, look past what you see, and truth shall find you."

Heinrich glanced anxiously at Lukas as tears blurred his red eyes. He held the woman's cooling hands in his. Emma's face whitened and her lips began to lose their color. She drew a halting breath, then slowly whispered, "Spread your wings, m'dear one, lift your head and turn toward the—"

The blessed woman lurched in her bed and cried out. A cold wind suddenly draughted the hearth smoke downward through the smoke-hole, and Emma's room instantly filled with a choking smoke. The weeping baker lunged to the door and flung it open. It was then, as the cold, clean air of All Souls' Eve poured into the good woman's cottage, that Emma's spirit fluttered away, like a summer's butterfly to her Maker's wondrous gardens now readied and waiting on the far side of the sun.

🙞

Emma's burial was as her life had been: simple and unassuming but touched by an unearthly beauty. Father Albert, Pious's new assistant, prayed earnestly for her soul while Heinrich, Wil, Karl, Brother Lukas, Richard, Herwin, and Varina stood solemnly around her grave. A warm southern breeze caressed the tear-stained faces staring sadly at the shrouded remains of their good friend. A few songbirds then lighted atop the sturdy tower of the ancient church and sang as though sent by the angels to soothe the aching hearts below. But when the final words were spoken and the last shovel of brown earth fell atop Emma's mounded grave, the birds flew away, and with them their sweet tidings.

With wet cheeks the mourners returned to the tasks and

burdens of the day. Each faced the labors of autumn as they had every year before. Herwin joined the men in the forests setting fences for the swineherd. Varina returned to her children and sat in her damp, smoke-choked hut to spin the fleeces of spring-sheared wool. Lukas slipped away to the banks of the Laubusbach, and Heinrich walked his boys home.

The baker led his lads slowly along the footpaths of the village and said little. Karl, however, babbled on and on in his cheerful way, chattering of the simple, happy times spent with Emma. "*Vati!* She made me laugh and she taught me riddles!"

Heinrich smiled. "Aye, boy. I've yet to solve the one of the rooster and the chick!"

Karl laughed. He was sharp as a saddler's needle. "Ha, *Vati*, and if you do, I've another!"

"Your riddles are stupid," grumbled Wil. "And this is no day to laugh, you dolt."

"Boys, no fights. Wil, the prior says you shall start school on Monday next. You'll join a group of fine young lords from other parts and a few oblates. 'Tis a wondrous thing. Frau Emma was so happy for it. Karl, in a few more years you'll have the promise too."

Wil wrinkled his nose. "I shall be with oblates?"

"Aye, mostly."

"But the oblates are most of good blood."

Heinrich nodded. "You and your brother are of good stock as well."

"The son of a baker and the grandson of a miller? Everyone hates Grandpapa, and you … you are plain and …"

Heinrich drew a deep breath. "Aye, lad. I am a simple man, but you and Karl are blessed with a special gift from a great-grandpapa who even I never knew."

The three then talked of other things until reaching their hovel where they entered the door to find Marta and Dietrich deep in conversation. "Father," Marta said dispassionately, "you know I shall care for you. I shall—"

"What is the matter?" asked Heinrich.

"The prior has ordered Father from the mill. 'Too old,' he

says. But Father is yet strong and the mill is working well and—"

"Enough, daughter," groaned Dietrich. "It is true, Heinrich. Others have been sent to run the mill. But I've other news as well." He looked at Marta nervously.

Heinrich sat on a stool and his boys leaned curiously against the cottage walls. "Yes, go on." Dietrich looked old to Heinrich. Indeed, the man was now in his fifties. What hair edged the sides of his head was white and sparse, his teeth were gone, and he had become bony and feeble.

"I've a bit of a problem. I've lost a wager with that devil Horst, the brother of Friedal. I thought sure of the thing and pledged m'house and chattels as good faith. I only wanted to win some shillings for a day such as this so you'd need not care for me and—"

"You lost your house and all what's in it?" cried Marta.

Dietrich hung his head. "*Ja*, 'tis so."

Marta stared at her father in disbelief. "If Mother were alive she'd ... she'd ... how *could* you—"

"Marta," interrupted Heinrich, "perhaps we can plead to Horst for charity and—"

"Charity? Nay! Never! My good word is all I've left to me and I shall not lose that as well, no, I shall not!"

Heinrich looked at Marta and at his sons with a stomach turning like a pail of curdling milk. "M'brother, Axel is to move out, methinks during the Advent. You shall live here and we shall provide for you." The words fell from the man's lips like heavy bricks. But Heinrich knew his duty.

Dietrich nodded and reached for his daughter. "Marta, Marta, I knew you would help. May heaven bless you."

The woman stiffened and stared at him hard-eyed and bitter. She had not forgiven him for little Lukas's death, though she was pleased he had suffered at least a bit for it. *Ach!* she thought. *Another sorrow to endure ...*

The man embraced her for a moment, then he turned to Heinrich. "I shall help you in the bake-house."

A pang cut through Heinrich's chest. "I've apprentices from the monks and m'boys, I've hands enough, I ..." A sharp look from Marta finished his sentence. "I ... might always use another, though."

Dietrich smiled. "Of course you can."

ॐ

Advent brought its usual cheer to what was otherwise a dismal time of year. The air was cold and damp, the slaughter finished. Taxes and fines were paid and the village now waited expectantly for the feasts of Christmas. The labors of this season were easier than many, for little could be done other than the repair of workshops, roofs, and fences. For both serf and monk it was a time of blessed respite, but for Wil it was a time for work to begin.

The cloister fast had started on the fifteenth of November and the monks were about one third through their suffering when young Wil was brought to the eastern gate. A cranky, hungry porter greeted the lad and his father with a curt and insincere, "*Deo gratias*. Thanks be to God."

Heinrich bowed. "I've my son to see the school."

The porter stared at the two in disbelief, but he gave them entrance and led them to the prior's chamber. Wil had seen the inside of the abbey only once before. He marveled at the busy workshops and granaries lining the wall, and gawked at the tall stacks of beer barrels. The gray-stoned church loomed large and ominous at the very center of the abbey grounds, its stout bell tower facing the east. Wil paused to stare at the church for a moment before looking beyond it into the maze of garden walls and orchards that lay beyond. He then looked to his right to study the collection of stone-and-timber buildings forming the cloister itself.

"Over there," Heinrich said, "is the refectory where the monks eat, the infirmary for their sick, the dormitories, kitchen, scriptorium, covered walkways, and, of course, the latrine."

"Where does Lukas live?"

"There, in that dormitory." Heinrich lowered his voice. "Lukas says he is going to take a vow of solitude with hopes of being put in a private cell. He says he finds the brethren a bit of a bother!"

Wil laughed, earning a stern glance from their escort. Heinrich pointed to Lukas's new herbarium standing in the center of a huge, cross-shaped garden to their left. "That is where our friend spends most of his day."

The porter led the pair along a well-worn, stone footpath past the gardens, a fish pond, and toward the abbot's grand residence and another set of buildings near the southern wall. He said nothing until they reached the prior's chamber. "*In nomine Patris ...*" The monk knelt before the two and washed their feet as he prayed for them. When the man was done he recited, "God, we have received Your mercy in the midst of Your temple."

Wil was wide-eyed and uncomfortable when the brother gave him a kiss of peace, but when he offered a sweet roll and a strip of salted fish, the boy grinned from ear to ear!

"Please, sit yourselves here. Brother Mattias shall join you shortly." The porter showed the two to a couple of comfortable wooden chairs setting adjacent to a blazing hearth and quickly stepped away.

The room was plain, damp, and shadowed, lit only by firelight and what sunbeams pressed their way through two shuttered windows on the southern wall. A large desk sat opposite the hearth and a smaller scribe's table was placed next to it. A few simple chairs and a stool were arranged on top of a woven carpet.

"Peace be unto you," a voice suddenly said.

Wil and Heinrich turned to see Prior Mattias and his clerk. "And to you," answered Heinrich as he and his son stood.

"You have been greeted and fed?"

"Yes."

"Good. Now, if it please you, I shall sit by my desk."

As Mattias and his clerk took their places, an official and two more clerks entered. Heinrich knew they were not of the brethren. The official wore a mantle of white squirrel over a long, magnificently embroidered green robe. His legs were covered in fine breeches that fell to his shins where red woollen hose led to his well-oiled ox-leather shoes. From beneath his sleeves peeked the cuffs of a white linen shirt, and atop his head sat an otter cap. His companions were more modestly dressed but were clearly free men of means.

"Heinrich," announced the prior as he pointed to the official, "this is Steward Hagan. Sire Hagan serves us from Runkel as did Erhard in years past. He handles our matters of law and accounting."

The baker and his son nodded, curious.

Mattias went on. "We've two matters of business to discuss with you, my children, and know that Abbot Udo has been appraised of thine issues and has charged us to bring all to proper order. Firstly, in the matter of this, thy son, Johann Wilhelm: I do have in my possession the abbey's pledge to your father's father. I see you have brought yours likewise."

Heinrich nodded.

"Our second point is a matter regarding thine inheritance of a holding once granted to our deceased tenant, Emma of Quedlinburg, of late a resident in Weyer."

Heinrich chilled. Lukas told him that Blasius would be transacting all business regarding Emma's lands. He feared any discussion on these matters without the counsel of either Lukas or him.

"Now," continued Mattias, "I do freely admit that on matters of law I am not well versed, but it would seem we have some concerns regarding both. For this reason, I have yielded to the better judgment of our steward. He is a lawyer in the realm and properly trained in these things."

All eyes turned toward Steward Hagan. The man was hawkish and cold. His beady, brown eyes were aimed dispassionately toward the pair of peasants staring blank-faced and nervously at him. "Heinrich and Wilhelm. Hmm. It seems we have some problems. It is my charge, under God, to protect the industry of the abbey so that future generations may benefit from its service to God's kingdom on earth. I have discussed your grandfather's ... covenant ... with the lawyers of the emperor and Archbishop Siegfried in Mainz, as well as the papal legate."

Wil whispered to his father. Heinrich, now anxious and sweating, hushed the boy.

"To speak directly to the first point, we wonder by what right any man might coerce the services of these Holy

Brethren?" The steward fixed a hard eye at the poor baker and waited for an answer.

Heinrich stammered, "I beg your leave, sire, but what is 'coerce'?"

The man smiled. It was a haughty, wicked, condescending smile. "Ah, but of course. You are but a baker! I beg your pardon, friend. To answer you, 'coerce' means to force by threat. So I ask again, by what right are you forcing these good brothers to provide your sons with learning?"

Heinrich looked helplessly at the waiting faces of the others. He drew a deep breath and stared at the cracks of gray light filtering through the shutters. He wished for all the world he could run home. *Oh, if only Lukas were here*, he thought desperately. But Lukas was not there. "I cannot answer you, m'lord, I know only of a promise and …"

"Ah, of course. You know nothing of this other than what's been told you by the other ignorant folk of your little village."

Heinrich sat still and tried to swallow. His lips were dry and he looked about for a flagon of beer or mead. He nodded.

Hagan continued. "Hmm. Well, good fellow, I must needs tell you that your parchment is in some doubt. The realm cannot have its subjects taking advantage of its Lord Protectors through threats and slanders. And, as a point of law, a pledge under duress is not valid. Ah, your pardon. 'Duress' is the pressure of a threat, you understand?"

Heinrich nodded again. "But I only know of an abbot's promise, I—"

"Enough, baker!" The steward threw off his mantle and leaned toward the confused man. No longer dispassionate, the man's eyes burned with anger and with purpose, only to suddenly soften as poor Heinrich dropped his eyes. The man released a long breath. "Hmm. You seem to be an earnest fellow."

Heinrich looked up hopefully.

"Perhaps we ought leave this matter for the moment and speak of the other."

Relief came over Heinrich's face and he relaxed.

Hagan slanted his eye ever so slightly toward the prior,

but it was a look that did not escape the sharp eyes of young Wil. "I have been asked to review the wills of our vassal, Gottwald of Oldenburg, and of his whore, Emma."

Heinrich bristled. "She was no whore!" he growled.

The steward smiled slyly, surprised at the spirit in the man. "Ah, Heinrich, I do sincerely ask your pardon. I had no right to use such a term for the mother of Gottwald's bastard child."

His wry tone belied his insincerity, but Heinrich had no ear for subtleties. "She was a good woman and I dearly loved her ... and, yes, I pardon you."

"Many thanks." Hagan bowed his head sarcastically.

The veins in Wil's young neck now bulged. He had a different instinct than his father.

"So, Heinrich, I was about to say that I have reviewed the wills carefully." He held Emma's will toward the fire of a wall-torch. "Nay, nay," he chuckled, "you've no need to fear. I am only reading the witnesses to the woman's name. Yes, yes, our own beloved Lukas and the Templar knight, Brother Blasius. Hmm. Well, no matter, all is in order here. I declare the woman, Emma of Quedlinburg, to have issued a proper charter of her earthly holdings and I concur that you, Heinrich the baker of Weyer, are her rightful heir by the declaration witnessed herein."

Heinrich raised his eyebrows and released a long sigh. He looked happily at the prior. Mattias smiled. "So I am the proper holder to her lands?" Heinrich asked.

"Yes."

Heinrich was relieved and delighted. "I am told the Templars store my rents and handle my fees and fines, taxes, and the like."

"That is so," answered Prior Mattias.

A long pause followed. Heinrich sat still, waiting for something else to be said. He stared about the circle of faces and began to fumble with his hands. "Well," he finally offered, "it seems the light is failing. M'son and me want to see the schoolmaster, and we've more than an hour's walk ahead and—"

"Heinrich," interrupted the steward, "I have been

authorized to propose an offer to you for your land."

Heinrich's heart began to race. He had often dreamt of negotiating his freedom. He had seen himself marching to the abbot's door and gleefully bartering his new land as manumission for himself and his family. He imagined the abbot grunting and groaning and pleading for better terms. And in his fantasy he saw the prior on his knees begging for the baker's charity, only to finally yield and grant the man his freedom and more!

"Heinrich!" Hagan bellowed. "Are you listening, man?"

"Oh, aye, of course, m'lord."

"And what say you?"

"Of what, sire?"

"Of your price!" boomed the frustrated steward.

Heinrich licked his dry lips and looked at Wil. *Oh, to set his household free!* he thought. He turned to the steward. "I ... I ..."

"*Ja? Ja?*"

"I would offer Emma's lands for ... for the freedom of m'self, m'wife, and our children."

Mattias' clerk began to cough and the prior, himself, reddened. Hagan put a finger on his lips and frowned. "Manumission? You offer this as manumission?"

Heinrich was sweating. "Aye, sire, lord sire ..."

"Prior Mattias," Hagan began, "would you join me in the outer chamber for a moment?"

The two slipped out of the shadowed room and whispered beyond the heavy oak door. Heinrich shifted uncomfortably on his chair and smiled at his son. Wil leaned toward his father. "*Vati,* they'll try to cheat you. I do not trust these men! Lukas says you needs be more the fox and less the hare!"

The man nodded. "I am trying. 'Tis not an easy thing for me. I ..."

The door opened and the prior and steward returned to their positions. The kitchener scurried in behind them and brought Heinrich and Wil tankards of cloister ale and wheat rolls. "Now," began Hagan again, "you know I dare not speak untruths on behalf of the brethren."

Heinrich nodded.

"So I speak truth when I say they would like very much to barter your land fairly and in accordance with their obligations as caretakers of that which God has given them. Now, it seems your land lies near some good ground that Lord Gottwald also granted them."

"Ours lies in the very center!" cried young Wil.

Heinrich hushed him sternly.

The boy folded his arms and scowled. The steward and the spirited lad locked glares for a long pause before the man continued. "You ask much of us this day, Heinrich, and we are somewhat surprised. You are known as humble and devout, faithful to private vows. You'd be a man known for his industry and you are no thief, at least not until this moment."

Heinrich looked confused. "Why this moment?"

"When you charge a man for bread, good fellow, how do you fix the charge?"

"The price is set by the abbey."

"And how do you imagine they set the price?"

"I never think of such things."

"Could you imagine they set the price in accordance to what is fair and necessary to all parties, that the price is set from charitable concern for the buyer as well as necessary concern for holy stewardship?"

Again Heinrich was confused.

The steward raised his voice. "Let me say it in another way! Do you think the brothers charge the very most they possibly can, or do they consider the buyers as well?"

The baker looked at the prior and scratched his head. "I surely do not know."

"I see. And I understand, for you are no man of business. You give little thought to things as these, and why should you? What I am saying is that Christian dealings account for all sides' welfare. You are charging a price for your land that considers only you! Greed, I think, is one sin in view here. And when one takes advantage of another, as in usury, it is called theft. Are your kin and kind thieves?"

"Nay. Scrumping is a grievous shame to us."

Prior Mattias leaned forward. "Sire Hagan, it is true. The man is no thief, not since he was a youth."

The steward nodded. "Hmm, most honorable."

Heinrich drew a long, uneasy draught from his tankard. A clerk hastened to refill it as the prior now stood and set a gentle hand on the baker's shoulder. Heinrich remembered a warning from Emma: "Be wary of the touch or smile of a churchman!" Heinrich drew a deep breath and waited.

"Worthy baker," said the prior, "if you had thy freedom, what would you do with it?"

Heinrich answered quickly. He had often imagined exactly what he would do. "I should stay and labor at the bake-house and when m'boys were done their schooling we would travel as free men to other parts where they might work as lawyers or physicians, even men of commerce, and I should join a baker's guild."

"Ah, a dreamer are you? We did not realize."

The steward and his men chuckled quietly as they snacked on bread, cheese, and a bottle of French wine.

Mattias continued. "You have no means of knowing this, but the abbey suffers lost revenue of every sort and we are in grave debt to the archbishop. We've given some thought to relieving our debt by offering bakeries and breweries to the archdiocese. Father Pious has already negotiated with us for control of Weyer's bakery.

"Now, should we give the bakery to Pious, I doubt he would keep you in hire as a freeman. Ambitious men such as he lust for control and free men are difficult to manage. Now, we are not pleased by some of Pious's ways but we have few choices at this time. But this goes beyond the point. I say this to you and I say it plainly: should we exchange thy land for thy freedom, you shall have no place of labor other than thy half-hide. Neither Pious nor we would employ you. And if you needs leave our lands, then your sons shall surely have no learning in the abbey school."

Steward Hagan interrupted. "Of course, prior, we have not yet settled on that matter."

"Ah, indeed, 'tis still a question."

Heinrich was now very confused and he looked desperately

into the dwindling hearth hoping for some miraculous rescue. His mind was jumbled and his heart pounded. The steward took the floor again.

"I can see, man, that you are troubled." Hagan spoke calmly, with an almost fatherly tone. "Here it is: your claim for your children is dubious, your inheritance intact. Your price brings problems, for if you barter your land for your freedom you shall have nowhere to enjoy it. And, if the brothers are willing to honor your parchment, your freedom shall surely forfeit it, for you'll needs live elsewhere. Add to that the worry the brothers have for your soul. It is clear to us, men more accustomed to the temptations of business than yourself, that you are guilty of the sins of greed and ingratitude."

"Ingratitude?"

"Aye. These Benedictines have cared for you and your kin for generations and have done so with generous hearts and at great cost. Now you wish to dismiss all thoughts of their kindness and charitable service in favor of your own gain. That, poor fellow, is ingratitude."

Heinrich lowered his eyes. *Indeed,* he thought, *perhaps I am wayward in this. Greed, theft, ingratitude, what else?*

The steward let the man be for a few moments, then motioned for the prior to join him in the outer chamber once again. With a wink and a nod, the two left the room. Wil leaned over to his father. "I saw the steward wink! He's a bad man, *Vati,* a bad man. I hate him! And I hate the prior and I ha—"

"That is enough!" scolded Heinrich. "You're not to hate at all, least of all a monk! What devils you, boy? Now sit and say not another word."

The prior and steward returned shortly and took a few relaxed moments to sip some wine and nibble on the tray of cheese now shared with Heinrich and his son. Prior Mattias folded his hands and spoke gently. "The day grows short and our steward would very much like us to close our business in time for thy safe return. He shall propose an offer I think shall serve all of us very well. Steward Hagan, would you explain?"

"Surely. Heinrich, Mattias has instructed me to make a most generous proposal. In exchange for the rightful deed to your land near Oldenburg, the abbey shall honor the pledge to your grandfather. And, though it was my counsel that such a concession was payment enough, they do most graciously and charitably offer you the rights of heritable ownership to the bakery in Weyer. You shall pay a fair rent and you shall keep the profits from the sales of your bread. They, however, shall set the price so as to protect both you and their other subjects."

Heinrich was weary and his mind was numb. It seemed to him that the ancient pledge should never have been in question at all and perhaps Lukas or Blasius could help him claim it at a higher court. As for Emma's lands, he was completely confused. If they bought it from him by granting his freedom he might be sent away only to find no employment elsewhere in these hard times. If he was allowed to remain, he'd have no job to pay his higher taxes and would have to offer military service or else pay the scutage. *And Marta wants no parts of freedom anyway*, he thought. Heinrich fumbled for words. "I needs think on this matter for some time, and—"

"Heinrich, I leave for Oldenburg on the morrow. You are aware that Lord Heribert is a cousin to the count in those parts. I must hurry there to secure the abbey's new lands that Gottwald granted us. We are hoping all is not already lost to the armies opposing the pope's emperor. You do understand, that if those lands are seized you'd have nothing to barter at all? If I were you I'd take this generous offer while I could. Also, I need tell you the abbot's charity toward you is encouraged by the expediency of this arrangement. In other words, you must agree now or the proposal is withdrawn."

Heinrich ground his teeth. He stood to his feet and paced the floor. Dressed in his common homespun he felt powerless and weak. *Perhaps I am being selfish*, he thought. *Perhaps their offer is best for all and maybe I ought take what I can while I can.* He tried to avoid the accusing eyes of Wil.

Heinrich suddenly felt ashamed for doubting the world

that ruled him. It was all too much to bear and the man yielded. "I ... I accept your terms." Heinrich sighed in resignation and collapsed into his chair, exhausted.

Chapter 16

LIFE

Heinrich's hand shook as he accepted the offer with a few carefully witnessed scratches of a quill on parchment. The deal done, the baker was hurried out of the prior's chamber and escorted to the novice cloister where he and Wil made a brief appearance before the abbey's lay-instructor, Herr Laurentius.

Laurentius fixed an intimidating stare into the face of the lad who would become his pupil. Wil stood stiff-jawed and silent and studied his schoolmaster with equal determination while he received a brief orientation of the day to follow. The boy said nothing but finally offered a respectful bow as Laurentius finished his lecture.

"Thank you, m'lord," said Wil. "I shall do m'best."

"Aye, the lad shall work hard," added Heinrich. With that, the pair stepped into the abbey's courtyard and began their journey home.

After a long period of silence, Wil finally spoke. "He's a terror. He held the rod like he loved it and I think he'll use it often!"

"If he uses it too often I'll use it on him!" boasted Heinrich. The two walked up the long slope leading away from Villmar and said little. Heinrich's mind ran over the business of the day and he shook his head. "Methinks I should have done better."

"Aye, you let them trick you."

Somehow knowing that Wil was right, Heinrich hung his head.

The two finally arrived home in the dark hours of that most difficult day. Wil knew only that he hated everyone he had met and was in dread of the morning's hike to his first day of school. Heinrich stared at his hovel door as nervous as a cat approaching an angry hound. He knew his wife would demand an explanation for all that had transpired, and he knew that his answers would likely be derided no matter what they were. He entered his home with trepidation.

"And where have you two been? The mush is stiff and cold; you've a few dried peas and a hard-boiled egg. 'Tis more than you deserve for coming home like this!"

Dietrich was half-asleep on the floor. He sat up to his elbows and groused, "What kind of man comes to his meal at this hour. I tell you, Marta, I wouldn't put up with it!"

Heinrich closed his eyes and drew a deep breath. "We've much to tell, wife," he began. He sat at the trestle table by the cook-fire and dipped his fingers in the mush bowl. "First, your son begins his instruction tomorrow by terce. His master is a young man from—"

"Cologne," interjected Wil. "And he's a brute. He hates me; I can see it in his eyes."

"Nay, nay, Wil," said Marta. "He needs keep good order. 'Tis no hate in that."

Wil grunted and looked carefully at his father, wondering how he would share the rest.

"And there's other news." All eyes turned toward Heinrich as Karl climbed playfully into his lap. The man hesitated. He would need to be more clever now than he had been a few hours earlier. "Wife," he began slowly, "what say you to bartering our land from Emma for our freedom?"

"Freedom? Nay! Better to stay safe in these times. I'd rather be rich and safe than poor and free!" She suddenly fixed a hard eye on her husband. "What did you do, Heinrich? What sort of fool thing did you do?" Her voice was shrill and loud. Heinrich wanted to stuff his ears with wool. Instead, he drew a deep breath and sighed.

"No, fear not, you are not free." Wil noted a subtle hint of sarcasm in his father's voice. The man continued. "What say you to keeping the lands for their rents?"

"Nay!" the woman growled suspiciously. "Your head is thick and filled with dung. I've told you time and time again we cannot trust land on the other side of the world, and I do not trust that Templar!"

Dietrich grumbled as he climbed to his feet. "You've always been a dolt, Heinrich. Your uncles, *ja*, those are men who are men! But you? Ha, you learned nothing from them. Your papa, Kurt, he was—"

"Enough, Father," ordered Marta. "Heinrich, what have you done?"

Heinrich would have liked nothing better than to throw the old intruder out the door. He bit his tongue, then answered his wife. "Would you have me barter the land for more land here, by Weyer?"

Marta paused. "Anka says we ought take silver, so when we've a bad harvest, all's not lost."

"But where would we hide so much silver?"

"The Templars."

"Aye, but, wife, you've said you do not trust the Templars."

Marta grew quiet. Heinrich found the brief interlude refreshing and he took a few bites. Finally, the woman pressed again. "So, tell me."

Heinrich wiped his mouth on his sleeve and sat cross-legged by the fire crackling in the center of the room. "I've bartered our lands, not the Weyer lands of course."

At this news Marta began pacing around the room. "You bartered them! For what?"

"I, dear wife, now *own* the bakery; the buildings, ovens, tools, flours and spices, and the sole rights to bake for Wey—"

"The bakery?"

"*Ja.*"

"We own the bakery?"

"*Ja.*" Heinrich began to perspire.

Astonished, Marta sat down slowly on a three-legged stool and stared at her speechless father. None in either family had ever owned an enterprise. She was dumbstruck and struggled to say what came next. "Heinrich, I think it a … a good thing you've done."

Wil grinned at his father and giggled as he burrowed into his straw bed. Heinrich smiled back, surprised at the unexpected and unprecedented approval of his wife. The feeling was delicious and he suddenly felt like a giant among men. His round face glowed and it stretched with a smile as he walked toward Marta in hope of a kind embrace.

News of Heinrich's gain followed the man like flies to the dunghauler. At every hut he passed, a curse or an oath, a jeer or an insult, reached his ears. Marta, too, suffered the jealousies of small souls. Few, however, were as outraged as Father Pious. The abbot had clearly outmaneuvered the ambitious priest, and the man was humiliated by the defeat. For Pious, Heinrich's simple bakery had suddenly become more than a coveted asset; it had, instead, become a symbol of personal pride. And symbols, of course, are given power greater than their substance.

The day before Christmas, Father Pious arrived at Marta's door. The woman was surprised to see the overstuffed priest and invited him inside.

"Greetings to you and your father," grunted the churchman.

"And to you," grumbled Dietrich from a corner.

Marta scurried to gather some beer, bread, and an egg for the priest. *She is a rare beauty, indeed*, Pious thought. He pursed his lips. "Good woman, I thank you for your kindness. I have learned of your happy news. Your husband now owns the bakery, a worthy prize for a servile man. Forgive me, sister, for my tardy well-wishes."

"Yes, father. Of course."

"It is duty that calls me here. I must take this joyous occasion to remind you that 'to whom much is given, much is required.' So says the Holy Scripture."

Marta wiped her hands and sat down to listen.

"Firstly, you needs be ever mindful of your tithe. God's blessings follow sacrifice and faithfulness. His wrath, however, follows unrighteousness and pride. Which brings me to my fear for you. I've heard from another that Heinrich is suspect of secret sins."

"I do believe so as well," answered Marta, "though I know not of what sort."

"Ah, with pardon, woman, I cannot divulge. I've simply come to warn you that God is not mocked. As long as Heinrich hides his sins, your gain is at great risk. It is my joy to shelter you from sorrow, so I beg you heed my words." The priest said nothing else, for he had sown his seeds of fear—seeds destined to sprout misery and discontent—tools of opportunity, indeed.

>

Wil suffered greatly through his first week in school. As his instincts had forewarned, Master Laurentius did hate the peasant boy. "No right!" he was heard screaming to any who would listen. "The peasant scum has no right to learn with these others." Indeed, Wil sat on the granite gradine alongside oblates of high birth destined to serve the Church or to rule petty kingdoms all over Christendom. His classmates hailed from castles up and down the Rhine and from manor houses from Staufenland to Saxony. Eleven in all, these were offered by their parents with a pledge that granted them to the cloister. It was hoped these young and promising gifts to the abbey would secure the salvation of both child and parent alike.

Wil was the only servile child and was not pledged to the monks. He sat stone-faced and proud through five days of taunts and mockery. His rough-spun tunic and close-cropped hair earned him more than a few fists in the face. His only joy at week's end was the knowledge that for every bruise he tended, another nursed a lump!

The baker's son began his training with three new oblates, each slightly older than himself. The four sat in the corner of the cold novices' chapter house atop long stone benches. The group was first taught to respect the Rule of St. Benedict. They were not to engage in conversation or activity with the monks until or unless they were admitted as novices.

"Boys," began the master the first morning, "the brothers spend their lives in service to God and others. They live by the strict code of the Rule and most of you shall follow them in their way of life. What they do is always for a reason. They scurry about with bowed heads because the Rule says, 'Whether sitting, walking, or standing, our heads must be bowed and our eyes cast down. Judging ourselves always guilty on account of our sins, we should consider that we are already at the fearful Judgment, and constantly say in our hearts what the publican in the Gospel said with downcast eyes, "I am a sinner, not worthy to look up to the heavens."' "

Wil thought of his father.

Master Laurentius continued. "The Rule further reads, 'we speak gently and without laughter ... without raising our voices.' You boys need to respect this. No feigning of bad ears just to hear a brother yell. I shall beat any who does such a thing.

"They are joyfully sworn to obedience, to chastity, to poverty, and someday you may be honored to take their vow. Do not tempt them with idle talk, with trinkets in your purses, with whispering deeds. The Rule says, 'every exaltation is a kind of pride.' Do not praise them for their flowers in springtime, their food, their piety ... nothing! The Rule and their customaries guide them in all they do. You shall treat them with respect, I say, or you shall be beaten until you do. Have you questions?"

"Do they bathe?"

"Three times a year."

"Where do they sleep?"

"They've a dormitory, like you. All must sleep in a separate bed, but the Rule calls for them to sleep in large rooms. The abbot has approved one corridor of private cells to be used for brothers who seek solitude during fasting or penance."

"Do they sleep dressed or naked?" The boys tittered. A stern warning from the master called them to silence.

"According to the Rule they—and you—must sleep dressed, but without knives."

The boys wondered about the knives. They looked at each other and shrugged. "I've heard they must eat in silence."

"It is so, and so it shall be with you."

"And when do they eat?"

"From Easter to Pentecost they eat at noon, with a light supper in the evening. From Pentecost and through the summer they fast until midafternoon on Wednesday and Friday. On other days they eat at noon. From the thirteenth of September to the beginning of Lent they eat in the midafternoon, and from Lent to Easter they eat in the evening."

"What do they do beside pray and sing?"

"They read, then they work in their fields or in their workshops. Some are copyists; others work at the brewery or the mill. Look around you, lads. It is a world within the world."

"Master, how is it you know so much of this place?"

"They are all near to the same, some larger, though none, I think, smaller. I was offered to a monastery as a young boy. Like you, I remember holding my parents' document in my hand and my hand wrapped in an altar cloth. Then some words were said by my father and a monk, and at that moment I belonged to a cloister near Aachen."

"But you took no vows?"

"Nay. I was weak-willed and proud of heart as a younger man. I have entered here to try again. So, in accordance with the Rule, I have endured much to be received as a novice once more, but 'brother' I am not ... as yet. Now, that is enough questions.

"You shall learn by phonics and by repetition. You shall learn the abacus ... for you, Wilhelm, a string of peas may do. We shall study the alphabet with the beginner's reader, the *Disticha Catonis*, which you shall read and copy over and over on your wax tablets. I am sure your right knees shall be well-calloused by winter's end!

"When you can read and write to my satisfaction—in about three years—you shall then study the *trivium*; grammar, rhetoric, and logic. Then, when these are mastered, you shall learn the *quadrivium*: arithmetic, geometry, astronomy, and music. Then, little men, you shall have mastered the seven liberal arts, after which you shall then study Donatus and Priscian; you shall learn more Latin. You shall learn Cato's *Moral Sayings*, at heart, and shall recite Virgil and Ovid.

"And, while you are studying these things, it is my desire to have you learn chess and backgammon and a bit of law. We want our future abbots to be able to converse with guests and pilgrims.

"Your instruction shall take many years." He paused and stared at them sternly. "We begin our journey together now and with this first truth: Christian mankind is divided into three estates: those that rule, those that pray, and those that toil. As learned men you shall serve God in the first or second estate. Whatever your call, it is for the glory of God, amen.

෮

On the twenty-fifth of April, 1204, the folk of Weyer gathered at the stone church to celebrate Mass. Having confessed their sins in a responsive, penitential prayer, the simple folk then received the Holy Eucharist through their priests. Ably assisted by Father Albert, Father Pious faced his flock with a face hardened for the precision required of the sacrament. Pious was draped in a white mantle for the season and confidently followed the Roman Rite to near perfection. His unscrupulous attention to detail provided great confidence to his ever-increasing congregations.

Marta was always apt to stand close to the altar. She ground the soles of her shoes hard into the earthen floor in hopes of drawing power and protection from the relics of bone recently buried beneath. She drew deep breaths as Albert incensed the air above the pyx, the paten, and the chalice and nearly swooned as the bread was set upon the tongue of Pious. Her sins now purged, she felt clean again, and so very grateful to her revered priest.

Heinrich also felt some burdens lift from his weighted shoulders. Unlike his wife, however, he preferred offering his confession to Father Albert, who allowed Heinrich the comfort of confession without the embarrassment of specificity. Heinrich believed Albert to be genuine and earnest—simple, yet thorough in his faith. His counsel was thought wise though less rigorous than that of Pious, and his demands for penance were generally eased by a quality of mercy. Ironically, however, it was the young priest's tender heart that gave pause to poor Heinrich, for the baker often wondered if he ought not suffer harsher penances than the gentle cleric called him to perform.

Marta provided an Easter feast that drew high praise from her household. She beamed as Wil and Karl applauded her presentation of fatty pork and boiled goose. To this she added a bowl of tripe, a loaf of her husband's wheat bread, a small saucer of honey she had bought from the monks, and a dish of cheese. Since Easter was late this year, she had picked a quarterpeck of early peas and added them to a pottage of wild scallions, ground acorns, and early herbs.

To Heinrich's delight and mild alarm, she then retrieved a gift from behind the table in her room. It was a flask of wine she purchased from a Frenchman on a pilgrimage through the village. He had stopped to pray at the abbey's new *Kappelle* built by the roadway to Münster. For an undisclosed price, the woman had wrangled the precious beverage for her family, and she beamed with delight as smiles spread around the table.

She poured the wine slowly, almost ceremonially into each waiting cup. She served her father first—a choice that did not escape the notice of Heinrich. Then came Karl, Wil, and her husband in turn.

Dietrich smiled and winked at his daughter as he stared into his cup. "Ah, now you've proved your success! You've the means to buy wine! I'd often wished I could run off with the priest's chalice." He laughed. "Thanks to you, daughter, and God's blessings to all. Now, all drink!"

Heinrich again wished he could toss the old man out, this time into the April mud. It was his own role to offer his household the blessing of the season; it was the money *he* had earned that bought the cursed wine, not Dietrich's. But Heinrich also wanted peace, so, with another sigh he took a swallow of the cherry-red drink. It felt warm and smooth as it rolled over his tongue, bursting with life and flavor.

Karl and Wil smiled and rolled their eyes in ecstasy as the last drops were tapped from the recesses of their wooden cups. "Mother, 'twas like nothing I've e'er tasted," said Wil.

"Aye, *Mutti, ist wunderbar.* Have you more?" chirped Karl.

Marta basked in her glory. She turned to Heinrich. "Well, husband, have we the means to buy more?"

Heinrich was surprised to hear a tone that was somewhat deferential. He answered with a smile. "Ah, I do surely hope for it. You'd be a hard worker, Marta, and it gives me joy to see you pleased. More wine and someday a cloak of otter or a headdress of silk?"

Marta immediately suspected him of sarcasm and she tightened her face. It was a sad moment, for the man had been earnest, and when he saw her face harden his heart sank. Before Heinrich could respond, Dietrich stood up and hobbled to his daughter. His legs were failing and his back was now stooped. But his face was lit as he presented a gift to the curious woman. "Here, I've made you something."

Marta received a chain necklace and laid it across her palms. Her father had spent his evenings at the smith's, most thought spinning tales or drinking beer, but it seemed he had learned to fashion links of steel. "Father, I … I can hardly speak!"

"No need to answer," boasted Dietrich. "You've tended me well in my late years. You've done well for me. Yer not like your cursed brother! I want you to have this gift of m'own hands."

Marta embraced her father and she clasped the links around her neck. "I shall treasure it always."

❧

May Day eve found Marta gathering bushels of flowers and greens for the next day's celebration. She closed her eyes for a moment and wished nothing more than to be chosen the Queen of May. At her last confession, Father Pious had assured her that she was more than worthy of the honor. As a young girl the woman had been selected thrice for her beauty. Perhaps she was not the youngest any longer, but she hoped the village men might see her as still attractive. She had kept most of her teeth and her hair shined silky and smooth in the springtime sun. Her shape was broadened some by the births of five but was still pleasing to the eye, at least according to the whispers of Father Pious.

In the morning, the priest rose in the new house near Oberbrechen that the carpenters had built for him. Placed conveniently between Oberbrechen and Weyer, it afforded him both privacy and access to his two little empires. Furthermore, it gave him discreet access to the housemaid he kept in residence.

Following the advice of his predecessors, Pious traveled first to Weyer in order to offer a restrained and rather routine objection to the springtime festival The first of May was not sacred, nor was it noted on the Holy Calendar. Instead it was born of the ancient Romans who had called the day *Festival Floralia* in honor of the goddess Flora. The sight of the village women adorned with crowns of green leaves atop their braided hair gave the man a reason to wink at the celebration, however. So, instead of trying to ruin the day, Pious settled for a village prayer and a psalm before reaching for a tankard of warm ale.

The young men of Weyer raised a tall birch pole high into the air. It was decorated with flowers and leaves and a bright red ribbon. Beneath, the village began to dance and drink until the bells of nones when the queen was to be selected. Reeve Edwin called all to order. He had been elected reeve in Dietrich's stead the year prior, though few respected or liked the harsh man of twenty-seven. "All gather!" he roared. The village quieted and circled around the maypole.

"Quiet! Quiet, I say." He paused. "Good people of Weyer, we sing this day for luck in planting and in harvest. Times are yet hard but we've seen worse. I am told to keep an eye for trouble from Lord Conrad. Watch the wood across the stream. But today, sing and drink! The sun shines, the earth is warming. Ring your bells to wake the ground, for winter is now past!"

The crowd cheered and a hundred little bells tinkled in the air.

"Father Pious has agreed to help judge the May Queen. Father, your blessing?"

Father Pious waddled to the center. He loved the attention and strutted to the pole like a peacock before its hens. Wil stood between Karl and little Otto, the five-year-old son of Herold the new miller. Wil pointed a finger at Father Pious. "Look at him! He looks like, like some overfed boar! His robes can barely hold that lard-arse of his!"

"You ought not speak of him like that," answered Karl. The boy was nearly seven but had the honed conscience of a righteous monk. "He is a man of God You ought not—"

"Put a stopper in it, Karl! You needs not teach me. I've teachers enough!"

Father Pious stood on a stump and raised his hands over his flock. "I cannot bless this occasion but I do bless you in the name of our Lord Jesus and the Virgin." He made the sign of the cross in the air. "Now, it is time for me to nominate five for the office of Queen. The elders shall then call the vote of the men." The priest clutched his robe with two hands and rocked on his feet as he surveyed the crowd pressing close. He basked in the moment before speaking again. "Ah, I needs remind you that the choice may be for either youth or beauty or for kindness. And in this year we shall also think of those who have aged with grace."

Those last words gave hope to all women over fifteen! Marta elbowed her way closer to the priest and fixed a smile on the man. Pious narrowed his beady eyes at her. "Hmm. I confess I see more beauty here than ever in Oberbrechen!"

Weyer roared its approval. The priest smiled and waved and begged for calm. Heinrich was leaning on a shed post grumbling into his beer. "If she wins, Richard, she'll be impossible to endure. And if she loses, it'll be even worse!" The two had spent more time together of late. They howled and laughed until tears ran down their cheeks.

The priest began to point to his candidates. "You there, maiden."

A cheer rose from her kin. "Me?" she asked timidly.

"Aye, you! Come to the fore."

A young girl of about eleven stepped lightly toward Pious. She was willowy and tall, blonde, and fair. She turned to face the others and blushed.

"And you ... there."

Another young girl stepped forward. She had a bold step, however, and Richard muttered that her legs looked thick under her gown. She was brown-haired, buxom, and spirited. "Better ahead of the plough than behind," he chortled.

"Hmm. I pray God helps me!" cried Pious. The crowd tittered and waited patiently. The priest scanned the pressing folk until he spotted Katharina. She was standing at the edge of the crowd, shyly, and eyes cast down. Heinrich saw her too and his heart beat quickly. He had not seen her for months, for her cruel husband had kept her indoors for nearly every winter's day. Pious stared at her for a long moment. Her form was as one kindly, graceful and lean. *A bit old*, thought the priest. *But ...* He hesitated while Katharina died a thousand deaths. "You, there! Wife of Ludwig the Yeoman." The man pointed a chubby finger toward the woman and beckoned her.

Katharina closed her eyes and drew a deep breath. She wanted nothing of this silly game. She had been pleased enough to feel the sunshine on her face and needed nothing more. As she moved reluctantly toward the front she smiled politely and begged the pardon of those she bumped against. She stood with the other two and licked her dry lips nervously.

Heinrich left Richard and pressed his way closer. He caught her eye for a fleeting moment and she looked quickly away. At the same time her brutish husband bellowed from somewhere in the crowd, "She's mine! Y've no right to look at my woman!"

Meanwhile, Marta simmered. *Why that cow before me?* Suddenly she worried that Pious would not choose another matron.

The priest shifted his black robe and craned his balding head. "A gourd!" sneered Wil. "His head looks like some swollen gourd and his eyes peek out from his flab like ... like little acorns."

"Quiet!" scolded Karl. "You'll be doing penance again."

"There, you," called the priest. He had chosen number four from the far side of the common. She was another young one, barely of marrying age.

"She's the sister of that redhead, Ingrid," added Wil.

"Aye, and y'think Ingrid to be pretty!" teased Karl.

"Shut up, y'dolt!"

Irene, daughter of Franz the yeoman, now stood by Pious and smiled shyly to her cheering family. She waved and giggled and adjusted the white *Maiglücken* blooms tucked neatly in her hair.

"I've but one left to choose," announced Pious. He stretched his neck and scratched his head, furrowed his brow and folded his arms. The names of this one and that were shouted from the impatient folk until, at last, he smiled and motioned for calm. "Ah, good people, I have chosen!" He smiled and pointed to Marta. The woman feigned surprise and blushed. "Me? You pick me?"

Heinrich groaned as Richard jibed him. "You are s–surely one destined to suffer!" he slurred. "Look at her. She walks like someone p–planted a great stick in her rump! She's got the way of a she-wolf on the prowl, and ha, poor Katharina looks like a d–doe tangled in the brush!"

Reeve Edwin called the crowd to order and thanked the priest, but Pious was not quite finished with his plan. He cleared his throat and beckoned for Marta. He laid his arm over her shoulder and spoke sternly. "Men, hear me, and hear me well, for nothing happens on earth that is not noted in heaven:

Your spelt and wheat and oats and rye
I pray do yield you well,
But choose not she who tempts your eye
Else you shall end in hell!

Choose with care, choose not in jest

A queen to bless your ground.
Choose one proven and one blessed
And one whose spirit's sound."

Wil groaned. "A riddle!"

Karl smiled. He loved riddles.

The crowd remained quiet. In times past choosing the queen was a frivolous thing, but Father Pious's poem made it seem worthy of more care. They suddenly imagined their crops to be at risk and the fun was gone. They studied the candidates and murmured amongst themselves until Edwin called for their attention. "Now, are we ready?"

The crowd nodded.

"Good." Reeve Edwin put his hand on the first maiden's head. "All for this one?"

She received a polite applause and a few distant cheers. The young girl hung her head and stepped backward.

"And for this?"

Again, the same.

"And for Katharina?"

Heinrich held his breath. He wanted to roar his approval. A larger cheer rose from the men and a few shouts. She was in the lead.

Edwin reached for Irene. "And for this?"

Irene was a fresh-faced beauty to be sure, but it seemed Pious's poem had frightened away all support for the young ones. A few shouts from a group of boys wasn't enough.

Edwin turned to Marta who stepped forward hastily and smiled with feigned shyness. Wil and Karl hoped she would win, else "we'll have hell to pay at our own hearth!" grumbled Wil. Pious was the first to cheer and with his lead the men of Weyer roared their approval. And so, for the fourth time in her life, Marta, daughter of Dietrich, wore the purple, silken veil of Weyer's May Day Queen.

As Heinrich had feared, his wife spent the summer lording about the village like she was queen. Her friends followed like hurried goslings behind a goose. Anka, the dyer's wife, scrambled hither and yon fetching and stepping to keep

Queen Marta in a humor worthy of her status.

By late July it had become apparent that the empire's troubles would not be easing and the profits of the bakery began to dwindle. Worried and growing fearful, Heinrich sought out Lukas as he was picking *Eberesche* and pulling nettles in the forest by the Magi. "Ho, friend!" called Heinrich.

Lukas straightened and smiled. He stretched his old back and put down his pots. "Ah, Heinrich. Always a joy to see you."

"And you. Have you a few moments?"

"Aye, indeed." The two wandered to a log at the base of the three trees and faced the shimmering stream.

"Lukas, I've some fears 'bout m'bakery. Hard times seem to never end and the villagers seem less willing than ever to buy m'bread."

"Hmm. You've also repairs, firewood to buy, a helper or two to pay, and Marta has dreams that need be fed by shillings."

"*Ja.* Shilling-dreams by day and endless fears of the Judgment in the night. I do what I can to please her. As for the bakery, the tax gets ever higher. I thought when I owned it I'd feel more free than I do."

Lukas shook his head. "Nay, the power to tax is the power to own. You must know that you cannot stop them from raising it. I fear they'll force you to give it back by taxing the life out of you."

"Never! 'Tis mine and m'lads' after me!" The two sat quietly. Heinrich tossed a handful of pebbles into the clear water. "I wish Emma were here."

Lukas nodded. A blackbird landed nearby, then a thrush. A flicker banged his beak against a tree deep in the forest's shade and a swallow swooped atop the water. "This is a good place, Lukas. A place to think."

"And a place to dream."

Heinrich shrugged. "Have you a thought for my bakery? I needs earn more from it."

Lukas lay on his back and stared at the canopy of leaves arching from the ancient trees around him. "Yes. I do indeed. I've a thought or two on the matter. First, try this: folks buy what they think has worth. If you think your work has worth, then they shall as well. I've heard the free bakers in the guilds mark each loaf with a mark of their own. You, friend, are the owner; this is *your* bread! Be proud of it. Show others it has worth to you and mark it with *your* mark!"

Heinrich glowed. "Yes! A mark like the monks'. I could have a smith make an iron brand with m'own shape!" The baker laughed, pleased with the idea and begging for more.

Chapter 17

THE DECISION

$\mathfrak{J}$t was the first Thursday in September when Heinrich returned from his busy bakery to the wails and laments of Marta. He charged through the door to find his wife weeping and lying limp over the body of her father. Dietrich had been a heavy cross for Heinrich to bear and the baker felt a twinge of guilt for feeling great relief at the old miller's death. Father Pious entered next, and though Marta had rejected all attempts by her husband to offer comfort, she eagerly received a lingering embrace from the priest.

Dietrich was washed, shrouded in an expensive deerskin, and buried in Weyer's churchyard. The day of the man's burial was quiet, for few had any affection for the cheating, abrasive miller. His was another wasted life, and few gave more than a moment's note to its passing.

In the hovel a tiny gathering of mourners huddled over a table of bread, salted pork, and cider. Arnold was distant and cold as ever. He spent most of his days in Villmar, "conspiring with the prior," as Lukas once complained. But as wealthy as he had become, his life was empty and void of value. Richard, on the other hand, was less broody than he had once been and had begun to laugh again. In the past few years he had struggled to reclaim his former self and he was apt to tease and play about the village once more. He had bravely accepted the loss of one dream and had found the courage to dream again.

The village smith stopped by Heinrich's hovel at day's end and gave Marta a hammer and a small anvil that Dietrich had bought to use in those late nights by the furnace. Marta burst into tears as she ran her fingers along the necklace her father had made, and thanked the man. Heinrich bade the smith farewell, then turned to catch him on the pathway. Karl and Wil came trotting behind.

"Smith!" called Heinrich.

The man stopped and looked. "Aye?"

"How much to make me a baker's mark? A small stamp to press into my loaves."

"Uh, that would depend on the shape. Have you a drawing?"

Heinrich turned to Wil. "Boy, can you write in the dust, can you write 'Emma'?"

Wil brightened. "Of course, it begins with an *e*." The lad drew an '*E*' in the dirt with his finger.

The four studied the letter for a few moments until Karl suddenly cried, "Look, *Vati!* Draw the middle line all the way through and you've a cross!"

The man smiled. "Good lad! There, smith—there is m'mark!"

੩

By St. Michael's Day the baker was proudly stamping every loaf, roll, twist, and bun with his brand. And as Lukas had imagined, the village loved it. No longer were they buying only bread, but instead were buying the handiwork of one who cared. He had also learned to season his loaves with herbs and even honey. The bakery was suddenly paying its tax and yielding a pleasing profit. But Heinrich's heart was softer than his fresh-baked doughs and it often broke for the little ones who came and begged. So his bakery had also become a source of Christian charity for those in want. He found ways to stretch his flours just enough to feed what needy ones he could. Far from reducing the gain for others, his prosperity became a means for many to have more.

Between matins and morning lauds Heinrich rose from

his straw-mound bed, kissed the heads of his sons, and walked briskly toward his bake-house and met his apprentices.

"Good day, Rolf, and to you, Reinl." The sleepy boys nodded. Karl, now nearly six, would join his father at prime to aid in selling bread to travelers along the road. *A good occupation for the little chatterbox!* thought Heinrich. *He learns of riddles and tricks, songs, and legends from all parts and sells lots of bread!*

The baker set his goods in baskets by the door and set his coin box in its place beneath a shelf as his first patrons arrived. The first hour passed without incident, and all seemed well until Brother Lukas peeked through a shuttered window in the rear of the bakery. "Pssst! Heinrich!" he called in a hushed tone.

Heinrich turned about. "Lukas?"

"Shhh!" The monk beckoned him to come close.

Heinrich stepped to the window. "Why aren't you in chapter?"

Lukas shrugged. "No matter. We've other business. Come with me."

"But ... but m'patrons, I—"

"Nay! Leave them to the boys. You come!"

Heinrich hesitated, then removed his apron and slipped out the door to follow Lukas silently through the day's early light. The monk said nothing as they crossed the plank bridge spanning the Laubusbach and entered the wood. "Lukas, really, I've no time today for a talk at the Magi."

Lukas's voice was tight. "Keep walking, friend, and quickly. Now listen, it seems there was quite a battle yesterday on Lord Conrad's land. We knew nothing of it until late in the night. Conrad suffered a terrible slaughter, but he escaped by dividing his army into several parts. The Templars separated to give chase but were ambushed by mercenaries held in reserve."

Heinrich stopped. "So why is this our business?"

"Blasius is missing."

Heinrich felt a chill. Heinrich could still see the good man weeping for young Albert at the gallows. He would give his life to help Blasius despite his being a Gunnar. The baker suddenly thought of the words Uncle Baldric had spoken long ago: "Never deny the Code or the cause!" Heinrich had honored the Code and kept it well, but on this day the cause must end.

The two ran past the Magi, then hurried past the boundary poles of the abbey. Heinrich grew nervous. He cast an anxious glance at the monk who winked confidently and pressed on. At last the monk stopped. "Just over there," panted Lukas.

Heinrich followed the man's finger to a dip in the ground. "Why there?"

" 'Tis something of a secret. Blasius and I oft spy this land. He for his master, me for the thrill! Knowledge, Heinrich, is power. The Templars want control of all these lands, at least that is my thought. Blasius was sent here to spy and he brought me along. In that hollow is a deep spring, heavy timber, two small caves, and a bounty of herbs and berries."

"I'm off m'lord's lands."

"Aye, but you'd be doing the Lord's work."

Under full light of day, the two trotted quickly through an open field, ever vigilant for what other eyes might be watching. They hid against the trunk of a huge beech where Lukas abruptly warbled like a thrush. Heinrich's mouth dropped in astonishment.

Lukas warbled again. This time it was answered. The monk laughed with delight and hiked his black robes above his ankles. He led Heinrich carefully along a deer path and downward into the heavy shade of the hollow. The two walked slowly through cold, damp air until a low whistle was heard off to their right. Lukas froze and cocked his ears. He answered the whistle, and it echoed back to him. "There." He pointed.

Heinrich peered carefully between the trees and saw nothing until he followed Lukas a little farther and saw the figure of a man slumped against a fallen log. Lukas raced ahead. "Blasius!" he called in a hushed tone.

"'Tis I," the man answered.

Lukas embraced the young soldier and checked his

wounds. Blasius was badly cut across his left arm and his face was bloodied. He held his belly and mumbled he had been "de-horsed by a hammer."

Heinrich looked into the man's eyes. "Brother, all shall be well. We've brought bread from the best baker in all the Empire!"

Blasius chuckled, then groaned. "Aye, for certain. No rye, please!"

Heinrich laughed.

"Lukas, three of us came upon a company. Then ... then others came and ... it was just ... just to the west a few hundred paces. When I awoke, my comrades were dead and I crawled here."

Lukas nodded. It was midmorning and he was certain that a grand hunt was already on by both sides. It was dangerous to move, especially with a wounded man, but all the more dangerous to stay. "Can you walk?"

"Aye, m'legs are well, but m'lungs cut me and I cough blood some. But, Lukas, my brothers shall surely come. Templars leave none behind; 'tis our oath."

"I understand, but Conrad's men are searching as well and I think it more likely for them to find you here than your fellows." Lukas studied the man, then glanced at the sun above. He bent on his knees and lifted a prayer to the Almighty, recited the *Doxologia Minor* and smiled. "Now we go."

With that, the three began a tortuous climb out of the hollow and onto the wide, sun-swept ridge above. They crawled in the cover of tall grass to the protective edge of the forest where Heinrich propped Blasius against a tree and wiped the blood oozing from his lips with a cloth he had wetted in the spring. Lukas surveyed the field behind them and suddenly pointed to their hollow. "Look," he whispered. "Conrad's men riding in. God be praised, we would have surely been found! We needs move off, and fast."

Blasius groaned and gasped as he stood to his feet. Lukas was troubled and he looked squarely into the young Templar's face. "Blasius, you needs take off the armor. Heinrich shall carry you."

The soldier hesitated. Chain mail was costly—very costly. A baker would need to work for a year to pay for one man's chain-mail coat. "Your life has value, as well," snapped Lukas. "Now off with it! I'll stuff it under these rocks."

With a few grumbles and groans, the man was stripped of his heavy armor and hoisted upon Heinrich's broad back. Their load now lightened considerably, the three tripped their way through the heavy wood to the safety of Weyer.

ॐ

Marta had worried and pleaded with Heinrich for months. "I hear rumors everywhere that you crossed the boundary to save a Templar. Yet you told Father Pious you did not! A mortal sin. If you lied to the priest you shall surely earn us all a penalty on this earth and beyond!"

The woman's shrill voice turned the man's stomach. He shook his head and walked away. "Just leave it be, woman, just leave it be!" Indeed, the priest had confronted him three times with the story. Since leaving the manor was a very serious offense, Heinrich had reasoned he'd rather add to his secret sins than risk forfeiting his bakery. After all, he could always counter with another penance.

It was mid-June and Heinrich thought the unusual heat was a mild discomfort compared to the unyielding badgering he continued to endure from his nagging wife. She was now convinced that every bad bake, each leak of the roof, the near fire that Karl started in the hovel—all were warnings of greater woes to come. Marta spent hours with the priest, begging him to squeeze the truth from her husband.

Father Pious found the woman's fears to be opportune. He coveted the bakery for reasons of both ambition and of personal pride. He had cleverly negotiated the transfer of the brewery in Oberbrechen to the archbishop in Mainz and had received a letter of commendation. Weyer's bakery would be another prize—one formerly denied—and he was now more certain than ever that he could plot its capture. He also found the woman desirable. He was happy to spend as much time near her as he could. "Dear sister, how might I serve thee?" asked Pious one warm afternoon.

"Oh, good father. I can hardly live each day. I am so distressed at my husband's deceits, I know that ill shall befall m'self or m'sons."

Pious took her hand. "But, dear woman, Karl and Wil are both now sitting under the lindens in the abbey. They are in the good care of their schoolmasters, learning of God's ways. They are surely safe."

Marta nodded. "'Tis true, father, and I thank you. B–but what of me? What price must I pay for that man's evil? What am I to do?" She leaned toward him.

"Hmm. As his wife, you must stay in submission."

Marta nodded.

"But you are correct to reckon your risk, for the Scripture says that you and he are as 'one flesh.'"

Marta nodded nervously.

Pious stood and pondered the opportunity before him. He was not sure exactly how to proceed, but he was certain an advantage was in view. "I think it best that I speak to the man. I fear his sins are both mortal and venial. His eyes must be opened."

While Father Pious was comforting Marta, Heinrich walked through the village. It was midafternoon and the other men were hard at work in the fields. He thought he should be checking on Herwin's son, Wulf, who was working his land that day, but he knew that Wulf was as faithful and as hardworking as his father. Instead, Heinrich decided to take an unusual hour's respite.

The baker left the village and walked through the narrow fields of fresh-cut hay that lay by the Laubusbach. He strained an eye to find Herwin, who now sat in the shade with the other old men, sharpening scythes instead of swinging them. He happily strode toward the haymakers with few cares on his mind. Actually, he thought his adventure with the Templar had changed him some. News of the man's complete recovery had given him a good feeling and he felt proud for his part, despite the twinges of guilt he felt for having crossed the border. Not finding Herwin, he settled contentedly under one of the great oaks lining the Oberbrechen road.

The baker surveyed the fields filled with men swinging scythes, women binding sheaves, and oxen pulling two-wheeled carts. He watched the haymakers' entrancing rhythm until his eyes grew heavy. He laid back and imagined Emma picking flowers in her summer garden surrounded by flocks of hovering butterflies. He heard Ingly laughing in the Laubusbach and Richard giggling in the wood. The cool grass, the sweet-smelling hay, the lowing of oxen all lulled the tired man into a deep sleep.

Heinrich awakened as the bells of vespers clanged from both Oberbrechen and Weyer. He sat up, startled and surprised. A strong breeze brushed the curls off his slightly sweated brow and he looked about at the final carts being led away. He knew he ought to start toward home, for he had tasks in his garden to attend. The man stood up and stretched, then thought of his wife's likely reception and lay down once again. He faced the blue sky but kept his eyes closed; it felt good to him to keep his vow. At last he yawned and sat up. He looked about and eyed the approaching form of a familiar figure. "Katharina!"

Katharina had gleaned the fields of what cuttings were left behind and was prodding an ox gently toward the road. Heinrich stood and stared. Katharina saw the man and bowed her head timidly as she nudged her ox forward. Heinrich's heart beat quickly and he was overcome with a desire to speak to her. He pushed a creeping guilt away and called to the approaching woman. "Katharina. You'd be a bit behind the others."

"Aye," she answered softly. She kept her face turned away.

Suspicious, Heinrich trotted toward her. "Katharina?"

The woman kept her eyes downward. The man gently lifted her chin with his forefinger. He gasped. "Katharina!" The woman's face was badly bruised and swollen. Fury filled Heinrich's heart. "I shall ... I shall kill him!" he shouted.

Katharina's eyes filled with terror and she shook her head. Her lips were so swollen she could barely speak. "N–nay, good Heinrich. I beg you." Her tone was desperate and pitiful.

The man was enraged, but also overcome with compassion. He reached his arms toward her and pulled her tightly to his breast. Katharina began to sob and Heinrich felt all the more a man until a voice from the roadway sent a bolt of lightning down his spine.

"What is this?"

Heinrich spun around, ready to attack the woman's cruel husband. He snarled and snapped, "Who speaks?" His chest then seized and he faltered for words for it was not Ludwig, but Father Pious.

"You know who I am! Sinners! Caught in a lover's embrace!" The priest was scolding and loud.

Heinrich felt suddenly sick and shame washed over him like a cold cloudburst in November. "Nay, father, I was only offering comfort. Look at her, father, see her face."

The priest dismounted his weary donkey and brushed through the roadside bramble with a wagging finger and heated words. "Add not lies, Heinrich! Add not lies!" He pushed between the two and hissed spittle and fury from his purpled face. "Sinners be damned!"

Heinrich backed away and dropped his eyes.

"Do not hide your lust in mercy, man. Do you think me a fool?"

Heinrich stood, speechless and confused. *Indeed,* he thought, *perhaps there was some desire.*

"And you, woman!" Pious shouted as he turned his back on Heinrich. "Wife of one, mother of three! Whore! Scourge!" With those words the priest raised his hand and slapped the quivering Katharina across the side of her head. She whimpered and fell.

Heinrich's change was sudden and complete. His eyes burned and his teeth clenched. He grabbed the priest's cowl from the rear and jerked the man around. Then, with a warrior's cry he smashed his fist squarely into Pious's flaccid, fleshy face, first once, then twice, then a third time.

Pious staggered backward until a fourth blow dropped him groaning to the ground. The man lay motionless and bloodied, staring at the evening sky of June in disbelief and shock.

Heinrich stood over him, his legs straddled across the priest's wide girth. His fists were tight and readied for more; his nostrils flared in rage and contempt. "See to it, priest, that Ludwig's punished, else I shall do it m'self. And if you lay a hand on this woman again, I shall do you worse!"

Katharina burst into tears. Then, with a grateful look at her friend, she scurried toward her waiting ox and hurried home.

$\approx$

It was a long fortnight before Father Pious came pounding on Heinrich's hovel door. The baker had spent the time in a private agony of guilt, shame, and fear, for he was certain a harsh consequence would surely be the fruit of his behavior. Pious had been vacant from his pulpit and Father Albert served at the altar in Weyer, but Heinrich could not miss the hard eyes of his favored priest and knew the man was not ignorant of his offenses.

"Open, I say. Heinrich, open thy door!"

Marta answered. She was tired and worn from a day of summer's tasks but seemed to brighten at the sight of men of God in her doorway. "Father Pious ... and Father Albert? And, and Bailiff Werner?" Her eyes lingered curiously on Pious for just a moment. His white-bleached skin was spotted with light green bruises and the woman wondered.

"Poor, dear soul," began Pious. "Is thy husband here?"

Heinrich had just returned from his fields and was in the croft repairing the fence. He heard the men and came slowly to meet them. "I am here." A cold, clammy sweat came over him. Thunder rumbled in the east and a gust of wind stirred the dust on the footpath.

Werner glared at the man. His brown eyes were close set and penetrating. "You needs get inside!" he ordered.

Heinrich drew a deep breath and nodded. The five gathered in Heinrich's common room as a summer storm drifted closer. Pious began. "Marta, poor and blessed woman. You have spoken truly of thy fears and of your jeopardy. Indeed, your husband brings grave risk to this household. Thy children and thyself shall surely suffer for his sins. As our Scripture says, 'the sins of the father shall be visited upon the children.' I must ask you first if he has confessed himself to you?"

Marta was speechless. She shook her head and stared blankly at her husband.

"Hmm. We feared it to be so. Thy husband is guilty of much and for his sins he must do a great and mighty penance else you shall bear God's judgment. One of his dark secrets has been revealed—he has been unfaithful to you with another woman."

Marta cursed and wheeled about with curled lips and a clenched fist. The man protested, "Nay, nay! I've been true to you, woman, I've—"

"Enough!" roared Werner. "Keep silent, for there is far more."

Pious clutched his robes and lifted his pursed lips toward heaven. "Ah, 'tis true. There is much more." He laid his beaded, fat-pressed eyes on Heinrich. "Tell me, man, can you recite the seven deadly sins?"

Heinrich nodded.

"Then do so."

The baker thought for a moment. His mind was spinning and he wanted to run away. "Anger, avarice, envy ... gluttony ... lust, pride, and sloth."

"Well done. And can you recite the Ten Commandments?"

Heinrich did.

Pious nodded. "Seventeen warnings from God. And, one other, the most important of all?"

Heinrich shrugged.

"Love thy neighbor as thyself! Have you kept this one?"

The baker hung his head. Pious smiled. "Ah, perhaps you have loved thy neighbor's ... wife?"

Marta's face became as dark as the sky outside her hut. "What is this about, husband!"

Bailiff Werner answered. "He has been seen holding another's wife, he has struck a priest, he—"

"Struck a priest!" cried Marta. "Struck a priest? My God, we shall all be damned! You fool, you wicked fool!"

Pious pointed his finger at Heinrich. "I have sought

counsel with my superior in Mainz and with my brother, Father Albert. We have all agreed that you have violated all these eighteen demands of God. Thy many sins are mortal. Thy miserable soul is worthy of utter damnation and thy household cannot but be in harm's way. I know no man more evil than you! You are known for your charity to the poor? Ha! A ruse. You are thought to be clever and shrewd in matters of business, but a deceiver is what I see! Hypocrite, liar, thief, adulterer, man of murderous intent, envious, slothful, haughty, greedy; I could go on!

"Your assault on my own person is worthy of penalty in both Church and lay court. With a word to Werner I can have you taken to Mainz and then to Runkel for flogging, or thumbing, or worse." He leaned forward. "Perhaps you ought lose the bakery?"

Marta was suddenly uncertain whether she ought to feel outrage or fear. She hated her husband for his offenses but feared the loss of the comforts he provided. She stepped forward and looked at Pious with pleading eyes. "Father, I fear so for m'boys. Could he not confess and do some heavy penance?"

It was the question Pious was burning to hear. He had already been told it was unlikely the man would forfeit his bakery—a harsh penalty like that would have created an unmanageable uproar among the free men of the manor. He paused and feigned merciful reflection. He lowered himself dramatically upon a squatty stool and picked at his ear. "Hmm. Perhaps. You are, indeed, a woman of tender spirit, one in touch with heaven. Hmm. I would not deny his absolution with proper confession, and I do imagine a heavy penance might reduce his temporal debt." He let hope prosper in silence. Marta held her breath and her eyes widened. The priest leaned forward and whispered, "Yet, I fear thy whole household must make a sacrifice fitting to the offense."

"*Ja, ja?*"

Father Albert was suddenly nervous. Lightning flashed across the evening sky and a clash of thunder shook the hut.

Pious sighed. "His confession must be sincere and if so, I shall not deny him God's grace. As far as the necessary penance, however, I should think for the Holy Trinity we need three shirtless belly-crawls to Oberbrechen while reciting the *Ave* and the *Pater Nostra*; for the disciples, twelve Sabbath fasts; for the two Testaments, two barefoot pilgrimages to the walls of the abbey. And one more ... hmm."

Heinrich was staring aimlessly. He had spent much time during the past two weeks considering his sins. *I was unfaithful in m'heart,* he concluded, *and had murderous intent, and was prideful, and filled with sloth that day.* He had already spent days reciting the Commandments and concluded he truly was guilty of all. Shame washed over him like the torrent of rain now crashing on the village.

"For Mother Mary, he must willingly release the bakery to the parish."

None spoke. The falling rain was all that could be heard. Father Albert looked at Pious incredulously and turned a now sympathetic eye toward the baker and his wife.

Marta gasped. "But, but father, if we lose his bakery then we all suffer for this miserable man's failings!"

"One flesh, dear sister."

Heinrich stiffened. Guilt-ridden or not, he had been pushed beyond his limit. Anger chased away his melancholy. He looked at his wife and wanted to vomit. Then he looked at Pious and his hands closed into fists. He fixed his eyes on the priest and held his stare for a long, agonizing moment.

The rain slowed to a steady patter on the thatch above and all waited. Heinrich's heart pounded within him, yet he said nothing. He listened to the rain and the trickling rivulets of water just beyond his door. His thoughts drifted the Laubusbach and he began to grow calm. His fury faded quickly and his mouth felt dry. In another moment his mind was seized again by accusing thoughts: *I am an evil man.* The baker could not speak. His fists relaxed and he sighed. Much of him wanted to surrender the bakery if only it would finally free him of the shame and the confusion that was driving him to madness.

Words of submission began to form on Heinrich's lips and Pious leaned forward, waiting anxiously. The baker paused. He suddenly pictured dear Emma by the Magi and he thought he could hear her voice whispering words of wisdom in his ear. Heinrich raised his chin. "I shall offer my confession to Father Albert, and will consider your penance under advice from others."

The satisfied twitch of Albert's lips told Marta that her husband would not lose the bakery. Frustrated and furious, Pious rose and leaned toward the baker. "You shall yield a heavy penance," he hissed. "For it is due me!" The priest cast a scheming eye toward Marta. "Poor woman. I shall pray for God to rescue you. Until then, stay clean in spirit and in flesh, for you are surely in grave danger."

~•

Heinrich wept on his knees alongside a sympathetic Father Albert. His confession was heartfelt, though rambling, yet the tortured man left the church still unsure of his heavenly absolution. With hope obscured by doubt, he spent the miserable harvest of 1206 doing every sort of penance Marta's wild imagination could demand. He reasoned that he truly needed to suffer harsh earthly penalties for the heavy sins forgiven in heaven, yet his instincts shielded him from Pious's self-serving demands.

By the bitter days of the Epiphany Marta insisted that Heinrich do a belly-crawl to Oberbrechen and Heinrich complied. His contrition was confusing him, however, for though he felt sorrow and shame for his imperfections and his failings, he also felt a growing hatred for the very penances intended to reconcile him to those offended. He found no relief and his only joy was in knowing that his sons were far away in the abbey and not witness to his embarrassing distress. Given his ambivalence, he was also further convinced that his soul and those of his family were surely in jeopardy of a terrible lingering in Purgatory, perhaps now more than ever.

By summer, poor Heinrich wished he might just fly away. He enjoyed neither his days in the bakery nor his Sabbath walks, for everywhere he went he did not fail to see the sneers on others' faces or the malice in their tone. Most now believed him to be filled with deceptions, ill-will, hidden hatreds, and untoward desires. News had also reached his ears that Katharina had been beaten by her husband more than once for the rumors spread about her and the baker. Heinrich confronted him twice but the man would not be goaded into striking first.

Good Richard remained faithful and true, and Lukas did what he could to encourage and embolden the man. On a few occasions even Blasius made a special effort to bring a cheery wish or kind word. So Heinrich endured. He denied himself all thoughts of Katharina and agreed with Lukas that such desires were, indeed, not in keeping with God's ways.

Yet, news of Katharina's beatings tortured him, prompting him to make the mistake of begging Father Albert to protect her. He was warned that any assault on Ludwig would cost him the bakery and land him in Runkel's lethal dungeon. Hopeless and desperate, Heinrich wanted to raise his eyes to heaven and beg for mercy. "Look beyond the sun," Emma used to say. "Hope lies in heaven, dear boy," she would cry. But he did not look beyond the sun, for he thought the keeping of his horrid vow to be his lone surviving virtue.

~

On a cool and blustery Sabbath day in early September, Father Pious returned to Heinrich's door. He was accompanied by a well-dressed man who identified himself as Bernd, a deputy of Lord Heribert. Bernd gawked about the hovel and lifted a lip in some contempt. "Heinrich," said Pious flatly, "'tis time your account is settled. I've come to you this day to spare your life and that of fair Marta."

Marta nervously bade the two inside, and scurried to fetch some bread and wild plums. She placed a pitcher of ale atop her table and two tankards, and cast a look at Pious that did not escape her husband's notice.

"As you know, baker, for the sake of thy wife and children I have been seeking counsel for your penance yet due."

Heinrich stiffened. He had known this day would surely come.

Pious's voice tightened. "And, good Marta, I've sought a way that preserves your own good standing." He had found little choice but to design a new path to his prize, one that required a few extra steps.

Marta smiled.

The priest pointed to Bernd. "This man comes with news that is most unusual and I am quite certain it is God's answer to my prayers. Sire, please tell of your needs."

Bernd studied Heinrich for a long moment. *Broad-built, though a bit old,* he thought. *A bit beaten of spirit? But seasoned, perhaps, and not one to risk mutiny or escape.* He cleared his throat. "How old are you, man?"

Heinrich wasn't sure. "I am not certain."

Pious interrupted. "Brother Martin tells me you are near the age of Christ at His death."

Heinrich shrugged. "How old was that?"

"Thirty-three," snapped Bernd. "That makes you older than many. You've survived much and I am told you are a good baker."

Heinrich shrugged again.

"Yes, and you understand that elder men are less important to a growing village than the younger ones."

Heinrich remained silent.

"Let me come to the matter. The Holy Church has called on my lord, Heribert, to support her in parts far north of here. As if the civil war was not enough, it seems Archbishop Hartwig of Bremen has a need to protect his diocese from some rebellious serfs who would deny their Church her proper taxes, rents, tithes, and the like."

Heinrich leaned forward. The words "rebellious serfs" were suddenly appealing. "What men are these?"

"Some wild and untamed Frisians; peasants who have strayed. Lord Heribert's cousin is the Count of Oldenburg and has called on Heribert to satisfy a debt by providing assistance."

Heinrich was curious. "And why, sir, are you here?"

"Yes, of course. My lord is sending a small troop to help

the archbishop, and I am charged to support them with servants, groomsmen, cooks, armorers, and others. We've a terrible shortage with our losses in the war, so I am to recruit some from the villages." He turned to Pious. "If you have not already learned, the pope has abandoned his support of Otto and now allies with Duke Philip."

Pious raised his eyes. "And then what of the Templars?"

"Aye, the blessed Templars. Like us they follow the pope wherever he may go. Seems they imagine him to be infallible. Incredible! The local preceptory is to send one of theirs with us—as a spy, methinks. The abbot has permitted us to take servants from among his serfs as payment toward his contract with us, and he has graciously offered free rents for the time spent. Father Pious and the bailiff have suggested you to go."

Marta looked pleased and she smiled at her priest.

Pious nodded. "*Ja*, Marta, this is somewhat easier than what is truly deserved, but I have seen that you have called him to tasks of obedience and suffering these many months."

"But what of my bakery?" quizzed Heinrich.

"The commission is for the usual forty days, a most manageable time."

The priest grunted. "You shall be home by Advent. And more, you may be pleased to know that your cousin, Richard, is a most eager recruit, as well. Seems he's a few matters of his own to settle under God!"

Heinrich was all the more tempted. *Oh, a chance to fly, to be away from this place—away from her, and an adventure with Richard ... like we are boys again!* He quickly condemned himself. *Nay, it is to be a penance ... a serving of the Church in her time of need.* He looked at the faces staring at him. "Forty days you say?"

"Aye."

Heinrich hesitated. The penalty seemed too light and he did not trust Pious. But he desperately wanted to feel clean and he wanted peace returned to his mind. Despite Lukas's pleadings to the contrary, he had become obsessed with the fear that his sons would soon suffer because of his failings. He needed to be sure this would save them all. "I am not certain, father, that this is penance enough for my sins. It seems ... somewhat gentle."

Bernd laughed. "Gentle?" the deputy scoffed. "It shall not be an easy time! Indeed not. You shall be required to carry firewood and cook, lift carts out of mud, push them through fords. The knights shall demand much of you. And worse, you are helpless in ambush and there are oft attacks. We've lost more servants than soldiers while traveling the Empire! The civil war has brought naught but confusion. If attacked, the knights have armor and you have nothing. When the enemy fears to engage our knights, they creep into camp to slaughter the servants, then disappear, leaving the knights to cook their own supper! Ha! It is not a light thing."

Heinrich was satisfied; the plan seemed to give God a wealth of opportunities to punish him properly. "Father," he asked, "this penance covers all my sins?"

"More than likely. You'll need report thy sufferings upon thy return."

Marta did not approve of that answer. "But father, if he fails to return and is not absolved, shall I be at risk for—"

"Fear not, sister. If your husband fails to suffer enough I shall find some other way to finally absolve you and your brood. You must trust in me." He picked a dark, caraway-seasoned roll from the breadbasket and lifted it to his nose with a wry smile.

Ignorant of his secret schemings she was satisfied and grunted her approval.

Heinrich listened carefully. He stared at Pious, aware that the ambitious priest was setting some kind of snare. *But what can happen in forty days?* he wondered. The baker looked at Marta. *She'll keep the bakery safe; she's too much greed to let it slip away. And if I die, Lukas shall surely protect the bakery for m'sons. I do own it.* He paused to consider Wil and Karl. *Only forty days, free rents to put in the strongbox, the lads released from my sin and still safe in the abbey—and time away from Marta.*

Moved by an anguished desire to feel clean and whole

and free, Heinrich's heart pounded as he wrestled within himself. Yet it was not reason, nor fear, nor shame, nor secret curiosity that finally prodded the man's assent. Instead it was an irresistible sense of something greater than himself urging him to fly. He closed his eyes and let his spirit yield to the call of a silent voice. The weary man nodded. "Yes! I shall go."

Book 2

*Die Verwandlung
(The Wandering)
1206 – 1212*

Chapter 18

FAREWELL

It was the ninth day of October in the Year of our Lord 1206 when Heinrich stood anxiously at his hovel's door. The bells of prime had just sounded as the man prepared to bid his family farewell. The air was damp and chilly; a stiff breeze brought a hint of rain from the east and the sky was gray. Heinrich had expected to leave by St. Michael's Day but there had been numerous delays—something the man hoped did not portend things to come.

Heinrich rubbed a set of bruised knuckles and cast a nervous glance at Reeve Edwin now racing along the footpaths in search of his gray, scruffy dog. The baker had always pitied the bright-eyed creature and now hoped he had run far, far away. But Heinrich had another reason to hurry and could delay no longer. He fussed with his clothing one last time, shifting about in his woollen leggings and hooded tunic. He stamped his feet and admired the heavy-soled boots that his new master, Lord Niklas, had sent him. The anxious man took a deep breath, placed a thick, brown, woollen cape over his shoulders, and slung a leather satchel across his neck. In this he had put some salted pork, a loaf of spelt bread, a flask of mead, and a withered, red flower from Emma's now abandoned garden. He also put a small, flat stone from the Laubusbach on which he had etched his baker's mark in memory of his beloved Emma and the bread of truth she had so lovingly shared with him. "Ah, Karl!" he said as he bent on one knee. "Stay happy, lad. Learn your riddles and your lessons well. And don't bedevil the monks!"

The round-faced redhead smiled, halfheartedly, then tightened his face to stifle the tears. "*Vater*, must you go? I want you to stay ... I may never see you again."

Heinrich's eyes swelled and a thick lump filled his throat. He loved the boy, now nearly eight, and suddenly wondered if he was making the right decision. Marta's crisp voice turned his head.

"They must be waiting by now."

Heinrich nodded. "Aye." He laid a tender hand on Karl's curly head. The lad tried to offer a brave smile but his chin quivered and his lips simply twisted. Heinrich next turned to Wil. The lanky lad had just turned eleven. His eyes were light blue and keen. His flaxen hair shimmered in the October sun, but his feelings were buried deep in dark places. Heinrich laid his hands on the boy's shoulders and Wil stiffened. Heinrich eased his touch slowly and sadly. "Wil, I ... I shall surely miss you as well. I will imagine you under the monk's linden, and I'll return after my forty days." Wil nodded and said nothing. He did not believe his father would ever return.

Heinrich turned a swollen, sorrowful face to his wife. "I ... I am truly sorry, woman, for what pain I have caused you and our children. I shall surely work to ... to give you what you have always longed for. I mean to restore m'soul to the proper ways and save you all from my shame." He glanced about the gray, smoke-choked village and handed Marta a small, folded paper with a trembling hand. "Here's the abbot's pledge that pays the rents."

The man wished he could do something more, something that might chase away the misery of what was and replace it with the glory of what might have been. He considered his sons and then his woeful wife. *What a failure I am*, he groaned to himself, *that I must do this thing to repair the mess I've made!* The broken man looked to Marta for hope. How he longed to hear her say something gentle, something kind. His heart would have soared at nothing more than a light touch of her hand or a forgiving smile. And, oh, how he would have felt had she offered even one word of contrition for her own vexing ways. For one such word the man would have forgotten and forgiven all to embrace her with a heart as big as the whole of heaven! But the hard, unyielding barrenness in the woman's eyes chased all hope away and the beaten man's chest released a weighted sigh.

Marta tightened her shoulders and folded her arms across the apron covering her simple gown. "Godspeed, husband," she stated tonelessly.

Heinrich nodded and turned once more toward his sons. He battled his melancholy to offer them a smile and, with a lingering, doubt-filled gaze, the man walked away.

❧

"Where have you been?" roared Richard from the sheepfold gate. "I've been standing here since the bells and I've heard quite a gossip!" He smiled and wrapped an eager arm around his cousin. "What of Ludwig? Eh?"

Heinrich glanced nervously over his shoulder. "We'd best hurry. I'd some hard time leaving."

"Ha, not me! Brunhild was happy to see me off. She's already spent the rents, methinks!"

"Then you've come to peace with our new master?"

Richard darkened. He held up his twisted right hand. "I shall never come to peace with that bastard, but I may yet find m'revenge on this journey."

Heinrich grunted in disapproval as the two strode quickly out of their village and hurried toward Villmar. A light, morning rain drizzled on the grumbling pair as they entered the village. The market square was crowded with oxcarts and pungent with wet dung and urine. The harvest had been good and barrels of apples and wild plums were filled to overflowing. Richard snagged a fat, red apple and pointed. "There, that looks like our lot!"

In the center of the market, by the well, waited a grumbling group of recruits atop a two-wheeled cart. They seemed confused and impatient as Heinrich and Richard approached. "Are ye two of Weyer, for Lord Niklas?"

"Aye," answered Richard with a mocking bow.

The cart driver stared at Richard's hand. "Does the lord know of that?"

"Aye, he ought!"

"Get in," groused the driver. "You'd be the last and yer late."

Heinrich climbed behind Richard onto the plank-floored wagon where the two met their fellows. Wishing to appear confident and self-assured, Richard barely acknowledged his new companions and chose to mumble an insincere greeting before leaning against the chest-high wagon wall.

Heinrich sat on the wooden floor and leaned his back against the tilting wagon. He surveyed the others and slowly made his acquaintance with them. "I am Heinrich of Weyer, and that man is m'cousin, Richard."

A young, brown-eyed lad, perhaps fifteen years of age, eagerly greeted Heinrich. "Good cheer to you, sir. My name is Emil of Runkel. And this is Rosa and her cousin Ita from Runkel as well."

Heinrich smiled politely. Rosa and Ita were young beauties, both of marrying age. Ita glared at him from within a woollen hood. "What ye be lookin' at, old man?" she barked.

Heinrich blushed. "Ah, maiden, I ... I was only wondering why you'd be joining us."

"Lord Niklas wants fullers, we're told. And he's payin' a fair price for the two of us."

"Ah, of course. Fullers." Heinrich turned toward the other three sitting quietly. "And who be you?"

Two men dropped their hoods. "I am Leo and this is m'brother Lenz. We'd be shepherds by Lindenholz." The two seemed friendly and earnest. Heinrich clasped hands with them and turned to the remaining man who was crouched tightly against the cart's front corner.

Heinrich stretched his hand forward. "I am Heinrich," he offered.

The man nodded curtly and looked away.

"He is called Samuel," offered Emil. "He's a Jew from Limburg."

Richard turned a hard stare. "A Jew? I've never seen a Christ-killer before."

The man spat and closed his eyes.

It was nearly noon when the wagon of servants arrived within the walls of Runkel's brown stone castle. The rain had eased a little and the conscripts were ordered to stand by a generous fire inside the castle grounds. They stood obediently and warmed themselves until two large knights strode toward them with shouts, oaths, and waving arms. Confused and frightened, the huddle of peasants backed against a stone wall where they stood to be inspected.

Each was eyed from head to toe, turned around, and poked and prodded like livestock at the market. "You've more teeth than most," growled Lord Niklas as he yanked Heinrich's jaw open.

"Huh-uh," offered the baker.

The knight stared at Heinrich. "Can y'bake bread that shan't kill us?"

"Aye, sire."

"Humph. And can y'cook other things?"

"Aye."

"You're a bit old ... you've some gray on that red head and gray stubble on yer jaw."

"Aye, sire." Heinrich nearly laughed out loud, for the knight was about the same age!

Niklas moved on to Richard. The two locked eyes. The knight grabbed hold of Richard's short-cropped hair with a laugh. "Glad to see y'found yer proper place!"

Richard pushed the knight's hand away and growled. With that, Lord Niklas jerked his sword from its sheath. He pinned Richard's head against the wall with the palm of one hand as he laid his blade's edge against the peasant's exposed throat. "You'd like to avenge yer hand, wouldn't ye? Eh? Speak, man!" Niklas grabbed Richard's crippled hand and held it high. "If your right hand offends you, cut it off!" he shouted.

Lord Simon joined the two. The aging knight was leathery and worn. Gray hair fell to his shoulders and a long, gray beard framed a face wrinkled by war and weather.

"Enough, sir! He's a good man and shall serve well. I stake my honor on it." The fire in Simon's dark eyes was enough to still the impetuous Lord Niklas.

Niklas leaned close to Richard. "Let the past stay there!" he muttered. "I meant you no harm then ... or now."

Richard's blue eyes never moved from Niklas's face. The knight sheathed his sword and moved on to inspect his other servants.

"Y'needs be more careful!" scolded Heinrich.

Richard was still bristling. "Put a stopper in y'mouth, cousin. 'Tis my fight, not yours."

A familiar voice turned their heads. "Peace be unto you!"

"Ah, and to you!" shouted Heinrich. He was smiling from ear to ear as his friend, Blasius, the Templar, approached. The two embraced and the warrior-monk turned to greet Richard.

"A wonderful day!" cried Heinrich. "Look at us! Together in a common cause, serving our Church and each other." The baker suddenly beamed with joy. It was an amazing thing for him to feel more than a simple tradesman. Instead he felt important and he delighted in the new sense of purpose.

A black hood peeked from around a corner. From deep within its recesses spread a huge smile. "Brother Lukas!" roared Richard.

"Shhhh!" hushed the jovial old monk as he trotted toward his friends. "I've been caught thrice out of the monastery and am supposed to be in prayer! Ha! I'd rather see m'dearest friends off on their adventure." Lukas gave each a mighty hug. "My prayers shall follow you where e'er this journey takes you. Now, on your knees, each of you."

Heinrich, Richard, and Blasius obediently bent and bowed as the monk laid his age-marked hands on each of them. He prayed loudly and boldly, urging the kingdom of God to offer them "shield and buckler from the wiles of Satan and the ignorance of man." When he finished he kissed Blasius and Richard on each cheek, but took Heinrich by the elbow.

Lukas walked the baker some distance from the others

and paused by a dozing ox. Lukas looked deeply into Heinrich's patient face and began to speak with a gentle, pleading voice. "Good man," he began, "my heart aches as I behold you here, in this place, about to leave in this service. My son, for all the many years I have loved you, I have prayed you might leave your darkened path. Your captive conscience binds the man that bears God's image deep within. You have allowed others to chain you to the madness that rules our world because you turn your eyes away from truth and have closed your ears to wisdom!

"You have denied yourself the joy of the butterfly. You have yet to pleasure in the glory of a wildflower. You've not warmed your face in the sun, nor washed your eyes in the colors of a rainbow since you were a mere boy! You have ne'er danced to the music of the Scriptures, nor delighted in your Maker. Listen, dear friend, I beg you. Abandon your wicked vow; oppose the deception of this empty world that is so terribly familiar to you. Dare to look beyond what you know! Truth is outside yourself, man, and is searching for you. Seek it with your eyes, listen for it; quiet your mind and let it find you, let it free you!"

The baker stiffened. "Lukas, I am in no mood for this! Look, there." He pointed to a knot of knights receiving their blessing from a priest. "And there." He pointed to a large wooden crucifix mounted against the courtyard wall. "And listen." The bells of sext began to ring. "All around us is the way I know. Is it so terrible? Is it so pointless?"

Brother Lukas paused for a moment. He laid a gentle hand atop the baker's shoulder. "Listen, good, faithful, devout Heinrich. It seems you truly believe that your way, your *Ordnung*, is neither binding nor blinding nor dark. Nor do you believe it is contrary to either Scripture or the way of nature."

Heinrich waited.

"So I ask you this as your old friend: if your eyes are ever opened to its terror or your heart ever iced by the draught of its empty void ... would you then turn and look beyond?"

Heinrich relaxed and thought for a moment. "I readily admit m'world is not perfect."

"Agreed, perfection is not yet come. But what if you discovered that your way is more than just imperfect? What if you find that it is so very imperfect as to offer little more than poor shadows of truth? Would you then turn from it to find a better way?"

The baker stood silently for a long pause as the knights readied their column. "Has the sound of Emma's song."

Lukas smiled at the memory of the blessed woman. "*Ja, my son.*"

Heinrich looked about the castle grounds at the knights, the kneeling priests, the banners fluttering under the scattering clouds. He felt good to belong to such a world. From this vantage, all seemed true enough. He hummed Emma's tune and smiled. "... Come flutter 'tween flowers, sail o'er the trees, or light on m'finger or dance in the breeze ... ."

The baker looked at old Brother Lukas waiting breathlessly for an answer. He remembered watching the black-robed rascal sneaking through the forests to gather his herbs before spending a day of laughter with his friends at the Magi. Heinrich knew he could not deprive the old man hope, not for all the world. Heinrich took Lukas by the shoulders and looked at him kindly. "Aye, good friend. If I find the *Ordnung* to be terrible or wickedly empty, I shall leave this way of things and let another find me. It is then, Brother, I shall break my vow and face the sun."

❧

It was a full fortnight before Lord Heribert's column was finally ready to make its journey northward. Several of his knights had traveled from manorlands in the Duchy of Bavaria, a few from lower Swabia, and one from Styria far to the southeast corner of the empire. The latter was delayed in the Brenner Pass and had suffered the loss of several servants to the swords of some highwaymen. Finally, however, on the twenty-third of October, Heinrich, Richard, Blasius, and a column of thirteen mounted knights, four mounted archers, twenty-two well-armed footmen and an assortment of some forty servants began their journey northward under the command of Lord Simon.

Heinrich's heart fluttered like the standards snapping in the wind above his head. He had never stepped foot on another's land, save for the time he helped rescue Blasius with Brother Lukas some years prior. Now he was about to march into a new world, one he had only imagined. He smiled at the knights' ladies who waved their colorful kerchiefs from tiny windows high within the castle walls and waved to the peasants staring enviously at him as he passed them by. Yet, despite his jubilance, he shared the fears of the knights who had earlier complained that they had no priest to accompany them. Without the protection of a priest they'd pass through dark forests and cross deep waters void of God's protection. The priest, it seemed, had fallen ill the night before and none others could be spared. It was an omen that troubled the whole of the column and fear hung as heavy over the company as the dark clouds above. Only Blasius, the warrior-monk, might serve to forestall the wiles of Satan's minions.

Since seventeen days had already passed since he had left Weyer, the baker also wondered about the "forty-day" contract. Blasius told him he had heard the march to be about seventy leagues. Considering they'd be transversing popular highways through a flattening landscape, the Templar reckoned their travel time to be about six or more leagues per day. According to his calculation, the company should arrive in Oldenburg within a fortnight. Leaving a week for battle, and another fortnight to return, he assured Heinrich they should all be safe in Weyer before Christmas.

Things rarely go as planned, however. Under a blinding torrent of rain, the column followed the swollen Lahn River toward Marburg where additional provisions were waiting with another small company of men-at-arms. Simon's army lost two wagons and an unfortunate servant in the currents of a flooded ford. The knights were now more certain than ever that this was the beginning of a doomed campaign.

After a brief rest in Marburg's hilltop castle the army returned to the highway that would lead them roughly northward toward the growing Hanseatic city of Soest. The meandering road was sometimes shin-deep in mud, creating a special hardship for the servants, like Heinrich and Richard, who were forced to push heavy wagon wheels through sucking ruts. Agitated and wet, the travelers slogged forward along the normally pleasant and crowded route.

Several miserable days later they entered the gates of Soest, where Lord Simon directed his cold, soaked troops, past the Petrikirch and into the warmth of the burghers' halls. It was a great relief to all and the generous addition of roasted meats and countless kegs of Westphalian ale soothed the men and lifted their spirits. Two days later and very much drier, the army resumed its journey.

It was Simon's hope that his sluggish column might hurry through Westphalia without further delay. His army was imposing enough to give pause to the roving bands of knights known to ambush many on this route, and no mere highwaymen would dare an adventure against them. Yet the cursed rain seemed to be the one enemy he could not dissuade, and the frustrated commander could do little more than turn his face against the gray sky and grumble.

The rolling land just north of Soest was covered in dripping pines and bothersome streams. Numerous moated castles were hidden in the center of forest villages, like the octagon keep at Bad Iburg, which sent a party of menacing knights to the shoulder of the road. Runkel's little army had no heart for drawing swords; they'd rather be drinking beer in the city of Münster some four leagues to the east. They paid a modest toll and pressed on.

The thought of Münster's warm hearths had been tempting, indeed, and as they neared the city the knights craved them all the more. Their fear, however, was the uncertainty of its position in the empire's civil war. Heribert's men had followed the pope's new choice, Duke Philip, but it was rumored that Münster was still supporting Otto.

Simon led his company toward the city with reluctance. Then, with the Budden Tower in view, he balked. He decided he would turn away from Münster after all, and despite the loud objections of his captains, he pointed his army toward a more certain reception in Osnabrück. Longing for a dry bed and hot soup, the knights complained bitterly as they followed their leader north through a lowering landscape and to the banks of the swollen Ems River.

"Old fool!" barked Niklas. "We can't cross here! We'll lose all."

Normally narrow and lazy, the Ems was typically a sluggish, easily forded river. Given the unusual rains of the season, however, it had risen over its banks and brown water now swirled at the ankles of the frustrated knights. Simon gathered his captains to review their situation. In the last week, two servants had perished from fever and one knight had turned back from the discomforts he claimed were beneath his station. The cold rain had kept the men limited to the warmth of a few smoky fires contained within some iron kettles. The baker's clay oven could not maintain its heat so no bread had been baked, and without boiled water the men could not even eat a peasant's mush. The impatient, pampered lords were accustomed to roaring hearths and hearty foods in their great halls and lodges. To the secret delight of their servants, they had been reduced to eating cold, salted pork and a few dried fish.

The conversation by the riverbank became heated. All finally agreed that Münster was a risk, but Simon's indecision had been inexcusable and had cost them valuable time. So, in less than half an hour, Simon's good friend, Lord Wolfrum, spearheaded a mutiny and assumed command. Crafty, fleshy-faced, and brutal, Lord Wolfrum had been favored all along. The new leader abruptly ordered the small army westward along village roads near the Ems until they found a creaking bridge near Warendorf. Once across the river he quickly directed his column to the trade route leading to Osnabrück.

The shivering, wet army set up camp each night, with the exception of two small monasteries that hosted them briefly. The wagons were pulled close together, the horses tethered to trees. Each servant scampered about his duties—except for poor Rosa and Ita who did their best to hide in the dark recesses. Since they feared the terrors of the spirit-filled forests even more than the soldiers, they rarely dared venture far from the camp's edge. Unfortunately, they were stripped of the dignity nature had kindly given them and suffered the sad consequences of their gender.

Heinrich shook his head each night. The glory he had felt in Runkel had slowly faded into a seething disgust as he watched the knights denigrate the women, or savage other servants with straps or sticks. It was Blasius, however, who gave Heinrich hope. The devout warrior-monk had not missed a single prayer in the weeks they had traveled. Each morning he dutifully recited twenty-eight *Pater Nosters,* and at each approximated canonical hour he sang or recited other prayers or psalms.

Yet Brother Blasius was distressed at heart. Outwardly he seemed strong-willed, resolute, and devout. Over chain-mail tunic and breeches, he proudly wore his white robe embroidered at the left breast with a vivid red, Templar cross—easily recognized from afar with its distinctive blunt, wedge-shaped arms. He dutifully bound his robe with a braided, leather cord, which signified his vow of charity. However, since Templars were to avoid the proximity of women, Blasius was uncomfortable with the presence of those accompanying the column. More than that, he was enraged at the wicked attention foisted upon them, and he had risen in defense of Ita on the first night of the journey. Blasius's master, Brother Phillipe de Blanqfort, had commanded the man's sworn obedience to the authority vested to the lay knights, and Lord Simon had ordered Blasius's silence on the matter. So, despite the cruelty he witnessed, he was trapped in a dilemma that worsened with each passing day.

At last, to the great relief of all, the nagging rain subsided. Heinrich and a dozen other servants were ordered into the forest to forage for wood. They dragged fallen boughs to the campsite where axe-wielding men shaved away the wet bark, exposing the dry heartwood beneath. By compline of one long day a series of small fires were beginning to snap to the cheers and hurrahs of the chilled travelers. The cooks were then set to task and midst the happy cries of the men-at-arms, cauldrons of bubbling gravies soon churned dried vegetables and chunks of pork and bacon. Finally, at long last, the famished knights were slurping hot stews.

The servants shivered in the cold as they waited their turn to eat. Rosa and Ita huddled close by Leo and Linz, the young brothers from Lindenholz. Richard noticed the four whispering and he shifted close enough to hear Rosa's voice choked with tears and anguish.

"What do you want?" barked Leo.

"Why, naught ... nay, I just was coming to see you," answered Richard. He looked at Rosa in the dim, yellow light of a distant fire. He could see bruises on her face and she cupped one elbow in pain. "Can I help?"

"Help in what?"

Richard lowered his voice. "Look at them. We can't let this keep happening any longer."

"Aye," muttered Leo. "But what do we do?"

"'Tis simple." The five were startled by a new voice. It was Heinrich.

"Münster's but a few days' quick-step behind us. None would bother follow back through those swamps." The girls looked so helpless to Heinrich. He nearly wept for them. He thought of the bruises on Katharina. "The men are drunk already. They'd be finishing their meals and coming for you soon enough. You'd best hurry."

The girls began to cry and Linz took Ita by the hand. "Leo, you and I shall take them! One year and a day in Münster and we shall all be free!"

"What of your family at home?" asked Richard.

"We've none. All died by plague this summer past."

"And what of you?" Richard asked the girls.

The two shrugged.

"Rosa! Ita!" It was drunken Lord Niklas calling from the camp.

"By God, you needs go quick!"

"How can I help?" Blasius's voice whispered from the darkness.

Startled, Heinrich nearly dropped at the sound. "Uh, brother, these four are escaping."

"Aye. If they are caught they shall be slain on the spot."

"We'd rather die than stay," answered Linz.

Blasius thought for a moment. More men began to cry out for the girls. "Get ready to run, and go with God." With that, the Templar burst into the firelight. He raised his sword above his head and roared, "I challenge any man!"

The camp grew quiet as the Templar circled round and round. He grabbed a shield and banged his sword against it until Lord Niklas took the bait.

"I challenge!" roared the drunken knight. "Prepare yourself, fool monk!"

As Lord Wolfrum reviewed the rules of the contest and his knights eagerly circled the combatants, Leo, Linz, Rosa, and Ita slipped away unseen into the forests of Saxony. Heinrich and Richard, having bade them a heartfelt "Godspeed," crept to the edges of the camp's firelight and watched as Brother Blasius skilfully attracted all attention to himself.

It took mere moments for the Templar to be fully engaged in a savage duel with Richard's nemesis. The monk circled and dodged, parried and ducked. He mocked and ridiculed, beckoned and harassed Niklas with his long Templar sword and a surprising repertoire of sarcasm. He strutted and boasted, taunted and jeered the tormented lord until the bedevilled man roared in frustration. Then, wily Blasius teased with riddles and rhymes as he parried with *riposte* and lunges. At last, the arm-heavy Templar reckoned the time to be right for a final, silent, savage assault. With a few deft strokes Lord Niklas was driven backward across the campsite and knocked flat on his back. He lay under the dark sky staring glumly up the shining flat of Brother Blasius's long-sword.

"Ha, ha!" howled Richard from the shadows. It was a disrespect that would not soon be forgotten.

Blasius withdrew his sword and reached a hand to his fallen foe. Lord Niklas dismissed the monk's chivalry with a sneer and climbed to his feet. Midst words of congratulations and newfound respect, the Templar bowed to his fellows and walked away quietly.

It was nearly an hour before the camp knew of the girls' disappearance. Lord Wolfrum ordered a search of the wagons and the forest, but took Blasius aside and studied him with a suspicious eye. "Do you know something of this?"

Heinrich was standing nearby and listened carefully. He wondered if a Templar dared lie. Blasius set his jaw and leaned close enough to Wolfrum's craggy face for their beards to tangle. "Nay, sire," he answered calmly.

Lord Wolfrum was not convinced. He paused for a moment—a long moment for Blasius, as the aging knight's breath reeked of garlic and beer. The old knight blinked first. "Humph! I've little choice but believe you."

৵

The next two days brought some relief to Heinrich and Richard. A brightening November sky washed the column in sunlight, though the cool air kept the roadways from drying very quickly. Despite wrestling the wagons through the mud, however, Heinrich found his journey rather pleasurable. The sky seemed larger to him here than at home, and the sprawling landscape was rich and fertile.

Osnabrück was a wealthy city renowned for its linen trade. Its mayor and resident bishop offered generous provisions to the weary men and provided a gracious feast. Wanting to hurry on, Lord Wolfram permitted only one night's stay, however, so at dawn of the next day the bishop blessed the kneeling army in front of the doors to his three-towered cathedral. With the sun shining overhead, the rested column then bade a grateful farewell and was soon traveling along an improving highway leading to the moated gate of Oldenburg.

The knights became ever-more pleased with Heinrich's baking. He fired his wagon-mounted, clay, domed oven each night about matins, and then began his bake in the hours before dawn. Now that he was better acquainted with his new oven, at each daybreak he delivered baskets of hot, fluffy wheat rolls, salted, hard-baked pretzels, and large loaves of wheat or rye. A friendly archer from Ulm taught him a recipe for honey-laced flat loaves, spread with cherry preserves, and rolled into a treat that won a roar of approval from the lords. Heinrich had earned a place of value and it felt so very good.

Richard, on the other hand, was more interested in adventure than service. He found himself always at the edges of a circle of drunken, gambling knights, or conniving with his fellows on wagers and contests. He had won a flask of liquor from a staggering footman and a flagon of Rhine wine from a carter, and was quick to drink them both. His drunkenness simply oiled his wagging tongue and numbed his better judgment. It did nothing to endear him to either friend or foe.

The night before the column would enter Oldenburg the men-at-arms had filled their bellies and lay about the camp comfortable and groggy. The servants were gathered in huddles by small fires and Heinrich was propped against the trunk of a large spruce thinking of home.

"Ah, good baker," announced Blasius as he joined the sleepy man.

"Aye, sit."

"'Tis a wonderful night and your bread was light as angel's wings!"

Heinrich chuckled. "I like m'oven. It heats good and loves m'doughs."

Blasius nodded. "You speak of it as though it were alive!"

The two sat quietly and listened to the snores and grunts of sleeping soldiers. A few horses snorted and the fires snapped lightly. "Blasius, I confess I do not really know why we are here. I've been told of a rebellion of peasants but I know nothing else."

"Aye. 'Tis so. Seems the land we travel to is now called Stedingerland. It was settled by Frisians and Dutch Saxons some hundred years ago or more. They came from the Low Countries over by the sea in the west. I am told they are a wild lot; hard-fisted, stubborn as rocks ... barely Christian in their ways.

"Of course, this Stedingerland needs folk of special strength. It is low and flat; a marsh that wars with the

Weser River year by year. The waters flood and freeze, they make the whole earth a sucking pit, yet these Stedingers know how to tame it. They build dikes to drain water from the marshes and claim new earth to graze their cattle."

Heinrich was fascinated. "And what is their crime?"

"Ah. Seems they were promised much. The archbishop of former times wanted this wasteland to be civilized; turned into something more than marsh-grass and bogs. He offered them freedom and low taxes. So, they came ... and who could blame them? They've formed a close bond among themselves. They've a militia and courts, even a name. They call themselves the *Communitas terre Stedingorum.*

"I am told they have resisted all authority from their rightful lord, Archbishop Hartwig in Bremen. Just two years ago they claimed their laws were abused and they attacked and destroyed the bishop's castles at Lechtenburg and Lineburg. They've built bulwarks and defenses, they've even resurrected the ancient Germanic gathering called 'The Thing'—where the chiefs and the people make their own laws. Under such claimed liberties they now refuse to pay taxes and tithes beyond what they accept as fair."

Heinrich was astonished. "They overthrew the bishop's castles?"

"*Ja.* They say their women were taken in the night by soldiers and their property raided. But rather than petition the Church court, they rose in rebellion and now threaten to undo the order of things. Seems Archbishop Hartwig fears for the whole of the northland if these Stedingers are not put into their proper place. The count in Oldenburg is equally nervous of such notions spreading through his nearby manors."

Heinrich was quiet. He could barely imagine peasants defeating the knights of the realm. He remembered his uncle Baldric unseating and dispatching a handful of rogue soldiers in Weyer so long ago, but he could hardly fathom an organized army of farmers.

Indeed, the legions of Stedingers posed a serious threat

to the whole of the empire's northland. Their ranks had been swelled with escaping German peasants who yearned for the liberty of their tribal forefathers. Stedinger villages and farms had become united in a spirit of common wealth and common purpose. They were becoming more than a population of free farmers, they were becoming a realm unto themselves, and more dangerous than even that—a symbol.

Such intransigence troubled the ecclesiastical and lay lords, for throughout all Christendom storm clouds were gathering. Peasants in Düdeldorf, Pickliessem, and Himmenrode had attacked their masters. The unhappy serfs of St. Pantaleon had planned a mass escape in the dark of night. The folk of the lord of Oberzel rebelled with the torch, the peasants of Gindorf with rocks, those of Goslar with organized sloth.

Blasius stared into the darkness. "I do confess some sympathy for these brave souls. I believe they have suffered abuses, nor do I doubt that they are entitled to special privilege on account of the archbishop's promises."

"So why do you come to fight them?" asked Heinrich.

Blasius was quiet again. "I never said I've come to fight them. My preceptor sends me to ensure that Templar silver is properly managed. Seems the count and the archbishop owe us a sum of one hundred and forty-seven pounds. They both claim they cannot pay until the Stedingers satisfy their debt of taxes and tithe. I am to witness their collection, then be paid our rightful sum. Afterward I am to arrange an escort of the silver to our representatives in Cologne."

"Will you fight against them?"

Blasius drew a deep breath. "I have suffered over that question since our journey began. I am not convinced they are in the wrong, yet they are in rebellion. I do swear, good friend, that I am caught in a dilemma. The Stedingers have just claims and grievances, yet their reactions violate all laws of God and man. If ... if I must raise my sword against these folk, I shall do so with pain in my heart." The soldier stared at his feet, blank-faced for a long moment.

Heinrich laid a gentle hand on his friend's shoulder.

"Brother Lukas once told me the only way to resolve such snares is to yield to the highest virtue."

Blasius nodded. "Ah, good Lukas. But it is just that which vexes me. Tell me, which is the higher virtue, Heinrich—order or mercy?"

The baker became very quiet. He drew a deep breath. "I once thought I followed the order of proper cause ... and I took another's life ... unjustly." He trembled and lowered his eyes.

&

Bright sunshine and merry spirits brought laughter and glad hearts to the high, rounded walls of Oldenburg Castle. The fortress sat squarely on the banks of the Hunte River, where its waters were diverted to serve as a moat. Beyond lay the growing city of Wasserburg, soon to take the name of the castle. With trumpet blasts and welcoming drums, the mounted knights led their column over a draw bridge and through the arched gateway leading into the smoky castle courtyard where the count and a company of his elite men spread their arms in welcome. The mail-clad knights of Heribert embraced their fellows with hearty hugs, and in moments brown ales and foaming beers were splashing into eager tankards.

Heinrich scampered about the castle with the other servants as they hurried the horses to the livery, carried stocks and provisions to the warehouses, and delivered the knights' personal trunks and barrels to valets. The knights would be bedded in stone-walled chambers within the castle walls and towers. The servants would be chased to timbered, thatch-roofed warehouses, stables, and sheds scattered haphazardly about the muddy bailey.

When Heinrich was finally directed to his own straw-filled cot he rested for a while. Uncomfortable and restless, he sat up, however, and gazed vacantly at the sorry lot of fellows crowding his low-roofed building. Weary, gaunt, and unkempt, his comrades were in stark contrast to the well-dressed, bold, fire-eyed knights they served. Heinrich sighed. He knew he was one of them.

"Heinrich!" barked Richard from the yard.

"Eh?"

"We've needs go. They've summoned all from Heribert's column."

The two soon stood in a long line of servants with their backs pressed against a cold wall. They faced their new foreman with dread and waited breathlessly as a broad-chested young man with an upturned nose and a well-fitted cloak strutted before them. "I am Falko of Wasserburg and I have news." He smiled wickedly and tapped his thigh with a heavy stick. "Yer lords have assigned me as yer master. I'm to fetch you when one of 'em needs you. In the meanwhile, you'll 'ave yer daily duties that I'll set you to." He gave them a hard look and raised his stick. "Keep in good order or you'll be meetin' m'friend here. Yer first duty is to get yourselves shorn and shaved." He walked to Emil, the lad from Runkel. "Y've runny eyes."

"*Ja*, sir master. And fever."

"Humph." He knocked the boy hard to the ground. "Get in yer bed and be ready on the morrow for fair day's work. Now, the rest of you hear me. Yer lords won't be warring against the Stedingers just yet; they've needs wait for more troops. Seems the Thurungians are late and the archbishop's troops are in a fight with Otto's men far to the east. The archbishop orders the count to hold fast until springtime."

Astonished, Heinrich groaned and he squeezed his fists angrily. *Springtime!* he thought. *Forty days, indeed!*

≈

Forty days became ninety and many more would come. The biting cold winds of late January had frozen the castle into a dismal stone cage. To the north, blinding snows sculpted the flat landscape into a blue-tipped desert of rippled white as far as shivering Heinrich could see. Each day the sky grayed with low clouds sagging southward from the nearby, ice-laden sea. Inside, the castle grounds were hazy with smoke trapped by heavy air within the high walls where peasants huddled around pitiful fires stoked with meager rations of firewood.

Within the halls of the nobles, great fires roared in ample

hearths and drunken men indulged their vices in boredom. Soon after the Epiphany, the more refined and civil pleasures of reading, fencing, chess, or backgammon had given way to heavy drinking, dice, bloodletting swordplay, lasciviousness, and brawling.

Brother Blasius was aghast at the blasphemous indulgences and spent long, lonesome days and nights praying in the chapel or breaking bread with the three timid priests who served Oldenburg Castle with dubious devotion. Joined by four faithful, Christian knights who also found the wanton behavior of their comrades too disheartening to bear, he stared at each morning's sky yearning for some harbinger of spring to offer hope in the winter's desolation. From time to time he visited Heinrich and Richard in their respective bakery or stable. Yet he dared not linger for fear of what penalties Falko might exact from his good friends.

Richard was grateful for the hours he labored in the pungent stables. The many horses kept the buildings warm, and he found comfort in the gentle eyes of the beasts. It was the days he was sent with forage teams into the barren, frozen landscape that he dreaded. Wrapped in fur cloaks and heavy boots, he and others would lead sleighs into a far-off western forest where they rang their steel-head axes against the frozen trunks of tall spruce. By the pink-hued light of dusk, they then hurried their heavy loads back across deepening snows into the confines of the castle where they stood before their small fires with numb fingers and toes.

Richard's crippled hand had adapted to the handle of an axe once again. Though awkward to the eye, the man had regained some measure of skill and quickly recalled the martial training of his youth. On Sabbaths he would race about the bailey feigning combat with his own shadow!

By March, the knights and other men-at-arms were nearly at their wits' end. They had blatantly disregarded the forty days of Lent. Their months of self-indulged excess had predictably failed to satisfy, so they were irritable, explosive, and seething for blood. The servants, too, were despairing. Day after endless day of cold and gray, of aches and chills and monotony had left them miserable and short-tempered. A few had died from fights within their quarters. Six had frozen to death, having slept at the farthest reach of the fires. Four had been killed in the forest and another went missing. Samuel, the Jew from Limburg, had been found murdered during Advent though it was of little interest to any. Eighteen had perished with maladies such as bloody flux, cramp colic, congestive chill, and St. Vitus's dance. Among the dead from fever was young Emil of Runkel.

The servants were not the only ones to suffer. Six footmen had died of putrid fever, one sergeant from milk leg, and Richard's former master, Lord Simon, from an infected wound.

It was Holy Thursday, the nineteenth of April, 1207, when Richard faced Lord Niklas once again. The knight was drunk with brandy cider and was accompanied by two escorts as he struggled across the castle bailey. The courtyard was a quagmire of mud and manure, and terribly rutted, so it was not uncommon for a pedestrian to lose a boot or find himself floundering, ankle deep in the brown muck. It was in just such a state that Lord Niklas was discovered by Richard as he passed by atop a cart of firewood. Having spent a winter of utter melancholy, having passed months with nary a smile or a grin, the blond peasant roared in delight. The loud laughter boiled the blood of the chagrined knight, and he responded with a string of oaths and blasphemies, scourges, insults, and mockeries that hushed the whole of the castleyard.

Richard seized his teamster by the shoulder and bade he hold fast. He turned and faced Niklas squarely. "Eh?" he cried.

"You heard me, y'son of Satan's brothel. You one-handed simpleton, you'd be playin' the fool your whole life, y'worthless coward!"

Richard stared silently at the knight who was shaking a fist at him. The disappointment of his life's dream had never truly left him. Despite all efforts to break free, his lame hand still held him within its grasp; like others, he suffered a wound of life that he permitted to define him. He suddenly pictured his father's face staring at his hand. He heard the man's words ringing in his ears: "Worthless!" Richard wanted nothing more than to release his itching anger and avenge his shattered hopes. He scrambled through the logs until he laid his hands on the axe he had wielded all that dreadful winter. He snatched it and held it high. "I challenge you, Niklas! Have you the courage to face a simpleton and his axe?"

With a haughty laugh and a snarl, Lord Niklas agreed.

Word spread quickly throughout the castle sheds that a duel was about to begin, and the combatants barely had time to face each other before a circle of foul-smelling, black-toothed peasants were cheering and mocking the both of them.

Niklas was clearly drunk, and he stumbled this way and that as Richard cut the air with his swinging axe. Yet the knight had been well-seasoned by combat and quickly sharpened his senses with each near miss.

Heinrich pushed his way to the front of the circle and closed his eyes. "Oh, Richard! Poor fool ... poor hopeless fool." He clenched his teeth and grimaced and groaned as his friend and kinsman lunged about the mud, red-faced and furious.

At thirty-one, Richard surprised most, particularly Lord Niklas. For an aging peasant with a lame hand, the impudent rebel gave a good account of himself. He had not forgotten his training under Lord Simon, and years of repressed bitterness now uncoiled into a fierce assault. He blocked Niklas's sword with skill, then swept his axe smoothly toward the knight's dodging belly; he followed with a savage swipe at Niklas's head, then swung another, and another.

But Niklas was no fool. He quickly discerned that his foe was driven by a fury that would blow itself away, like a gust on a cloudless day. The seasoned knight dodged and ducked, turned and stepped. He blocked and did not counter until Richard's blazing eyes began to cool.

The flex in Richard's joints slowly stiffened. His movements became less fluid and more lurching. His legs began to wobble, and soon sweat dripped heavy from his brow. Richard sucked air through a gaping mouth and his chest heaved. The white grip of his knuckles faded and his forearms burned. He cast one fleeting, desperate look at Heinrich and the baker held his breath.

Richard never really had a chance against the knight, and his vain effort finally earned only scoffs and ridicule from the circle of spectators. His arms now began to fail him and the axe weighed heavy. On burning legs he sloshed backward against a rapid flurry of Niklas's sword. But, with a loud cry, Richard rallied what reserve of hatred he had left and charged forward one last time.

With a sneer, Niklas deftly dodged the assault, then plunged his sword through Richard's lungs. The woeful cry of Heinrich filled Richard's ears with their last sounds on earth. The pierced peasant stood wide-eyed for a moment, impaled nearly to the hilt of Niklas's blade. The knight then yanked his sword away with a sickening sound and Richard toppled forward. Heinrich ran to his friend, only to have Falko hold him while Niklas rolled Richard over. Mercifully, the man's soul had flown away and he was unaware of his final indignity as Niklas scraped his muddy boots across the bridge of his nose.

Heinrich claimed Richard's body quickly. He washed and shrouded the bloodied corpse, and a willing priest said the final prayers as he and Blasius dug a grave beyond the castle wall. Then, as a spring cloudburst added yet more misery to the sad day, Richard's body was lowered to its eternal rest.

Chapter 19

THE CHOICE

A fortnight passed and the castle quickly filled with fresh troops finally ready for the campaign against the obstinate Stedingers. Soldiers of the archbishop had arrived from other places and now bivouacked in tents scattered throughout the bailey. The first days of May were filled with the sounds of their drills and training.

At last, the Count of Oldenburg appeared in all his finery to address the gathered army. He was a vain man, given to the same bloated sense of self that prompted his forebears to claim the title of "count" in the first place. With smug satisfaction he surveyed the rows of armored knights now lined in parade formation at his feet. They were fully bedecked in their colors and proudly bore the standards of their liege lords. Behind them gathered ranks of mounted sergeants—soldiers nearly equal in skill to a knight but from a lower station. Rows of archers formed the next line, and behind them stood an orderly throng of footmen dressed in leather jerkins and grasping maces, axes, lances, and glaives. Heinrich and the other servants were sent to their places amongst a long row of wagons and packhorses laden with provisions for the march that lay ahead.

The count shouted words of encouragement and introduced the army's commander, one Lord Egbert of Hamburg.

He, in turn, announced the knighthood of three former squires. The trio had pledged their fealty in a ceremony of homage that very same morning in which they had knelt before their liege lord and placed their hands within his. After reciting their pledge and receiving the prayers of the archbishop himself, the three were touched upon each shoulder and the head by their lord's long-sword, forever sworn as his obedient vassals.

The archbishop's army was comprised of men from all parts of Christendom. Fear of the Stedingers had spread as far as sunny Spain, for it seemed that spontaneous peasant armies were beginning to display astonishing acumen in many parts of Europe, and the kings' courts were growing nervous. A few English lords had considered sending a company of footmen to join the cause but did not. Perhaps the heritage of liberty savored in that good land had blunted their enthusiasm.

The Archbishop of Bremen's cause was served by thirty knights from the empire, forty mounted sergeants, and a host of footmen numbering nearly a hundred. In addition, the dukes of Lorraine sent sixty footmen, five mounted sergeants, and four Norman knights under contract. Distant Cordoba offered two black-haired knights on fine, Arabian mounts. Added to these were an entourage of teamsters, cooks, bakers, smiths, groomsmen, armorers, priests, women-of-the-camp, and physicians. The castle of Oldenburg had become host to an encampment of a vigorous and impressive army.

To the surprise of all, Archbishop Hartwig suddenly emerged from his guest chamber bearing his scepter in one hand and his sword in the other. *"In nomine Patris, et Filii, et Spiritus Sancti!"*

The army fell to its knees as the great bishop prayed over them. "Have mercy on us, Lord." Bishop Hartwig bowed to the priests at his side, then descended the steps toward Lord Egbert's mount and offered his sword and standard to the commander. The trumpets lining the battlements sounded and a thunderous cheer rose up. Then, as Egbert waved his army forward, the knights of the Church passed beneath the outstretched arms of their bishop and through Oldenburg's high gate.

Heinrich felt the hairs on his neck tingle and rise as he took his first steps forward. There he was, a simple baker from little Weyer, marching midst trumpets and cheers beneath the snapping pennants of a castle keep. He suddenly felt as though he were more than a breadmaker. His chest rose and his stride lengthened as he imagined himself a soldier in God's army, commissioned to help bear the sword against evildoers and the legions of Lucifer! Tears of inexplicable wonder blurred his eager eyes as he strained to find Blasius.

Heinrich smiled as he spotted the noble monk trotting briskly a short distance ahead. The Templar was surrounded by an enlarging group of devout knights from far-off places that shared his faithful love of God and duty. These true soldiers of Christ wanted little to do with the shameful ways of their fellows and were drawn to the piety of the warrior-monk. They were the flower of Christian knighthood, the lingering fragrance of a fading glory.

The sun shone brightly as Heinrich passed beneath the outstretched hands of the bishop. He closed his eyes to feel their power bring him strength from the Almighty. He breathed deeply and smiled and marched across the drawbridge to the long roadway lying before him.

The army followed the Hunte River for a short distance, then turned southeastward toward the prosperous town of Hude lying in the very center of Stedingerland. The day slowly faded, like the thrill of its beginning. Heinrich's heart did fly in those early hours of that special day, but it would have soared to even greater heights had it not been tethered to the memory of poor Richard. *Why, Richard? What a foolhardy, stubborn, selfish thing to do!* As the baker stepped to the rhythm of his wagon's turning wheel he reflected on their boyhood together. His mind carried him to happy times in Emma's garden and beneath the boughs of the Magi. He thought of Ingly and how the three of them had sat in speechless awe to hear Emma's tales of sprites and gnomes, of Dragon-rock and the Knight of the Swan.

He remembered lying between Ingelbert and Richard beneath the warmth of a kindly summer sun to discover faces in the clouds. *Ah, to gaze at the heavens again,* he thought. Heinrich sighed and shook his head.

Within the hour the column had traveled well within the marshy world of the Stedingers. Though its boundaries had spread over the years, Stedingerland was generally considered as lying east of Oldenburg with the River Weser as its original eastern boundary and the Hunte as its northern. The ground was primarily marshland that had been claimed from the flooding Weser by its ingenious settlers through series of ditches and locks. As the land drained, the farmers used their livestock to compress the soil, eventually leaving large areas of hardened fields within protective grids of low dikes. They then built access roads along these dikes connecting the tidy towns and villages that sprouted as vigorously as the hay fields of their ever-widening meadows. Their communities had become prosperous by the third generation.

In a show of strength, the archbishop's army passed numerous small villages and near noon was ordered to make camp. Here plans were set for a morning attack against a redoubt that protected access to the town of Hude. By smashing the fortress guarding the Stedingers' largest town, it was believed the rebels would quickly yield their taxes along with heavy dues with which the army might be paid a bonus. Heinrich hurried about his tasks to ensure fresh loaves for both the night's supper and the next morning's first meal.

After his duties were done, Heinrich was glad for the conversation of a friendly company of footmen grateful for his hearty rye.

"Your bread is as good as I've e'er eaten!" said one. "Come, sit with us."

Heinrich nodded. "M'thanks. You'd be the last left to serve and I'm happy for a rest." He sat between a huddle of contented soldiers and pulled a spelt roll from his pocket. "I am Heinrich of Weyer, from the region of Runkel and Limburg-by-the-Lahn."

The group introduced themselves as coming from numerous manors or towns of the empire. Each was a yeoman—a freeman who owned land but owed military service as part of his obligation to the lord who protected him. "Forty days! Ha!" grumbled one. "My lord had better credit us three years or more for this."

The group nodded. Heinrich listened quietly as the men spoke of their reluctance to oppose other free men. "From what I've learned they're our brothers. Free like us, cheated like us." He lowered his voice. "If we could join together, we could resist as well!"

"Hush, Roland! Are y'mad?!"

"Humph ... we must all be mad to be in this army. We belong in the other!"

"Under God I do wonder which cause is just," whispered one. "I am sworn to follow m'lord, and I dare not oppose the Holy Church ... yet I see justice in the Stedingers."

"But not in the *way* of their grievance," blurted Heinrich. "Their cause may be just but their ways are not."

A young soldier levelled a hard gaze at the baker. "You spent the winter as us ... bound in that stone coop with the likes of drunken, debauched lords. You might just as easy say the same of them."

A grumble of "ayes" circled the ring. Heinrich shrugged. The man had made a good point. "But what of the Church ... one cannot oppose the Church."

"Methinks the Stedingers 'ave priests praying over them as well. Who's to say which of God's men are speaking for God?"

The circle approved of the fellow's logic but grew suddenly quiet. The dilemma was more than they could handle the night before a likely battle. Heinrich brushed flour from his arms. "Well, I am glad my conscience needs make no choice in this!"

A leather-faced soldier shook his head and curled his lip. "Eh? Methinks y'know better than that. You feed this army ... we live on yer bread. Y'might as well be raising a sword against these folk yerself! You'd be a fool and a coward to hide behind yer doughs. You'd be no better'an us, so on the morrow do not think yerself clean and pure whilst we shed innocent blood!"

The soldiers stared at Heinrich with steely eyes, and the baker hung his head in shame.

≈

Dawn broke red and glorious as the army of the archbishop prepared to launch its attack. It was to be a short march across lands as flat as a table stretching toward a wide horizon. A northerly breeze wafted cool air through the camp, and Heinrich sucked clean air through his nostrils and sighed. He turned his eyes to the tender green grasses of May that blanketed the marshlands spread before him and he wished he were home. The grasslands were dotted with butter flowers and white lace, wild rhododendron and white clover. The sandy road ahead was dry and clear, lined with tall hardwoods such as oak and walnut.

The army began its march with a blast of trumpets and the roll of kettledrums. The servants and their wagons were ordered to follow close by, for the commanders wanted no risk of ambush to their supplies. So Heinrich mounted a cart and bounced along a straight roadway. His attention was quickly taken by the long, narrow fields that ran at right angles to the road. They were evenly divided by hand-dug trenches that marked the owners' boundaries and disappeared far into the distance. "One denier per year per holding," grumbled a footman.

"What?"

"I say, one penny per year for the tax on all of that." He pointed to a Stedinger field. "I'm told they were granted about thirty hectares and their freedom for one penny per year tax!"

Heinrich shook his head. "I am taxed two hundred a year for m'bakery alone!"

"Aye," answered another, "but did y'build a dike around it?"

A round of chuckles followed. Heinrich grumbled. "I'd dig a river round m'whole village for a tax like that, and I'd drain the Rhine for m'freedom!"

"And me as well!" cried a voice.

Along the road, also at even intervals, stood the tidy Stedingers' houses. Each house stood at the head of the farmer's rectangle of land, and the houses were strung in lines of some twenty or thirty, creating villages known as "*Marschhufe,*" or "marsh holdings." The houses were well kept and exuded a pride that naturally followed the liberty that was enjoyed under each roof.

As the archbishop's army passed by one such village, Egbert dispassionately ordered its destruction, and, with no hesitation, his army obeyed. To Heinrich's horror, its simple cottages were put to the torch and those inhabitants who could be found were slain.

About one league past the burned village stood the earthen fortress that straddled the road leading to Hude. Built some years prior with heavy clay dug from the riverbanks, it was a rectangular bulwark reinforced by large timbers. The ten-foot-high walls were steep, but green with spring grass that waved softly in the breeze. At the walls' rounded tops were periodic eroded notches similar to the more even-spaced ramparts of stone castles. Within were a few wattle-and-daub sheds used for shelter and storage. The small redoubt looked heavy and squat, sturdy—but vulnerable. A timber gate barred the road in front of it and a series of wet trenches were dug along its sides to provide an additional obstacle for an enemy.

Commander Egbert stared at the quiet fortress and feared the peasant militia were poised to strike. He abruptly ordered his army into position. Midst shouts and trumpets Heinrich's cart was ordered to turn and take a position in the distant rear. Suddenly nervous, the baker eyed Blasius galloping near. "Godspeed!" he cried.

The Templar reined his horse and loped toward his friend. The man's mount snorted as the soldier stared at Heinrich with an expression uncharacteristically despairing.

Heinrich was pale and confused. "Blasius, tell me we are in the right."

The Templar shook his head and tried to speak. He fumbled for words and shook his head. "Follow conscience,

Heinrich, or follow duty. Perhaps one may be righteous."
His cheeks were drawn and his lips pursed. He adjusted his
helm and shield, then stretched his sword toward Heinrich
and laid its flat upon the simple peasant's shoulder. "God
be with you, my friend." Blasius lingered for another
moment as if to wish them both to a better place.

The earth began to shake and tremble as the armored
cavalry thundered to its place. The warrior-monk drew a
deep breath, then turned his horse sadly and galloped to
the line. Heinrich climbed atop a wagon to survey the army
now gathering quickly before him. In the center of the front
line sat the commander atop a white charger. Beside him
was his standard-bearer, and on both sides were the broad,
cape-draped shoulders of Christendom's knights waiting
impatiently on their pawing steeds. Behind this first line
pressed six other tightly formed ranks of knights, together
forming a seemingly impenetrable mass of shields, swords,
chain mail, and leather. A series of signal flags ordered a
swarm of helmeted footmen to their place behind the cavalry and three rows of waiting archers then hurried to form
their lines in the rear.

All eyes faced the peasant fortress from which no single
sound had yet been heard nor a single defender seen. The
captains of the army waited and watched, but only the
rustling of their own horses, the tinny sound of shifting
armor, or the clearing of nervous throats broke the silence.
At last, the archers were ordered forward with their arrows
set ablaze. They drew their strings.

At that moment, the gate was flung open and a contingent of Stedingers appeared marching forward with their
colors tipped downward in submission. "Hold bows!" cried
Egbert.

Three representatives were sent forward to receive the
Stedingers midway between the army and the fortress.
Heinrich craned his neck from atop his wagon and waited
anxiously as the urgent discussion determined the day's
destiny.

The army's agents returned at a gallop and huddled with
the commander and his captains. It seemed the Stedingers

were in no mood to resist. They could ill-afford another war, and they thought their villages were filled with widows enough. They had met in loud, chaotic meetings at The Thing, as their assembly was called, and had reluctantly agreed to pay the taxes as demanded. They desperately needed a season of peace in which they might be left alone to prosper in their liberties.

News of the Stedinger capitulation rolled through the army like the low rumbling of dry thunder. It was met with some cheers and a few satisfied nods, but mostly with grumbles and oaths, sarcasm and jeers. Blasius was among those few cheering the moment, and he was glad-hearted as he witnessed the counting and removal of the taxes from within the fort.

By the time Hude's distant bells rang nones, the business of the day was completed and an unsettled Lord Egbert gathered his captains on the roadway. The man was content to have his tax in hand and had even exacted a heavy duty besides. Yet he was hardly satisfied. "These rebels cannot simply buy us like we are marketplace whores!" he seethed. "They need see the power and might of God's army. Tear down these gates and burn whatever stores you find in this pitiful fortress. Slay their delegates and put their heads on pikes. Burn their banners. When your business is finished, I shall lead this army through the town and show this wayward flock what doom they bring atop their heads if they dare oppose the Holy Church ever again!"

To the horror of some and the joy of others, a company of eager knights dashed into the fortress and slayed the woeful yeomen. Then, as ordered, the timber gates were pulled over and burned along with a meager quantity of stores found within.

In the meanwhile, Heinrich was ordered by Master Falko to help harness the wagons and pack the horses. He was busy racing hither and yon when Blasius appeared with a contingent of some dozen mounted soldiers.

"Heinrich!" he called.

The baker turned and shielded his eyes from a bright sun above. "*Ja?* Ah, Blasius!"

The monk dismounted and embraced his old friend. He looked at the baker closely. "In this light I see yet more silver in those red curls of yours!" He smiled. "And the look of many burdens."

Heinrich shrugged. "Aye, but a few have lifted today. I am pleased you've no need for battle against these people."

Blasius shook his head. "Ah, I wish the day was so pure. Egbert ordered these to be butchered without Christian mercy and without cause. I raised my voice against him but was silenced. I am only grateful we've no larger war to fight, for as God is my witness, I do not know that I could raise my hand against them. I spoke with a few while we were collecting the tax. They are good men, Heinrich, good Christian men. They work hard and only want to be treated under the law as free men ought. They've no stomach, for war but their blood boils for their liberties. I pray God blesses their fellows, and I pray for the souls of those just slain. Ah, but I am here to bid my farewell."

Heinrich's chest seized. "Farewell?"

"Yes. I have collected the Templars' due and must escort it to our preceptory in Cologne at once."

"But ... but, I ..."

Blasius laid his gloved hands atop the baker's shoulders. "Good and dear friend. There's to be no war. You shall be leaving for home within days and methinks by midsummer you shall be with your boys and wife in Weyer once again!"

Heinrich sighed. He grasped the Templar's hand in his own and squeezed it. The two embraced before Blasius mounted his horse. "Until we meet in Weyer!" he cried. With that, the monk and his company urged their horses forward and dashed away.

Heinrich stood still as he watched his friend disappear on the roadway. "*Bis Weyer.*" With a heavy heart he turned away and soon was marching with the army through the smoking bulwarks of the Stedingers' stronghold. He peered at the headless bodies of some twenty freemen strewn about the place and wondered if their murder truly served the cause of greater good. Rolling his Laubusbach stone between his fingers, he turned away and followed his wagon.

The archbishop and a contingent of his elite guard suddenly appeared from the west and soon joined the army as it marched toward Hude. Whispers down the line confirmed the bishop's pleasure with the tax collection, but he was apparently displeased with Egbert's bloodlust.

The servants were in good humor, though wishing to return home. A tiny village appeared in front of them. As they passed through, loud wails from a hand-wringing host of women greeted their ears. They wailed as they saw their men's heads staring at them lifelessly from atop the horrid pikes.

"Toss them to their wives," barked the archbishop. "The taxes are paid; let them bury them as Christians."

A large series of fields now separated the army from Hude, and in them were men working at spring labors. These paused to stare warily at the passing column, still ignorant of the day's sad news. Heinrich looked carefully them, men not unlike himself. They and their sons stood proud and broad-shouldered with short-swords and daggers in their belts. They lifted their heads and faced their would-be oppressors squarely and without fear. Heinrich felt an odd kinship and sudden respect. He did not imagine them to be Lucifer's pawns or the demons of darkness after all.

The army soon passed by the fresh brick of St. Elisabeth's Church and entered the gates of Hude. The stockaded town lay along the small, muddy Berne River on the edge of the marshes. It was prosperous and crowded with brick or timber homes arranged in neat rows. Many were thatched, but some were roofed with clay tile. Heinrich was amazed at the wealth he witnessed and could not help but marvel at the dignity and self-respect with which the people carried themselves. Weavers, carpenters, tinsmiths, wheel-wrights—tradesmen of every kind were hard at task. Heinrich understood the pleasure of heritable ownership—the satisfaction of creating wealth that would serve generations to follow. Ah, but to be free to move from

town to town, to pay a fair tax, to have some say in what and
why the tax should be; to have the honor of bearing arms to
defend oneself, one's kin, and neighbors! The baker of
Weyer was moved.

Archbishop Hartwig was not. He glared and scoffed like a
jealous spinster at her sister's wedding. "No right!" he
grumbled. "They've no right to have so much. Their very
presence mocks us and our ways ... they pay a pittance and
turn their backs as if they'd be our better!" He sat pouting
in his saddle with a nose lifted high in contempt as he
ordered the army to spend the night in Hude's market
square.

Hartwig slept in a pleasant room provided by a wealthy
merchant of the town. He found it bittersweet to enjoy the
man's bounty, but was particularly annoyed to be awakened by the bells of prime pealing from the town's church.
Hartwig was aggravated that the souls of these rebels were
aided by the very Church he, himself, served so faithfully. It
was a paradox that spoiled a good breakfast of eggs, bacon,
cheese, and fish. He grumbled a sour thanks to his host,
then rushed back to the church with barely a nod to the
three priests bowing respectfully as he passed them by on
his way to the altar.

Hude's new, red-brick church was, indeed, a beacon of
hope in a dark world. Like the folk it served, it delighted in
the joys of liberty that truth beckons its beloved to enjoy. It
was a good and decent refuge for wounded and weary
souls. Humility was its very breath, and the light that burst
through its simple windows filled its nave with goodness.
The simple priests who served the town were wise and caring, scrupulous in their piety, honest in their charity, and
blessed with uncommon grace.

Hartwig blustered to the altar where he prayed a revolt-
ing, self-aggrandizing prayer. He administered a hasty
Mass to himself and the three priests, then left the altar
filled with the illusion of an even greater self. He chided the
town's three bowing priests with a diatribe of rebuke and
remonstration that must have nauseated what saints' spirits dared linger in his vulgar wake. Finally, his dark shadow

left the sun-washed church, and he stormed toward his army to lead them home.

᧞

Grumbling, cursing, and still dissatisfied, the army returned to Oldenburg where, over the next few days, its knights began dispersing to their various manors throughout Christendom. Resettled in the castle, Heinrich felt a flutter of excitement as he imagined seeing his boys again. He paused to wonder, however, if his service had been misery enough for what penance he owed. A twinge of nausea filled his belly as he suddenly wondered if Richard's death was related to his penance. The sound of Lord Niklas's voice interrupted his thoughts.

"You'd be the last from Villmar, y'miserable dolt, and I the last from Runkel," the man muttered.

Heinrich stared at him with a look that betrayed his utter loathing. He hated the lord and wanted nothing more than some terror to come upon him. He could still see the monster wiping his boots across Richard's face—it was a memory he'd never forget.

"Get that look out of yer eyes!" shouted Niklas. "Y'might pass for a Stedinger!"

Heinrich liked the sound of that. He set his jaw and kept his eyes fixed hard on the drunken knight.

The lord was tired of obstinate peasants. He backhanded Heinrich with a ferocious blow that knocked the baker to the ground. "Now, bend the knee to me, y'worthless fool."

Heinrich stood. He would not obey.

"I say bend!" roared Niklas. He grabbed the baker and threw him into the shadows of a nearby stable.

Heinrich found his feet and stood defiantly. The baker had spent a lifetime bending and stooping, scraping, bowing, yielding, submitting—but only when he believed such compliance to be proper and just; only when it was right and in order. Lord Niklas had misjudged his tractability for timidity, his meekness for frailty.

Niklas struck him again and again. Bleeding and silent, Heinrich returned to his feet over and over, stiff-necked and ready for more. Frustrated and furious, the bulge-eyed knight suddenly jerked a dagger from his belt and thrust it toward Heinrich's throat.

The baker dodged the blade and grabbed hold of Niklas's arm. A fury rose within him, a familiar rage that had once filled him on a rainy night along the Villmar road. He held the knight's wrist with a viselike grip made strong from years kneading heavy dough. He tossed the soldier over his leg, slammed him hard onto the earth and pounced atop him to keep him close. He held Niklas's dagger hand fast to the ground with one hand, and with the other he seized the knight's throat and squeezed with all his might. Niklas gasped and squirmed, trying to roll. He dug his fingers into Heinrich's eyes as his swelling face began to purple.

Heinrich grunted and squeezed with all the strength his thick hand could muster. Pictures of Richard filled his mind and he tightened his grip even more. The moments passed slowly as the baker's unyielding grip stayed fixed to the lurching lord's throat like wet leather drying around a post. Niklas's flailing body rose and fell as he struggled against his gritty foe. His mouth stretched open wide and gaping, his fingers desperately digging at Heinrich's flesh. At last, the knight's eyes rolled and his hand dropped. His torso relaxed and Heinrich slowly, warily, released his hold. A gurgle and wheeze escaped the dead knight's chest and all was silent.

Heinrich stood and straddled the corpse. A cold shiver ran through him and he spun his head from side to side. He spotted a mound of manure against a far wall and quickly dragged the man by his boots toward it. In moments, he was desperately digging an unseemly grave in which he hurriedly buried the knight.

Once certain the man was well covered, the baker peeked beyond the stable door. With hurried fingers and a rag, Heinrich picked bits of straw from his leggings and wiped manure off his boots, then he slipped into the bustling castle courtyard without a notice.

ॐ

The night seemed endless as Heinrich stared at the dark rafters above his head. The halls of the castle were glowing in torchlight and restless knights' swords clanged in good-natured contest. A large contingent of tardy men-at-arms had arrived that very evening from Pomerania in the east. Rumors abounded among the servants that these rough-hewn soldiers were veterans in the empire's wars against the pagan Prussians. Claiming devotion to Church and emperor, they could be heard above the din shouting for vengeance against the Stedingers. "Next these dogs shall be filling their villages with witches and stealing infants from Christian homes!" one cried. Heinrich groaned.

The baker was worried the dung-haulers would be about the stables in the morning. His only hope was a comment he had overheard in which there was a complaint noted by the count that the castle latrines must be cleaned. It seemed his lady was aghast at the hordes of flies and the army's reeking piles of excrement yet to be shovelled away. *Perhaps*, he thought, *perhaps I might be halfway to home before they find Niklas.*

But Heinrich wondered if it would be better for him to simply unburden his soul by confessing his deed to the constable. After all, he reasoned, it was an act of self-defense, and who would deny even a servile baker the right to life. Yet, prudence was with the man. The lines edging his eyes and furrowed on his brow had been ploughed by years of wisdom's teaching, and a voice deep within told him plainly that his confession would send him to the gallows. He turned his mind to the state of his soul and wondered if God would require penance for such an act. *But self-defense—surely God would forgive. Yet I did think of Richard and hateful vengeance was in m'grip.* Heinrich groaned and begged the night to pass.

It was Wednesday, the sixteenth day of May, when the sun rose again to shine atop the baker's world. Nervous and distracted by his secret, Heinrich went about his duties anxiously, delivering baskets of fresh-baked breads to the knights grumbling from their chambers. He passed quietly through the halls of the castle, then into a garden courtyard where he overheard something that would change the simple man forever.

A group of French captains were whispering among those recently arrived from Pomerania. Believing justice had not been served, these knights were convinced of their right to exact a higher price than what the archbishop had required. Since Hartwig and his soldiers had departed for Bremen with Lord Egbert two days before, none could deny them the opportunity. Furthermore, it was rumored that the count was enraged that the Templar had taken away the entire debt, leaving him with scarcely enough to meet his other obligations—including paying the army. They plotted a raid.

Heinrich listened carefully before hurrying to his wagon where he swallowed a long draught of cider. *What am I to do?* The man's mind whirled and he wanted to vomit. With Richard dead, Blasius far away, and every other soul from his homeland gone, he felt so very alone. It was then he also realized that he had no way home! *I'll be attached to a strange lord ... I'll be stolen away, never to see m'lads again.* Panic gripped him and his mouth dried. He plunged his hand into his satchel to find his Laubusbach stone. *Ah, Emma ... if only you could guide me. And Brother Lukas ... if I could but hear one word of counsel from you now.*

He closed his eyes as words from his past came to him. *Emma said that sunshine is hope and moonlight is mercy. But I cannot lift my head to either. I am supposed to live m'life "by the law of love."* She told m, *"'tis higher than that of any man."* He took a deep breath and another draught of cider. He loaded his strong arms with large baskets of bread and returned to the knights' tables where he cocked his ears.

Some Normans had joined with the Frenchmen, and a footman had overheard them talking about a wealthy village within reach. "They wants to loot a rich town along the Weser called Berne," the man whispered to Heinrich. "It's north, just below the Hunte and they say there's less a militia there. But the booty ought be plenty since it trades heavy from the seaport. Then, they says, they'll come back to the castle, collect their wagons, and go home."

"Are you footmen going?" Heinrich feigned disinterest.

"Aye. They'll be makin' us quick-step the whole way!"

Heinrich nodded. A hard tap on the shoulder sent a chill through the baker. He turned slowly, expecting the worst. He was staring at Falko. "You! Baker."

Heinrich paled.

Falko narrowed his eyes and leaned close. "'Ave y'seen yer lord?"

"Lord Niklas? Nay, sir master, not for days. Methinks he must be with the ladies, else drunk in the halls."

Falko said nothing but kept a cold gaze on the baker. Heinrich felt perspiration beading above his upper lip but he did not move or look away. Falko nodded. "Aye. You needs shave that stubble and shorn that mop! No beards, no long hair on servants." He pulled Heinrich by the sleeve and whispered, "And one more thing. You and the others need bake early. Some soldiers'll be leavin' 'fore dawn."

Now Heinrich knew it was certain. He also knew Falko to be dimwitted and loose-tongued. "Aye, sire. And ... for how many ought I bake?"

Falko leaned closer. "'Bout a hundred, methinks ... two score mounted men and some footmen. Say no word of it to others. If asked, say you've been told some companies be leavin' for home in early morn." The fool winked.

"Aye." Heinrich's heart raced and his mind spun as he hurried toward his wagon. He muttered to his helpers, "I'd be suffering colic, methinks." He held his belly. "I'd needs an hour in m'bed." Once out of sight he leaned against the cold stone of the castle wall and closed his eyes. *I'll not raise m'hand against them nor help those who do. God forgive me, but m'lords are wrong.*

Heinrich scanned the castle grounds for a safe way out. He quickly climbed the steps leading to the battlements where he fixed his eyes on the green fields beyond the drawbridge. "Wildflowers!"

The man raced down the steps, through the courtyard, and into his bakery where he grabbed a basket. He hurried to the gatekeeper and spoke boldly. "I'm the baker ... been ordered to gather flowers to flavor m'lord's sweetbread and tasties."

The guard grumbled a word or two, then waved him

through the portal. Relieved, but trembling, Heinrich crossed the drawbridge spanning the curve in the Hunte and slowly headed toward the open fields. Soon he was bending to pull spring blooms from the sod. The soldiers on the wall gave him little heed and by vespers he had managed to wander far enough to find cover midst a clump of willows by the riverbank where he hid until twilight.

Under a merciful moon the man ran eastward along the river roadway. The night was quiet and all he could hear were the sounds of his boots pounding the road and his lungs wheezing for air. At this time of year the darkness would be short-lived, and the urgency of his cause pressed him onward. Yet he was not as young as he once was and Heinrich finally collapsed at the side of the road gasping for breath.

After resting a few moments alone in the silver nightscape, the simple man from Weyer felt suddenly important. Heinrich cleared his lungs and began to run again. He had reckoned the distance to be about four leagues—about a three-hour quick-step, less if he ran hard. On and on he pressed despite the ache in his weighted legs and the agony of his heaving chest. It was sometime after matins when the gasping baker finally collapsed at the door of Berne's simple church. The man pounded on it until a wary priest arrived with a candle. "Please," Heinrich begged. "Please ... let me in."

The priest helped the exhausted man through the doorway and onto a stool. He called for a drowsy novice to bring a tankard of beer with which Heinrich quickly slaked his thirst. "Knights are coming!" he cried. "Warn your people the knights are to attack the town."

The priest gasped and immediately ordered the church bell rung. Within moments, bleary-eyed militiamen began streaming into the church. Upon hearing the baker's report, messengers and scouts were sent in all directions, and a defense was quickly planned by Berne's elected captains. Then, before Heinrich could protest, he was herded into a wagon and delivered to the redoubt guarding the main road leading to the town.

In the next hours, anxious farmers poured steadily from villages far and wide with swords and pikes in hand. Some had shields, most not. Some carried axes, others flails, forks, or hammers. None had armor. They gathered into tithings and arranged themselves quickly into proper order as they awaited more news. Once organized, they learned of Heinrich and his brave decision. One by one they sought him out and embraced him. For the baker, the hours were a blur of confusion and fear.

&

The first rays of dawn spread bright pink across the huge sky of Stedingerland. The wind had changed to the south and a light breeze wafted a bit of warmth to the chilled peasants preparing their defense. They stood around their earthen fortress facing west, still within sight of the steeple of Berne's church that guarded their rear. From time to time some turned to face the squat tower as if to draw strength from it. And why not? The red-brick church was stout and sturdy, its square steeple unpretentious and efficient—like the people who had built it; like the people it served. It was a worthy reservoir of hope.

Heinrich stared about in disbelief. He had been given little time to consider his predicament, and he gaped numbly at a group of men munching hastily on cheese and swigging beer. He thought his new fellows to be a handsome race. Almost to a man they were tall, ruddy and blond, blue-eyed and sharp featured—very much like the Northmen of Emma's legends. They spoke a dialect that the baker struggled to understand—a form of German, though more guttural and harsh like the Dutch of their ancestors. Some Pomeranians from the east were mixed in, as well as a few converted Prussians and a handful of Thuringians from farther south.

A militia chieftain, a thick-chested, aging man named Lars, stroked his beard and tossed his long, grayed mane to one side. He gripped a fearsome battle-axe and used it as a pointer. "They'll come in close along the road so their horses don't bog in the marshes they suspect on either side," he growled. "You, Devries, hide three companies in the ditches over there and there." He pointed to the far edges of the field. "We'll stand here, in front of the fort. If need be we'll fall back behind the walls, but I'd rather fight them in the open. After they hit our center, you flank them." He turned to Heinrich. "We owe you much, friend. Stand with us and see how liberty is defended."

The baker bowed. Being called a friend of men such as these felt good to him.

A priest scurried toward the commander and his resolute little army, and within moments Heinrich found himself suddenly kneeling shoulder to shoulder with free men as a priest prayed over him. He was bedevilled by his new dilemma. These strangers now expected him to fight the knights of his own world—the protectors of his life's order. And he was receiving a blessing from a priest who served the same God as Father Pious and Archbishop Hartwig. *Or does he?* Heinrich had no time to reflect. It was as if his decision had been made for him, for he surely knew he could not simply walk away. Nor did he want to, for he was drawn to these astonishing people and felt strangely compelled to defend them.

A white-haired fellow smiled and handed Heinrich a weapon. It was a glaive, a long-handled lance of sorts, with a sharp blade-edge on one side and a hook on the other. He was told the hook could be used to unseat a rider and the blade could be wielded "like a sword tied on a pole."

Heinrich grasped his glaive in both hands and stared at it for a moment. Suddenly, rough words directed him to his new company where his commander placed him in the center of a tight knot of militiamen.

A hard-faced youth instructed Heinrich how companies of tithings would stand in the open field in close formations, separated by large spaces. "Their cavalry either attacks one of our clusters with its whole, or it spreads to get us all. Either way, we get an advantage." The lad had barely finished speaking when a rider came charging from the west. "They're coming," he roared.

The peasant militia numbered about seven score. The yeomen stood at the ready and Lars asked the priests to pray for howling winds that might blow aside the enemy's arrows. "There!" he cried. A column of horsemen and infantry could be seen advancing rapidly. Even from a distance their arrogant posture could be spotted, and the simple freemen hated them for it. Emotions stirred. "Easy, men," ordered the captains. A chant began to rise, louder and louder. "*Vrijheid altijd, Vrijheid altijd!*"

The surprised knights from Oldenburg's castle reined their mounts and stood in their stirrups to survey the motley lot grouped oddly before them. "Someone warned them!" groused one.

"Good, m'sword needs to be wet again!"

They studied the landscape and noticed a few waterbirds flying from the ditches to their right. The heavy drops dripping from their legs convinced the knights they would be clever to avoid the muck and mire of a likely swamp on that side. To their left the ground appeared firm, but the knights were unsure. "We needs keep tight to the roadway," stated one.

"Aye. We've thirty-six mounted men. We ought drive nine wide and four rows deep ... each row with two knights. We go straight down their center and scatter 'em wide. We'll seize the fort with our footmen and give chase on solid ground. Once they've dispersed, we'll loot the town and be back in Oldenburg by nones!"

Heinrich was set in the middle of a tithing in the center of the road. The position was one of honor, Lars had said. The poor baker wasn't so sure. He stared breathlessly at the sight before him. Under colorful banners and atop impressive steeds, a steely line of mail-clad knights prepared to unleash their fury on an unkempt army of wool-clad yeomen. Their trumpeters sounded and cheers were lifted. Armored stallions snorted and tossed their heads as they pawed the earth. Heinrich closed his eyes. The order that was arrayed before him was *his* order. The pennants that rolled so easily in the morning's air were the same that shadowed the world from which he came. He fixed his eyes on that which was about to strike, and he wondered.

The earth began to shake and the wind carried the sound

of a thousand tumbling boulders as the cavalry charged. Closer and closer it roared, and behind it came a host of spinning legs bearing a forest of lances, axes, forks, and pikes. Heinrich's heart pounded, his body chilled.

Slowly, ever so slowly, yet with earnest confidence and unyielding resolution, a defiant cry rose up from the Stedingers. It grew louder and louder until it roared like a great and wondrous bellow from the Lion of Judah Himself. It was hosanna; it was liberty's reply. These free men would not run!

Heinrich clenched his jaw and gripped his glaive, and when the first wave crashed atop him he did not yield. He leapt into the battle like a man gone mad. He thrust and jabbed, swiped and yanked his glaive in, at, from, and through knights' flesh and horse with no more thought to reason or to cause. He lunged about the tempest as time fell still, and as suddenly as it had begun, it ended.

The gasping baker stared at the heaps of groaning men strewn across the once green grass. He could hardly hear his commander put his ranks into a new formation, and he took his position while gazing numbly at his blood-smeared glaive. In the pause his mind suddenly flew to Weyer and his boys. He could see their faces in the shine of the steel and the memory jolted him. He bade them farewell.

The astonished knights retreated in humiliation. They had not expected either courage or skill-at-arms and were dismayed at the ardor of their foe. They suffered damaging losses to both mount and rider, and their footmen had received enormous casualties from a surprise flank attack. The furious lords hastened to salvage both their pride and their army's resolve as they regrouped to lead with cavalry once more. The knights hunched forward in their saddles enraged and determined. They would form a column and drive forward like an iron lance.

Brave Heinrich stood in the first line, nervous and unsure. He breathed quickly and gripped his weapon with fists squeezed white with fear. Behind him and to each side crowded the woollen horde of angry peasants. They chanted and cursed and raised their spears and axes in defiance of the ordered ranks of knights preparing to charge them once again. A long trumpet blasted and the earth began to shake.

Heinrich licked his dry lips and closed his eyes. A warm wind blew through his curly hair, and it felt good as it brushed across his stubbled face. Yearning only for peace, the simple man seemed always beset by strife and disharmony. He had spent his life offered to the bondage of things familiar, yet he was ever pursued by the disrupting purposes of something greater than himself. Persistent, patient, and persevering, truth had labored to stir and prod, to urge and teach until, at last, the poor wretch might be freed to lift his eyes toward the light beyond his own dark world. Now he had been placed in the center of the greatest paradox of all his troubled years.

The mighty warhorses raged closer and closer like a furious tempest bearing down upon a helpless village. The thundering hooves filled Heinrich's ears with dread, but the man held shoulder to shoulder with his stouthearted comrades. Steely-eyed and bearing all the confidence of their station, the knights crashed into the stubborn line of these lesser men.

With a shout and a lunge, Heinrich entered the whirlwind. All around him swirled the blurred images of horse and knight, the flash of swords and the splatters of blood. The stench of butchered men and slaughtered beasts filled his nose and choked his lungs; his ears were crowded with the thuds and clangs of hammers and steel, the cries of men and the whinnies of stallions lurching about the mêlée. Heinrich jabbed his glaive this way and that, impaling whom he could and dodging others. The man fought well.

But somewhere in the fury Heinrich's world fell silent. He dropped to the ground gently and closed his eyes as if to sleep. It was then, it seemed, his spirit was lifted like a hawk on the wind far above the bloody plain. Higher and higher he climbed until he felt he was soaring and drifting in the sun's kind currents. There he sailed and fluttered free, like a butterfly on a summer's day. His weary heart was glad and he sang with joy as the warmth of the merciful sun bathed his wounded soul. Calmed and steadied, he was touched by hope and returned to his struggle in the world of time.

Chapter 20

A NEW JOURNEY BEGINS

ein Herr? Mein Herr? Can you hear me?" A gentle, middle-aged woman bent anxiously over the stranger. The fevered man stirred ever so slightly, then returned to a deep, dreamless sleep.

Anna sat back and sighed, then whispered to her daughter-in-law, "He has come and gone from us for a fortnight or more." She ran her hands through her gray hair and smoothed her apron. "God's will be done."

Anna's young daughter-in-law stood at her side. She was blue-eyed but dark-haired, unlike most of the Stedinger women. Her ancestors were settlers from somewhere near Bruges, a crowded Flemish city in the Low Country north of Normandy. She was willowy and intelligent, strong featured and compassionate. "Mother, he is bound by fits all the night, he calls names and cries aloud. I fear the spirits haunt him."

"*Ja*, Edda, I fear the same. Day by day he suffers so, yet methinks his body agonizes less than his soul. He seems to be in the grip of devils. But, devils or not, he only swallows a bit of broth. He must eat more else he shall surely die." The older woman sighed. She was plump and weathered by the wind. Blue-eyed and ruddy, she had spent her life struggling against the land she dearly loved.

Edda nodded and wiped the stranger's clammy brow.

She pushed damp curls off his forehead. "Husband is glad to bind us to this stranger."

"Indeed I am!" bellowed Cornelis as he strode to the table. The dark-eyed farmer sat down and wiped the summer sweat off his broad, bearded face. He lifted his young son and daughter to his lap and poured a tankard of beer. He cut a thick slice of cheese and said, "He's yet to waken, Edda?"

"Aye, husband," answered his wife. "He seems fevered again. His wraps are clean and tight … the infection is clear and your mother seared the stump in places again this morning."

Cornelis grimaced. He gestured toward the unconscious man. "That, m'*kinder*, is who saved your *vader*." The young man tilted his head to pour a long, welcome draught of beer down his parched throat. He set his tankard down hard, then sat silently in thought. A hot June breeze rustled the thatch atop the brick-and-peat farmhouse.

Anna waited patiently and smiled lovingly at her grown son. A few years prior her husband had been killed overthrowing Lineburg Castle, but before that he had fought with the militia in several skirmishes. She was no stranger to the way men faced the haunting recollections of bloody combat.

Cornelis dragged his sleeve across his lips and stared blankly. "None knew his name—from the first he seemed confused and uncertain. Yet when the horses were upon us he fought like one of us … all say so. When the bishop's footmen waded in at the second charge, I was behind him when he was struck hard by a mace. I can still see the way his head bounced sideways … like a bladder ball with a good kick … and as his face spun toward me I saw his eye was gone. Yet he turned back and jabbed his glaive hard into the man! Next I knew, I was on the ground. … All I remember is looking up at a huge knight with an axe. He was swinging at m'fellows—this way an' that, like a harvester cutting tall grass! Then he saw me at his feet and smiled. … Ach, dear God in heaven, I can still see that smile!"

Cornelis reached for his beer and turned his eyes toward

the suffering stranger lying quietly on the nearby bed. Edda and Anna looked patiently at one another. They had heard the story countless times.

"But then he came—this stranger. He sees me down ... I know this because his good eye locked on mine. I struggled to m'feet as he swiped his glaive at the knight. I tried to help but it all happened too quick. ..." He closed his eyes and nodded. "Aye ... aye. The axe came down hard and chopped into the poor wretch's arm like a cleaver into ox-flesh. The good fellow fell to one side and collapsed into m'own arms. I remember the peaceful look on his face as I laid him down— I shan't e'er forget it."

Cornelis sighed and cut another slice of cheese before adding, "I must confess it was sweet to see that cursed knight dead on the field at day's end. Devils! I swear, some-day we shall throw them off us for good." Angry, unshed tears welled up in the man's eyes.

Edda stroked her husband's hair and filled his tankard. She sent her children to their garden chores while Anna tended Heinrich.

It was Wednesday, the thirteenth day of June in the Year of Grace 1207 when Heinrich's fever finally broke and he opened his left eye wide. He stared about the tidy farmhouse, disoriented and anxious. He was weak and trembling as he raised his right hand to his face. He gin-gerly pressed his forefinger into the socket where his right eye once sat and groaned as he gently probed the empty hole. He suddenly felt sick and tried to lift himself by his elbows. A terrible pain shot through his left arm and he reached his right hand over to grasp it. But, to Heinrich's dismay, his hand found nothing but air. He looked to see and released a low groan when he found no arm at all.

Edda heard the wounded man stirring and hurried to his side. She held his head softly and soothed him with calm reassurances. She wiped his brow with the fever-rag and settled the poor man back against his pillow. "Anki, run for Papa." Her daughter scrambled to the field.

Cornelis came running from a distant pasture and burst through the doorway panting and perspired. He ran to

Heinrich's bed and fell to his knees. *"Prijzen God! Hoe maakt tu het?"*

Heinrich stared blankly, then mumbled, *"Wo bin ich?"*

At a neighbor's home, Anna had heard the commotion and returned quickly. She entered the room with a smile as big as the Stedinger sky. "He is German! We must speak in his tongue." She turned to the bewildered man. *"Wilkommen,* we will help you. *"*

The man was suddenly relieved, but still confused. He offered a timid smile. "Many thanks." Heinrich's voice was rusty from lack of use. "It seems you have helped me already." He looked uncomfortably at his stump.

Anna motioned for Cornelis and directed her daughter-in-law toward a kettle of early peas and fish. Like most of the Stedingers, Cornelis and his wife spoke a dialect that was a mixture of Frisian and German. Furthermore, since life near the sea made contact with people of other lands inevitable, many could speak a little Norse, some Danish, even French and English. Cornelis was primarily a farmer but had launched a prosperous trading business in nearby Elsfleth that had required he learn other tongues. He laid a strong hand on Heinrich's shoulder and spoke this time in German. "You are in the village we call Weserfeld, not far from Berne. You were injured in the battle and we brought you here." He then introduced himself and his family. "This is my *Frau,* Edda; my mother, Anna; and my children, Anki and Bolko." He asked a few questions of Heinrich, then turned to his family. "Our friend is named 'Heinrich,' and he is a servile baker from the village of Weyer in the center of the empire. He is a landowner, but bound to a monastery in a place called Villmar. He has two living lads, Wilhelm and Karl, and a wife."

Anna beamed. "A baker! So, you must tell us how one might prepare—"

"Leave him be," laughed Cornelis. "By heaven, Mother, let the man recover first." He turned to Heinrich and slowly repeated the story of the battle and how it was that the baker had come to his home. Heinrich's memory began to return, though he had few recollections of the battle itself.

"The last I remember is pushing m'glaive under a foot-man's jerkin. I remember because I think I knew him ... I fed him bread the day before." His voice trailed away and he sighed. "As for the rest ... it is nothing but a vague dream."

"Just as well. Now, friend, eat."

Heinrich had lost a great deal of weight. His face was drawn and his legs were spindly. He was helped to the table, one not unlike his own, and he slumped into a simple wooden chair. He glanced about the farmhouse and felt good. The house was tidy and bright, clean and airy. It was part of a small village placed at the juncture of the Weser and the Hunte at the northern border of Stedingerland.

A northerly breeze brought fresh, sea air through the open door and Heinrich breathed deeply. Despite the heat of the summer day he felt chilled and Edda wrapped him in a warm cloak. He patted little Anki atop the pale braids piled on her head and he smiled kindly at shy, little Bolko, the farmer's son. That day friendship sprouted in a seedbed of gratitude—a place where trust and devotion send the deepest and most lasting roots.

By mid-August Heinrich had regained much of his strength. At thirty-three years of age he did not heal as quickly as a younger man might, and he found the long recovery to be frustrating. His patient caregivers were unrestrained in their generosity, but few things troubled the man more than receiving without giving in kind—it was a veiled vice rooted in the subtleties of pride. He did what he could to serve Cornelis's household, but with one arm and one eye his opportunities were severely limited. He pulled weeds from the kitchen garden with the children, helped Edda herd the cattle from field to field, and did what he could to bake bread for the family and their friends.

By the Feast of the Assumption Heinrich's face had healed completely, and on the morning of the feast day Edda presented him with a leather patch she had fash-ioned from a well-tanned cowhide. She tied it neatly around his head with a cord of hemp her daughter had braided as a gift. Heinrich thanked the six-year-old with a gentle kiss on her cheek and squeezed Edda's hand with heartfelt appreciation.

Anna then stepped forward with a smile and presented their patient with more gifts. She and her daughter-in-law had sewn the man new leather leggings, a wool tunic, a leather vest, and a winter cloak of sealskin. "This is no empire wool!" boasted Anna. "This is Danish wool. It looks rough but wears smooth. And the cloak comes from Norway. The breeches are of mallet-softened sheepskin! They ought last to the end of your days. Ah, and here, we've made you good linen under-breeches as well!"

Heinrich received the gifts with a trembling hand. He felt the fabrics and knew they'd last him many, many years. "I … I—"

"Ah, you've no need to speak, good sir!" interrupted Anna.

Heinrich sat speechlessly and stared at his hosts with wonder.

"We didn't want you to be worried about the winter to come."

The man embraced each woman as best he could with one arm. "I've no right words to thank you. I shall gratefully wear them on m'journey home."

Cornelis had been watching quietly from a corner chair. "You need another month, maybe more, to get your strength."

"Nay, sir." Heinrich shook his head. He yearned to return to Weyer. "I must leave soon, else I risk an early winter."

Cornelis beckoned all to gather round him. He looked at Heinrich with compassion but with a firm expression. For a young man of twenty-two years he was strong and wise, brave enough, but prudent. "First, I've news … Duke Philip has been assassinated and that means the empire's in greater confusion than ever. Alliances are shifting and the lords are in chaos. I must confess it makes me smile some!

"But, I've other news that makes a problem for us. Seems common talk has put us all at risk. Word of a runaway servant has found its way to Oldenburg—a runaway that helped us set a trap for the soldiers." Cornelis shook his head. "Our neighbors know of you. They love you for what you did and always shall. But this village is filled with idle tongues and men who ought know better! Word of a stranger always moves quick, especially one with a story. Methinks they've talked of you from place to place over the summer, and the words have even found their way to Bremen. From there ... news travels the world.

"Our friends tell us the count and the archbishop have heard of a one-armed, one-eyed peasant who may have betrayed them. There's talk of a search to begin."

Cornelis turned to the women. "And there is more. It seems the soldiers whom we defeated claim they were passing through peaceably on their way to worship in Bremen. Ha! They say they went north to the ferries at Berne and we ambushed them without cause, so now the archbishop is considering another attack to punish us. The chiefs meet in a fortnight."

Heinrich rose. "There'll be no single death on my account! None. I'll surrender myself in the morning!"

"Listen, friend, you do not understand. The archbishop and the counts seek every possible excuse to war with us. Your capture would only prove their rumors to be true and add strength to their claim. This much is certain: you are in grave danger here and you cannot travel to the south—it's where you'd be expected. You'd stand no chance in Saxony or Thurungia, none at all."

"What is he to do, son?" asked Anna.

"I've another plan." Cornelis faced Heinrich squarely. "A group of us have struck a deal. We're to trade our rye and oats for skins with Kjell the Swede from West Göthland. Our own captain, Groot, has agreed to our fee and is sailing in a fortnight from Elsfleth. Kjell is an old friend of m'father's—he'll hide you for the winter."

"The winter?" Heinrich stared blankly.

Cornelis understood but wanted to be very sure the man did as he was told. "Listen, friend, and listen well. You saved my life and I shall ne'er forget it. But hear me plain: if you are captured, this village and m'family shall be slaughtered in God's name. You cannot travel south—not now. I cannot allow it." He leaned close to Heinrich and narrowed his eyes. With a resolved whisper he repeated, "I *will* not allow it."

The baker turned away and stared at the wide horizon. *Another winter away from home!* He struggled with his predicament and concluded that his host was right. Stories of Cornelis's offered sanctuary would be confirmed, and he had seen what sort of justice the lords served. He looked at little Anki, at Bolko the toddler, the patient eyes of Anna, and the kind face of gentle Edda. He could do nothing to bring more risk to any of these.

Another thought had been haunting him for some days. He thought of his missing eye and touched his right hand to his stump. *I've sinned greatly and am forever crippled for my shame*, he moaned within himself. *Dear God, have I added more to my debt? I've needs pay a great penance to keep m'sons safe. This winter might begin the season of sufferings that may finally cleanse me.* He nodded sadly and answered, "Forgive me, Cornelis. Surely, I shall do as you say."

The next two weeks were filled with restless anticipation. Heinrich was anxious to be on his way, but was forbidden to leave Cornelis's farmhouse for fear a passing spy would confirm the rumors in Oldenburg and Bremen. Cornelis was busy with his fellows finishing the harvest in the higher ground to the west. There, the grain crops had done well that year and the eager landowners worked tirelessly in a cooperative effort that benefited everyone. Heinrich only wished he could take part and aid his gracious host.

It was late on Friday, the fourteenth day of September when a messenger hurried into Cornelis's door. The fellow whispered an urgent message to the nodding farmer before disappearing into the heavy river mist blanketing the village. Cornelis touched a coal to a torch and called his wife and Heinrich. "We have news. The count sent the bailiff and a company of men-at-arms from the castle at noon yesterday and they've searched Altenesche and Hude. Our spy says they will be searching the villages along the Hunte next."

Edda gasped. "Husband, they shall surely slaughter us!"

Cornelis gathered his wife in his arms and held her tightly. Mother Anna joined the two and laid a comforting hand on the young woman's shoulder. Cornelis answered, "Nay, Edda. No doubt the militia's being called as we speak. The count has been given no permission for this search ... he'll be turned away. But," the man turned to Heinrich, "now 'tis time, good friend. You must board Groot's ship. He would have sailed by midweek anyway—he's almost loaded. A few days in the bottom of his stout vessel is a small price for your life ... and ours."

Heinrich agreed.

Cornelis clasped hands with the baker and beckoned his wife to quickly gather an ample stock of provisions to send with their guest. Within minutes, Edda and her mother-in-law handed Heinrich his satchel, stuffed with smoked fish, cheese, salted beef, and dried apples. He hung the bulging leather bag across the shoulder of his new brown tunic and draped his sealskin cloak over his back. The man looked rugged, almost fierce. His graying auburn curls hung over his ears and brushed the base of his neck. He had grown a beard, like the free men who had hosted him these four months, and the weight he had regained padded his broad shoulders and thick chest. The patch over his right eye and the stump hanging at his left side added a quality of mystery and adventure. Anna thought him to have the look of the pirates who pillaged the nearby sea.

Cornelis handed the man a final gift, a long dagger with a gleaming, polished blade. "This gift is from the chieftains as a token of their thanks. Your warning saved many and your bravery in battle is worthy of honor."

Heinrich was stunned. He received the gift with a trembling hand and stared at it almost fearfully. An unbidden voice hissed within him and reminded him that a servile man was forbidden to own such a weapon. He grunted to himself and lifted the blade to his lips for a kiss of acceptance and a humble bow.

Cornelis smiled. "The blade is Saxon steel. Its edge is hard and sharp enough to split a hair. The handle is fashioned from the bone of an elk taken from the great forests of Norway. Old Wit van Ness was commissioned to make it for you. And see there, an inscription of our battle cry, *"Vrijheid altijd,"* which means "Freedom always!"

Heinrich answered quietly, "I am not worthy of such honor, Cornelis. You have returned my simple act tenfold. I told you before, I did not choose to fight with you. It was as if I was carried along by an unseen hand. I confess I do still wonder if my soul is in greater peril now, or in less." His voice trailed away and he sighed.

Cornelis smiled and clapped him on the shoulder. "And as I've told you, you think too much! Now, 'tis time we get you to the dock. Wife, he's well supplied?"

Edda nodded as Anna took Heinrich's hand and squeezed it warmly. "Thanks be to God for you; you saved the life of m'son." The man smiled and turned to touch each sleeping child lightly on their heads. "May God's blessings be upon these little ones ... and you all." He faced his hosts. "You have shown me more kindness in these few months than I have seen in many years. I've no words to thank you but I pledge I shall ne'er forget you. When I am home I shall ask a special friend of mine—Brother Lukas is his name— to pray for you each day, and when I meet another— Brother Blasius, the Templar—he, too, shall pray for your safekeeping." Heinrich followed Cornelis to the door and turned one last time. *"Veel danken ... Vrijheid altijd."*

ॐ

Groot was a leathery seaman of Frisian roots, born at the mouth of the Weser River some thirty-five years prior. Being Heinrich's elder by only two years, the man treated his passenger with more respect than he did the four young oarsmen who served him. Gruff and coarse by the standards of more genteel folk, the sailor was courageous, intelligent, and ambitious in the finest sense of the word.

He stood aft on the sturdy vessel he had purchased from a Danish shipwright ten years before. It was wide and squat, blending the features of a traditional Nordic design with the features of the popular Celtic cog. Skillfully crafted of planks hewn from ancient Swedish oak, the ship was worthy of the wright's skill. It lay some thirty-eight feet long and sixteen feet wide and maintained a generous freeboard even when weighed heavy with cargo. It had a flat bottom, like the cogs, and a straight sternpost. The vessel was powered by a large square sail and four long oars, and like the Viking ships of years past, it was steered by a large rudder attached to the side of the stern. Its tall, upward-curved bow ploughed the waves with the self-respect and unpretentious determination of its master.

Groot stared quietly at the gray September sky. His ship's hold was filled with baskets of grains from the Stedinger farmers as well as wheels of cheese, leather goods, and some handcrafts. He was paid a handsome fee to brave both the perils of an autumn sea and the violence of Nordic pirates, but only once had he failed to return with a profitable exchange. A stiff breeze from the west gave him pause. The Danish seas were usually calm and blessed with light winds in summer, but late September and October were often given to strong westerly storms. He looked carefully at the dark, western horizon and reasoned that the pirates would be equally wary to sail. *Do I risk high seas or evil men?* he wondered. Groot looked at his waiting crew and at the one-eyed stranger staring blankly at the gray water lapping hard against the smooth bow. "Cast off!" he cried.

The four crewmen scrambled to throw their heavy ropes onto the dock before pulling hard to set the sail. The oars were lowered and the squat ship began to lightly roll with the falling tide of the Weser.

Heinrich's heart soared within him as he peered into the wind-drifting mist of the river. He had never been on water before and he immediately turned his ears toward birds screeching above. His nostrils were filled with the smells of fish and of river mud. He gathered his cloak around him to chase the morning chill and pulled his hood over his head.

The sun was rarely seen that day as Groot sailed northward across the widening Weser. The river's spreading banks were flat and empty, the sky growing ever larger. Heinrich stood with legs spread wide atop the thick planks of the ship's foredeck as it began to rock into the river's mouth. The man breathed deeply of salt air and turned his face to either side where mud flats and reeds stretched as far as he could see. He looked forward and saw nothing but gray water that met the sky somewhere beyond his sight. The simple baker from Weyer was speechless and awestruck. The wind blew hard through his hair as sea birds cried overhead.

The increasing wind had made Groot quiet and ill-tempered. His ship was tacking due north in a stiff westerly and his large hands and forearms worked hard on the heavy rudder. Heinrich noticed the man's obsession with the sky and he could see concern in the man's tight, sun-etched face. Groot motioned for his passenger to come close and Heinrich lurched his way to the stern. "Go below," Groot bellowed.

"Aye, sir. Is all well?"

"*Ja.* We've nearly a hundred leagues to the tip of Jutland. With a heavy cargo and light winds we would've made about ten leagues a day. With this wind we'll be doubling that, but if it blows harder we'll begin to slow. She tacks good in strong wind, but poorly in high."

Heinrich nodded politely. He knew nothing of the sea. He did know, however, that he could walk more than one league in an hour so he was surprised to learn the ship normally only traveled ten leagues from dawn to dawn. "I thought the ship might go faster."

Groot shook his head. "Not these merchants. The old Vikings could travel six or seven times what we do, but their fighting ships were sleek and made for speed. Now, you needs get below; the wind's up."

Heinrich ducked beneath the deck and found a comfortable corner atop a few baskets of oats. There he lay the rest of that day and all of the night following, but he awakened as sick and miserable as any man could be. His belly rolled and his skin turned a clammy white. He scrambled to the deck frequently to vomit into the water, believing for all the world that he might die. By midday and all the night next he lay and wished that he had been slain in the battle. "If God has mercy, let Him take m'soul from this cursed boat!" he groaned.

On the fourth day the winds eased and Groot permitted his passenger to crawl onto the deck once more. The crew greeted the baker of Weyer with howls of laughter as the poor wretch dragged himself to the high wedge of the bow. There he let a cool wind soothe his haggard face. A kind oarsman handed Heinrich a tankard of beer and a strip of salted fish.

"Oh, dear God above," groaned Heinrich weakly, "I cannot! Methinks I shall surely die."

The sailor laughed and slapped him on the back. "*Goed man, je leven!*"

On the sixth day, Groot navigated his ship around the point of Denmark and steered his ship east-southeast toward the Swedish town of Götheborg in the lands of West Göthland. He was relieved to have seen no pirates but was surprised to find that only a handful of merchantmen were on the sea. September was usually safe, and the first to get a harvest to dock earned the highest profits. "Heinrich, we've but five days to port. Can you live a bit longer?" He laughed.

Heinrich was feeling a little better and smiled halfheartedly. "Aye, sir, methinks so, but can y'not keep the sea still for me?" He leaned across the smooth rail of the rolling ship and stared at the blue horizon. Somewhere in the distance the sky and the sea merged into one and the man marveled. He scanned the distant view and watched the water shimmer, reflecting all the colors of the rainbow. "Ah, *Frau* Emma," he sighed, "if only you could see this!"

The ship rose and fell rhythmically on the North Sea's waves and Heinrich sat comfortably with his back against the salt-worn walls of the ship's deck. He closed his eye to enjoy the music of the groaning hull, the sailcloth in the wind, and the rub of ropes. But thoughts began to creep over him like an army of shadows consuming a fragile light. His mind began to fill with the images of Weyer and his past. He suddenly saw Baldric's face and he chilled. He saw the stern faces of abbots and monks, priests, stewards—and

Marta, staring at him with contempt and cruelty. It was as if he could hear them shaming him for his betrayal. The man felt sick. He was so very confused, so very disoriented that he did not know which world was real and which was not.

He opened his eye with a start. *Sins and penance,* he groaned inwardly. *I've yet to know how to save m'lads or Marta from m'wicked past. Oh, dear saints! I've truly forfeited all I've come for. My soul and theirs may be in greater jeopardy now than when I left!* A nervous flutter tickled his empty belly and his mouth went dry. *I raised m'arm against the army of the Church! I am a runaway; I have coveted the freedom of the Stedingers, filled my heart with pride; I've indulged m'self with joy ... Oh wicked man that I am! Surely, I must find a great penance.* A grumble from Groot distracted Heinrich from his internal diatribe.

The captain's face was turned to the west; his round nose was lifted like that of a hound scenting the air. Heinrich climbed to his feet and followed the captain's gaze to a menacing bank of clouds mounting in the western horizon. What he did not see, however, was what only a seaworthy Frisian could see. Some distance behind the ship a darting wedge of wind had ruffled the sea's surface. To port another patch was stirred, then another. A pocket of cold air swelled the sail and the ship lurched a little.

"All hands tighten the ropes aft! Prepare to set two oars; you, sailor, lend me your back at the rudder."

Heinrich sensed something was about. He groaned aloud. "Only one more day to dry land!"

Groot knew what was coming and within the hour his wooden ship was riding the white-capped sea like a squire tossing atop an unbroken colt. A howling western wind drove hard into the stretching sail while ropes and timbers groaned. Stinging salt water broke over the high bow and crashed atop the struggling crew.

The sturdy craft heaved and plunged atop the sea all through that afternoon while Heinrich trembled deep in the hold. It was sometime just past dusk when the cloth sail ripped. It split into two ragged pieces and, like the

rending of the temple's holy veil, its cleave changed everything. Cries sounded from the deck and the ship suddenly
spun. Groot and his seamen grasped and grunted at the
rudder, straining against the mighty waves. Unable to
have its bow turned toward the wind, the ship drifted sideways to the storm. Water poured onto its deck and the hold
began to fill.

Heinrich clambered up from his flooding refuge and
sprawled on the slippery deck. With only one arm he
could do little more than lie helpless and terrified in the
darkness. A desperate sailor hollered in his ear, "Follow
me!" The baker obeyed and slid on his belly back to the
hold.

"Groot says heave the cargo!" shouted the sailor.

Heinrich nodded and helped drag bushel after bushel of
Cornelis's precious harvest to the deck above. The man
strained and groaned and used his back and legs to help
his aching arm lift what he could. He wrestled wooden
casks, wicker baskets, carts, and crates to the deck while
other hands tossed one after the other into the angry sea. It
would prove to be a futile effort.

The night's storm redoubled its bluster like a zephyr
gone mad. The wind that had formerly only howled now
raged with bitter squalls of raw and unyielding malice as if
blown from the fearsome lungs of a leviathan. Groot's ship
was quickly filling with water and listing farther with each
crashing wave. No human hands could hold the rudder,
and the captain finally bellowed to his crew, "The ship is
lost! Find a barrel or plank!"

Heinrich had no time for fear. He could not swim, of
course, and knew he was in grave peril. His mind worked
quickly. He removed his eye patch and dagger and placed
them deep within the satchel he secured over his shoulder.
He bound his cloak with a belt and grabbed hold of a wide
plank he had secretly prepared for such an unlikely
moment. The baker slipped along the tilting deck and followed the sounds of voices until he was huddled with his
fellows. A mighty, black wave suddenly lifted and rolled the
squat merchant ship high. Then, as if a mighty hand

pushed hard from port, the ship tumbled over on its star-board side, plunging all hands into the foaming sea.

Heinrich held his board with all his strength and sucked a mighty breath of air into his lungs before he disappeared beneath the water. For an awful moment the baker's world was black and suffocating, strangely quiet and nearly still. The oak was not meant to sink, however, and the man rode it on a vertical shot to the surface. Heinrich's face broke the water with a gasp. Sputtering in the salty spray and with all the might his arm and legs could muster, he pulled and kicked until his upper body lay draped atop the bobbing board.

With legs dangling in the cold water, Heinrich peered desperately into the night's darkness for his fellows. The man strained to hear, but his ears were filled only with the whistling of wind and the wash of water. Unable to do more, he spent the rest of that awful night hanging desperately to his plank.

By daybreak the wind had eased and a cold rain pelted the flattening sea below. The six men were scattered across a wide area but were within view of one another. In a few hours they managed to kick and paddle their way together. Groot knew he needed to find either a ship or landfall soon, and he strained to see through the cold rain that now washed over them. For hours, the hapless seamen floated aimlessly at the mercy of the sea's currents until Groot's ears finally cocked. "Shh." The six bobbed quietly. "There! Can y'hear it?" A church bell was ringing. "The blessed bells of sext! 'Tis noontime, lads, and we're drifting toward land! Tide's up ... that's good. Now kick and paddle!" His eyes brightened and a huge smile crossed his face. Ahead was a flat ribbon of land, and as the rain eased all could see the spire of a church.

"*Prijzen God!*" they cried.

By midafternoon a rolling tide tumbled the shipwrecked party onto the sandy beach of the large Danish island of Slotshlomen. The men stumbled out of the surf and col-lapsed, shivering and numb but grateful beyond words to reach land alive. Groot stared toward the distant town.

"Heinrich, I'm not sure where we are. Seems like we'd be near to the mouth of the sound. That would make Havn some two days away by land."

"Havn?"

"Aye. Some call it Copenhagen. 'Tis a good port built on the marshes. The Bishop of Roskilde owns it from the other side. 'Tis where all Christendom gets its salted herring for Lent! We needs get help in this town, then maybe walk to Havn."

"I needs get to Götheborg and winter with the Swede." Heinrich shivered.

Groot shook his head. "Nay, sir. I'll not be going there now. I'll get m'men to Havn where we'll ferry our way south, 'round the islands to Schleswig. Then I'll needs overland them to home."

Heinrich stared blankly. "But, I ..." He was exhausted, cold, hungry, and confused.

"First, y'needs get dry and warm, be fed, and see where we are. And y'needs cover that hole in your face!" Groot roared.

Heinrich nodded, slowly. He reached into his satchel and put his patch back over his eye. He was relieved to find his dagger safe and he secured it in his belt. He pinched the Laubusbach stone between his finger and his thumb. Then he smiled. "Here." He offered his fellows a generous portion of the food that Edda had sent with him. The six feasted on his cheese, fish, and salted pork, and in a few moments the company was hurrying toward the belltower of the church.

ᔥ

Groot's instincts were correct. His crew had washed ashore at the north end of an island some two or three days' journey from Copenhagen, and they were now the guests of a hospitable Danish fishing village. The local priest fed the six and led them to a roaring hearth where they sat naked under wool blankets held wide to capture the heat of the snapping blaze. Three weeks later the same priest arranged their transport with a wagonload of sympathetic monks from a monastery in Sweden who were traveling to an outpost in eastern Pomerania, just north of Poland.

The six were introduced to a Swedish priest, one Father

Baltasar, who was escorting the monks. The gracious young father insisted Heinrich and the sailors take positions in the tall wagon while he and his white-robed Carthusian brethren walked alongside the wagon's solid wheels. Looking over the side at the hooded heads bowed and bobbing beneath him drew Heinrich back to visions of the monks in Villmar. He stared at these men, quite aware that their gesture was an act of true Christian piety. Amazed and profoundly moved, he was suddenly disturbed by their kindness. He closed his eye and groaned within himself, now certain he had betrayed the good that yet was in the world of his past.

As promised, the priest and his monks finally delivered the sailors to Havn where they bade a humble farewell. Groot and his men would need to find a ferry back to the Jutland peninsula before marching overland to home. The churchmen, on the other hand, would ferry southeastward to the mainland at Stettin by the mouth of the Oder River near the eastern borders of the German Empire.

Heinrich had reasoned that he would follow the monks to Stettin and then travel south through the Oder River valley until such time as he might make a move westward toward home. It was a plan counseled by Groot and not without wisdom. Heinrich dared not venture into any of the lands influenced by news from knights returning from Oldenburg, and numbers of them had come from manors all over nearby Brandenburg, Saxony, and Thurungia. Nor did he dare wander farther east into the perilous lands of the Poles. By transversing the Oder Valley he should be safe in between both dangers and hidden in the wilderness until he was far enough south to make his turn.

The sailors could offer the monks nothing more than their heartfelt thanks. For their part, the brethren seemed genuinely pleased to have served their fellow man. Groot and his companions then turned to Heinrich and embraced him. Each offered him a hearty "Godspeed" and Groot whispered a final word of advice: "Say nothing to the brothers or their priest. Do not tell them of your past ... of where you come from, or how you lost your arm and eye. Even the tongue of a good monk can slip ... and one slip might surely be your doom. I've told them all that they needs know about you."

"What did you say?" asked Heinrich.

"I said you were a pilgrim doing penance. Godspeed, Heinrich. Perhaps we meet again!"

"But ... but, Groot ... wait—" With a saddened look to the men that had become so quickly familiar, he waved a final farewell. It was a painful moment for the baker. Though he had known the sailors for only a short time, he had grown close to them. Sharing the terror of the shipwreck and the joy of survival had knit the six together in a way only such a shared adventure can. "Ah, indeed. Perhaps we meet again."

⁊

It would be several more days before Heinrich finally boarded the ferry with the monks. He had done his best to keep a polite but necessary distance from the priest and the brothers, for he was uneasy about what questions might be posed. "Follow us—we are ready to sail, good pilgrim!" cried Father Baltasar.

Heinrich drew a deep breath and nodded. "At last," he grumbled. It was already two days past All Souls' Day and the world had turned gray and cold. He wrapped himself tightly in his cloak as he stepped out from the church that had been his safe haven. He thanked the priests, then followed the silent column of monks through the village streets. In less than a quarter of an hour he stood facing a rough-looking galley filled with sad faces. Heinrich gaped at the eyes peering at him, for though he had heard of slaves before—and even had known a few in Weyer—he had never seen them like this.

Before him sat tight rows of Slavic pagans, "Lithuanians," some voice muttered, "else eastern Poles." Dirty, shivering within their thin wraps, the score of broad-faced men and a handful of women sat chained to the ship's deck. Heinrich thought of his friends, Telek and Varina, and his heart sagged. Christian knights had captured these Slavs in their campaign into the wild and untamed reaches of the Baltic lands and Poland. The wretches would doubtlessly be sold in the popular slave market of Lübeck.

The baker followed his hosts along a wide plank joining the dock and the ship, and he stepped onto the smooth planks with a measure of anxiety. A crewman led Heinrich and the clerics past the hapless cargo of souls to a set of benches in the stern.

Father Baltasar handed the captain a small bag of silver as payment for the passage before sitting next to Heinrich. "So, my son. 'Tis a chill in the air but the captain promises a smooth sail to Stettin." The priest had a calming way about him and smiled kindly. Heinrich thought him to be about twenty-five and believed him to be a good and decent man, though somewhat nondescript. He was plain to look at—mild brown eyes, light brown hair, average height, and plain face. It was only his Christian charity that set him apart from other men—that, and a quality of humility that bred an air of quiet confidence.

Heinrich was hesitant to engage the father in conversation and had hoped to sit amongst the silent brethren without uttering a word for the entire journey. Instead, he smiled self-consciously at the loquacious priest and groaned inwardly. It was not that the priest was unpleasant company. On the contrary, the man was cheerful and intelligent. Heinrich was simply fearful of those reasonable questions any leisurely discussion might present. *What if he asks me of m'home ... how do I answer him?* he wondered. *And what of m'arm and eye ... and my penance—he's not yet mentioned it! Ach, dare I lie to a priest? And, by the saints, exactly what did Groot tell him?*

Chaper 21

ENDLESS GRAY

he single-sailed galley rolled atop a gentle sea as it pitched and lurched southward toward the northern shore of the continent. The ship was longer than Groot's and served by eight oarsmen, a slave-master, a master-of-the-deck, and the captain. The crew was Norwegian, all except the brutish slave-master, a Wend from the nearby island of Rügen.

The captain treated Heinrich and the churchmen well and commanded the ship to a respectful silence whenever the monks conducted their prayers and psalms. The brothers were sober and contemplative. They devoted much of their day to saying the three offices: firstly, the Office of the Day; secondly, the *de Beata,* which is the Office of Our Lady; and finally the Office of the Dead. They ate only one scanty meal per day and repeatedly declined generous offerings of fish or cheese from the ship's crew. Unlike their Benedictine counterparts, these Carthusians were clean-shaven and their habits were white, not black, though they, too, shaved the crowns of their heads in the tonsure. Their willingness to deny themselves even the most meager of personal comforts made them good candidates to bring the Word to the farthest, most uncomfortable reaches of Christendom. Father Baltasar and his monks were being sent to a new monastery in the marshes of Pomerania near the western borders of pagan Prussia.

As Heinrich had dreaded from the outset, Baltasar soon launched a series of questions that brought beads of sweat to the baker's brow despite the biting cold of the Baltic air. He knew he could neither betray the Stedingers nor lie to a priest of God. The poor fellow did his best to elude and evade, but the dual assault of the father's curiosity and his own pricked conscience made the experience unbearable. Each new probe evoked a more clever hedge, and with each hedge Heinrich felt all the more like Jacob, the great deceiver. He wished the sky would blacken with a mighty tempest; that the sea would roll giant mountains toward them so the flapping jaw beside him would be stilled!

It was on the third day of Heinrich's present agony that his verbose companion loosed a bit of news that cornered the simple baker. Father Baltasar did not intend to torment the man so, nor was he aware of the misery that Heinrich now suffered. He was genuinely curious about the stranger and wanted to shepherd the fellow's soul to good places. So, when he yawned and nonchalantly shared that which Groot had told him, he had no malice.

Heinrich paled and gripped his seat. Huge streams of sweat ran into his beard and he gulped. "What, father? What did you say?"

"Ah, my son. It seems you have barely listened to me all this voyage! I said that your friend Groot told me you are a pious man and are on a pilgrimage to Rome to do a great penance. He said that in your humility you wanted others not to know, hence I have been shy to embarrass you with my knowledge of it. Forgive me for mentioning it, but I do wish to be your encourager in this."

Heinrich stared at him blankly. *Rome?* he thought. *A penance to the Holy City?*

"My son? Are you listening? Have you heard what I said?"

Heinrich's mind whirled; the news was a shock but suddenly became something of an epiphany. *Rome? Of course Rome!* he thought. *Indeed! Other than Jerusalem, 'tis no better place. There I might truly free our souls ... Rome could forgive me, cleanse me, free m'family from judgment, and put me truly on the proper way again.*

"But 'tis so very far ... how would I get there? How long a journey?" Heinrich was mumbling.

"Aye? Did you say something, my son?"

"Nay father, I was talking under m'breath."

"Ah. So, again ... forgive me but I should like very much to pray for you and am happy beyond words that a freeman like yourself would walk away from temporal things to serve God."

Heinrich was barely listening. He fumbled for words. "F–freeman?'

"Aye!" laughed Baltasar. "Of course, a Stedinger man! Groot also says you are a fine baker ... and that your arm and eye were lost when your family perished in a great slaughter by rogue knights in your youth."

"He said that?"

"*Ja.* Is it so?"

Heinrich licked his lips, "Groot has a way of ... of spin ning a tale. He ... he makes a big sail of small threads."

"Ha! Like a good sailor ought!"

Heinrich nodded. His tangled mind was churning and he faced the horizon with tight lips and a tense face. The man ached for his sons and a twinge of doubt suddenly brushed against the idea of Rome's remedy.

"So tell me about your hopes for Rome."

The baker's mouth was dry and he closed his eye. *What to do?* he wondered. *I am caught in a snare. If I speak against Groot's word, then suspicion is aroused and more questions. Ach ... and there ... the crew is listening! They'll take word of suspicion far and wide.*

The captain leaned forward. "Father, did I hear y'say this man's on pilgrimage to Rome?"

"*Ja,* my son."

The old, weathered Norseman looked at Heinrich with piercing blue eyes that chilled the baker. Heinrich was sure the man suspected something. The captain stared for a long moment, then slowly reached into his shirt and pulled a necklace over his head. It was a valuable silver chain bearing a long, curved tooth. "My grandfather's grand-father took this tooth from a water-dragon in the shoals off

Iceland. The silver comes from a Scot pirate who m'grand-father's father killed near the Shetlands. 'Tis the only thing of value left to me, besides this leaky ship. My own three sons 'ave been lost to the sea and I've none to pass it to.

"You, stranger, needs take this to the Holy Stairs in Rome; m'mother told me of them from a bishop who once climbed them. Lay it there and have a priest say a prayer for me and for m'lads. I must do something for our souls' sake. … Judgment is fast coming. Surely the Virgin would look kindly on us for such a gift. Take it, man, and I shall return the monks' silver for their passage." He leaned close to Heinrich's ear, then whispered, "And I'll say nothing of the runaway rumored 'bout the ports."

Heinrich groaned. The man knew.

Father Baltasar laid his hands on Heinrich's shoulders. "My son, serve this man as you have been served; charity for charity. Take his treasure to Rome with you."

Heinrich turned his eye away from the smiling monks, only to lay it on the beaming face of the hopeful priest. The Norseman bowed and laid his necklace into Heinrich's opened palm. "Swear to me, stranger, by the Holy Virgin and to her servants on this deck that you shall surely do this and you shall do it directly. I've not many years left in me."

Heinrich knew once he vowed this service to the captain he must surely go. After all, the Virgin and the saints were listening.

He closed his hand around the necklace. He wanted nothing more than to return to his beloved sons and once again smell bread baking in his own ovens. He longed to walk along the Laubusbach and sit beneath the Magi on a summer's Sabbath day. He sorely missed the comforting counsel of Brother Lukas. Yet he would neither endanger the Stedingers nor return to Weyer with the souls of his family in even greater peril. The sad-eyed peasant had little choice. Like a weary dog entreated to oblige his master, the poor man yielded to his chosen destiny. He moaned within himself, then answered, "I so swear."

❧

Snow was falling when Heinrich followed the monks along a slippery plank and onto the dock in Stettin. He bade the captain farewell and assented once more to his pledge before hastily following Baltasar to the town's church. He was heavy-hearted and depressed. His shoulders slumped and he plumbed the dark recesses of his soul in search of reasons for his predicament.

The man trudged thought the town, soon thinking of nothing other than the hurt his further delay would inflict on Wil and Karl. *More than a year!* he moaned within himself. *I've been away more than a year ... and now I've sins enough to send me to Rome! I pledged only forty days to Pious.* The pitiful man realized something else as well. It was November and he would not travel very far before winter would close around him.

It was as if Baltasar could read the man's mind. "You must spend the gray days with us, my son," he offered. "We journey overland to a monastery near Posen in the land of the Poles. We plan to winter there before traveling farther east in springtime."

Heinrich was beaten and knew he had no other choice. He had no money and no means of transport. He grit his teeth and yielded. "I cannot repay you, father. But I can serve in the monks' bakery if they'll have me."

"Aye! So, 'tis true you are a baker!"

"*Ja,* father."

Baltasar nodded compassionately. "It must be hard work with only one arm. Pity, you have lost the other along with your family."

Heinrich shook his head. *Enough of this,* he thought. He turned to the priest. "Father, it is my wish that you ask me nothing more of my past. I choose to think only of my coming time in Rome and the cleansing of my miserable soul."

Baltasar nodded and bowed sheepishly. "I humbly ask your pardon, my son. I am content to know you as you wish to be known."

Heinrich sighed and thanked the father, then reluctantly climbed into a large, four-wheeled wagon. The group traveled for about a week over rough roads and through a flat monotonous wilderness buffeted by blustery winds. They followed the Oder River south until the point at which it converged with the Warthe. There they turned east past countless lonely, desolate villages of German colonists until they were deep within the Kingdom of Poland. At last, on a cold, damp night they arrived at the tiny monastery in Posen.

The Carthusian cloister was little more than a single-naved church surrounded by a pathetic ring of stone and timbered buildings that served as the refectory, infirmary, stable, chapter house, and such. The porter greeted the new arrivals with the customary welcome, and the group was hurried to the chilly chambers of the ruling prior. Tankards of beer and a tray of cheese were offered, but they were presented with neither enthusiasm nor joy. A few dutiful words were exchanged and soon all were directed to their night's quarters.

Wrapped in his sealskin cloak, Heinrich lay atop a board bed and shivered beneath a thin wool blanket. A small, meaningless fire burned in a smoking hearth at the end of the dormitory, giving as little heat as light. The man stared at the underside of the thatch roof and wondered why and how it was that he was lying in some forgotten place in Poland with only one arm and one eye, penniless, despairing, and cold. He would have wept had not the first tear of self-pity so shamed him that he clenched his jaw.

In the morning of his first day he was assigned to duties in the kitchen as the baker's helper. The cloister's baker was a lay monk, one whose vows did not require the piety of the choir monks nor demand the same devotion to either self-denial or charity. He was a sullen, blond-haired Pole named Radoslaw who had no affection for either Germans or their language. With utter disdain, he grunted and directed Heinrich to his tasks with pointed fingers and lips curled like a seething wolf.

Heinrich served his master without complaint. He labored hard, for kneading dough with one hand proved difficult. He was an expert in formulas, however, and meekly showed Radoslaw better techniques for preparing the oven and shaping rolls, pretzels, loaves, and the like. It was a miserable, unrewarding relationship, however, making the harsh winter seem all the more endless.

The Advent came and passed, then the Epiphany, and finally the self-inflicted sufferings of Lent were also over. Easter was the sixth of April in the year 1208, and on that day Heinrich complained to Father Baltasar about his confinement in the dreadful place. He had wanted to begin his pilgrimage long before but had been frustrated by delays due to heavy spring rains that had made the roads nearly impossible to travel. Father Baltasar and his monks were equally eager to begin their journey and preparations for their departure were underway. Unfortunately, the skies of April were unyielding and day after day the deluge continued. The priest made every effort to calm the man. "Heinrich, you are to be honored for your zeal. Surely your heart's desire is to stand before the Lateran Palace of the Pope and receive the merits of your faithfulness. Ah, 'tis a wonder to behold a common man who is not common at all! Tell me, my son, does your heart soar as you see the Holy City in your mind's eye?"

Heinrich was in no mood for this. He wanted to escape the bells, the chants, the prayers, the fasts, the incense, the huddles of head-bowed shavelings, and all their somber ways. He had no interest in another conversation with the verbose young priest and at that moment would have preferred to share a bench with some rough-tongued drunkard! "Aye!" He shouted the lie and as soon as it left his lips his heart sank again. The bite in his tone caught the priest unawares, though the answer pleased him.

"I thought as much," he answered, smiling cautiously. "Might I beg you one small favor?"

Heinrich closed his eye in dread. He knew the skill with which churchmen cloak obligation in just that sort of innocuous query. He nodded and held his breath.

"You are a good man. Come with me a moment." The priest walked Heinrich through the mud and rain to a corner of the cloister church where a dusty, gray beam of light strained to chase a few stubborn shadows. He reached into a satchel hanging by his side and reverently withdrew a long silver chain suspending a gold medallion. The coin twirled in the muted light of the church. Heinrich watched it, entranced and somewhat mesmerized. Something about it seemed vaguely familiar.

"This relic is a gift from Archbishop Anders Sunesen of our diocese in Göthland. An astounding man of God, is he; a poet of extraordinary skill. Ah, but no matter. It is said he received this from the Archbishop of Mainz in exchange for herring. He then presented it to our former prior upon the cloister's endowment. Our prior, in turn, has sent it with us along with a lock of hair from Saint Cyrill, once the Bishop of Jerusalem. He prayed these relics would protect us on the sea from pirates and from the pagans by land.

"Since our sea journey was already blessed, some of the brethren believe the new monastery would be best served if one of these would be taken to Rome and presented to a church that cares for the poor. So they have chosen the gold medallion for you to take."

"Gold?"

"*Ja*, friend. 'Tis a gold bezance ... see here ... it appears one of the ancients bit into it with a broken tooth!"

Heinrich went nearly faint. He grabbed the coin and stared numbly at the dashes made by one good tooth and one broken. "Father ... tell me what else you know of this."

Baltasar paused, surprised at the man's sudden interest. "My son?" He paused, then continued slowly. "The archbishop was informed that this very medallion was touched to the Holy Sepulchre by the Grand Master of the Knights Templar and so blessed by him. It bears the power and wonder of our Lord's body."

Heinrich's eye blurred with tears. He held the necklace to his breast and collapsed to his knees. "Oh, Mother!" he muttered. "Oh, dear Mother, it is your golden secret come to help me!"

Father Baltasar was pleased with the man's apparent veneration and laid a hand on Heinrich's trembling shoulders. "Good and worthy fellow. You are entrusted with a sacred thing. Our prayers shall follow you on your journey."

Heinrich rose slowly, still holding the medallion to his heart. He faced the priest, dumbfounded and speechless, and listened as he was given final instructions.

"Brother Ignatius prayerfully and humbly offered a candidate Church to receive this relic. Ignatius was an orphan in the city of Rome and raised with Christian charity amongst other destitute children in the church known as *Santa Maria in Domnica*. It is agreed that this church should be granted the relic for the blessing and protection of its lowly flock. It is our wish that you should deliver it to the superior of that particular church along with this." Baltasar handed Heinrich a folded paper sealed with wax. "Present this letter as witness to the nature of our gift and the sacrifice of your service."

Father Baltasar then took the chain away from Heinrich and walked slowly to the altar. He laid the coin atop the bronze table and prayed loudly. Then he motioned for Heinrich to approach and he lifted the necklace over Heinrich's head. He laid the golden medallion gently on the man's heaving chest and prayed, "Angel of God, my dear guardian, to whom his love commits me here; light and guard, rule and guide."

Heinrich opened his eye and wiped the tears off his face. The priest embraced him and together they returned to the rain-soaked courtyard of the barren cloister.

For the next week it mattered little to the man whether the world was wet or sunny. In the mornings he awakened with his hand closed tightly around his mother's relic, and when he drifted to sleep he held it all the more. Its presence around his neck restored him to the world from whence he came and he embraced it joyfully.

The rains finally began to ease by the end of April and the roadways were reported to be nearly passable. The cloister was busy with the tardy planting of early peas and the ploughing of its few well-drained fields. Lay-monks scurried about during the few days of warm sunshine in a rhythm of tasks that was familiar to Heinrich.

At long last, it was agreed that conditions were right for the pilgrim to begin his sacred journey. He was called from his bed at morning lauds, sometime before the bells of prime. He rose to receive the blessing of the cloister priests and to hear a psalm sung by the monks in his honor. As he approached the church, however, he suddenly felt faint. Heinrich took a few steps, then lurched forward and caught himself on a stone column just inside the church door. He looked up to see rows of white-robed monks sitting on their gradines and staring at him solemnly. It was all that he remembered.

Later that morning, Heinrich awakened in the cloister's infirmary sweating and delirious with high fever. "*Debilitas*, winter fever ... possibly bilious fever?" The cloister's infirmer was neither well-trained nor confident.

Father Baltasar was grave. He leaned over the man and prayed. "Heinrich, can you hear me?"

Heinrich groaned.

The priest and his monks gathered together with the infirmer and the prior. It was decided that God's will would hardly be thwarted by a simple fever and that the Devil was no doubt fearful of the man's mission. It was further agreed that the man's fever was most likely not a result of personal sin, for Baltasar was convinced the man was devout. Nor could it be from immoderate living; none were witness to any excess in greed, gluttony, or impure behaviors. Instead, the consensus was that the man suffered maladies resulting from the oppression of the Evil One. Since all were convinced of the man's calling as the relic-bearer, all believed he would be healed.

Father Baltasar was so certain of Heinrich's healing that he counseled his Carthusians that they should press on to their own calling without the slightest reluctance. He vouched for Heinrich's piety and uncommon devotion. He assured all that the relic would be safe and they need not do more than pray as they left him behind in the safekeeping of the cloister.

The matter settled, Heinrich received an anointing of oil, a quiet song, and a bathing of scented water from the priest. Baltasar and his monks then bade the sleeping man a whispered farewell and began their perilous journey to the eastern frontier.

Poor Heinrich wrestled with his fever for days. He awoke in the darkness beset by night terrors and hallucinations. He cried aloud when he thought he saw the hand of Baldric's ghost grasping at his medallion. With a whimper he returned to half-sleep only to be awakened by nightmares of Ingly drowning in a flooding Laubusbach. He felt both his hands stretching to rescue the desperate lad, but he could not quite touch him. When Ingly's eyes rolled and his white hair sank out of sight in the brown water, the man lurched awake, weeping. By day the man dreamt of fresh breezes in the sun-swept cottage of Cornelis. He drew breath through his flared nostrils and was sure he could smell the clean air of that glorious, free land. It was those pleasant recollections that brought some peace to his bed.

Unable to stand, Heinrich could barely lift his head to receive infusions of sweating herbs such as thyme, hyssop, or chamomile. Depending on the position of the moon, the frantic infirmer poured either barley water or raspberry vinegar down the gagging man's throat.

By the end of the third week it was rumored that Heinrich might surely die after all. Having tried all manner of ministrations without success, the weary prior and his worried infirmer yielded their patient's ultimate end to the Healer of the universe. They prayed earnestly for Heinrich's restoration and sufficed to do what service each day required. The man's fever lingered, however, and he spent more days in dreamy places.

It was sometime in the afternoon of Pentecost when the baker of Weyer finally awoke. The infirmer was in the church celebrating the holy day so Heinrich stared at the ceiling before serving himself a tankard of thin, warm ale that was sitting by his bed. He glanced about the room and saw his cloak, tunic, leggings, satchel, and eye patch set neatly on a distant stool. In the bed next to his own coughed an old monk suffering consumption, though greatly relieved at Heinrich's sudden improvement. Heinrich rolled from his straw mattress, only to find his legs too weak to hold him. He pulled himself back into his bed and lay still.

Between nones and vespers the infirmer returned and rejoiced to see his patient in better health. He quickly ran to the kitchen and returned with a hot pottage of lentils, spring peas, boiled cabbage, and bits of smoked pork. Heinrich smiled and slurped weakly from the man's spoon. And so it was from day to day for the next week.

But it was as though forces greater than the man bedeviled him. Whenever his fever broke and good health seemed to blossom, another bout of debilitating illness seized him and he was on his back once more. Heinrich began to wonder if it was his mother's relic that had cursed him. "Not worthy," he groaned in his sleep. "Am I not worthy to wear it? My heart is black with sin and shame."

On a day in early July the hapless baker was feeling somewhat better and he wandered beneath a sparse young linden to ponder his suffering. He held the medallion in his hand and considered the state of his life. "I was sent from m'village to do a penance for sins known and unknown. Surely, I needed to do that thing, for my lads, m'wife, and m'self were in peril of the Judgment. Yet I failed to pay the proper price! Instead of suffering pain and remorse I delighted in my journey and my heart filled with pride. Then I coveted the liberty of others and deceived myself to join them as if I were one of them. I raised my arm against the army of the archbishop. God took one of m'arms as payment for my rebellion and he took one eye for m'envy." He buried his face in the palm of his hand. "My sin followed me to the sea ... it caused the shipwreck and the loss of Cornelis's harvest. They should have cast *me* out.

"I deceived a priest to believe I am a devout pilgrim in order to protect those who rebel against God's order. Now I wear this holy relic as if it were mine by right ... my heart covets the thing for mine own.

"Wicked man that I am, 'tis good I go to Rome. There I shall beg God's mercy; there I shall sink m'self into what is right and true. I shall walk home clean and whole ... m'sons shall be free of my penalty." Heinrich sat up and drew a deep breath. He removed his mother's necklace and placed it in his satchel with the captain's. He coughed and wheezed and stumbled back to his bed.

All that long summer Heinrich suffered recurring bouts of fever or malaise. As kindly as the monks attempted to be, they, too, were becoming impatient with his recovery. By the Feast of the Assumption in mid-August he seemed to be making true progress, however. By the early days of September strength returned to his legs and he helped drive the oxcarts laden with firewood from the forests in the south. Unfortunately, a fall in the garden caused him to seriously sprain an ankle and he was bound to a crutch.

On St. Michael's the frustrated man received news that drove him nearly to the point of madness. Brother Radoslaw had died. No one knew why or how; the man simply did not awaken from his sleep. His apprentice had been a novice who had been dismissed from the cloister for insubordination at Lammas, so there was none to operate the bakery. Bread, of course, was that most important symbol of both temporal and spiritual nourishment. It would not do that the brethren should suffer their deprivations without that one sacred foundation. Monks in monasteries everywhere wanted fresh, warm rolls in the morning. And, since it was they who gave Christendom the joy of bread in the first place, perhaps they deserved it.

The prior asked the obvious. "Heinrich, have we been charitable to you?"

Heinrich groaned. It was another question laced with the scent of obligation. "*Ja*, brother," he answered warily.

"In these difficult months past we have lost six of our score of brethren to disease or injury, Brother Radoslaw being one of them. A novice was sent away for his rebellious spirit and another has taken flight. Our fields are in desperate want and we, now, are in need. Would you serve us as our baker until another is sent?"

It was as if a hand seized Heinrich's heart. He knew he had little choice. He dreaded another delay but considered the immensity of his soul's present debt and quickly calculated what credits the agonizing service might yield. "How long do you think it shall take for another to come?"

The prior darkened. "How long?" his voice was sharp and cutting. "How long? I answer you thus: as long as God's pleasure requires."

How might any man challenge such an answer? "Ah, indeed," mumbled Heinrich.

≈

It was a dull day between the Feast of the Assumption and St. Michael's in the year of Grace 1209 when a timid monk in a well-pressed scapular appeared at Heinrich's bakery door. The prior introduced the new member of the cloister as Brother Wienczyslaw. Heinrich dusted his leather apron with a huff and repeated the bowing monk's words. "Aye, 'peace be to you' too. 'Ave y'any knowledge of baking?" he asked curtly.

The prior smiled and ducked quickly out the door. "Nay, good baker."

"Nay? *Ach, mein Gott in Himmel!*" Heinrich was exasperated. He walked to the door and felt the cool air of late September. "If I don't leave this place I shall go mad!" He turned about and scowled. "Well, you'll be getting some now!"

For weeks the baker furiously pushed his exhausted apprentice through every stage of baking. The poor monk did his best to learn quickly, and by early October Heinrich hastily declared to the prior that the Pole was fit. "I find him to be a bit slow, but willing. And I needs begin my journey. I made a vow to the ship's captain that I'd deliver his token directly! That was nearly two years ago!"

The prior nodded. "I do have one question, good Heinrich."

The baker set his jaw. There would be nothing the shaveling might ask that would obligate him to a single added duty. "*Ja?*"

"Would you be sure to receive our song of blessing before you leave on the morrow?" He smiled.

Heinrich nearly laughed out loud. *Free to go!* his heart cried. *Can it be so?*

The sun had barely broken over a new day when Heinrich received the prayers and blessings of the brethren at Posen. The white-robed men waved kindly and sang a final psalm as he passed by them. A few secretly worried that the man may have gone mad in the dreadful winter past and, judging the way he then turned and raced from sight, others thought he surely had.

"At last!" cried Heinrich aloud as the smoky columns of the horrid cloister faded behind him. The man was quite convinced that no misery he might ever face again could equal the damp grayness and unrelenting monotony of that place. He looked ahead to the flat road that lay in wait and he smiled. He felt suddenly strong and vigorous. His clothing was clean and mended. His dagger was sharp and his eye-patch, like his leather boots, soft and well oiled. He had secured both necklaces at the bottom of his satchel along with the Laubusbach stone. The rest of his bag was stuffed with an assortment of foods and a generous pouch of silver pennies given to him by the monks.

October's crisp air was bracing and enlivened the man's stride. Upright and resolute, the one-armed man with a swirling beard and graying tangle of auburn curls marched against a warm southern breeze, grinning and greatly relieved. By day he walked southward through the wide, green, Oder River valley past villages of German or Slavic inhabitants. At night he wrapped himself with his cloak and lay upon the cooling earth on pine boughs or wilting weeds. The Oder River gave him water, a few passersby bits of bread or cheese. From time to time he would stop to kneel with a pilgrim priest at one of the many, simple prayer *Kapelles* and from them he learned much about the larger world they traveled.

He was not certain where he would spend the winter. He was told the signs were warning of early snows, particularly in the great mountains of the south. "You should not dare the passes this autumn, my son," counseled one journeying priest. "However, you might have time yet to press on to Vienna or Salzburg."

Heinrich shrugged. He had no idea which city to choose and gazed at the priest helplessly. "Hmm, it seems you have little knowledge of either?"

"Nay, father."

"You have stated you are on pilgrimage to Rome?"

"Aye."

The priest scratched his head and thought for a moment. "From here either path could lead you to Rome. Hmm. Vienna is a most lovely city and I believe 'tis a free one now, though I am not certain of it. But, Salzburg may be free as well ... I know not. No matter. The Kingdom of the Huns borders Vienna and I do avoid every sort of border that I can. I've learned over my life that all boundaries, whether those of kingdoms or of persons, are places where troubles collide, places of sure conflict, risk, and peril.

"If I were you, I would press south and westward to Salzburg. It is deep in the Duchy of Bavaria and places you along a good, direct line to Rome for your springtime journey."

Heinrich nodded. He was at the man's mercy but his words seemed reasonable. The priest bent over and drew a map with a stick in the roadway. "Here ... here is where we are. You must leave Poland behind you, travel due west through Silesia, and find the Elbe River in the Kingdom of Bohemia. Follow the Elbe Valley west to Prague." He lifted his head. "Take care in Prague. 'Tis another place of borders. You needs skirt the city, else your winter may be there and I doubt that would be a good thing.

"Now, after Prague follow the Moldau River south. Be warned of the Bohemian forest. 'Tis a fearful place, filled with bogs and horrid marshes called the *Sumava*." The priest crossed his chest and prayed before continuing.

"The Moldau turns hard to the west. There you must find a small roadway that travels to the wondrous Danube River. 'Tis a glorious blue ... like sapphire! Follow it west to the confluence of the Inns River at the town of Passau. Follow the Inns south to its split, then travel along the narrow Salzach River upstream into Salzburg ... you shall see a mighty fortress on a hill just outside the city."

Heinrich drew a deep breath and nodded. The priest made him recite the directions six times. Then he let the troubled baker rest. With a friendly embrace the priest offered one more word of advice: "Be on the watch for rogue knights and men-at-arms whether German or Slav ... and highwaymen as well. It would be better for you to find the company of a caravan … but we must leave that to God's wisdom." With a final hug and word of blessing, the kindly priest disappeared along the lonely road leaving Heinrich to his own devices.

The peasant reordered his leggings and his cloak, counted his foodstuffs and coins, then pressed on, relieved to have a plan but feeling a bit anxious for the perils ahead. Ignorance had been a more favored companion.

The days passed without rain, but the wind now blew from the east and delivered a damp coldness that chilled Heinrich to the bone. Despite his growing discomfort, the man set a spirited pace. Then the heavy rains came just as Heinrich entered Passau. He quickly negotiated shelter in a grain shed and carned a silver penny and two meals for one-handing the latrine's shovel for a full day. On the following day, Heinrich watched a wagon of Slavic slaves roll through the town's muddy streets. He stared at the wretches from his latrine as they passed him by and his heart broke. He was particularly troubled by the face of an attractive young woman that he thought he remembered from his passage on the ship so long ago. She was packed into the jostling wagon with a dozen or so men, two children, and a few other women. Each was scantily clad in threadbare homespuns and shivering in the cold rain. They were filthy and unkempt, and all but she sat slumped in their places. It was her erect posture and the fire in her eyes that had caught Heinrich's attention on the ship and he swore he recognized it again. Perhaps it was that she looked so much like Varina.

The man found sleep to be elusive that night and it was with a mysterious compulsion that he arose before dawn's first light. He pulled on his boots quickly and followed his instincts through the sleepy footpaths and alleys of the smoke-heavy town. It was along such an unnamed alleyway where he stopped and listened carefully. *There!* he thought. *Over there.* Heinrich walked silently toward the shadow of a building. He heard a slap and a groan, a bit of laughter and a shout. Heinrich followed the sounds closer to the thatch-roofed smith-shed where he placed his eye against a small chink in the wattle walls. In the yellow light of several thick-handled torches he saw a group of prisoners bound with ropes. They were the same Slavs he had seen enter the town the day before. The slaves sat helpless, though defiant, and they could do little but stifle the outrage that rose within them as two of their captors made sport with one of the women.

"Soldiers," muttered Heinrich. He studied the slaves carefully and found the woman who had reminded him of Varina standing defiant and hard-faced as she awaited her inevitable turn. The baker thought quickly. He looked about and grunted. The rainy dawn was gray and dark. A thick smoke from sagging hearth-fires filled the streets with a heavy smog; it was a fortuitous blanket of cover.

Heinrich slipped quietly to the far side of the smith-shed and opened a small door that was set deep within the building's shadows. From there he crept inside the shed slowly and eased his way along a dark wall where he paused. No one had seen him. He looked about and noticed a loft of hay mounded high with dry fodder. The soldiers were busy grunting and belching and trifling with their prey. With their backs to him, Heinrich saw his opportunity. He took three long strides toward a torch, then jerked it from its holder, and tossed it into the hay. As the dry tinder began to snap, he crouched into a dark corner and drew his dagger.

The slaves cried out. They were bound by ropes to the shed's posts and their eyes bulged wide in sudden terror. The soldiers turned in astonishment and raced toward the rising fire to beat it with their capes. They coughed and gasped for air as flames licked the underbelly of the thatch roof. Realizing the cause was hopeless, the rogues abandoned both the building and the slaves, cursing as they fled.

Heinrich lunged from his cover and dashed toward the panicked prisoners. His dagger cut through their ropes like it was passing through soft fruit, and he quickly released them into the smoke-choked streets. From there they stormed through the chaos of the rousing town and into the forest standing just beyond the timber walls.

Heinrich ran with them deep into the Bohemian woodland. He followed them to a clearing where a large male took charge of his kind and gathered a circle of panting faces. Heinrich's eye swept the dim glade until it fell upon the woman he remembered. He stared at her for a moment until a voice turned his head.

"*Dekuji, dekuji,*" repeated the leader. Heinrich bowed. He received the man's thanks graciously and smiled at each of the dirty faces inclined respectfully toward his own. The German bade farewell and watched the band of pagans disappear into the forest. They would need to travel a great distance to reach whatever villages they had been taken from. Heinrich hoped God would watch over them, yet he wondered if such a thing were possible.

Heinrich wisely slipped back into the village. He was sure he had not been seen by anyone, and if he had gone missing the angry magistrate might hunt him all the way to Salzburg. He quietly returned to the latrine where he watched the townsmen scrambling to douse the fire. Despite the rain and cold, the man was glad-hearted and joyful. He pictured the band of Slavs vanishing into the wood and he grinned.

The pleasure of his secret kindness was short-lived however, for Heinrich had no sooner finished his inglorious labors when a furious magistrate turned a penetrating eye on him. Heinrich paled and bowed to the officer and the priest at his side. "You there!" growled the officer. "What do you know of this morning's bad business?"

"I've seen the smoke, sire, and heard 'bout the fire and some words of escaped slaves."

"Aye? You've heard things already?"

Heinrich gulped. "Aye, sire. I've spent the morning at the latrine ... lots of noise there, sire."

Some soldiers laughed.

"Silence!" barked the officer. "Where are the slaves? Has anyone spoke of them?"

Heinrich's mouth was dry. "Uh, nay, sire. None said

anything of them ... except they've gone missing."

The man stared hard. He was blustery and red-eyed. The town's mayor had guaranteed the slave-master the safe-keeping of his cargo and the magistrate would be held accountable for their disappearance. The man pressed his face close to Heinrich's. "Swear to me before this priest that you've no knowledge of the slaves."

Heinrich groaned within. He glanced at the priest standing stern and impatient by the bailiff's side. He hesitated, then remembered the happy faces in the glade. "I do so swear."

Chapter 22

SALT AND LIGHT

t was a bright and sunny day, the first of November, *Annos Dominus* 1209 when Heinrich of Weyer stood in wonder before the city of Salzburg. He crossed a timbered bridge, pausing for a few moments to marvel at the icy, blue-green of the curving Salzach River running swiftly beneath the man's feet. He gazed into the crystal waters and imagined he was staring into a heaven-sent liquid poured out of angels' golden pitchers. "Oh, my blessed Laubusbach! Pitiful copy of this!"

He lifted his face to the dark stone-and-timber walls of the city, then above them to the imposing fortress perched atop a steep cliff. His eye lingered on the castle's heavy walls and battlements until it was drawn across the southern landscape. There the mountains stood watch as the first rank of the realm's most glorious sentries. For many days Heinrich had marveled at their distant silhouette and had often stopped to stare in awe. *They rise from the land like great, jagged teeth from the bottom jaw of a sleeping Colossus!* he thought. He felt a chill of wonder run along his spine. Another thought then gripped him. The mountains rose higher than the spire of any church in view—he had broken his vow!

Cursing himself, Heinrich crossed the bridge and marched through the crowded south gate struggling and confused. Mercifully, the city's sights quickly stole his

attention. He passed rows of tidy homes and shops, wagons filled with winter stores and well-dressed folk busy at
task. He paused before an open fire to warm his hand and
answered a few greetings. He looked about and suddenly
felt better; he liked Salzburg.

Salzburg was named for the salt, or *"Salz"* that had
blessed the entire region with uncommon wealth for centuries. Ancient Celts had once mined the mountains to the
south and built a large settlement where the city now
stood. The city endured much hardship in its earliest days.
Converted to Christianity in the fourth century after
Christ, it later was ruined by the onslaught of pagan bar-
barians from all sides. By the eighth century, Salzburg had
been restored to Christendom and St. Peter's Cathedral
was erected to serve its archbishop. A monastery was built
and filled with Irish monks. Soon the lucrative business of
mining salt had assured all the city's citizens the most
agreeable of temporal comforts.

For Heinrich, this "salt city" was like nothing he had
ever seen. He walked through its snow-whitened streets
dumbstruck and astonished at the endless stalls of
guildsmen and merchants. He passed a row of cobblers, a
strip of fowlers, four goldsmiths, then a tinker. His head
turned this way and that; tanners and weavers, grocers
and wheelwrights. His eye studied the mysterious
banners and signs that hung above the doors. Had the
man been more learned he might have known it was the
name of St. Catherine that graced the shops of wheel-
wrights. After all, Catherine's body had been broken on a
wheel. The needlemakers were marked by signs of St.
Sebastian, the martyr slain by arrows, and the image of
St. Mary-Magdalene hung above the perfumers' doors.

Heinrich walked slowly until he came to a bookmaker's
shop. He paused and peered inside. The proprietor smiled
and bade Heinrich enter. The baker ducked through the
low door and greeted the man politely. He gazed about the
dim-lit shop and felt a lump grow in his throat. "Wouldn't
Emma be pleased?"

"Eh?"

"Ah, good sir, m'pardon. I was remembering an old friend that worked in parchment." Heinrich surveyed the shelves of ink, raven quills, knives, binding stitch, and the choirs of folded pages, and the leather stretched on drying racks. It was a shop for people of wealth. He smiled and nodded approvingly at this and that until he discovered a colored page of such beauty and astonishing craft that his very breath stopped.

The proprietor smiled. "Ah, the blessed knots and links of the Irish! *Gloria tibi, Domine!*"

Heinrich's eye remained fixed on the artwork as though a prisoner of its comforting sublimate.

"God's Word honored with a bit of heaven's glory, I say," added the proprietor. "Color and light ... the Irishman who does this work says it is the very essence of our hope."

Heinrich nodded without speaking. He stared at the parchment's hues: dark reds and blues, yellows and greens. Within the artist's curls and graceful turns, gold leaf glittered and shimmered. It was as though the colors of Creation's rainbow were lit by the sun and offered in all their glory on this single page of Scripture. The man began to weep.

Heinrich hurried from the shop and leaned against the cold stone of the three-story building. He covered his face to hide his tears and in the blackness of his palm he saw Emma smiling at him, pointing him heavenward. "Oh, Emma," he groaned. His mind carried him to her garden of wildflowers and butterflies. He imagined lying within the blooms of June, staring at the bright blue sky with Richard at his side.

"Are you in need, man?"

Heinrich was startled.

"May I help?" a sickly young man pressed further.

"Uh, nay, good sir. But m'thanks to you."

The man nodded. He was leaning on a makeshift crutch and his leg was bandaged with a discolored wrap.

Heinrich would have preferred to hurry away but his heart held him fast. The young man was thin and drawn, slightly yellowed and hollow-eyed. "Methinks you'd be the one in need," observed the baker.

"Ah, my leg's been shattered in the archbishop's mine and it seems my time is short. My name is Dietmar of Gratz." He coughed and shivered.

"Gratz?"

"'Tis in the Duchy of Styria near the Kingdom of the Huns."

"The Huns. Ne'er met one."

"You needs hope you don't. They raid the borders from time to time. I lost my lands to their treachery three years prior."

"You are a freeman?"

"Aye. You?"

Heinrich wasn't sure any longer. He no longer felt like the property of Villmar's monks, yet he assumed the law would say he was. His delay caught the notice of Dietmar.

"A runaway?"

The title snagged Heinrich. His heart skipped and his belly fluttered. "Runaway? Nay, sir. I am a pilgrim from ... from Stedingerland in the far north."

Dietmar nodded approvingly. "I have heard of your people. Seems word of your ways is troubling many a lord's court throughout all the realms." He paused to gather strength. "When I was a lord, I was troubled by the likes of you as well. Now, it seems, I find your rebellious ways delicious!"

Heinrich smiled. The young man seemed earnest and honest. "You say you were injured in the mines?"

"Ja. I worked for the archbishop's steward, Laszlo. The man's a Christian Hun. He's a clever devil from Pest along the Danube. I was one of his clerks. He sent me to the new mine at Hallein to do a reckoning of charcoal." Dietmar paused and sat atop a keg. He coughed and wiped some spittle off his chin with his sleeve. "A timber fell from a cart and broke my leg ... hasn't even begun to heal in near a month and now I fear I've mormal in the wound."

"Mormal? You'll die for sure." Heinrich grimaced at his words.

"Aye. We all die for sure." Dietmar chuckled lightly, then became faint.

Heinrich steadied the man and handed him a flask he had bought for himself. Dietmar drained a long draught of air-chilled ale.

"Many thanks, stranger. What is your name?"

"Heinrich. Heinrich of … Stedingerland." He hated to lie.

"Well, Heinrich, your pilgrimage is to where?"

"Rome."

"Ah, the Holy See. For a penance?"

"Aye. Have you been there?"

Dietmar shook his head. "You plan to winter in Salzburg?"

"Yes. But I hope to leave as early in the spring as possible. I hope before Easter."

"The mountain passes are often closed until Pentecost, sometimes later. You ought travel through the Brenner. It is lower and clears a little earlier."

Heinrich grumbled. "Perhaps I should hurry and find a caravan. I am told they sometimes dare the passes late in the season."

"Some years the snow is late … sometimes early. Perhaps strange fortune and south winds might make for an odd season next year, but I can tell you that this year is too late."

Heinrich sighed. The two sat quietly for a short time while Dietmar rested, then Heinrich offered his new friend a meal. The two found their way to a tavern within the shadow of St. Peter's near the town's center. Dietmar ravenously chewed a thick slice of soup-soaked bread and wiped his fingers through a hearty mash. Gangrene had indeed spread within his poorly set break and fever was besetting the young man. "This fare is some of the best I've eaten!" said Dietmar cheerfully. He grimaced and reached for his leg. "Cursed physicians! I have spent far too much on them. All they do is squeeze the ooze and sprinkle bits of salt on the rot."

Despite the physicians' shortcomings, salt was a powerful agent for healing. Just as it preserved the sausages, hams, bacon, fish, fowl, beef slabs, cheese, butter, and nearly every other food necessary to winter the growing population of Europe, it was found to protect life from many diseases. Salt was precious and expensive, yet, along with sunlight, a necessary ingredient in a dark and corrupted world.

Heinrich listened compassionately to Dietmar's story and happily paid the man's meal from the monks' pennies. He then helped the man from the table and led him into the late daylight that still warmed the courtyard of the cathedral. The two found a comfortable bench and leaned against the wall of a merchant's house.

Heinrich stared in awe at the massive stone church. Its towers were squat and heavy, like the little church in Weyer, but on a much grander scale. Its walls were massive; it was a fortress that would surely hold fast against the assaults of Lucifer's legions. The simple man of Weyer had seen few such edifices of God's kingdom and he sat in spellbound astonishment.

Dietmar noticed the man's excitement and asked Heinrich to follow him into the sanctuary. Heinrich entered reverently, almost fearfully. His eye widened at the arched buttresses and thought the huge columns lining the nave to be like orderly plantings of ancient trees. He walked quietly toward the altar standing so very far away. His leather soles padded lightly on the stone floor, and as he walked he leaned his head back to behold the carvings gracing the heights of God's castle. "This place," he whispered, "it points me to God."

Dietmar nodded. "What our eyes see, our tongues taste, our noses smell, our ears hear, and our fingers touch do much to call upon the spirit within us. They are important parts of our worship."

The pair stood quietly near the altar where they lingered for some time. At last, an annoyed priest spotted them and chased them out the door, complaining he had chores for the All Souls' services in the morning. The two stumbled out into the courtyard laughing.

"My new friend, look there." Dietmar pointed to a mountain towering over the edge of Salzburg. "Look up, Heinrich! An old Bulgarian priest once taught me to 'Let the eyes climb the summit, then let them fly higher and higher! Let them take you to the God that this poor little chapel chirps about.' 'Tis good the works of man remind us of bigger things, but look, see how the mountains point us higher still." He turned to see Heinrich staring at the snow edging the tops of his feet. "Heinrich ... ?"

"I ... I am under a vow."

"A vow?" Dietmar was confused. He stared at the baker. "What sort of vow keeps your eye from heaven?"

"I do not wish to speak of it. Now, let me help you home."

Dietmar said nothing. He was saddened for Heinrich, and the look on the baker's face nearly broke his heart. But Dietmar was failing quickly. He felt suddenly weak and faint and halfway to his home he begged Heinrich to sit on a bench for a brief rest. He sat quietly for a while, then handed the baker a ring. It bore his family's seal. "Take this. You have been kind to me and I've none other to leave it to. Show it to the archbishop's steward of the mines, Laszlo. Tell him I sent you. He's a monster but he always respected me and he owes me a favor or two. He can employ you through the winter."

Heinrich stared at the silver ring. "I am forever in your debt, sire." He let it fall into his palm.

Dietmar shivered and Heinrich wrapped his sealskin around him. "Before you begin your journey for Rome," said Dietmar slowly, "take the ring to the tinker by the well. Ask no questions, simply do as I bid."

Heinrich nodded curious.

Dietmar sighed and pulled himself to his feet. "Now, good fellow, we've just a few streets farther."

The pair shuffled slowly through the narrow alleyways of Salzburg until they arrived at the young man's modest home. There, Heinrich was offered shelter until he could secure his employment at the mines. The grateful baker accepted Dietmar's kindness but spent the next two days doing nothing other than tending his dying friend. On the third day the landless lord handed Heinrich a few silver pennies and shrugged. "It is all, Heinrich. It is all I've left here. Buy some food and drink. I'll not be calling the physicians again. The fools are stealing my money and the cause is long lost."

"But—"

"Please … do as I say." His voice was weak and imploring.

Heinrich left quickly, only to return with an ample provision of meats, some dried peas, a fresh chicken for a good soup, and a flask of red wine. He also dragged in a canvas bag filled with firewood and a pouch of precious salt. "Now, Dietmar, sit by this better fire and warm your bones! I shall cook you a soup you'll not soon forget and we'll dress this wound."

Tears rolled down Dietmar's gaunt face as he huddled close to the fire. He poured a tall, clay goblet of wine with a trembling hand and smiled. "Thanks be to God for you, friend." He knew Heinrich had dipped a heavy hand into his own bag of pennies to bring a bit of cheer and hope to a dying man. "Heinrich," he began in a weakening voice, "I am but a young man … but raised by a wise one. He once told me …" Dietmar faltered. "He once told me that freedom is not granted by men. Freedom, like hope, is a birthright from God. Your vow is a terrible thing that keeps you bound within the ways of others. Break it, my dear friend, brea—" Dietmar would say no more. He toppled lightly to his side and stared open eyed into the snapping fire.

Heinrich lifted the young man's head to his breast and wept for him. He did not know why this stranger had become his friend nor how he had become so. He only knew that a good man was gone and he was saddened for the loss.

≈

Heavy-hearted, Heinrich used the rest of his pennies to pay a priest the fees necessary for Dietmar's burial and stood by a strange-looking woman hidden under her hood as the sole witnesses to the man's interment. He lingered by the grave for a time and wished he could have known the man longer.

The man from Weyer sighed and bade a final farewell. A cold wind rustled through his shoulder-length hair and lifted his long, gray-laced beard. He pulled his cloak tightly around his shoulders and lifted its hood over his head. He secured his dagger and satchel and rolled Dietmar's ring around his finger. In the safety of the cathedral's tall spire he lifted his head to look at the fortress perched on the cliff overlooking the city and drew a deep breath. It was mid-morning and he must get on to things that needed doing.

Heinrich climbed the long, curving road that led to the castle and upon reaching the gate he requested a brief meeting with the archbishop's steward-of-mines, Laszlo the Hungarian. He was led to a cold corridor where he waited for several hours. Soldiers of the archbishop tramped by in disinterested companies and a few velvet-caped merchants meandered past. Finally, a fur-capped gentleman escorted Heinrich to the steward's chamber where he was seated on a short bench at the wall farthest from the heat of a roaring hearth. He was introduced as a "country yeoman in want of a moment." Heinrich grunted. He remembered the steward's chamber in Villmar's abbey and he was not comfortable. "I bear this ring to beg ... a moment."

Laszlo stared from dark eyes. He was an arch-nosed, pinched-faced fellow. His frame was lean, almost skeletal, and he looked short on his high chair. Yet he commanded an intimidating presence that few dared challenge. "What's this?" he grumbled. With a wave his secretary removed Heinrich's ring and handed it to Laszlo. "Hmm. Dietmar of Gratz. So, you've killed my secretary and have come for something?"

"Killed him?" Heinrich was baffled. "N–nay, sire. I cared for him until his death from injury ... suffered in your mine at ... at Hallein. He said I ought bring this to you and ask if I might labor for you this winter."

"Ha! Ha!" Laszlo laughed loudly, then rose to his feet and slammed his palm hard atop his oak desk. "What would I do with a one-armed, one-eyed murderer?"

Heinrich paled and he stammered for words. "M–m–murderer? Sire, nay, I am innocent ... there's been no murder. Ask the priest who buried him! He prepared the body ... he saw the mormal that rotted his leg—"

"Humph," snorted Laszlo. He stared at Heinrich for another moment. He enjoyed toying with men of lesser station. What Heinrich did not know, however, was that laborers were desperately needed in the mines. Laszlo tossed the silver ring back to Heinrich. "I believe you to be a runaway."

The words shocked Heinrich even more than the other accusation. His mind raced. He had just arrived a week before. *Who would have told him?* he wondered. Heinrich gulped. He had been told that a runaway could be hung on the spot where he stood. He licked his lips. "Nay, sire. I am a freeman on a pilgrimage to Rome."

"Can you prove it?"

Heinrich's mind raced. He drew his dagger from its sheath. The flash of his steel had barely glistened in the torchlight when three guards were upon him. He was pushed to the ground roughly.

Laszlo laughed. "Bumpkin! Dolt! What sort of fool are you. Why did you draw steel against me?"

"N–nay, sire. I thought to show you I was armed ... only free men bear them and—"

"Enough!" Laszlo walked to Heinrich and leaned close. "Pity you're no runaway. Those who escape their manors to live here and work for me for one year and a day leave with my seal on a passport ... forever free ... and their heirs as well." He stared slyly at Heinrich, then returned to his desk. "Have you any skill, freeman?"

Heinrich was still pondering this new opportunity. He knew that any who lived in an imperial city for a year and a day were considered freemen—it was a problem for the landlords of the realm. He hadn't known that Salzburg was such a city.

"Are you listening, man?" roared Laszlo.

"Aye, sire. I am trained as a baker."

The steward nodded and smiled. His workers needed bread, and neither the city's bakers nor their apprentices could be coaxed to stay in Hallein for very long, especially in winter. Laszlo stepped from behind his desk and leaned his face close to Heinrich's. "Well, pilgrim. I suppose we could use a baker. He tossed the man back his ring. Aye, you are assigned to the bakery at Hallein, where you shall make dozens of the Church's faithful laborers very happy. For your service you shall be paid in salt like the Roman legions with their *salarium*. This 'salary' as we call it, can be exchanged for coin at our moneychanger's stall in the city when you are given leave." Laszlo then set his lips by Heinrich's ear to hiss, "And when you are ready, we shall talk again about your freedom."

~

A two-day cart ride delivered Heinrich to the village of Hallein that was nestled within the Dürnberg Mountains. He was given a bed in a worker's dormitory and introduced to his new master, one Ladislav of Moravia. Ladislav was a dark-eyed, violent man of twenty years who possessed a poor grasp of the German language and even less Christian charity. His task was to squeeze the most production possible out of each worker and he had no patience for fatigue, hunger, cold, or infirmity. Heinrich knew his objective would be to keep as much distance between himself and the impetuous Slav as possible.

The baker was soon working long hours in the bakehouse. He had become proficient in using his one arm in the mixing and kneading of dough and was suddenly grateful for the woeful years in the dreadful cloister in Posen where he had learned to retrain his body. His apprentices watched with admiration as the handicapped man worked the doughs, shaped the loaves, and shuttled the paddles in and out of the brick ovens. More than that, they marveled at the excellent product the newcomer presented to the eager workmen each day.

Through the long winter Heinrich worked faithfully. He was fed amply, his canvas cot was reasonably comfortable, and the dormitory was surprisingly warm. A monumental amount of wood had been stripped from the mountainsides in order to fire the huge furnaces necessary to produce the salt. The relatively small quantities taken for the personal comfort of the workers was barely noticed.

Hallein's salt mines had been closed for several centuries. In ancient times the Dürnberg Mountains had been mined by the Celts who carved tunnels deep into the mountains. Here they had chiseled clumps of red salt from the narrow veins that spidered their way through the mountain. The clumps were then carried outside where they were smashed into granules, washed, and poured into barrels. One Sabbath afternoon, however, Heinrich learned of the archbishop's better way. His curiosity called him up the trail from the village to the mine entrance, where he hesitated. He drew a deep breath and picked up a pine-torch. He lit it on the coal bucket and stepped timidly into the tunnel where he immediately saw a dull, curling flame some distance ahead. He walked slowly toward the light until he came upon a sleepy guard dozing against a timber brace.

"Nice and warm in here," yawned the guard.

Heinrich nodded. He was surprised how comfortable it was.

"Aye, no need for hearth fires. ... Good thing else we'd choke on smoke!"

Heinrich grunted and stared about.

The guard was bored and happy to humor the curious man. "See here," he pointed to a vein of salt. "We needs not hammer away at it. Look, there." He pointed to some sawed lumber and then held his torch to a hole recently drilled in from above. "We'd be some furlong into the mountain, and about the same distance 'neath the church that sits atop. In here's a maze of tunnels from long ago. ... They go all ways. See here, the carpenters build a dam in the tunnel, then the workers'll pour water in from that hole above yer head. They'll flood the place in springtime."

"Flood it? Why?"

"Ha ... that's the wonder of the new way. The water dissolves the salt from the walls, then carries it out when the dam is broke into the big vats they're building down below. Then we'll boil the water to dry the vats and you've salt left on the bottom!"

"Ah!" Heinrich understood.

"Methinks it clever."

"Aye ... very." Heinrich walked past the guard and moved deeper into the lonely tunnel.

The guard's voice followed him. "*Glück auf.*"

"Huh?"

"*Glück auf* ... 'tis the miner's well-wish."

"Ah. *Glück auf* to you."

"M'thanks ... and beware the bodies and the lake."

"Bodies?"

"Aye."

Heinrich stopped walking and called back to the dim torch and the hollow voice beneath it. "W–what bodies?"

"We finds them from time to time, dead men preserved by the salt. You'll have quite a start if you walk by one with your torch. And up ahead 'tis the lake. Better if you don't go for a swim."

Heinrich paused, then turned around. Perhaps he had seen enough of the mine!

&

News of caravans gathering in Salzburg reached the ears of Heinrich on a rainy day in late April of 1210. Immediately, he set off to inform Ladislav that he would be leaving his position and was ready for his final salary. Ladislav was in no hurry to lose his master baker, however. Heinrich was good at task and had treated both Ladislav and the numerous agents of the archbishop to delicious honey cakes and sweet treats that had lightened the drab fare of winter.

"I needs permission from Laszlo."

Heinrich was agitated. "I needs be on m'way. The caravans are forming in the city now."

Ladislav grunted. "Go without your salt, then."

Heinrich hesitated. He had been frugal all winter. Actually, he had not converted any of his prior salt payments for coins. A wise old miner had bartered him some wisdom for a pretzel. He told Heinrich that salt was more valuable farther from the mines. He'd get a better price with the Italians. The thrifty baker had lived all winter eating from the bakery and sleeping for free. He had not needed any money, but wanted his final payment.

"Then I shall go m'self to the steward." Heinrich was firm. It felt good to him to deal as though he were a freeman.

Heinrich jumped aboard a cart bound for the city and as soon as he arrived, he climbed the road to the castle once more. He waited all that day and far into the night before Laszlo would see him. At last, he was ushered into the steward's shadowy chamber.

"Aye?"

"Sire, I am Heinrich the baker at Hallein."

"Indeed. I've heard your work is good. Why are you here?"

"I've come to collect m'salary for I'm to leave on m'pilgrimage with a caravan."

Laszlo motioned for his secretary to leave. He walked toward his hearth and motioned for Heinrich to join him. "Sit, Heinrich. There, on that stool."

Heinrich sat obediently. A sense of dread began to creep over him. He nervously adjusted his clothing and stared into the fire.

Laszlo sat close by and stared into the flames. His bony face was etched in deep shadows and when he turned to face the baker his dark eyes seemed to glow. "Have you ever seen a man hang?"

Heinrich's mouth went dry and he sputtered an awkward, "Yes."

"Look at me, baker. Do you think me a fool?"

Heinrich felt dizzy. "N–nay, sire."

"Hmm. I have employed runaways for many years, runaways from all over the empire. Do you imagine I am such a fool as to not spot one with ease?"

The long pause was interrupted only by the crackling of tinder. "Nay, sire."

"Heinrich, I have it within my power to hang you on the morrow, or to offer you and your heirs freedom. Do you understand?"

Heinrich wanted to run. His mind whirled. *My punishment!* he thought. *For all the lies, for all m'evil doing, oh dear God!* His heart pounded and his belly turned. He had no clever retort; he'd no place to go but to truthfulness. "Aye!" he blurted.

"I serve the archbishop in many ways, and it is my duty to see that his holiness earns a good profit for his diocese. I suppose that end is hardly served by hanging a good baker in Salzburg's market square, do you agree?"

"*Ja.*"

"Naturally. So, then. You came into my employ in or around the first day of December in the year past."

"Actually sire, 'twas mid-November."

Laszlo chuckled. "Of course. I shall have my secretary set the date for November the fifteenth. One year and one day from that date sets you free. You've already served us in these environs for five months! So, you shall remain another seven and may come to me after the sixteenth day of November next for your passport."

Heinrich trembled. *Another seven months!* He groaned. *Yet I shall be free ... and Wil, Karl, and Marta, and I'd still have the bakery.* His spirits lifted. He stood and bowed to Laszlo. "Aye, sire, until November."

෨

Honor among men of commerce is a rare thing. For whatever reason, the tinkling of coins is a bewitching music that has the power to incite every vice and cruel ploy of the imagination. It seems that the seductive twins of wealth and power are indeed Sirens whose presence ought alarm both those whom they seek and those who scent their presence. Heinrich, therefore, was without excuse. He had often suffered the wiles of men more clever than he. Laszlo's odd offer ought to have piqued his suspicions; he should have dared ask others about the man. So, upon his learning of Laszlo's deception, he should have been neither surprised nor angered at anyone other than himself.

After spending all the summer and most of the autumn that followed dreaming of his life of liberty, it was drunken, miserable Ladislav who finally dared expose the truth of the matter. "Fool!" slurred the master. "Ha, ha! Dolt, stupid king of idiots!" He laughed. "Laszlo has no authority to grant y'freedom!"

Heinrich jumped to his feet. "You'd be lyin', y' drunken Slav!"

"No, he's not lying to you," answered a sober, well-groomed soldier standing near. "And you've not lived in the city, anyway, you've been here, in Hallein." He narrowed his eye at the astonished Heinrich. "Are you a runaway, then?"

Heinrich panicked. "N–nay, sire. I ... I am servile to ... to a Lord Dietmar of Gratz."

The soldier nodded. Ladislav laughed out loud. "Ha! Good one!"

Heinrich turned away. It was Sabbath evening, the fourteenth day of November. He wanted to cry, to kill someone, to run. He stormed into his dormitory and gathered his things. He jerked the dagger from his belt and considered driving it into the belly of Laszlo. He stuffed it back into its sheath and packed his satchel. He trotted past the bakery, ignoring the greetings of his apprentices, then paused to return. He chased the workers from view and plunged his hand into the salt bin where he helped himself to a month's salary. It was a crime that could cost him dearly. "And now some extra for Laszlo's lie!" Heinrich scooped more salt into his sack and hung it on his shoulders.

The angry man strode from the bakery and descended from the village to spend that night in an abandoned stable. The next morning he decided he would follow the Salzach upstream through the mountains until he crossed paths with some caravan. He was relieved that the month had been unusually warm. "Southern breezes—just as Dietmar said might come." With that, Heinrich suddenly recalled the ring Dietmar had given him. He paused and pulled it from deep within his satchel. He stared at it for a moment. *'Take this to the tinker by the well,'* Dietmar had said. Heinrich hesitated. *Why? I wonder what this could be about?* The man turned wearily for Salzburg.

Heinrich arrived on Wednesday at noon. It was market day and the city's main well was positioned in the very center of the square. The ground was covered with colorful tents and booths that offered every imaginable trinket or staple from all ends of the empire. Ells of woven cloth, baskets of fish, pretzels, spices, woollens, salted pork, barrels of kraut, kegs of ale; it was a seemingly endless, wonderful blend of color and sound that was nothing like Heinrich had ever seen. He wanted to pause at every table to study the work of the goldsmiths, the leatherworkers, and the glassblowers. He would have lingered over the bakers' wares, but a sense of fear hung over him like a pall. He glanced up at the castle staring from high atop its cliff and he knew he must hurry.

Heinrich arrived at the tinker's door and entered. A woman greeted him. "*Grüss Gott.*"

"*Grüss Gott*, m'lady." Heinrich spoke slowly. He was startled by the woman's appearance and found her hard to look upon. He then remembered her from Dietmar's burial and he asked curiously, "Is the tinker about?"

"*Ja.* 'Tis me." She giggled.

Heinrich was surprised. Tinkers were something of jacks-of-all-trades. Generally poor, they primarily mended pots and kettles and the like, and were rarely women. "Well, I see." He fumbled for his ring and presented it to the woman.

The lady studied the ring quietly for a moment and as she did Heinrich ventured a look at her pox-scarred skin and homely features. He felt sad for her, yet quite taken by her manner. "Lord Dietmar gave this to me 'fore he died."

The woman studied Heinrich for a few moments and became slightly wary. She remembered him, too, but his appearance gave her some pause, for his hair was very long and shaggy, and his beard had grown bushy and wild. The eye patch and stump did not help his cause. She thought he had the look of a highwayman. "I remember you from Dietmar's burial, but I had m'doubts then as I do now. Tell me about him," she said quietly.

Heinrich was in no mood for this. He wanted out of the city as quickly as possible. He sighed and recounted his times with the man. As he told his story, however, he relaxed and the pleasant memories of his brief friendship brought an earnest smile to his face. "And he told me ... he told me that freedom and hope are found beyond ourselves. 'Twas at the last."

The tinker's eyes twinkled. The stranger had indeed known Dietmar. The woman stood up and asked Heinrich to wait. She climbed past crates of tin pots and stumbled over a basket of ladles before disappearing into the darkness of a back room. She returned in a few moments with a flask of wine, a roll of rye, and a heavy pouch. "As a child I was a friend to Dietmar's mother when she came to the city. 'Tis a long story I'll not burden you with. Dietmar fell from fortune, as you know, but he saved this pouch that he hid here. A tinker's shop is ne'er thought worthy of thieves! He asked me to give it only to the presenter of the ring. But, the ring, sir, I shall now keep ... I made it for his mother, and Dietmar promised I could have it."

She reached two warty fingers into the embroidered leather pouch and retrieved two gold coins. "Dietmar also promised me two. I swear by the blessed Virgin I've not scrumped a single other. The rest, stranger, are for you."

Heinrich stared wordlessly at the woman as she set the pouch in his outstretched palm. She smiled and nodded. "May God protect you from the dangers of this little bag and those who would take it from you."

Heinrich still could not speak. He had never held a gold coin other than his mother's relic. He believed a ducat was worth about two shillings, or twenty-four pennies. The pouch probably held over fifty ducats. At a laborer's wage of three pennies per day he quickly reckoned he was holding nearly two years' wages in his hand! "I do not deserve this!" he muttered.

"Probably not," answered the tinker. "But there you have it. Now beware to use it wisely and keep it hidden in your satchel. You have the look of a traveler."

"Aye. I'm on a pilgrimage to Rome."

The woman smiled. "Ah, Rome! I was in Assisi for a time and I did a pilgrimage with some sisters."

Heinrich was surprised. He looked about the shop and then at her.

"I see the questions on your face. Dear man, as I've said, my story is far too long and I've the sense you needs be on your way."

"Where is Assisi?"

"In the countryside north of Rome."

"Ah. Did you like it there?"

"Indeed. The valley is broad and beautiful. The sky is pale blue and warm and the flowers bloom bright. I had the feeling it was a special place. Now, tell me, why do you go?"

"For a penance."

"A penance. Hmm, 'tis a good place for that. The only place better is Jerusalem. How long a penance?"

Heinrich shrugged. He hadn't thought about that.

"What are your sins?"

Heinrich was a bit annoyed at the woman's sudden directness. "My story is too long," he answered.

The tinker laughed and poured him a goblet of wine. "Good sir, I am not easily surprised by the sins of man. My father was a bishop. Aye ... a bishop." She chuckled. "And m'mother was a nun! Some say 'tis why I look the way I do. So, you'll not be shocking me and I may be able to help you determine a proper plan."

Heinrich thought for a few moments, then yielded to the woman. She seemed trustworthy and wise, though he was not certain she was the well of wisdom that Emma had been. He proceeded to tell her of his theft and lies, of misplaced desires, of sloth, of envy, greed, and hatred. The more he revealed, the more he wanted to reveal. He told her of his vow. He whispered of his fight for the Stedingers, and even of his recent pillage of the salt box. By the time he had finished he was melancholy but lightened of a great load.

"Hmm," mused the tinker. She closed her eyes and sat quietly for a few moments. At last she moved. She lit a candle by a coal and turned a tender eye toward the curious baker. "I spend my days with broken things." She took Heinrich's hand and held her candle by his eye. "You are a vessel within a vessel. Each is cracked, but each is yet filled with darkness. Both must be broken to let the light in." She paused and squeezed Heinrich's hand hard. "If you must go to Rome, expect that which you do not."

She released her grip and leaned forward. Her tone was firm but kind. "Now hear me. For each of the Commandments do penance for one month; for each of the seven deadly sins, one month; for the Golden Rule, one month. Serve in Rome for eighteen months. Suffer the bells, suffer the smoke, suffer the suffering ... it is the only way."

Chapter 23

PENANCE

einrich hurried from the tinker's shop somewhat confused by the proprietor's riddle but decidedly purposed and his mind fixed on the plan. He strode the roadway with a chin set hard in defiance to both the archbishop and his miserable steward, and as he climbed the rising slopes he felt all the more relieved to be leaving the waste of that foolish year behind.

He was determined, yet troubled. Though he had been lied to, Heinrich was well aware that he had been blessed beyond measure. Over his shoulder was slung a satchel stuffed with provisions and coins, and on his back hung a well-waxed rucksack filled with precious salt. He had left home to suffer, yet it seemed he could not escape mercy. *Even m'boots don't fail me!* he thought. Indeed, the boots Lord Niklas had given him years before were worn, but neither torn nor leaking. They had become comfortable like two old friends sitting close by a warm hearth.

Heinrich filled his thick chest with clean mountain air as he followed the sparkling Salzach southward. His thick legs stepped lightly along the dirt road and his broad face beamed under the cloudless sky. The man was not ignorant of the risks involved in daring the Alps in November. It was already the third week of the gray month, yet fortunately, the southerly wind continued to rule the air. With continued good fortune he thought he might enter Rome by Christmas Day!

The pilgrim traveled alone through a landscape that filled him with wonder. He dared lift his eye from time to time to marvel at the towering mountains rising to touch the floor of heaven itself. Grand valleys of mist curled and lapped along these giants' feet and disappeared midst the mixed-hued greens of ancient forests. Heinrich's nostrils were filled with the intoxicating scent of pine and spruce, and he rejoiced to hear the screech of eagles and hawks soaring bold and free above.

He reached Bischoffen in good time. There, where the river bent westward and narrowed, he joined a small caravan of Syrian merchants hurrying home with a summer's bounty earned at the fairs in faraway Cologne, Champagne, and Frankfurt. They spoke enough German to barter food for Heinrich's services as a cart-driver. It seemed they had lost a young Bavarian carter who thought their late rush through the passes unwise. In any event, Heinrich was glad to rest his feet and grip the reins of a two-horse team.

The caravan consisted of two score of men; most were pagan followers of Mohammed. Heinrich found the company of these dark-skinned men to be somewhat uncomfortable, but not totally disagreeable. He had spent his life, as had his forebears, instructed in the evil ways of these infidels. They seemed ever poised to seize upon the lands of Christendom and had ruled Spain and half of France. They were a constant menace in the Christian east and for centuries had persecuted the Christian faithful in Palestine. In Jerusalem they now required Christians to wear leather girdles as a symbol of their servitude and forbade them to learn the Arab tongue, for to do so would be to defile Allah's people.

For generations Christ's faithful had endured alternating seasons of harshness and tolerance while they quietly suffered the added offense of watching their most holy places fall one by one into heathen hands. A small corner of the Holy Land still remained under Christian rule, and pilgrims continued to go in an unrelenting stream; they saw their lot as that of Christ's and suffered in hopes of a final deliverance. Deliverance had surely been delayed, however. The black-and-white tents of the terrible Turks under Suleiman now dotted the plains and mountains of that land, and Christian pilgrims had become the targets of cruel torture and death. To these challenges the knights of Europe were still hoping to rise again in Holy Crusade.

As he bounced through the valleys tightening around him, Heinrich began to wonder why these Syrians could peddle their spices and their silks unharmed, while Christian knights were dying on the bloody sands of Palestine. He stared at them as they knelt to pray and wondered if they were asking Allah to strike down the Christ. He knew Jerusalem had fallen to their kind less than twenty years before. He also knew that a remnant of Christian Palestine was hard-pressed on every side by a rising storm of infidels, perhaps kin to the ones he now served. Heinrich slowly became incensed. *Look at 'em! They strut about like clever peacocks in their foolish turbans and silk. They think our lands are theirs for the taking!* The man began to bristle.

Finally, in the early twilight of that same day Heinrich reined in his horses and dismounted the wagon. He snatched a loaf of stale bread and a flagon of ale from the caravan's provisioner and walked away. He'd not serve them another step. Midst a volley of blasphemies and curses, the man spat and marched north toward a village he had seen from higher ground. He could hear a distant bell ringing compline and he quickened his step to find shelter before nightfall.

Heinrich arrived in a small village set neatly against a starlit lake. In the silver moonlight he could see the silhouetted ring of mountains securing the modest hamlet at its center, cupping the village as if to shelter it from the evil world beyond. A stout, stone church squatted near the lake's edge and he knocked on its heavy wooden door. A kindly priest named Father Wilfrid answered and welcomed the pilgrim inside to spend the night by a pleasant fire.

It was a good night for Heinrich. The priest was cheerful and earnest, his bread soft and sweetened, and the fire bright and warm. Heinrich slept like a happy child and awakened to a charitable first-meal of porridge and cider. Father Wilfrid blessed him with a traveler's prayer and an embrace. Heinrich looked about the warm surroundings and smiled. *This one feels true,* he thought. The priest begged him to delay his leaving for a few moments so that he might show him something in his workshop by the lake.

Heinrich followed the eager man into a shed containing slabs of marble. "I collect these, my son. A man can only do so many baptisms, so many Holy Masses, so many burials before ..."—he glanced about to be sure no other was listening—"before it gets a bit tiresome!"

Heinrich chuckled.

"So I carve the wisdom of others into rock for the ages to come. See, here." Wilfrid pointed to several finished pieces. Most were inscribed in Latin but a few were in German. He translated them. "'Open me this beautiful day and lead me into the house of God. Here at this place my soul shall be happy.' This goes over a church door."

Heinrich liked it. "Where is such a church?"

The priest shrugged. "I pray to find one!"

Heinrich laughed again. He liked this fellow.

"And here. '*Starke und Hilfe in alle Not.*'"

"Ah." Heinrich nodded. "'Strength and Help in all Need.' Would that it be so."

The comment did not escape the priest's notice. He paused, then showed Heinrich another. "'*Sei getran bis an den Tod,*' 'Be true until you Die.'"

Heinrich was silent. He looked about the shop and admired the priest's eye for wisdom and for beauty. He nodded, then ducked through the doorway and stood by the lake's crystal waters. "This village has a name, father?"

"*Ja,* 'tis called Zell. Zell by the Lake."

Heinrich stared at the shimmering water and the snow-laced mountains that rose around it. His glance lightly followed the shoreline and over the knotty boughs of oak and maple, the delicate bared branches of white-trunked birch, and the yellowed wands of bending willow. He turned to the father. "How does one know what is true?"

Father Wilfrid was not accustomed to such questions—his flock was more apt to ask how best to boil swan! But the young priest had a mind that was deep like the lake he loved, and clear like its waters. It was a matter he, too, had struggled with often. He answered slowly, but with conviction. "It is wise to know what it is, for it is the only thing worthy to serve." He paused and tossed a few pebbles into his lake. "I believe, dear stranger, that truth is what remains when all else fails."

                                   ☙

The priest of Zell gave Heinrich good directions to the Brenner Pass, and soon the pilgrim was hurrying through tight, twisting valleys squeezed between the steep-sloped mountains. Amazed, humbled, awestruck, and overwhelmed at every turn, the simple peasant of distant Weyer pressed on. He was pleased his journey took him through some simple hamlets where he could buy bread and cheese from cheerful, pink-faced villagers.

Heinrich finally found his way through Innsbruck and followed the rising Sill valley until he arrived at the white cliffs of the Brenner Pass. Here he found himself suddenly crowded by many others urgently pressing toward their destinations. Merchantmen, legates, men-at-arms, and pilgrims from all parts of the Holy Empire met to face the toll keepers.

Heinrich thought the toll a bit pricey for one man with only a rucksack and a satchel. But standing in the queue he heard something that was worth the half-shilling toll—he learned that a caravan of Syrians had just been slaughtered by a band of rogue knights returning from Palestine. Their bodies were found stripped and their wagons burned. The only evidence of the "crime" was a torn sash bearing the crest of a Norman lord.

From Brenner, Heinrich hiked with a company of legates and couriers in a rapid descent into warmer environs. One fellow traveler was a longwinded messenger from Rome who was able to give the man some idea of where he might locate the church he was seeking. "Ah, *si*. *Santa Maria in Domnica*. *Si*, it is on the Caelian Hill. I know it well. It is a bit south of the Coliseum and not so very far to its west is the basilica of *St. Giovanni* and the pope's palace in the Lateran. *Si*, my friend, I know it well. But how do you?"

Heinrich grew more excited. His cheeks felt warm and his veins pumped. A miner in Hallein had told him many things of the ancient Romans. He knew something about the Coliseum and its horrors. Heinrich explained his need to present a letter to the superior of that particular church.

The man loosened the fur collar of his shin-length tunic and laid his cloak over his arm. He removed a silk cap from his head and tossed a head full of long hair in the warm sun. "My *matrona* left me at the door of Santa Maria's while I was yet a babe. This church ... it serves the poor well. It stands where St. Lawrence once gave alms to the needy. Ah, good stranger. Wait until you see the mosaic! 'Tis, 'tis beyond words." You see, the church's art is Greek. It is a church made beautiful by rebels!" He swallowed a draught of red wine from a flagon slung from his shoulder. "Have you any interest in these things?"

"Aye! Indeed I do. I'm rather fond of the work of rebels!" Heinrich's eye beamed. "Please, we've days ahead; go on!"

The traveler nodded. He was cheerful and had been well-schooled by a wealthy Lombardian family who had adopted him from the church when he was six. Now a man of middle age, he was fluent in Italian, Latin, German, English, and French. In the following days, he taught Heinrich much of the history of Rome and its influence on all of Christendom.

Heinrich was intrigued. He had known no more than what legends were passed from the elders in Weyer, or what little news had come from passersby. Suddenly, he was beginning to realize that his life was but one story told in a moment, yet an integral part of others gone before and more yet to come.

The travelers descended quickly through the hardwoods of the Tyrol, past Balzano, Trento, and Verona. By mid-December Heinrich was striding through the warm, flat plain of the Po Valley. Here he marched past fallowed fields of rich soil made fertile by centuries of erosion from the Apennines and the Alps.

In Bologna, Heinrich bade farewell to his fellow traveler and thanked the man profusely for the wealth of knowledge he had imparted. This effusive man had taught the simple baker that the world was an intricate tapestry. "It is textured," he had said, "with Creation's mountains and valleys, deserts, rivers, oceans, endless forests, and fertile fields. It is hued by colors born under the sun; it is sprinkled with the races of man and the creatures over which they are given dominion. As time turns, this great tapestry is revealed in greater dimension, while fingers of the unseen Weaver deftly add more wondrous threads to this Story of Stories."

~

The Apennines Mountains arc in a long, sweeping turn from Genoa's Ligurian Alps in the northwest through the length of the Italian Peninsula. Somewhere in the stunted forests of these rounded hills Heinrich huddled beneath his cloak and waited patiently for the end of a heavy, pelting rainstorm. Indeed, he took the inconvenience in stride and soon found himself pressing southward around Firenze, through the olive orchards and birch forests of Umbria, by numerous villages of rose-hued stone, and beneath the uncomfortable watch of cliff-topped castles. At last he spotted what his informative friend had told him to seek: a Roman aqueduct! Stretched before him was a long, multi-arched, bridgelike structure that filled the gap between two rolling hills and disappeared from sight far in the distance. "Follow the aqueducts to Rome!" the man had said.

Heinrich was nearly bursting with excitement as the roadway gradually clogged with more and more travelers. Merchants, farmers, carts laden with goods, impatient consorts, and companies of cavalry jostled and hurried along the now dusty road. Heinrich had been told to circuit the city and enter from the south—it would be a more advantageous route to the little church.

The well-worn roadway was arrow-straight and flat, made of dark gray, almost black blocks of basalt. On either side were ancient ruins pilfered for their narrow, red-brown bricks or covered by creepers and vines. The blocks beneath his feet were about a man's forearm square, rather rounded with age and often grooved by what Heinrich imagined were iron wheels from long-ago carts and chariots. To either side were gardens and ploughed fields, cypress trees and umbrella pines, chestnut tree and rhododendrons. A few modest farmhouses sheltered dark-eyed folk who seemed unimpressed by the steady flow of traffic passing them by.

The man was eager but growing more nervous. He moved to the side of the road and took a brief respite. He watched the colorful pageant passing by, then stared wistfully ahead. He drew a deep breath and imagined Rome to be filled with the songs of angels and the aroma of heaven's gardens. He closed his eye and pictured golden streets, jeweled portals, and silk banners. He could hear brass trumpets summoning the Virgin to bless penitent pilgrims such as he. He imagined the pope stepping lightly down the Holy Stairs, the *Scala Santa*, to receive the old Norseman's pitiful necklace. He felt better.

A voice interrupted Heinrich's thoughts. "Saints Peter and Paul stepped there."

Heinrich opened his eye. "Eh?"

It was a young Saxon lad who Heinrich judged as a novice by his robes.

"Saint Paul stepped here, and Saint Peter, too."

Heinrich looked about. "Where?"

"Here. On this road. This is the Appian Way, the road Rome's legions traveled and the road the apostles walked."

Heinrich stared in disbelief.

"'Tis true, pilgrim. Ahead are the holy catacombs ... tombs of our brethren gone on before some thousand years ago. Then farther is the *Porta Appia* through Aurelian's Wall. The wall is nearly a thousand years old itself!"

Heinrich stared at his feet. He was about to tread where saints had actually walked. He lifted his foot toward the block of pavement and hesitated. When he set it down it was as if a surge of power entered his body. He muttered to himself, then bowed his head.

৵

It was dusk on Friday, the thirty-first of December, 1210, when a weary and dejected Heinrich finally stood at the door of *Santa Maria in Domnica* church. He paused and glanced over his shoulder at the ruin of an ancient aqueduct standing nearby. Beyond it, where the city sloped downward in the distant center of his view, he saw the gray walls of the infamous Coliseum.

Rome had already disappointed him. From the moment he had passed through the deep gate of the massive, double-arched city wall he was sickened by the septic stench of stagnant sewers and the putrid odor of human waste. He had walked past run-down and abandoned villas on the broken cobbles of the Caelian Hill. Goats and sheep grazed between the columns of a once-mighty empire. Bricks lay in heaps aside collapsed homes, and weeds grew where lush gardens had once boasted blooms from all regions of the known world. The few green sprigs of Advent hanging here and there did little to add the cheer of Christmas to a place that had fallen so very far from glory.

The City of Seven Hills was the heart of an empire that had once ruled the earth from the bogs of Britain to sun-baked Arabia. Its power and might had made Rome a city of glory in the center of a world forever changed. Yet great cities, like empires, always crumble under the weight of things greater than themselves, and by the time Heinrich arrived in Rome it had become a pitiful shadow of its former self. From its zenith of some one million inhabitants it had decayed into an overgrown, diseased, and gasping home to fewer than twenty thousand.

Heinrich grimaced at the horrid odor curling within his nostrils. He longed for the clean air of the mountain spruce or the briny breezes of Stedingerland and the sea. He surveyed the faded tile rooftops of the dismal city and sighed. *'Tis a certain place to do penance.* The sun was setting and the shadows were growing long. Heinrich gathered his courage and knocked on the door.

None answered, so he knocked again, harder. At last a

small window within the door opened and an eye peered out. *"Si?"*

"G–guten Tag," stuttered Heinrich. "I am a pilgrim come to do penance."

"Si? Avanti!" The window closed with a slam.

Heinrich scratched his head and knocked again. Twice. The window opened and a few sharp words were hurled at the dumbfounded baker. The window slammed shut again.

Heinrich sat on the dirt in front of the church and thought carefully. "Ach, dolt!" he muttered to himself. He reached into his satchel and dug for the relic and the letter from the Carthusians. When his fingers brushed against his mother's medallion, however, he hesitated. Then, with a measure of resolve, he lifted it from its sanctuary and dangled it from his hand. It twirled in the cool evening breeze and he thought it a most beautiful thing. His mind flew to his hovel and to his mother. He grasped the medallion in his hand and wept.

Whether it was the tears or gold none could know, but the church door suddenly creaked on its rusted hinges and opened slightly. A little man stepped from its recesses with a wary eye on the stranger. He had been watching the visitor all along. "German?"

Heinrich was startled. *"Ja!"*

"Humph."

"Pater?"

"Si."

The priest stared at Heinrich for a long moment. He was a short, aging man with a close-cropped ring of white hair running from temple to temple. His complexion was olive; he was dark eyed, round faced, and slightly rotund. His eyebrows angled upward at the far side of each eye, giving him the appearance of perpetual anticipation. "And what to do for you?" His German language skills were weak, probably by choice. Romans had been annoyed with their shaggy German guests ever since Charlemagne and his heirs dared claim the name of "Holy Roman Emperor."

Heinrich handed the priest his letter of introduction and followed him to a dimly lit chamber attached to the church's sanctuary. The priest lit several candles, read the letter with increasing interest, then turned to Heinrich. "The relic?" His tone had changed.

Heinrich said nothing for a moment. He looked around the little room and wondered. With reluctance he extended his fist, then opened it to reveal the treasure lying in his calloused palm. The father knelt and crossed himself, then lifted the medallion reverently and laid it gently on an open Bible. He knelt again and murmured another prayer. Heinrich waited respectfully, then followed the little man down a dark hall and into a larger room where dozens of children prepared for sleep. Attending them were two more priests, a novice, and three nuns. Heinrich followed farther, past an infirmary filled with coughing, fevered children, and finally to a small cell with a single candle and one cot. The priest lit a stubby candle with his own. "Your room."

Heinrich stared.

"I am *Don* Vincenzo. We speak in morning." With that the little priest vanished and left Heinrich to his first night in the Eternal City.

෨

It was squeals of laughter that awakened Heinrich from an unhappy dream. He sat up with a start and stared about his dark, little cell. He quickly checked for his rucksack and satchel. All was in order, except for the unfamiliar noise.

The man gathered his things and followed the happy sounds into the larger, straw-covered room he had passed through the night before. The children stopped playing and stared in terror as the one-eyed man with long red curls stepped toward them. Heinrich peered into each little face and smiled. *Children!* he thought. *'Tis good to hear them laugh!* A voice caught his attention. It was Father Vincenzo. "Come."

Heinrich obeyed and followed the priest through a maze of short hallways and rooms to a small office. He was seated in front of two other priests and one ancient woman dressed in a habit. Heinrich assumed she was a nun.

Vincenzo introduced each by name. "Father Arturo of Rome, Father Florian of Lombardy, and Sister Anoush of Armenia. Only sister speaks your tongue well."

Heinrich nodded to each, then turned to the aged nun. He bowed respectfully.

Anoush wore a simple nun's gown, a homespun white habit with a plain black apron. Her hair was covered by a black hood. Nearly bent in two by more than eighty years of life, the kindly sister smiled and took Heinrich's hand in her own—one curled and knotted by years of difficult labor. "Dear boy," she began, "sit with us." Heinrich felt good; he hadn't been called "boy" for a very long time! The sister's voice was as clear as her shining brown eyes. "*Don* Vincenzo has shown us your letter, and we spent the New Year's Eve in fasting and prayers of thanksgiving." She was pious, but not pretentious. She leaned close to Heinrich and wiggled her finger for him to lower his ear. She whispered, "Truth is they spent most of their time speaking of today's Feast of Fools at the Ruffini's!" She chuckled.

Heinrich smiled. He felt safe with the aged nun. Her face was wrinkled and spongy, her smiling mouth vacant of all teeth. She was tiny and frail and her expression wistful, yet she exuded a quality of love that struck Heinrich as heaven-sent.

"Dear boy," she said slowly. "I am instructed by *Don* Vincenzo to entreat your cause for penance. It is time to bare all to these three priests."

Heinrich had dreaded this moment from the day he left Stettin. The litany of his sins and failings was one that he was weary of recounting. Yet duty was now upon him and it was time to sit before God's chosen to receive their wisdom. The judgment was imminent and he must not falter.

The man lowered his head in shame and told his story. He began with Baldric's scorn for his sloth as a child, then spoke of his release of the reeve's dog, the vow, the slaughter of the Gunnars, his hatred of Baldric, his hatred of Marta, and his affections for Katharina. He wandered through his life backward and forward. He confessed his temptations to break his vow, the confusions of his faith, and finally admitted to the killing of Richard's murderer and the striking of Father Pious.

That done, he went on to acknowledge his treason on behalf of the Stedingers; of lies and ill-will, of selfishness, pride, and of undeserved joy. The man groaned and wept for the better part of an hour, earnestly descending into each dark chamber of his heart in a desperate search to fling open every door. He feared to forget a single act, lest his penance be futile.

When finished, he stood exhausted and trembling. Anoush wiped tears from the deep furrows of her cheeks and held the man's arm with her two hands. She leaned against him and prayed while the priests huddled.

After a half hour of low murmurs, Father Vincenzo announced they had come to a decision, and Anoush was asked to interpret as he spoke the pronouncement.

Heinrich stiffened and waited bravely. The priests folded their hands and bowed. "*In nomine Patris, et Filii, et Spiritus Sancti*, I begin."

Anoush held Heinrich's sweating hand in her own. She looked up at him sadly over a shoulder now stooped even farther as if the weight of the man's melancholy had come upon her as well. Her voice was strong and soothing as she translated the edict of the priests: "As the relic-bearer you have earned a right to our charity and we are here to return you to the fold of God's beloved. By your own witness your sins are both mortal and venial. Your words accuse you rightly as an evil man in grave peril. But our Lord is not without mercy, nor the Virgin Mother.

"First, this very day you shall enter into the confessional to receive absolution.

"Second, for your temporal indulgence hear this. We concur that eighteen months is a fitting time for you to serve God and man in penance. Now hear us: you must wear the hair shirt and breeches each day and each night. You shall be the bell ringer for this church at every ringing of every day, bar none other than if excused for other labors. Whether by sickness or by injury, by weariness or distress, you are without excuse. In mornings, you shall assist in the baking of bread for the poor children we serve. In afternoons, you shall serve this humble church as courier, transporter, wagoner, and the like. In evenings, you shall lie prostrate before the altar and recite two *Pater Nosters* for each known sin committed, and one *Ave Maria* for each known sin yet harbored in your heart. At the bells of matins, you shall awaken and walk barefoot to St. Giovani's. There you shall lie prostrate at the base of the *Sclara Santa* and recite alternating *Aves* and *Paters* for each of its twenty-eight steps."

To Anoush's horror, Vincenzo then yawned and sighed. He shrugged as he continued. "These are our commands; these are the words of your Holy Church. Kneel before me and swear now that you shall keep this penance and the vow of your own past. Swear to keep it whole."

Heinrich's mouth was dry and he was sweating. He felt bound again, trapped within the order he had hoped would save him. He wanted to run away. For no apparent reason, a vision of Katharina and the Christmas star falling through the night's sky at Weyer's church suddenly filled his mind. For all its pleasure, the simple memory damned him all the more. With a groan the man bent slowly to his knee and yielded. "I ... I so swear."

"Strength and mercy to you, my son. Come to us on the thirtieth day of June in the year 1212 and swear on the relic that you have brought that you have so obeyed your penance, and we shall bless your return home, you and your family absolved in heaven and on earth from all your wicked past."

Heinrich could not speak. He lifted his head and swallowed hard on the lump clogging his throat. He looked to Anoush whose eyes were filled with compassion and whose cheeks were wet with tears. She led the poor wretch from Vincenzo's chamber and toward his cell. Somewhere in the dark corridors he heard her murmur softly, "This is not the way."

≈

At dawn, Heinrich exchanged his own clothing for a shirt

and breeches made of unscraped leather worn hair-side against his own skin. Thin sandals were bound to his feet and a threadbare, woollen, hooded cape hung atop his shoulders. Anoush escorted him quickly through the church's dormant gardens and hurried him toward the sanctuary. She paused outside the door as the bells of prime rang, waiting patiently to present him with a gift. She smiled. "The sun is just right!"

Santa Maria in Domnica was a simple rectangle some thirty-five paces long and twenty-two wide. It had been built of gray stone blocks nearly four hundred years prior to Heinrich's arrival. Its modest exterior belied a nave of rare beauty, for the stones of the interior walls were alternating pastels of pink and gray, some further graced by borders of blue or gold. It was designed like a small basilica in that it had a broad nave separated from side aisles by ten columned archways that rose to form the outer wall of a second story. The rear western wall was built as a large, semi-circular apse which contained the altar.

"Come, Heinrich, my boy. Enter with me. I should be pleased, however, if you would drop your eye to the floor until I ask you to raise it." She was giddy as a young girl on May Day morn.

Heinrich had about enough of head-bending, and the hair itching at his skin was making him irritable. He obliged the tittering woman, nonetheless, and let her lead him like a blind man down the center aisle toward the altar.

The woman positioned him carefully and took a deep breath. "Now, Heinrich, look up!"

Heinrich lifted his head and as he did his mouth dropped open. His throat immediately swelled and tears formed. The morning sun of the new year was pouring through the windows of the wall behind him and splashing its light across a glittering mosaic that filled the concave apse. Shimmering before him were the colors of the Creation: green and blue, red, gold, and white. But there was more. It was a mosaic like none other in all Christendom, for in the concave hollow of the apse it displayed the Virgin and the Holy Child surrounded by angels and seated in a *garden of flowers!* "Flowers! *Mein Gott*... 'tis Emma's garden!" he cried.

Slowly, Heinrich moved closer. The vault was bordered by strips of gold and flowers of blue and red. To one side stood Moses, on the other, Elijah, both with flowers at their feet. Above the arch sat the Christ on a rainbow "Ach, a *rainbow!*" exclaimed Heinrich. "And look ... are they the apostles approaching him from either side?"

Anoush was weeping for joy. "*Ja,* good Heinrich." She had sensed something special about the melancholy pilgrim from the moment she had first seen him. The way his spirit rose to the beauty of the mosaic affirmed her hopes. She was sure that he, like her, might understand what such light and color said about the true heart of the God they served.

The stoop-shouldered sister and the shaggy German stood silently before the glory of the ancient display until *Don* Vincenzo grumbled his way into the nave. "To work!" he commanded. The two hesitated, then, with sighs and obedient nods, they parted. Sister Anoush bade Heinrich a reluctant farewell and scurried to her beloved children. For his part, Heinrich pulled his lingering eye away from the enchanting vision and followed Vincenzo to the bakehouse in the garden behind the church. He began his first day of penance with his hand deep in dough.

After ringing the bells of midnight matins, Heinrich took the Norse sea captain's necklace from the bottom of his satchel and began the quarter hour jaunt to the Palace of St. John Lateran. St. John's, or St. Giovanni as the Romans called it, was known as the "Mother and Head of All Churches in the City and the World." The first basilica built in Rome, it was the official church of the early Roman Christians. The infants of these ancient Christian families had been baptized beneath the waters of its black tub for centuries.

In the palace attached to the basilica, the pope maintained his residence as his predecessors had done for nearly a thousand years before. And on the second story of the eastern end of the massive complex was the pope's private chapel, the *Sancta Sanctorum*, the Holy of Holies.

That dark night, Pope Innocent III prayed in the *Sancta Sanctorum* while, unbeknownst to him, Heinrich of Weyer stood trembling in a nearby courtyard. The pope had recently excommunicated Lord Otto, his original choice for emperor of the Germans. Surrounded by relics such as the thorny crown of the Christ, nails from the cross, and, as some had sworn, the very heads of Saints Peter and Paul, Innocent now prayed earnestly for his new choice for emperor, the child, Friederich II.

Heinrich fidgeted with the Norseman's simple, silver necklace while he followed directions to the *Scala Santa*. The Holy Stairs once led to Pilate's judgment hall in Jerusalem; it was the very same stairway that Jesus had tread upon on the way to his trial before his crucifixion. Removed to Rome some eight hundred years before, they now brought comfort and assurance to the many souls wishing to follow in their Savior's steps. Penitents through the ages had climbed the deep-set, twenty-eight marble stairs upon their knees, pausing at each to pray or recite an *Ave* or *Pater Noster*. Some fortunate few would be greeted with a holy kiss by the pope himself, to whose residence this stairway climbed.

Heinrich would not be so fortunate, but he felt awed and humbled in the cold night's air as he bent his knee to the first step. Pausing to recite his words, he then climbed upward, one at time, slowly and carefully. He was told the blood of Jesus still stained the gray marble, but in the torchlight the man could not see to kiss the marks. Upon reaching the top, he laid the silver chain on the last step and recited both an *Ave* and a *Pater*. A grumbling guard snatched the necklace and put it promptly into his pocket. He muttered something in his own tongue and motioned for Heinrich to descend.

The pilgrim paused, certain the old sailor would have been disappointed, then obeyed by backing slowly downward on his aching knees. He reached the bottom and stood quietly, then turned and walked the long slope up to his little cell in *Santa Maria in Domnica*.

᷇

The weeks that followed proved to be difficult for the baker of Weyer. His skin was badly broken by the hair garments. Rashes became oozing sores, especially over his shoulders and thighs. But he reasoned that such agony was fitting for a season of penance and refused the pleas of Sister Anoush for treatment. Finally, however, on Holy Saturday, the twenty-fourth of March, the miserable man relented. He reached into his hidden rucksack and sprinkled salt upon his miseries and did so for the fortnight to follow.

By May Day his sores had healed and his skin had roughened in a way that it no longer suffered the abrasions of the clothes. Though the man was relieved for it, he felt ashamed as well. He had come to pay for his past, to immerse himself in a baptism of misery that might wash away his failings. It was the way of his order and he clung with desperate resolve to the notions it had planted so deeply within his soul.

But Heinrich could scarcely bear the frustration he felt and the growing contempt in which he held himself. "I come to pay a penance, yet I yearn for comfort and healing. I do duties that become easier each day. Woe to me ... woe to me!"

On a rainy day near May's end he handed old Anoush his remaining salt. "For the children. I have been greedy and selfish ... I should have given it before." He then reached into his satchel and retrieved his gold coins and what silver pennies he still had. "And take these idols from me. I've no right to them. Feed the poor, clothe the naked." He set the pouch into the astonished nun's palms and turned away.

On the first of June he announced an added penance. To Anoush's horror and the priests' affirmation, he would begin to crawl on his belly to St. John's each night; it seemed a way to suffer more. So for weeks on end the man did just that. In the dark hours past each midnight he dragged himself through the rough rubble and fouled gutters of Rome to the Holy Stairs where he muttered his repetitions. He then crawled home to lie alone in his cell until prime when a new day of hard labor would began.

Heinrich lived this way through the months of June and

July, but after ringing the bells of prime on a glorious August dawn, the man collapsed in tears. He moaned like a wounded bull as he railed against himself with yet more failings. "Methinks me mad! I hate this penance and in m'hatred I sin again!" He lay trembling and confused until the gentle hand of Sister Anoush startled him.

Sister Anoush had spent hours in her gardens reflecting on her friend's misery and in earnest prayer on his behalf. "Dear, dear Heinrich. How can I help you?"

The haggard, gaunt penitent sat up, hollow-eyed and drawn. His beard was long, his hair unkempt. He had lost his bulk, his clothing smelled, and his breath was hard. "I … I fear I am beyond hope."

"Nay, never." Anoush took him firmly by the hand. "Poor wretch, you are bound to something other than wisdom's way. You must find the courage to change … the courage to turn outside of yourself."

Heinrich looked away.

The old woman embraced the man. "I pray this caterpillar bursts from his bondage … I pray you become a butterfly and fly away from the gutters of Rome!" Her words chilled the man.

By St. Michael's Day, Anoush's prayer was not yet answered. Heinrich stubbornly held to his vow and sank ever further into an abyss of melancholy and despair. He sought new ways to purge whatever undeserved respite tempted him from his path, and to Anoush's great sadness, he finally refused to look upon the mosaic, once cursing it for the gladness it had given him.

His obsession became entangled with depression which, in turn, gave way to indolence. His sluggish ways did not go unnoticed, and on a cold Advent evening Father Vincenzo lost all patience with the man. "Sloth is a vice!" he shouted. "And sins require penance!" Heinrich groaned.

Vincenzo, of course, was surely a poor model. Content to mutter his liturgy and slump about his chambers, the man had little business crushing reeds already bruised. No longer a zealot who simply misused the faith, he had become indifferent to the pursuit of truth altogether.

"Give no more heed to *Don* Vincenzo ... or Father Arturo for that matter," pleaded Anoush. She now admitted a deep and secret heartache long denied. "They suffer a worse terror than you. They are miserable, cruel men who serve a meaningless god. They are men of religion and not of faith."

Poor Anoush was exasperated with Heinrich. She pleaded and consoled, admonished and instructed. She urged the man to abandon his penance and save his life. She urged him to listen to the counsel of songbirds instead of priests, and to hear the wind whispering for change. But, alas, January had passed and February was upon them. The songbirds were silent and the winds blew damp and cold. She could do no more than help the stubborn sufferer to his bed and weep for him in the dark of night.

Chapter 24

ANFECHTUNG AND PURPOSE

He is being called the 'Worm of Santa Maria's!'"
Father Vincenzo laughed. "I think the name is
good. Look at the fool."

Sister Anoush laid a hard eye on her superior. "This
'worm' is an uncommon man, *Pater*. He has taken your
ways deep within himself ... far to excess, perhaps to their
natural end." She doubted that Vincenzo had the courage
to do the same.

"Ah, the ways," scoffed Vincenzo. "The blessed ways."

Anoush helped Heinrich to his feet after he crawled the
final few rods to the church door. It was a cold night, the
sixth of February in 1212. Though it was three hours past
midnight, the priests and nuns were gathering for prayer to
begin the Great Lent. "Dear boy, dear boy," groaned
Anoush. "You must end this penance before you die. I hear
you in the night, wheezing and coughing." She held a
smoky torch over her head. "And I see you've lost more
teeth."

Heinrich could say little. He was weak and desperate,
obsessed with purging every vestige of comfort or island of
strength that might yet be found within. Even glimmers of
hope needed to be extinguished, for he imagined the very
sense of any good thing was undeserved. Each night's
painful crawl to the Holy Stairs was a tortuous punishment, yet with every sharp edge that cut into his belly the

man felt relief. Even his relief, however, caused him shame, for he was certain that such odd pleasure was, itself, a joy that voided the very purpose of his penance.

Anoush led the trembling wretch toward his cot. *"Tantatio tristitae!"* she whispered. "Beware the temptation to despair. You are not without hope, my son." Heinrich groaned and stared up at the sad brown eyes of the bent-backed saint. "You don't understand, sister. I must *lose* all hope. Hope brings joy."

On the morning that followed, Heinrich stood on trembling legs at first-meal and tore his rye in two. "Through this Lent I, too, shall deny m'self. Until Holy Saturday I eat half and share the rest with these poor." Those gathered simply stared.

The man's decision was another one rooted in deception. He believed his beaten, ravaged body was little more than the prison of his spirit; as if his outward shell was an unjoined appendage, a lesser thing, an unworthy annoyance to be abused and neglected ... like the reeve's dog. But the man, like all men, was a whole. His body, though long-suffering, would not allow such inane abuse—and it finally rebelled. On the night of Holy Thursday, in the third week of March, the "Worm of Santa Maria's" lay unconscious on the seventh step of the *Scala Santa*.

The night guards of the pope's palace knew the man well and sent a messenger to the church. Sister Anoush, of course, was the first to react. She yanked a big novice from his bed, harnessed the horse to its cart, and prodded the beast to hurry. She then marched up the Holy Stairs with her novice in tow, sharply dismissing all demands they climb on their knees. She laid a kind hand on Heinrich's sweated brow as the novice lifted him.

Heinrich was delivered to his bed midst the loud complaints of Fathers Vincenzo, Arturo, and Florian. They were in no mood for this. Their own Lenten fasts made them irritable under the best of conditions, and now they were rousted from a good night's sleep to carry this foul-smelling Teuton to his stale cot. "No more!" growled Vincenzo. "I wash my hands of him!"

Heinrich awakened somewhere in the afternoon hours of Holy Saturday. He had been bathed and dressed in clean linens by Anoush, who had also trimmed his hair and beard. He was sallow and sweated, too weak to even mutter a word, but when he heard another ringing the bells of nones he knew his mighty penance had failed.

The man closed his eye and his chest began to heave. Trembling, he rolled away from the blessed sister and moaned. Soon his breathing was halting and his shoulders began to jerk. Anoush gently laid both hands on him. He began to shake and lurch as the frightened Anoush prayed loudly. Suddenly she stopped and simply held him close, for the man was not wrestling in the throes of death, but rather sobbing like a child.

ॐ

Heinrich lay in the care of his aged nurse for weeks. His fever had passed but his body was frail. By late April he was baking bread once again and helping the novice with the bells. In exchange for lodging and food, broken Heinrich humbly asked to serve in whatever ways his improving health might allow until he was strong enough to begin his journey home. His request was reluctantly granted with the stipulation that he not remain past the first day of July.

In the warm weeks of springtime, Heinrich spent hours listening to the words of Sister Anoush as he helped tend her gardens. She was wise and encouraging. She worked in apparent vain to teach him the *proper* order of things, that nothing on earth—no king, no pope, no village priest or reeve, nor high-minded notion—ruled with authority unless it ruled according to God's Law of Love.

Despite her kindness and her instruction, the man remained numb, empty, and woefully shamed. His penance had miscarried, and he believed his many years away from home had been in vain. It was a new weight of sorrow he could scarcely bear. More than that, he had no more solution, no goal in view that might lighten the millstone hanging heavy on his shoulders. Everything had failed him, including himself. His spirit was wounded and scarred, barred from wisdom, closed to hope. He suffered the horrors of *Anfechtung*—the aching, unrequited contest for the soul.

In early June, Sister Anoush begged the priests to allow Heinrich the tasks of the carter. She hoped a change in the man's monotony might kindle some spark of life. So, with some hesitation, the man was given charge of the two-wheeled cart and sent about Rome delivering eggs, carrying children to adoptive homes, fetching foundlings, bearing dispatches, and other sundry chores.

Bouncing atop Rome's cobbles helped awaken something within the joyless man. He was particularly taken by the beauty of the Pantheon. Once the grand temple of the Roman gods, it had become a Christian church six hundred years before. The pilgrim stared up at its huge, domed ceiling, opened in the very center to the blue sky. Heinrich quickly looked down. "Cursed vow!" he grumbled. He wasn't sure it had meaning any longer, but he was not ready to abandon all.

The man began to enjoy his days riding in the Italian sunshine. He marveled at the ruins of Rome's glorious past, now mere mounds of stubble rising up from the dirt and debris of the centuries. He passed the forum and imagined the voices of the senators echoing amongst the goats now chewing grass atop what once had been the world's seat of power. He trotted his little horse through Constantine's arch and pretended to be a charioteer in a Roman legion following the emperor to the far-flung reaches of the world.

By Midsummer's Day, Heinrich thought the decaying city to be redeemed, in part, by its scattered gardens and wildflowers, songbirds and the few fountains that yet sprayed water in the sun-bathed air. He watched a few squealing children splash in one and Heinrich paused to think of his own good lads. He could see them frolicking in the Laubusbach. The man reached into his satchel and retrieved his stone. He swished it in the fountain's waters and chuckled. "There, little charm, you'd be baptized in the waters of Rome!" He rubbed the smooth stone between his fingers and thumb, then dropped it back into his bag. "Home," he resolved. "'Tis time."

Indeed it was. And in the early hours of the first day of July in the Year of Grace 1212, Sister Anoush walked her dear friend before the marvelous mosaic of *Santa Maria in Domnica*. There, the ragged, broad-shouldered German and his frail, stooped, Armenian friend stood silently together one last time as the rising sun illuminated the flowers of the fields and the robes of the angels. The golden halo of the Holy Child sparkled like a ring of jewels against the deep blue robes of the Virgin, and the saints glowed all around.

Heinrich's eye lingered along the gold-eyed, red blooms and his mind flew to Emma and her corn poppies. His heart filled with the colors of the rainbow; the fruit of the sun. He lifted Sister Anoush's knotty hand to his lips and kissed it tenderly.

Don Vincenzo broke the silence. "Sister, tell him I've come to release him."

Heinrich's mood changed as he was led to the confessional. There, he dutifully offered a short list of committed sins, but he had already reasoned it was probably useless. Whatever absolution God might have granted by His grace would certainly be rejected out-of-hand, for the man had held his own soul in the scales—and he found it wanting. God's love was surely conditioned on his sincerity, and his sincerity was disproven by his failings. Not only did he expect his eternal state to be in the gravest peril, but his temporal indulgence would not now be granted either. His incomplete penance would leave a reckoning still due on earth, one that both he and his family must pay as penalty.

At Anoush's insistence, Vincenzo charitably pronounced the man's sins forgiven in heaven and remitted on earth. The priest let his words ring with the authority of the Church, but Heinrich's heart was now cold to things of the order. To the baker of Weyer, it—like he—had failed.

With a bow and a final mumble Vincenzo disappeared from the nave, leaving Anoush a few final moments with her friend. Heinrich was sullen, though he did not complain of his unhappiness. He quietly slipped away from

Anoush to the crypt below the altar, where he stood before his mother's medallion. The relic had been draped gracefully over the neck of an olive-wood crucifix standing alongside a small painting of the Virgin. The man knelt alone in the candlelit chamber and recalled many moments of his former times. It was a bittersweet respite. Suddenly weary of such recollections, he sighed, then rejoined Anoush. He wrapped an arm lightly around her frail shoulders and bowed his head.

Anoush stood by her weary friend and would have stayed there all the day had not she heard the man draw a deep breath. She knew the time had come. She turned him toward her face and bade him to kneel. She laid her hands gently on his head and smiled. "Ah, dear, dear Heinrich. I shall pray you fly free from your cocoon." She smiled tenderly. "In the meanwhile, I have stuffed your satchel heavy with cheese and fruit, some dried fish and vegetables pulled by my own hand. The children have stuffed your rucksack with bread and some preserves." She stopped to fight back tears.

"Now, if you would allow, I should like to send you with my blessing." The wise woman closed her eyes and tilted her head upward. *"In nomine Patris, et Filii, et Spiritus Sancti.* Attend to my cry: for I have been brought low indeed. Deliver me from my persecutors; for they are stronger than I. Lead my soul out of prison, that I may praise Thy name." Her eyes blurred and her voice trembled. She embraced Heinrich, then walked him to the door.

Heinrich could barely speak. "I ... shall always remember you, Sister Anoush. You saved my life; please pray for my soul and that of mine household."

Anoush nodded, unable to utter a sound.

"And I shall think of you always and of what you taught me ... and of this mosaic." Heinrich turned to gaze upon the sparkling field of flowers one last time. He embraced the woman, then turned quickly away.

The man hurried for the door, but before he reached it he heard the old saint's trembling voice calling after him. "I shall lift up mine eyes unto the mountains, from where shall my help come? Mine help comes from the Lord God, who made heaven and earth. To you, O God, I lift up mine eyes to you who are enthroned above the sun. As the eyes of servants look to the hand of the master, so our eyes look to the Lord until he is gracious unto us."

Heinrich could not look back. His eye was blurred and his heart was filled with grief; he would never see the good woman again. Yet leave he must. Confused and ashamed, he was too weary to think. No longer could he weigh the perils of his soul, nor consider his plight. He needed to go home.

ೲ

Heinrich chose a circuitous route out of the city in order to linger along the shores of the Tiber River one last time. He arrived at its mucky banks sometime past sext and paused to watch the bluishgreen waters ease through its wide bends. He set his back against a thick, scaly-trunked pine and stared into the patches of seaweed and the scattered white rocks along the river's muddy bottom. "What tales those rocks could tell," he mused.

Heinrich stood and followed the Tiber northward, past the bridge leading to the ancient, round fortress known as the Castel Sant'Angelo. The man hastened along his route, past scurrying clerics and their acolytes, merchants, pilgrims, men-at-arms, misfits, castoffs, fugitives, and beggars. The sunbaked brick and broken marble of a former time now barely drew his notice, for he began to dream of the spruce-scented air of his own northern forests.

He hurried by the home-fortresses of Rome's elite—the walled villas guarded by well-armed soldiers as if they were miniature empires in danger of a siege. He passed churches and abandoned temples, gardens and neglected orchards. At last Heinrich arrived at the *Porta Flaminia*, the northern gate in Aurelian's ancient wall. He paused for barely a moment and gave one final look to the tile-roofed city. He wiped the sweat gathered across his brow, then shook his head and drew a deep breath.

ೲ

Heinrich of Weyer was now thirty-eight years old. Most of

his generation had passed into their graves, but those who yet lived were now likely to survive another seven or even ten years, and a few fortunates, like dear Anoush, might live three score and ten or beyond. Thanks to the old nun, the baker had regained much of his former bulk and he now walked with a healthy stride. Remarkably, he still retained a good deal of the red in his hair, though his freshly trimmed beard was nearly all gray. His shoulders were thick again and broad. His face was full, even fleshy, and his blue eye keen. His back was straight and his legs muscular. With his dagger in his belt, a patch over his right eye, and a stump for a left arm, fellow travelers were apt to keep a wary distance. Despite his physical health, however, the man's mood was still somber and devoid of hope.

Heinrich marched north in the uninvited company of pilgrims, couriers, and caravans of traders. The summer season had crowded the roadways with columns of men-at-arms, long convoys of wagoners, horsemen, oxen, two-wheeled carts, and groups of monks huddled around their donkeys. Heinrich made good time through the rolling landscape of Umbria, but did better yet across the wide plain of the Po Valley. Pouring much of his frustration into his stride, the man covered six and sometimes seven leagues per day.

Milan was a city worthy of a traveler's rest, and Heinrich delayed one day to duck a heavy summer storm that pounded the flat fields of Lombardy. He found shelter with a fellow baker with whom he exchanged some ideas for sweetening bread. In the afternoon he dozed, only to suddenly startle awake to see a quick-footed, fair-haired imp make off with his rucksack.

"Ach, poor wretch," he murmured.

"Eh?" A tall man walked by.

"I said, poor wretch. She took m'bag."

"*Ja*. She nearly ran me over on the way by. She's sure to be one of those pitiful child crusaders. My name is Horst, from Frankfurt on the Rhine."

"Child crusaders?" asked Heinrich.

"Aye. You've not heard? The pope cries that the cause is

lost in Palestine, so it seems an army of children is marching south on a fool's errand to save the Holy Land themselves! A lad in Cologne had a vision. Now thousands of the little waifs are coming, most in a large column from Cologne, but rumors are that others 'ave heard the news and come in little bands this way and that. Some say they're bringing pestilence and God's wrath with 'em."

"It cannot be so." Heinrich shook his head. "'Tis madness. Even if they could get to Palestine, the Turks would slaughter them like lambs. The priests would ne'er let them go."

"I speak what is true!" Horst was indignant. "Most claim the sea shall open for them so they'll cross over like the Hebrews did the Red Sea ... but I should think ships to be the more likely way. And the French children are coming as well; they'd be marching to Marseilles! They think God will convert the infidels by the purity of their hearts."

Heinrich still doubted that such a thing could be true. *But, if it is*, he thought, *Marta would ne'er let m'lads follow.* He changed the subject. "Frankfurt? I've a sister in Frankfurt. She married a merchantman named Jan." Heinrich hadn't thought of his sister in a long time. He smiled at the memories.

"Hmm. Jan." Horst brightened a moment. "I've business with a shipper named Jan ... and methinks I've heard a word 'bout his Frau wearin' the breeches of the house!"

"Ha! Could be her! What can you tell me of them?"

Horst paused. "I'm sorry, stranger, but I've no business with him lately."

Heinrich sighed. He was disappointed. "What other news 'ave you, sir. I've been on pilgrimage for years."

"Ah, the world is much the same. The pope still favors young Friederich for emperor. That little switch had brought some confusion to the lords! Seems whenever the pope belches the wind changes. I'm glad to be a freeman. Were I a vassal I'd fear to rise in the morning."

Heinrich nodded. *A freeman*, he thought, *I shall never be.*

The days were warm and the sky was cloudless as the baker pushed north into the southern range of the Alps. *Lago Como* was so beautiful that even the downcast

Heinrich was unable to pass it by without a brief rest. The man collapsed in the tall, green grass, hungry and exhausted. He stared at the lake's blue waters and wondered what recourse was left for his miserable soul; to what source might he finally appeal? There was little left for him in the order of things as he knew it. As he drifted off to sleep, long-ago whispers nudged him to seek another way.

Heinrich awoke to the pleasant sounds of water lapping a pebbled shore. He gazed at the southern slopes of the Alps rising all around him, but he still did not dare lift his eye too high. He spat, then dug his hand into his satchel to find his treasure from home; his little stone with the etching of his mark. He wiggled his fingers beneath the layers of compressed fish and cheese that Anoush had stuffed inside until he felt an odd-shaped pouch. He paused and let his hand test the pouch's size and shape before he withdrew it slowly. It felt heavy, as if it were stuffed with coins. His heart began to race as he pulled the string that bound it closed, and to his utter astonishment the pouch was filled with nearly all the gold coins he had given to the church. "Anoush!" he exclaimed. "You ... you—" The man's heart lifted. Yet it was not the sight of gold that filled the man with something fresh. It was the unconditional love of one who cherished him despite his shame. Stunned, humbled, gladhearted, and suddenly hopeful, the man from Weyer stood to his feet.

ॐ

The busy roads leading to the Julier Pass were tight and crowded. The Julier was the most popular mountain pass in summertime and had ushered migrating tribes and travelers north and south since before time was recorded. From the south the approach wound its way higher and higher through forests of long-needled pines. Jagged peaks edged each side of the roadway, and as Heinrich marched upward the trees grew scarce before disappearing altogether. Here the mountains were wet with rivulets of rushing water plunging clear and clean from unseen heights.

The walk above the tree line was one full day, but

Heinrich barely noticed the thinness of the air nor the ache in his straining legs. Instead he felt oddly serene in the calm desolation of the place. He turned away from the trail near the summit's toll to sit alone atop a boulder where he could eye the rugged panorama spread before him. Sitting quietly in the eerie silence, it was as though he could hear the words of Anoush's farewell whispering softly in the wind. "I lift up mine eyes to you who are enthroned above the sun." The psalmist's image beckoned the man to another way; it pointed him to things beyond the world he knew. But, despite the hallowed hush of that high and holy haven, the melancholy peasant still dared not turn his eye upward.

He drew a deep breath and trembled. In the distance, snow-capped peaks stood immutable and grand. Below, great rivers of mist coiled round these pinnacles' feet like white serpents sliding gently midst an army of giants. This was a place of hush and awe; a most splendid and astonishing abode of all things mighty, of all things magnificent. It was as if his pitiful soul had been swallowed up, engulfed, yet wonderfully embraced by the sheer enormity of things eternal. At that moment the man felt dwarfed, like a tiny, helpless creature sitting impotent and ineffective on such a stage as this.

Overcome by the glory of such incomprehensible stillness, he rested in the simple beauty of the wildflowers gracing a crevice at his feet. And in that ominous wilderness, that place of wonder where others fail to pause, broken Heinrich was touched. The *kosmos* was far greater than he and, so too, was the wisdom that guided it. It was here that Heinrich began to see.

శ

Basel was an ancient city set squarely on the Rhine. Heinrich arrived there at midmorning on the sixth of August. He was impatient and weary, dusty and hungry. The sun was shining and the man was warm. His sealskin had been stolen while he slept somewhere between Lago Como and the Julier Pass. His boots were still sound, but his satchel was nearly empty of food, though still weighted heavy with gold. With a determined step he walked beneath the swoop-necked griffen-of-the-gate and strode toward one of several docks where he'd wait to board a ferry bobbing on the river of legends and myth—the mighty Rhine.

He hadn't taken more than a few steps, however, when his eye was drawn from the hard-running, muddy river to the amusing sight of what appeared to be a mad churchman yanking on a crook that was wedged in the planks of the dock. The white-haired cleric was shouting a plethora of oaths that turned more than a few heads. His black robes were threadbare and, as Heinrich approached the wiry old scamp, he thought him likely to be some outcast priest. "Good day, old fellow. It would seem as if you've a small problem."

The man wrinkled his brow. Heinrich thought him to be as old a priest as he had ever seen. He had a narrow, white-bearded face, a head full of wispy, white hair, deep-set, fiery blue eyes, and bowed, spindly legs. Yet it was the single yellow tooth suspended in the front of the man's mouth that made Heinrich want to laugh out loud.

"Aye. And it seems that you've a good eye for what's plain to see," answered the priest.

Heinrich jerked the man's crook free and extended it to him.

The priest sighed in appreciation, "Well ... bless you, my son. I suppose I am in your debt."

Heinrich smiled and nodded and set his hand on the man's bony shoulder. "It would seem so. And I might add, sire, that by your look y'be—or at least once were—a priest?"

The old man blushed.

"Aye. And so I knew. Now, forgive my boldness, but y'd be the better for your cause if y'd be a bit more mindful of your tongue."

The priest's eyes sparkled and he laughed heartily. "I am undone by such a gentle rebuke, stranger, and am in your debt again. I should like very much to repay both your kindnesses with a tall tankard of ale."

"Ah, father, thank you, but it seems we be traveling in opposing directions."

But the priest insisted. "Of little import, good man. Your

simple kindness must needs be honored. I beg you to join me over bread and a quick ale."

Heinrich hesitated; he wanted to continue on his journey but there was something special about the gangly fellow and the twinkle in his eyes. "I ought press on; perhaps some other time in some other place?"

"Should you take a moment to study me, you'd be sure to see I've but a few more times and places left to my account," noted the priest. His twinkling eyes snagged their prey.

"Ach ... so! Very well, old man. I yield to your magic!" He followed the priest's amusing gait through the winding streets of Basel, where the two talked of easy things. They made their way up a steep narrow street to a welcoming inn and sat at a long table atop a warped bench.

"So, stranger," the old man looked at Heinrich with a twinkle in his eyes, "by God, in all my many years I have n'er drank with someone whose name I did not know."

Heinrich felt suddenly uncomfortable. It was as though he could hear the snickers in Rome, "Worm ... Worm of Santa Maria's!" What shame he felt, what sudden reservation. He balked at claiming his past, yet he did not know what he had become.

The old man broke through Heinrich's reverie. "Your pardon, sir. Did y'speak your name?"

"You ought be content to call me 'Stranger.'"

The priest wrinkled his nose. "Nay, 'Stranger' is no name ... ah, but you've yet to learn of mine own! I am known as Pieter ... and y'may be content to call me Pieter." He grinned.

Heinrich smiled. "I'd rather forget m'name," he said quietly. "And I've fair cause."

Pieter was a wise man. Spirited, clever, and quick-witted as he was, he had been blessed with uncommon charity as well. He looked into Heinrich's face gently. "Might I at the very least call you 'Friend'?"

The word was comforting to Heinrich. He nodded.

"There you have it then," said Pieter cheerfully. "I am Pieter and you are Friend, and I am most content with that." He turned to an ale-maid rushing past and blustered, "You there! Ale-maid! A tankard for Friend and Pieter!" He chortled like a schoolboy until he faced the buxom wench standing over him, palm open for payment. Perspiring and suddenly red-faced, he fumbled for words. The bag at his shoulder was empty.

Heinrich laughed and tossed a penny of his own atop the table, and soon the baker was reaching for more as he and his new friend toasted each other, glad-hearted and merry. But after preaching from the tabletop and wheezing in fits of laughter, Pieter pressed the ale-maid just a bit too far and was soon staring up at the hook-nosed woman.

Suddenly, his eyes toward the door. *"Mein Gott!"* he exclaimed. "My children! Friend, come with me, quickly. I needs find my children."

Heinrich was confused. *What could this old man have in the way of children?* he wondered.

The two hurried through the crowded streets and finally to the ferry docks where a chorus of singing voices could be heard above the din. "Ha!" Pieter grabbed Heinrich by his tunic and dragged him forward. "Ho, ho, my children!" Pieter bellowed as he stumbled toward them. "'Tis so very, very good to see you. I humbly beg your pardon for my delay."

Heinrich stared at a group of fresh faces scolding Pieter and a gray dog licking the old man's hand. His heart stopped as his eye lingered on a tall blond boy with piercing blue eyes. *Does my sight betray me?* he wondered. Chills ran up his spine and he nearly burst into tears. *Wil? Could that be my Wil?* He scanned the others, ranging in age from five to perhaps fifteen. Most were dressed in tattered tunics, some bearing red crosses stitched over their hearts. Many were shoeless and nearly all carried simple wooden crosses in their hands or belts. His gaze fell upon a ruddy, round-faced lad of about thirteen. He had a tumble of red curls atop his head. Heinrich gasped quietly. *Can it be?*

Several children plied Heinrich with questions, but the man had hardly time to think before Pieter turned and dragged him back into the city, where he found himself suddenly surrounded by the children and a scruffy dog the priest referred to as Solomon. One child explained to Heinrich that they were on crusade to save the Holy City.

The baker nodded, but was barely able to comprehend. He only wanted to study the two boys. It had been six years since he had left his village. He knew he must look very different from when he left, but surely, would they not know him? *They would have grown into young men ... those two must be mine!* His mouth was dry and he faltered. *If it is them, what do I say? I left them so long ago ... they'll not understand ... surely they must hate me!* His heart pounded and he felt suddenly very weak and timid.

A dozen men-at-arms burst upon the group. "More brats for the rats!" one cried. The deputy immediately ordered his men to bind the startled children, and he abruptly charged them with theft.

"Thou hast no just grounds!" roared Pieter. "None at—"

"Silence, old fool!"

Pieter was endowed with a large range of mood. He could be a comfortable friend, or he could be a raging warrior, consuming the wicked with tongues of fire! At that moment the priest's blood began to boil within his pulsing veins. He laid his long nose against the deputy's and loosed a blistering vituperation of expletives that could have toasted the ears of a seasoned knight.

Seeing that the guards were distracted by Pieter and his barking dog, Heinrich quickly begged Wil to order the children to put what treasures they had into his opened satchel. The children complied and several trusting little hands dropped a pitiful assortment of bread crusts, rotted turnips, half-eaten strips of salted pork, and sundry trinkets. Then Heinrich watched Karl drop a steel-chain necklace into the bag—Marta's necklace!

At long last the soldiers silenced Pieter and bound the terrified score of children with a heavy rope. With loud oaths they then drove them through Basel's winding streets by the sharp points of their long lances.

Heinrich followed at a safe distance. He had wanted, of course, to do nothing other than draw his blade and strike the villains dead. Perhaps were he a younger man he might have followed such an imprudent course. Instead, he took Pieter's dog, Solomon, by the collar and faded into the growing shadows of the city where he plotted his course.

The child crusaders and their faithful priest were rushed to the city's horrid dungeon set deep in the city's center. They quickly vanished within a cavernous gate guarding its dark chambers. Heinrich peered from a nearby alley and listened to the satisfied comments of city folk who were glad for it. "I hear they carry plague," grumbled one.

"Aye, they've scrumped and murdered their way to our good city. I say hang 'em all!"

Heinrich said nothing, but secretly vowed that the innocents would not stay the night in the belly of that place. He paced the streets, struggling to concoct a plan. The dog bounded away, only to return dragging Pieter's crook. Heinrich praised the dog and held the staff to his breast. "I've need of a plan, Solomon, a sound scheme."

Before long a confident smile stretched across the man's weathered face. "You there, guard!" he shouted as he ran toward the dungeon. "You there. Answer me at once!"

"Who speaks?" grumbled the guard as he pulled his torch from the wall. "Who speaks?"

"I speak."

Unimpressed, the guard groused, "*Ja, ja.* And what's this about?"

"'Tis said you've dragged a band of children through these very streets and they'd be bound inside."

"Aye. And what business is it of yours? Had I a say, they'd all be drowned in the river."

"What's m'business? Ha! Y'd be a dolt if ever one lived. I tell you what m'business is!" said Heinrich. "My business is your business. You've brought plague through these streets and you've set it just behind you. We've both business here and, aye, the mortuary shall soon have business as well!"

The soldier stiffened. "Y've no proof of such a thing."

"Nay? I've seen the yellow sweat on 'em up close, and I've seen the marks on their faces. Y'think me to have nought else to do but bother with a pack of little brats as they? By God, man, use that dung-filled head of yours."

"None else has spoke of it and—"

"Listen, fool! I can swear to what I've seen. Call your magistrate. Wake him from his bed and have him stand close to look with his own eyes. Aye, and you'll be needing a new magistrate in a fortnight!"

The guard hesitated, then shook his head. "If your words be true, then the worst of it is for that bunch inside … no loss to me."

"Walls can't contain plague, y'dolt!" boomed Heinrich. "Plague is plague—have y'forgotten Bern during the Whitsun Feast just two years prior? Any brushed by a single breath of the sick were cold and stiff in a winter's hour."

The uneasy guard was familiar with the stories of Bern, and imagining Basel filled with smoking biers was enough for him to beckon his sergeant and whisper a few hushed words. The sergeant abruptly ordered him to summon the captain of the jail who emerged from his quarters in an impatient rage.

"What say you?" the captain barked.

Heinrich narrowed his eye and growled, "Your dimwitted deputy paraded plague through these streets but a few hours past. Have y'ne'er seen plague? I have. And I'm here to warn y'that y've brought death and misery upon us all. Y've time to expel them yet … while the streets are empty … and I swear by the Virgin Mother and the Holy Church, if you simpletons don't, I'll stand in the square on the morrow and tell all of your murderous deed this night!"

The captain began to perspire. Heinrich leaned closer. "Have you ever seen plague?"

The captain shook his head.

"Well, I have and I've seen what it does. It seizes a stout and sturdy man like your very self and rots you from the innards out. From your toes to your scalp, your skin shall blacken and bleed, and you'll soon cry out in pain as you suck for breath. You'll be set in a row by others who share your plight until your miserable soul is snatched to the Pit and your putrefied body piled in a wagon and hauled to the fires. And, were that not enough, your pathetic name shall be stricken from the memories of all but Lucifer, who shall bind you in his furnace forever!" Heinrich was surprised at his own eloquence, but gave no clue of insincerity. He bored his eye into the captain's.

"And ... and which prisoners bear this ... plague?" queried the captain, suddenly anxious.

"Aye, the children. I saw the marks on most, and 'tis certain y've heard how they've carried such a curse over all the empire."

The captain stared blankly at the prison gate. "*Ja*," he answered slowly. "Perhaps I ought inform the magistrate."

"Ach. I knew y'to have more wit than the louts following you about. 'Tis a good man who spares his *Volk* such an end. If y'fail to exile those whelps, your city will be filled with the litter of a thousand black corpses by Assumption ... and y'dare not hang 'em, nor put them to the torch and risk the wrath of the Church. But why call the magistrate? I'd wager he'd put a foot to your arse for trussing him to such a blunder!"

The captain's lips twitched and he wiped his sweating hands on his leggings. "I've the authority to arrest and dismiss at my will and ... methinks it best to rid this city of any risk of plague. You, sergeant, drag them beyond the walls and be quiet about it. Let 'em die in the mountains." He turned a sly eye to Heinrich.

"And I suppose we are in your debt, stranger? You ought be rewarded for such a warning and for your ... discretion, *ja*? Take this silver and begone."

Heinrich restrained a smile and placed the silver coins in his stuffed satchel. He assured the captain of his silence, then disappeared into the darkness with Solomon at his side.

The surprised crusaders were quickly chased from the unspeakable horror of their dungeon and herded through the dark streets of the city. They were tumbled out through the gate and soon stared in disbelief at each other alongside the banks of the moonlit Rhine. Then, before any could speak, Solomon burst from the darkness and leaped into Pieter's trembling arms. A happy voice followed. "Ha!

You're free! Pieter, have you all the children, each and every one?"

"Oh, dear God in heaven!" cried the old man. "Good Friend. *Ja, ja,* we've need to count."

Wil ordered his company to their positions and Pieter counted twenty-six. "So? It seems we've grown!"

A few new faces stepped forward timidly. They had been imprisoned for a fortnight and were desperate to escape. Pieter warmly embraced them and welcomed them while Heinrich paced nervously along the line. "Were any left behind ... any at all?" he asked. He had seen Wil's lanky frame but had not found Karl.

Wil answered. "I think not, stranger."

Heinrich's heart raced. "Aye ... is the redheaded one here?"

"*Ja,* I am here."

Heinrich released a quaking breath. He could say nothing for a moment. His mind was whirling. He so desperately wanted to cry out his name, to hold his sons. He mustered his courage and took one step forward. He opened his mouth but could not find the words to say. *In the morning,* he vowed to himself. *By the light of morning I shall tell all.* He licked his lips and finally said, "Ah, 'tis good. I ... I wish you all God's mercy. I must be on my way." He set down his satchel and laid the children's effects on the ground. He handed Pieter his staff and the guard's pennies, and received the old man's embrace. Midst a chorus of voices the man prepared to leave. He stretched his hand slowly toward Wil's tall silhouette, stopping just short of touching him. "I ... I wish you all Godspeed," he choked. "'Tis past time for me to take your leave." With that, Heinrich turned and disappeared into the darkness.

Poor Heinrich walked away from his sons with the weight of all time heaped upon his shoulders. He could not sleep that night, for his mind was spinning with what words he might speak at the bells of prime. The man wandered to the docks and stared into the black waters of the surging Rhine. "I ought not wait," he murmured. "I ought wake them and tell them ... tell them now!"

The man hurried along the river's bank, only to halt and hesitate. "I ... I ought *not* wake them. Nay, 'tis better in the morn. I ... I shall buy them bread and cheese, some fruit ... aye! Fruit and fish ... and some cider. They've need of food!" Heinrich felt better.

It was an hour before dawn when the first booth of the day's market opened. Heinrich pounced on the peddler for a basket of his bread. Then the man raced to the next, and the next, until, at last his arm ached for the baskets hanging off his elbow and his neck. He then lurched and stumbled through the streets, and as the bells of prime struck in the city's steeples, he hurried to the grassy bank where he had left his beloved sons and stared among the ferries at dockside.

Heinrich quickly arrived at the very place where the crusaders had camped just hours before. He peered through gray light at the dewy grass flattened like the nest of small deer. No one was there. He ran farther down the bank. No one was in sight. He turned around and around, running this way and that, to the far side of the gate and back. They were gone! "You there!" Heinrich shouted to a pair of workmen ambling along the city wall. "'Ave y'seen a company of children ... with a white-headed priest?"

"Nay," they answered.

Desperate, the man ran inside the city again. He charged about the market square, the fish market, and the guild rows. Up and down the hilly streets he ran, until, fearing the worst, he sprinted to the dungeon and quizzed a guard. Relieved, but still distressed, Heinrich raced back to the grassy bank and collapsed. He rubbed his hand aimlessly through the crushed grass and he pictured his boys. The man then set his jaw and packed his satchel full. "I shall find them!"

Heinrich burst onto the roadway leading south like a madman, stopping only to annoy passersby with questions of the local geography or of the young crusaders' whereabouts. His feet pulled his leaning body forward through the low, green mountains that gently rose below Basel and into a nameless village where he needed to make the first of many decisions. After questioning a local peasant he sighed. *Do I follow the road westerly along this river or south to some place called Olten?* He paced about, then reasoned the valley seemed logical. A traveler had convinced Heinrich that the crusaders' next destination was likely Bern, and the wide road could lead him there. Heinrich wondered. He knew the children's provisions were low, and it seemed more logical that they might hurry for the closest town of some size, which would be Olten in the south. Nevertheless, the baker followed the other's suggestion and charged through the Birs Valley.

His decision proved unwise. He knew his own pace had to be considerably quicker than that of Pieter's, and after almost three days of hard marching he had not overcome them. Frustrated and angry with himself, Heinrich decided he must retrace his steps in hopes of intercepting the company in Olten. "Surely, they shall pause for rest and food."

He wanted to press through the night, but the skies opened and a deluge unlike any the man had ever known poured over the land. Great flashes of lightning lit the sky and thunder roared through the valleys. Heinrich hid in a goat shed until the rain eased. In the morning the roadway was a long, brown quagmire.

At vespers on the sixth day from Basel, an exhausted Heinrich stood at the gate in Olten's walls. He peered past the guard at the timber-and-mortar, steep-pitched houses, the fishponds, and the muddy streets busy with morning business. He turned to the sentry. "Have y'seen a company of children ... young crusaders ... with crosses stitched on their breasts. They'd be traveling with an old priest?"

The soldier stared down his long nose. He raised an eyebrow. "*Ja.*"

"And are they still here?" Heinrich's tone was impatient.

The man looked at the one-eyed stranger for a long moment, then called for his captain. The two whispered for a few moments, then the officer scurried off. "Wait here."

Heinrich paced about, slapping his hand against his side

until a beautiful young woman came to the gate escorted by a small troop of soldiers. Heinrich repeated his question.

The woman looked at him carefully. "And what are these to you, sir?"

Heinrich set his jaw, hard. He narrowed his one eye. "I am father to two of them. The leader, the one with long, blond hair named Wil, and his younger brother, a cheerful red-headed lad named Karl."

The woman looked at Heinrich's own red-gray curls and smiled kindly. "Please, she said, follow me." As the group made their way through the muddy streets of the noisy town, the woman introduced herself as Dorothea, the daughter of Bernard, Lord of Olten. She went on to explain how Pieter had healed her father from the torment of a fouled tooth and how the old priest had outwitted him in the barter!

Heinrich smiled. He could imagine that.

A loud, brash man emerged from the doorway of a rich man's house. It was Lord Bernard. "Ha, daughter! Another shaggy scoundrel? Look at him!"

Heinrich bowed as Dorothea introduced him. Bernard was smiling despite the fact that his summer sandals were sunk in the mud from the terrible storm. He rested his hands on the folds of a long, red doublet and said, "So, you are the sire of two of the lads. Ha, a braver company I've ne'er laid eyes on! And that scallywag Pieter!" The man tilted his head and roared a hearty laugh. "He outwitted this sly fox like none before. But he was true to his word … my tooth is cured. Now, stranger, how may we serve you?"

"M'lads are gone?"

"Aye … a'fore the storm." The man's voice saddened. He turned to the skull-capped secretary standing close. "Fetch them."

As the little man scurried away, Lord Bernard explained. "The company left late in the day they came. I sent them with provisions enough." Bernard turned and greeted two lads as they approached. One had a splint on his wrist and the other on his leg. He laid his hand atop the head of the one leaning on a crutch. "These two came wandering in the day following. Tell him, boys, tell him what you know."

The boy identified himself as Jon and told how the camp had been washed away in a surprise flood by the Aare River less than a half-day's march to the south. "A few of us was drowned and Solomon went lost. Wil made us two come back here. The others wanted to keep on."

Heinrich listened carefully. "And Karl?"

"Good," answered the younger one, named Friederich.

Heinrich closed his eye in relief. "And Pieter?"

"Spared, but hurt."

"How many days ahead are they?"

The boys shrugged, but Bernard answered, "Only three … you can surely catch them."

Heinrich nodded. "I leave at once." He turned to Jon again. "Are they taking the main roadways?"

The boys both shook their heads. "Sometimes. Pieter knows the ways. He usually keeps us to the sheep trails when he can; he says the roadways have danger."

Bernard furrowed his brows thoughtfully. "I heard some say they wanted to be in Burgdorf by the Feast of the Assumption, four days from now. He could surely make it there by then, even with injured children. From there they will probably go to Bern for more supplies, then turn directly south and follow the lake roads to the Grimsel Pass."

"Bern again," grumbled Heinrich.

Dorothea was thinking too. "Father, why not the valley of the Emmental. It is more direct to the Grimsel, it has many villages to help them, and—"

"Nay, daughter. They knew of pestilence in the villages and Pieter knows Bern is filled with plenty." Bernard's tone was firm and had the added weight of confidence. He looked at Heinrich. "If you miss them in Burgdorf, press on to Bern. You're close, man. God go with you!"

Chapter 25

THE FINAL PURSUIT

einrich left at once. It was near nightfall on the twelfth of August, and he desperately wanted to be in Burgdorf before the feast day. He had been told the town was about fourteen leagues away and the roadway was poor, but with some effort he should be able to get there in two days. So, the anxious man hurried on heavy legs for an hour or so before collapsing in darkness along the banks of the Aare River.

He awoke to a sunny dawn and reached into his satchel for some salted pork and a bit of smoked herring. The river was still carrying debris from the recent flood and was littered with piles of broken branches and brush that had collected in its shallows. The man stared and shook his head sadly for the children who had been lost. He rose slowly and stretched, then drew a deep breath and began his journey upstream.

Heinrich hadn't traveled more than a furlong, however, when he stopped suddenly. "I wonder." he said and then he heard the sound again. Heinrich trotted along the muddy bank following the whine of a dog until he came upon a webwork of river clutter. In the center of the shadowy labyrinth of tree limbs and bramble was snared a desperate dog.

"Hold on, fellow!" cried Heinrich. He splashed into the

brown river and pressed through thigh-deep waters until he reached the tangle. Carefully, he extended his hand between the knots of brush until he laid it securely on the dog's head. "Good creature," he said calmly, "hold fast." Heinrich struggled with the branches as he slowly pulled one from the other. As he did, his grateful new friend began to wiggle and squirm until he finally leapt from his troubles, free and happy!

Laughing, Heinrich lifted the licking dog by the belly and cradled him under his arm as he returned to the roadway. He cleared dried mud from its eyes and checked for deep wounds and broken bones. Content that the beast had been spared serious harm, he held him by the chin and stroked his head. "Solomon?" The dog lifted his ears and licked Heinrich's hand. "Ah, Solomon!" Heinrich laughed. "Won't Pieter be happy!"

He rubbed the dog's muddy head and studied him more carefully. Though low-bred and scruffy, there was a special light in the dog's eyes that Heinrich found oddly familiar. With a chuckle, the man reached into his satchel and fed the grateful beast a generous helping of cheese and pork. "We'll rest in the sun for bit, but we needs press on to find your master."

Within the hour, the ragged man and his shaggy companion were striding quickly southwestward, first following the Aare, then veering onto the narrow roadway leading to Burgdorf. Darkness fell and the path became so obscured that it was impossible to see. Heinrich reached for a new flint that Bernard had given him and struck some kindling afire. Before long, the two were curled alongside a crackling blaze under cover of the stars.

Daybreak found the two hurrying on, Solomon trotting ahead, nose down and excited. "Soon, good fellow!" panted Heinrich.

Indeed, by vespers of that second day the baker and the dog arrived at the gates of Burgdorf. "Ho, there, guard," called Heinrich.

"Aye?"

"Can y'tell me the whereabouts of a band of children and

an old priest? They ought to have come in the town a day past or so."

The guard shrugged and asked another, then summoned his captain. "He wants to know of any children and a priest."

The captain picked his nose and spat. "Aye. They come two days past and we sent 'em on. We've no need for the likes of 'em here, and by the sight of you, y'needs move on as well."

Heinrich stared angrily. "You sent them on?" he cried. "Did you give them food?"

The soldiers laughed. "Food? By the devil no, man. They've brought fever to all the villages about. We've no need of 'em here."

The baker growled and squinted. He laid a hand on the hilt of his dagger. With that, the guards lowered their lances and laid the points against the man's chest.

"Leave, cripple, whilst y'can still breathe," hissed the captain.

Heinrich glared a moment longer, then stepped back and turned away, cursing. He and Solomon returned to the road and the man sat on his haunches, angry and anxious. "Where? Where did they go from here?" He scratched the dog's ears and shook his head.

"Bern!" he grumbled. "They've surely gone to Bern like Bernard said."

The frustrated baker hurried along the roadway south until he came to a fork in the road where he needed to be sure. The man hesitated. "Right or straight? Right to food, straight for time? Which did they choose?" He sighed and stared at the dog, who had lost any trace of scent midst the many feet that had converged at the intersection. "Food. I say they went for food and for the feast in the city." Solomon followed obediently.

Heinrich's decision again quickly proved to be an unfortunate one, for Wil had chosen to stay the course and not add a detour to the west—not even for food. Fortunately, upon entering Bern, a spice merchant told Heinrich about a strange old man he had seen begging food for a tattered company of children in the Emmental villages south of Burgdorf. The raging baker ran out of the city gate and retraced his steps, unable to speak a word! Then, two days after he had made his decision, he returned to the fork and turned right—with a loud curse!

It was nearly a fortnight after he left Basel when Heinrich passed through the splendid Emmental and began the ascent into the passes of the Alps' northern slopes. For days both man and beast traveled through magnificent hardwood forests until the steep-slanted groves of beech and maple gave way to barefaced cliffs and spruce. The two soon crowded with other travelers through rocky channels of lichen and high-mountain moss. Along the way they paused only briefly to view the blue-green waters of a breathtaking mountain lake lying still and shimmering far below. "Where are they?" Heinrich moaned.

The pair pressed on. They had not been able to cover much ground—the roads were rocky and narrow, steep, and, at some places, treacherous. In addition, the poor baker had turned an ankle badly on a rock and had been limping for days. They finally descended into the flat Aare valley and the village of Meiringen. Exhausted, Heinrich led Solomon through the small village toward a pair of old men sitting on a bench. "'Ave y'seen a band of children with an old priest come through here from parts north?" Heinrich was impatient and irritable.

A white-headed, ruddy-faced fellow wiped froth from his mouth and set down his tankard of ale. "Hmm. Methinks to see some children on yester noon ... or was it this morn? Axel, can y'not remember the strange *Kinder*?"

The other man, a bald, wrinkle-faced farmer in a badly torn tunic, belched. "Aye ... nay ... hmm." He paused. "*Ja*, Edel, to be sure. They took the trail yonder, the one to the keep." He pointed vaguely.

"Ach, nay, y'old fool," answered the first. He shook his head and whispered to Heinrich. "M'friend's a bit dim. Happened when he took the fall some years back."

"Well, what of the children?" Heinrich chafed.

Edel wrinkled his nose and squinted. He grimaced and

grunted and took another drink. "*Ja*," he answered.

Heinrich tapped his hand against his side and waited as Edel swallowed more. His eye was beginning to bulge. "And?" he bellowed.

"You needn't shout, stranger. Now what's it y'want?"

"Did you see the band of children or not?" Heinrich roared.

"I already said so."

"Well ... where in God's name did they go?"

"Ach, you never asked me that."

Heinrich growled. "I'm askin' y'now!"

The man took another drink and shrugged. "Methinks they followed the highway south."

"Are you sure?"

Edel shrugged.

Heinrich gawked at the old men and wondered who was dim and who was not. He turned to Solomon and shook his head. "Edel or Axel ... whose word do we take?" He chose Edel—but he was wrong. Axel had, indeed, spotted Pieter taking the peddler's trail. It led to the small keep of a lord built just beyond the roadway where the priest had hopes of begging food for his hungry company. So, while the crusaders followed Pieter on his short detour, Solomon followed his new master due south and deeper into the mountains—just *ahead* of the crusaders!

For the next several days the pair climbed higher and higher, finally struggling through knee-deep snow in the Grimselpass and dismissing the kindness of two French wayfarers before beginning their long descent into the Rhône valley. Frustrated and straining to find Pieter's little column, Heinrich followed the rushing Rhône River southwest through the narrow, wooded valley etched deeply into the heart of the Alps.

A day later, in the village of Fiesch, Heinrich bought some mutton and a fresh-baked loaf of bread, a flagon of red wine and a spoon of honey. He wandered to a flat rock that sat squarely on the river's edge where he and Solomon enjoyed both their meal and the pleasant sounds of a little man singing on a small dock.

Heinrich smiled. It was good to hear music again, and the tiny minstrel with the funny hat made him laugh. The fellow wore pointy-toed shoes and had a pointy black beard, just like a marionette Heinrich had once seen in a peddler's basket. The little man strummed a wooden lute with fingers not much bigger than a child's, but he had a voice as clear and as strong as the river running below his feet.

The following day Heinrich arrived in the village of Brig, weary and slow-of-foot. He entered the timber-walled town and looked carefully for any sign of the elusive crusaders before collapsing on a tavern bench. "Has anyone seen a band of children?"

"Crusaders? Most are west, we'd be told," answered a merchant. He was seated with a group of fellows grumbling about their troubles.

"Why west?" asked Heinrich.

"Who could know what those fools are thinking? Why are they west?" he shrugged. "Why are they anywhere? I only know what's been said."

Heinrich bought the group a round of ale. "No news of any in these parts?"

Another answered. "None of late. Methinks some weeks past. Most stay by the highways near the monasteries, more to the west."

Heinrich thought for a moment. How very much he wanted to find his sons along the way, but if he couldn't, he rightly reasoned that he should get to Genoa before them. "Tell me, sirs, which is the most direct route to Genoa?"

The merchants paused and bickered a bit among themselves until one finally answered. "The most direct way is to cross the river here and follow the trail to the Simplon Pass, then along the Toce River to the lake. You needs follow the lake to the Ticino and then to Pavia. From there many roads lead to the mountains and the city."

≈

Heinrich and Solomon left Brig the next morning, not knowing that Pieter's crusaders had sped down the Rhône by raft and would arrive in Brig later that very same day! The baker and his panting dog climbed the long, winding ascent to the Simplon Pass at a pace much slower than before. At the summit Heinrich's aching legs dragged him to a sun-warmed boulder where he rested for a time. The man faced the splendor of green gorges notched and shadowed beneath distant, snow-capped ridges. But as his eye followed the magnificent landscape, the wind rustled the needled forest around him and he shuddered. It was as if he suddenly heard Father Pious's voice hissing words of judgment on he and his sons. Heinrich stood. His belly twisted and his chest tightened as he wondered if his sons would perish for his sins. He closed his eye and lowered his head; he thought he might go mad.

As if he understood, Solomon licked his new master's hand and leaned against his thigh. He whined a little and stared into Heinrich's face with hopeful, twinkling eyes. Heinrich coughed and scratched Solomon's ears, then forced clean mountain air into his wheezing lungs. He bent to pluck a wildflower and held it to his nose. Its scent was sweet and gentle, its colors cheerful and pleasant. He sat and stared at the beauty held between his thumb and finger. "Could there be another way?" he murmured.

For the next several days Heinrich and Solomon hurried south, past a menacing castle bracing for battle and through a lowering landscape to the source of the Ticino River. From there they followed a valley roadway that paralleled the blue-green river. They rested infrequently, but when they did they loved to lie atop the warm, white rocks that were scattered along the pebbled shore. Here they slept, both twitching and smiling while dreaming good things in the warmth of the Italian sun.

॰॰

Heinrich and Solomon finally reached the foothills of the Apennines and panted their way higher and higher into the mountains. The Apennines were rounded, like lumpy shoulders, but steep. The irritable German grumbled to Solomon about their lack of beauty and glared at the tangle of softwoods now surrounding him. "These trees are useless and disordered!" He wished he could prop himself against the sturdy trunks of his mighty Magi. He longed for the clear air and vibrant green of the mighty forests of the north. "Solomon," he muttered, "some say this is a charming land of music, good wine, and beautiful women. Ha! I say it is charming like ... like a dimwit smiling in the sun!"

The two pressed on for another day until they crested the mountains at a dramatic curve, where they paused. Heinrich smiled and a lump filled his throat. "There, Solomon! There!" He pointed across the treetops to the distant city of Genoa and the magnificent blue expanse of the Aegean. "Smell! Can y'smell the salt sea? Hurry! We needs hurry!"

The two rushed along the road as it wound its way downward. But it was then that fear rose within the man once again. With every step he felt a renewed urgency, a desperate need to hurry. He dared not be late! The pair trotted anxiously, pushing themselves through shuffling crowds of annoying travelers until they slowed alongside a patch of wildflowers surrounding a fresh grave. Heinrich felt a chill spread through the whole of his body as Solomon dashed toward it.

The grave was a mound of dark, crumbled earth and small rocks. It was overspread with a thin layer of freshly picked flowers whose blooms had not yet wilted. At its head was a simple wooden cross—one like the crusaders carried in their belts. Heinrich felt sick. He called to travelers coming uphill from the city, first to this one, then to that. Few could understand him and those that could knew nothing. At last, a huddle of brown-robed monks sauntered by, whispering amongst themselves with bowed, tonsured heads. Heinrich called to them.

An elderly brother answered kindly. "Nay, my son, we've no knowledge of the grave, but, yes, we passed the ones you describe. No doubt they entered the city just hours ago."

Heinrich's chest heaved. "Brothers, I beg you. Tell me of a tall blond lad and a younger redhead ... with curls."

The monks mumbled and shrugged. "Ah, forgive us, but we know nothing of either boy. We remember only their mad priest."

Heinrich's breath quickened. "In the city! In the city,

Solomon!" He took a long look at the mysterious grave. Something within urged him to cast off the rocks and dig beneath the flowers to find a face. *Vile thoughts! I am a vile and wicked man.* He accused himself a sinner and hung his head. Then, with a deep, resolute breath, Heinrich of Weyer turned his face away and hurried on.

శ

The port city of Genoa was large and unfriendly. Its palaces boasted the wealth of a merchant class enjoying the bounty of sea trade; the crowded alleyways of the poor just dingy and wretched. Smoke choked the narrow streets and the air reeked of septic and garbage. Its olive-toned folk gawked and grumbled at the travel-worn Teuton and his ragged dog. But Heinrich cared little and gave them no heed. His only purpose was to find his sons before they boarded a ship bound for Palestine.

The man hurried past towers and palaces, past marble colonnades and splendid fountains until he arrived at the city's docks, where he rushed about, frantic and afraid. He shouted to seamen and to priests, to merchants and to *matroni* ... but to no avail. Heinrich did, however, come across other little fair-skinned crusaders wandering aimlessly about the dangerous port. These pitiful wretches were confused. They had been told that the waves would miraculously part as they did for Moses at the Red Sea. They had been told that they would march to the Holy Land on dry ground. Instead, they now needed to either beg money for ship's passage, hide in a city that did not welcome them, or face the trials of autumn in the cold Alps. While they floundered for a decision, these sick, hungry, and fearful lost lambs had suffered the further miseries of others' contempt and the abuses that followed. They were shamed and spat upon, assaulted, molested, neglected, ridiculed, and mocked. After all, they had failed in their journey of faith.

So, despite his own compelling cause, Heinrich's tender heart could not ignore the dirty, hungry waifs that had begun to follow him. Night was falling and he could only imagine what horrors these children would soon endure.

With a painful groan he suspended his search in favor of mercy; he yielded his purposes to a circle of sad eyes. Heinrich hurried to the market and spent some of his gold on two carts full of provisions with drivers to deliver them to a hasty camp he set by the seaside. Here, surrounded by a growing throng of grateful little faces, he tossed a blanket to one child, then one to the next, all the while feeling the weight of a heart heavy for his own. With a forlorn eye on what could have been, poor Heinrich hugged, fed, and clothed the little strangers pressing close on all sides.

Solomon was happy to play with the tattered children and brought joy to faces that had almost forgotten how to smile. He licked and rolled, wagged his tail and pranced about midst squeals of delight. And as the dog warmed their hearts, Heinrich built a fire. Its light drew dozens more from their hiding. Homeless, wandering waifs slipped to the baker's fireside from alleyways and sheds, from beneath abandoned boats, and from the crevices of the rocky shore.

That night the man sat on the dark edges of his camp determined to protect the sleeping children. Many had suffered the vices and lurid concupiscence of humanity's most ravenous and disgusting debris, and it was merciful that a guardian had come. The night seemed endless to the exhausted baker, however, and he could only groan as he imagined his sons aboard a ship that may have set sail in the evening just passed. He stared at the silhouettes of rocking masts lined tightly along the city's docks. "Perhaps they are yet here, waiting somewhere to board at dawn." He saw a fire at the far side of the curving shoreline and wanted desperately to search it, yet he dared not abandon the little ones sleeping safely all around. A lump filled his throat. "I have failed again! Oh, dear God, hurry the dawn!"

Sometime before prime, sleep cast its spell over the exhausted baker and he tilted slowly to the earth where he lay long after the first hint of light eased over the rim of the round-topped mountains. The children quietly encircled the snoring man and watched him respectfully until a little girl nudged him awake. "Huh?" muttered Heinrich. He opened his eye and stared about the circle. Confused for a moment, he suddenly lurched with a start. "Dear God!" he cried. He jumped to his feet and peered anxiously at the docks. "Listen, children. The sun is up; you are safe for now. Quickly, I needs know if any has seen crusaders with an old, white-haired priest?"

A tattered, thin-faced lad of about eleven called out, "I have, sir."

Heinrich ran to him. "Tell me, boy. Did he sail—he and his company?"

"I don't think so."

"Do y'know where they'd be?"

The lad shrugged. He called to a friend. "Ludwig, remember the old priest? He gave you half an apple."

A little boy smiled. "Aye."

"Where is he?"

Ludwig thought hard. He was about seven and barefooted. His feet were bloody and his tunic was so tattered that his protruding ribs and sunken belly were plainly visible. "Don't know."

Heinrich's breath quickened and his face went taut. He leaned toward Ludwig and spoke slowly. "Do y'know if they've sailed?"

Ludwig shook his head.

Heinrich drew a deep breath, then surveyed the press of hopeful faces staring at him. He licked his lips. "Hear me. I needs find about m'children, then I shall help you. I swear it. Run, quick, all of you and see if you can find me the old priest. If y'find him, tell him he must wait. Then come find me ... I'll be along the docks; you'll spot me easy!"

The children scampered toward the docks, toward the marketplace, and to the far reaches of Genoa's shoreline as Heinrich and Solomon charged to the ships. The sun was now a bright disc climbing boldly over the mountains in the east. The sky was clear and glorious but Heinrich gave it no heed. He ran hard, but by the time he reached the water's edge several ships had already cast off and their sails were filling with a fresh breeze. The man ran from ship to ship, then bellowed across the rippling harbor. "Children! Have y'children on board?" He stared hard at each ship, first one, then the next. "There!" he shouted to himself. "There!" Heinrich's eye had caught the glimmer of yellow hair in the morning sun. He stared hard, straining to see more.

"*San Marco*," muttered a man with a hoarse voice.

"What?" answered Heinrich.

"*San Marco*." The dockman was peeling an apple and pointed his knife at the slow-moving ship in Heinrich's view.

Heinrich's heart stopped. "Good man, can y'tell me if children are on board ... children—*bambini* and a *padre?*"

The man swallowed his apple and held out his palm.

Heinrich grit his teeth and jammed his trembling fingers into his satchel. He retrieved a silver penny and pushed it at the fellow. "Well?"

"*Bambini, si, padre, no.*"

Heinrich was confused. "No priest?" His mind whirled and he paced the dock. "What to do?" A squeaky voice from a small, panting little girl interrupted him. "What, child?"

"I says the old priest is yonder." She pointed toward the far edge of the harbor where a jetty of black rock projected into the sea.

Heinrich stood on trembling legs. "There?"

"*Ja.*"

"Ah!" The man kissed the maiden hastily on the cheek. "Little one, I shall return for you!"

Heinrich bellowed for Solomon and sped across the harbor's wharves. Anxious, he raced past rows of houses and shops, the shipwright's building and the caulkers' guild, the sailmaker and the open door of a loud inn where he suddenly heard laughter and the mention of *bambini.* Heinrich paused and hesitated. He peered toward the distant jetty then ducked into the tavern.

"Who speaks of children?" Heinrich roared. "A flagon of wine for words of the crusading children!"

The sailors grumbled, then ignored him. Panting, Heinrich grabbed a wine jar from the cupboard and slammed it atop their table. He pressed his hand hard to the cork. His grief had turned to fury. "Now, you, yellow-beard, tell me what y'know!"

The sailor stared at Heinrich and then at the wine. "Aye. Two ships of northland whelps sank a week ago. All hands lost."

"You've got more to say! Tell me of the *San Marco*!" bellowed Heinrich. He grabbed the surprised man by the beard and slammed his own broad head against the stunned sailor's. The man collapsed to the floor as Heinrich snatched the Stedinger dagger from his belt. He laid its sharp edge against the throat of another. "Say more, or, by God, I shall slit you now!"

The sailor stammered. "Aye ... by the saints I shall tell you!" The man's face was tight with fear. "The *San Marco* is captained by Gaetano ... the most wicked captain in all of Genoa. He . he is in league with a Frenchman to sell the children to the slave markets in Bougie ... maybe Kairunan ... I hear he's found a fresh cargo of 'em."

Heinrich's stomach cramped and his face drained of all color. His chest tightened as he charged out the tavern door. *What to do? What to do?* His mind raced. He first turned toward the city, then toward Solomon. "'Tis too far to be caught ... is there no way to warn them?" He stared at the *San Marco* now lurching forward in a fresh breeze. "Perhaps when they near the point!"

Heinrich sprinted toward the jetty. His legs burned and he gasped for breath. At last he stopped and bent in two, wheezing. He lifted his head, and to his great delight, he saw Pieter seated on a large boulder by the sea. A host of children were gathered around the old man like goslings by a gander. Hopeful, the man strained to find his lads. None had the lean look of Wil nor the red curls of Karl. He closed his eye and clenched his jaw as if to hope his wishes true. Then, with a loud cry he shouted for Pieter and rushed forward.

The breezed carried Heinrich's cry to the ears of the old priest who now turned. Spotting the oncoming stranger he rose with a firm hold on his staff. Then, like a spindly spider, Pieter climbed across the black rocks to the path's end where he planted himself in defense of his beloved children.

Heinrich cried louder, "Father Pieter! 'Tis me!" Suddenly, Solomon's ears lifted and his eyes brightened. The dog bolted away from Heinrich and toward his old master like a gray comet speeding across the sky. And when he drew close, old Pieter's legs went wobbly and his arms opened wide. The priest fell to his knees and cried for joy as his shaggy friend leapt into his happy embrace.

Heinrich finally reached the old man who was now tumbled onto the earth by his wiggling, licking companion. "Hear me, Pieter!" panted Heinrich as he scanned the faces of the curious children behind him.

Pieter stood and squinted. He shielded his face from the sun, then gasped. "Friend!" He lunged toward the man, speechless and wet-eyed. "By the saints above ..."

Heinrich was in no mood for pleasantries; he was thinking only of his sons. The burly baker stumbled past the priest and over the rocks into the wary throng of children gathering about. Impatient, he cried, "Where are my sons?"

Confused, Pieter stared blankly. "Who ... who are your sons?"

"Karl and Wil ... My name is Heinrich, Heinrich of Weyer! Where are they?"

Dumfounded, Pieter pointed to a ship warping toward them from the docks. "Wil is aboard—"

"Hear me!" interrupted Heinrich. "The children needs off the ship. ... They're to be sold as slaves!" The frantic man stared desperately at the *San Marco* whose sails had gone limp and now bobbed lightly in a dead calm. His worst fears had come true.

Staring at the one-eyed, wheezing man in horror, old Pieter did not know what to do. "Are you sure ,man?"

"Aye! I heard it with my own ears in the tavern just beyond."

Pieter turned his face quickly toward the approaching ship, then rushed with all the others to the water's edge where he fell to his knees in prayer. "Father, shield them, shield my lambs, my Frieda and Otto, Wilhelm and m'little

Heinz! Protect them all, oh Father, save them this day!" The ship was now almost close enough for the cheerful faces of its crusaders to be seen smiling and laughing at their comrades on shore.

Heinrich jumped up and down, waving his arm in heart-wrenching desperation. "Wil ... Karl!" he choked. If only he could fly across the waves!

Pieter suddenly leapt to his feet shouting, "Everyone, everyone, the signal ... the signal! I have a signal ... it shall call them to come!" The old man stretched his arms wide, like man on a cross, and began to spin. "Do this!" he cried. "Do as I do!" Round and round he turned, stumbling and falling atop the sharp rocks, only to stand and spin again. Solomon whirled, then one perplexed child, then another, all mimicking the strange secret signal.

Heinrich's chest heaved, his mouth was dry, his mind raced. His eye fell upon Wil's shining hair, and his hands naively waving less than two bowshots away.

"Herr Friend!" squealed a young girl. "Spin ... y'must spin! 'Tis Pieter's call to come!"

Confused, Heinrich raised his arm to shoulder height and began to twirl, round and round, trusting the old priest and his mysterious signal. The man spun the best he could. He turned and turned like a wobbly top until someone cried, "Look, Father Pieter! There ... They're jumping!"

Indeed, over the side of the wooden rail dropped one child, then another and another. "Could it be?" The anxious man sucked short gasps of air. His ears cocked to the muffled shouts and oaths that could be now heard above the cries of swooping gulls and splashing surf. He winced as he saw a flash of steel and groaned as a swarm of wool caps rushed from port to starboard, then fore to aft. Another crusader dropped over the rail; a stout lad, neither Wil nor Karl.

Splashing into the surf, Heinrich strained to see the little heads now bobbing anxiously in the waves; he scanned from bow to stern and then again. At long last he spied his eldest son, now dashing frantically across the deck. The brave lad had waited until the very end, until each of his

comrades had fallen to the safe blue waters below.
Heinrich's muscles knotted and twitched and he moaned
aloud. Feeling like a useless, aging cripple, he staggered
about, bawling loud, anguished cries. And while he
floundered in the rising tide of his own helplessness, young
Wil's life was imperiled on fortune's delicate edge.

Heinrich could do little more. He stood paralyzed in
thigh-deep water weak and confused, lost, and utterly
helpless. Like a red-budded poppy closed and drooping
beneath the weight of a deluge, Heinrich stood slump-
shouldered and bowed by the burdens of his woe. He felt
impotent; stripped of all he had ever hoped to be. He had
failed his Order and it had forsaken him. Shamed by his
weakness, he stared, vacant and mute, empty of
confidence, void of hope.

Then it seemed as if the ocean's breeze whispered words
from far away and long ago. Heinrich's hungry heart began
to stir. The voices of wisdom past nudged and prodded him
once more to break his horrid vow, to tear off the final
shackle of his ways and, at long last, seek hope beyond
himself. The man trembled and groaned as truth battled
for his soul.

Warm waves rolled and their low-toned rumbles and
soothing salt sprays seemed to urge the man all the more,
for it was as if they carried Emma's tender voice, imploring
her beloved Heinz to remember. The struggling man listened and as he did he was carried away to memories of the
Magi, of the dappled Laubusbach; to the colors of the garden, and of butterflies floating 'neath the summer's sun. It
was then as if the wind and the waves conspired to boast
more loudly the words he had been offered so very long ago.
Heinrich closed his eye and strained to remember Emma's
soothing voice: "Someday, when your strength wanes and
your virtues fail, when you long for hope once more, turn
your eyes upward and find another way."

It was enough. Heinrich seized upon her words and his
spine tingled. He stood upright and boldly faced the sea.
Then, with a loud cry, he gladly yielded to that which had
pursued him all along. Like a springtime bud unfolding in

all its wondrous glory, the simple peasant stretched his opened hand to the blue sky above. And as angels' wings bore brave Wil toward the shimmering sea, the "Worm of Santa Maria" was no more. With his heart unfettered and his soul set free, Heinrich of Weyer broke free from the darkness to lift his tearful eye upward to the warm welcome of the smiling sun.

THE END

Readers' Guide

For Personal Reflection
or Group Discussion

READERS' GUIDE

$\mathcal{S}$ince the very beginning, humankind has labored in bondage. Adam and Eve ensured that each new life would be born under a curse of slavery, and for generation upon generation there was no hope of freedom. But when Jesus came, he declared, "The Spirit of the Lord is on me, because he has anointed me to preach good news to the poor. He has sent me to proclaim freedom for the prisoners and recovery of sight for the blind, to release the oppressed, to proclaim the year of the Lord's favor" (Luke 4:18–19). Finally, through the death and resurrection of Jesus Christ, humankind need no longer be enslaved by sin. Regardless of temporal circumstances, men and women alike can once again walk in the Garden with God.

The simple, yet remarkable story of Heinrich of Weyer is a tale of God's immeasurable grace and unconditional love. In twelfth-century Europe, few men were free. Heinrich, like those before him, was bound to the land and shackled by the Church. But Heinrich did not understand the true glory of the Gospel: that even a slave can be free in Christ. His story illustrates the battle that wages for every soul—and presents each of us with the opportunity to choose whether we will be slave or free.

Consider the following questions as you follow Heinrich's journey. Though separated by centuries, our lives are ruled by the same Truth: God longs to walk with us in the cool of the day; to have us delight in His Creation. He longs to bring color and light to our lives. For whether our bodies are slave or free, rich or poor, young or old—He is the hope of every soul's quest.

BOOK 1

Chapter 1

1. This story begins by establishing the theme that we all approach life from a context, whether it be familial—as in this chapter—or community (subsequent chapters). How in your own life might you test the perspective from which you live? How do you find the courage to change that point of view when called (or compelled) to do so?

2. Kurt pronounces a blessing upon his son, that "his eyes would be turned toward heaven and lit by the sun." Yet Berta reaches to shield Heinrich's eyes from the sun's rays. Aside from a mother's loving concern and attention, what symbolism is found in Berta's action?

3. How is Berta defined by her beliefs? How do they control her? In what ways are Kurt and Berta markedly different? How do these differences affect the development of Heinrich's character?

4. Jost addresses his family and demands that the feud against the Gunnars continue at all cost. He tells his family they "live to avenge, without quarter and without fear." What price does Jost's family pay for such a foolish vendetta? In what ways does this contradict Jost's intelligent wit and undermine the value of his inheritance?

Chapter 2

5. Jost dreams of being honored by his family long after his death, and dies believing himself a "good and worthy man." Is this a fair judgment? Is being good and worthy a sufficient legacy?

6. Emma willingly accepts Martin's rebuke—even thanks him for it. In what ways is Emma a living paradox? Who is a better example of Christlikeness—Emma or the monk? What sets her apart from the other women of her time?

7. Sieghild is beaten and raped by the Gunnars and then is further brutalized by the insensitive treatment of her family. Which is the greater tragedy? How might love and compassion offered in those critical moments have altered her fate?

Chapter 3

8. Matthew 18:3 says, "Unless you change and become like little children, you will never enter the kingdom of heaven." How is Heinrich's loving acceptance of Ingelbert an example of this principle? In what ways do judgment, prejudice, and fear keep us from accepting others? How can Christians justify this kind of behavior?

9. Kurt willingly accompanies his brothers on a mission to avenge his family. Is there any honor in his death? What does the family of Jost gain from this ongoing feud? What do they lose? What significant, life-altering impact does Kurt's death have on Heinrich?

Chapter 4

10. Why does Berta need someone to blame for her unhappiness? Why does her faith fail to offer much-needed comfort? How would a true relationship with Christ have made a difference in the outcome of Berta's life—even in the midst of tragedy?

11. Despite her past sin and status as an outcast, of all the villagers only Emma offers Berta real friendship and love. What do these two women have in common, and in what ways are they strikingly different? When have you found acceptance or love in unexpected places? What does this teach us about Christ's grace and compassion?

Chapter 5

12. Father Johannes is described as ignorant, yet "sincere and eager to do God's work." Is it possible to accomplish good things for God while being ignorant of His ways? How does Father Johannes's misguided sincerity harm the villagers?

13. Baldric is a bully who torments many who cross his path. What motivates his behavior? Why does he decide to turn back and defend the village against its attackers? Is it possible for someone who is abusive and cruel to behave with honor? Might Baldric be considered heroic?

Chapter 6

14. Heinrich faced a moral dilemma when he considered the dog's suffering: compassion was set against the law. How do we resolve such problems? Why does Heinrich choose to set

the reeve's dog free, despite his fear of the consequences? What similarities exist between the dog and Heinrich?

15. After his act of mercy, Heinrich is severely punished. How is mercy often rewarded? What is the true significance of being prohibited from "looking up"? What effect do humiliation, guilt, and terror have on Heinrich's understanding of God?

Chapter 7

16. Emma tells Heinrich, "knowing who hates you can teach you much about yourself." What wisdom can be found in this statement? Who hates Heinrich and why? What does this reveal about his character?

17. Lukas, Heinrich, and Richard discover that Emma is an "illuminator," using artistry, light, and color to bring beauty to the written page. What is the "light" she speaks of? In what ways does she illuminate the lives of those she touches? What characters might be said to see life as black and white, and who would see the world in shades of color? How does this reflect various worldviews?

Chapter 8

18. Lord Tomas is determined to punish Ingelbert for the murder of his son—despite compelling evidence that points to his innocence. Why is Lord Tomas unwilling to listen to reason? Does he truly desire justice or is he seeking to fulfill some other need?

19. Ingelbert is unable to defend himself against those who desire to kill him. Simon, an honorable knight, chooses to fight in Ingelbert's place and saves his life. What prophetic picture can be seen in these events? How does God defend and rescue His children when there seems to be no hope?

20. Lukas makes a provocative comment about how virtues can easily "become objects of our arrogance." Why would this be true?

Chapter 9

21. When Heinrich fights (and helps murder) the Gunnars, Baldric declares he is now "proud" of his nephew. Why is Heinrich suddenly empty of fury and void of joy? What was the source of his rage unleashed during the fight? Why is he not

happy to finally receive his uncle's approval?

22. What is the significance—both eternal and temporal—of Heinrich's role as the village baker? Why is Heinrich given such a remarkable opportunity, when he would normally have only worked the fields?

23. What possible motivation does Baldric have in "selecting" a wife for Heinrich? Why does Baldric choose (and Pious approve of) Marta? How are Heinrich, Marta, and Katharina each victimized by the arrangement? What are some reasons that we will allow others to control us?

Chapter 10

24. As a young girl, Sieghild has a reverence for the holy things of the Church and desires to do what is right. What changes within her? Is she driven by insanity or hatred? What tragic consequences result from her choices? What can be said about human limitations?

25. Heinrich is manipulated into a marriage that he despises. Why did he not break the engagement when Baldric dies? Which is the greater wrong—to break his vow, or to marry one woman when he loves another? How does this one decision affect the entire course of his life?

Chapter 11

26. What does the pomp and pageantry of the Feast of Lammas reveal about the people of this kingdom—rulers and peasants alike? How do the different classes relate to one another, and what purpose does each serve? Are all equally vested, or do some receive more than others? What pertinent biblical lessons can be seen in the festivities?

27. The Church dominates every aspect of the peasants' lives, and they live in constant fear of eternal judgment and damnation. What key components are missing from Christendom's "gospel?" How can we differentiate between superstitious legalism and God's uncompromising truth?

Chapter 12

28. Heinrich is unable to deny his feelings for Katharina, yet he also is uncomfortable in her presence. Is this due to his overly developed sense of guilt, or is God speaking to him?

How might the two be different? Could Heinrich have "willed" his feelings to change? Is Heinrich unfaithful to Marta? Does God always expect the same commitment to what is right—even when our circumstances seem unbearable?

29. What symbolism can be found in the Laubusbach? What is significant about the fact that the same water source that brings Emma and Ingly life, joy, and comfort is also responsible for Ingly's death?

30. Like others, Emma has suffered many terrible losses in her life. Why is she able to grieve without becoming embittered? How does she continue to find joy? Why is she uniquely able to understand the tragedy of Heinrich's marriage?

Chapter 13

31. When Heinrich and Marta lose two of their sons, she bitterly accuses him of "secret sins." By banishing him from her bed, is she really punishing him or merely protecting herself from more pain? What different choices might both Marta and Heinrich have made that would have changed their marriage?

32. Heinrich places his confidence in penance and vows and labors. He claims to have achieved humility by "keeping his face to the earth." Is this really humility or an expression of pride? What does the Bible say about living life with a "works" mentality?

Chapter 14

33. When speaking of the peasants of the manor, Abbot Stephen says, "We guard their souls, [Prince Heribert] their flesh; I oft wonder which they treasure most." Which do they really value more? How can contemporary ministry be prone toward the same trap? Does the abbey really protect the spiritual lives of the people? What evidence suggests otherwise? If the people saw more of Christ in their "shepherds," how would that affect the way they view eternity?

34. Why is Wil tormented by visions of the hanging? What wisdom does Heinrich share that changes the boy's perspective and allows him to conquer his fear? In what ways has Heinrich failed to take his own advice?

35. Do you agree that mercy is greater than justice? Why is there tension between these two godly attributes?

Chapter 15
36. Karl is a cheerful child and offers much-needed comfort after Emma's passing by recalling happy memories of times spent together. Does Karl really belong in the village of Weyer? How does he maintain his innocence and joy in the midst of such melancholy and oppressive surroundings?

37. Heinrich loses much of the value of Emma's inheritance during his "negotiations" with the monastery's steward. Why is he so easily manipulated, while Wil is quick to discern their true intent?

Chapter 16
38. Marta tells Heinrich that she would "rather be rich and safe than poor and free!" What does this statement reveal about Marta and the choices she has made? In what areas of her life is she enslaved? What hope is there for those who don't want to be helped?

39. Why do the villagers resent Heinrich for his prosperity? Why is Pious particularly furious? Is there something about Heinrich's character or person that Pious envies? What heavy price does Heinrich pay for foiling Pious's plans?

Chapter 17
40. The fathers of Heinrich and Blasius are both killed on the same night—possibly by each other's hands. Why does Heinrich insist on finally breaking his family's "code" in order to save the wounded Templar? What is significant about his willingness to risk his own life for his "enemy"? How does this special friendship reveal God's ability to work for our good even in the most tragic circumstances?

41. Pious accuses Heinrich of being guilty of all seven deadly sins: anger, avarice, envy, gluttony, lust, pride, and sloth. Yet Pious himself is guilty of all these and more. Why does Heinrich accept this accusation as truth, when Pious himself is so obviously wicked and hypocritical? What does this say about the danger of religious abuse?

BOOK 2

Chapter 18

42. Heinrich deeply regrets leaving his family behind, but sees his "penance" as the only way to protect those he loves. After initially sensing so much purpose, honor, and even glory in taking up the cause of the Church, why is Heinrich so quickly disillusioned by the purpose of his adventure? What moral question of justice is he forced to confront in taking up arms against the Stedingers?

43. Why does Richard challenge Lord Niklas to combat? What does he hope to gain by facing his old nemesis? How might his life have been different if he had learned to master his emotions and impulses at a young age? What valuable lesson can be gleaned from the tragedy of Richard's life?

Chapter 19

44. Despite the Stedingers' complete capitulation, they are massacred and their property is destroyed in order to satisfy the bloodlust of a few zealous knights. Is this a surprising turn of events? What judgment does this bring upon the Church? What does the Bible say about how God judges those who rule unjustly?

45. Why does Heinrich warn the Stedingers of the impending attack? In what other situations has he taken a stand in his life—often ignoring his own personal risk? What seems to be the common factor in these circumstances that pushes Heinrich from submissive acquiescence to defiant rebellion?

Chapter 20

46. After suffering life-threatening injuries in battle, Heinrich is nursed back to health by a loving, free Stedinger family. How does his interaction with his new friends change him? How is his valor and bravery rewarded?

47. Proverbs 16:9 says, "In his heart a man plans his course, but the Lord determines his steps." Heinrich's journey takes many unexpected turns, including the storm at sea and the resulting shipwreck. Might there be a divine purpose that "redirects" Heinrich's path?

Chapter 21

48. Father Baltasar asks Heinrich to deliver a relic to Rome. Is there any authentic spiritual value or power in this item? Is it mere coincidence that Berta's bezance is returned to Heinrich after so many years? What does the relic represent to Heinrich, and why does he long to claim it for his own?

49. Heinrich is forced to take shelter for the winter in a remote monastery, and he is prevented time and time again from leaving to continue on his journey. What work does this long-suffering accomplish in his life? What is the reason for those times in life when nothing seems to work out?

50. Why does Heinrich risk everything to free the slaves in Passau? How does this, along with his other acts of bravery on behalf of those who are oppressed, signify his struggle with his own freedom? Why is he so moved to set others free, but content to remain shackled in his own life?

Chapter 22

51. Jesus said, "I tell you the truth, anyone who gives you a cup of water in my name because you belong to Christ will certainly not lose his reward" (Mark 9:41). How is this truth illustrated when Heinrich cares for the dying Dietmar? What is the reward for his selfless, compassionate service? How do we avoid making the reward our purpose in serving others?

52. What is the meaning of the Tinker's riddle, "You are a vessel within a vessel. Each is cracked, but each is yet filled with darkness. Both must be broken to let the light in"? How is Heinrich cracked in both body and spirit, but not fully broken? Why would the wise tinker later tell Heinrich to "suffer the suffering"?

Chapter 23

53. The kind priest at Zell tells Heinrich that truth "is what remains when all else fails." What "truths" have already failed Heinrich throughout his life? What else must fall before only God remains?

54. Heinrich finally arrives in Rome, only to find that the Holy City does not live up to his expectations. How are the Roman priests similar to those in Weyer? Why does Heinrich continue to pursue acts of penance when it has always proven futile in

the past? Why does the physical pain provide relief from his mental anguish?

Chapter 24

55. Heinrich departs on what is supposed to be a "forty-day journey," yet is gone for several years. How does this compare with the wilderness wandering of the Israelites? Who or what is responsible for the continued delays, setbacks, and disappointments? What is God trying to teach Heinrich in his "wilderness experience"?

56. In what ways does Sister Anoush demonstrate the true love of Christ, while other members of the Church have not? How does Heinrich respond to the nun's unconditional acceptance? Why is it important for the church today to open its arms to those who are hurting and confused?

57. How does Heinrich react to seeing his sons again? Why doesn't he immediately make himself known to them? What is the source of his fear and what does it cost him?

Chapter 25

58. Heinrich desperately chases after his sons, only to miss them several times. When he finally locates the children, they are already aboard the slave ship. Why does God allow the situation to come to such a critical point? What would have happened to the other children if Heinrich had found his sons earlier and headed home?

59. What finally causes Heinrich to break his vow and look up to the sun? What breakthrough does this action signify? In the end, who was Heinrich's greatest oppressor?

60. What do you make of the suggestion that in all these years, while Heinrich thought he was the seeker of Hope, the fact was that Hope had been seeking him all along? How would you describe your own spiritual quest? Did you find God, or did God find you?

GLOSSARY

The Medieval Clock

Medieval time was divided into twelve hours of available daylight. Therefore, a summer's hour would have been longer than a winter's. The corresponding times below, typically called the seven canonical hours, are approximate to the modern method.

Matins: midnight
Prime: daybreak (6 A.M.)
Terce: third hour of light (9 A.M.)
Sext: sixth hour of light (noon)
Nones: ninth hour of light (3 P.M.)
Vespers: twelfth hour of light (6 P.M.)
Compline: twilight darkness

The Medieval Calendar

The Seasons

Winter: Michaelmas to the Epiphany. A time of sowing wheat and rye.
Spring: the Epiphany to Easter. A time of sowing spring crops (oats, peas, beans, barley, vegetables).
Summer: Easter to Lammas. A time of tending crops.
Autumn: Lammas to Michaelmas. A time of harvest.
Note: The medieval fiscal year began and ended on Michaelmas.

Holy Days and Feast Days

• Feast of Circumcision / Feast of Fools, January 1: celebration of circumcision of Jesus / a secular feast marked by uproarious behavior honoring those normally of low standing.
• The Epiphany /The Feast of Three Kings, January 6: celebration of the three wise men's visit of Jesus.
• The Baptism of our Lord: the Sunday after the Epiphany.
• Lent: begins 40 days before Easter, not counting Sundays. A time to deny oneself in order to meditate upon the sufferings of Christ.
• Palm Sunday.
• Holy Thursday, Good Friday, Holy Saturday.
• Easter Sunday.
• May Day, May 1: Not a holy day, but celebrated throughout much of Christendom as a time of renewal.
• Ascension Day: 40 days after Easter, usually early to mid-May. Celebrates the ascension of Christ into heaven.
• Pentecost: 50 days after Easter, usually late May or early June. Celebrates the coming of the Holy Spirit.

- Midsummer's Day: Not a holy day, but rather a celebration of the summer solstice, June 21.
- Lammas, August 1: beginning of harvest.
- Assumption of the Virgin, August 15: celebrates Mary's assumption into heaven.
- St. Michael's Day (Michaelmas), September 25: celebrates the archangel.
- All Hallows' Eve, October 31: a vigil that anticipates All Saints' Day.
- All Saints' Day, (Hallowmas), November 1: the honoring of all saints, known and unknown.
- All Souls' Day, November 2: commemoration of all the faithful now departed.
- Martinmas: November 12: Celebrates St. Martin of Tours who spared a freezing beggar by sharing his cloak.
- Season of Advent: begins 4th Sunday before Christmas and lasts through December 24. It is the anticipation of the birth of Christ.
- The Twelve Days of Christmas: Christmas Day to the Epiphany.
- Christmas Day: December 25.
- St. Stephen's Day, December 26: to honor the martyr.
- St. John the Evangelist's Day, December 27: to honor the disciple.

Miscellaneous Terms:

abbess: female superior of a nunnery.

abbey: an autonomous monastery ruled by an abbot.

abbot: the title given to the superior of an autonomous monks' community.

alles klar: German for "all is well."

almoner: official appointed to distribute alms to the poor.

avanti: Italian for "keep moving."

Ave Maria: Latin referring to a prayer to Mary.

arpent: unit of land roughly equivalent to an acre.

assart: the clearing of woodland.

bailey: inner courtyard of castle.

bailiff: chief officer of a manor, typically supervising general administration and law enforcement.

balk: an unploughed strip of land serving as a boundary.

bambini: Italian for "children."

benefice: a grant of land or other wealth.

bienvenues: French for "welcome."

bitte: German for "please; you're welcome."

bloody flux: dysentery.

bon: French for "good."

bowshot: unit of measurement equivalent to approximately 150 yards.

Bube: German for little boy.

castellan: governor of a castle.

cellarer: monk charged with providing food stocks for the kitchener.

cerebritis: inflammation of the brain.

chain mail: body armor made of small, interlocking steel rings.

chalice: the cup holding the wine of the Eucharist.

chapter: the daily convening of a religious order for purposes of discipline and administration.

chapter house: the building attached to a monastery facilitating the chapter.

chin cough: whooping cough.

cives: Latin referring to the aristocracy.

cloister: a place of religious seclusion. Also a protected courtyard within a monastery.

commotion: concussion.

confiteor: the formal expression of repentence.

congestive chill: accumulation of blood in the vessels.

corruption: infection.

cottager: a bound person of the poorest station.

crenels: the gaps in the parapets atop a castle's ramparts.

croft: small yard adjacent to a peasant's cottage, normally used to grow vegetables.

demesne: the land of a manor managed exclusively for the lord.

dowry: originally a gift of property granted by a man to his bride as security for her old age or widowhood.

ell: a unit of measurement equivalent to four feet.

flail: a hinged stick used for threshing wheat. Also a weapon consisting of a long rod with a swinging appendage on a hinge.

forester: manorial officer managing the lord's woodland, usually under the supervision of the woodward.

frater: Latin for "brother."

Frau: German for "wife, Mrs., or woman."

furlong: a unit of measurement equivalent to 220 yards.

glaive: a weapon with a blade attached to a shaft.

glebe: a parcel of land owned by the Church for the benefit of a parish.

Gloria Dei: Latin for "praise God."

gratia: Latin for "grace."

grippe: influenza.

halberd: a lance-like weapon.

hauberk: a heavy, sometimes quilted, protective garment usually made of leather.

Hausfrau: German for "housewife."

hayward: official charged with supervising the management of the fields.

hectare: a unit of land measurement roughly equivalent to 2 1/2 acres.

herbarium: the building in a monastery where herbs were stored.

heriot: death tax.

Herr: German for "husband, Mr., or man."

hide: a unit of land equaling about 120 acres.

hogshead: a unit of volume equivalent to 2 barrels.

holding: typically, heritable land granted to a vassal.

Holy See: the seat of papal authority.

ich bin: German for "I am."

ja: German for "yes."

Junge: German for "boy."

Kind/Kinder: German for "child/children."

king's evil: swelling of neck glands.

kitchener: the monastery's food overseer.

In nomine Patris, et Filii, et Spiritus Sancti: Latin for: "in the name of the Father, the Son, and the Holy Spirit."

lago: Italian for "lake."

league: unit of measurement equivalent to 3 miles.

list: area of castle grounds located beyond the walls.

Mädel/Mädchen: German for "maiden/young girl."

manor: the land of a lord consisting of his desmesne and tenant's holdings.

manumission: fee required to buy freedom from the lord. Also, act by which freedom is granted.

mark: a unit of weight or money equaling roughly 8 ounces of silver.

matrona: Italian for "mother; woman."

mead: a fermented beverage made from honey and water.

mein Gott/mein Gott in Himmel: German for "my God/my God in heaven."

merchet: a tax paid for the privilege of marriage.

merlon: the solid segments in the gapped parapets atop a castle's ramparts.

milites: Latin referring to the military class.

milk leg: inflammation of the leg.

monastery: a religious house organized under the authority of the Holy See.

morbus: disease.

mormal: gangrene.

mortal sin: according to the Roman Church, a sin so heinous as to rupture the state of grace between a Christian and God.

Mus: German for "mush," a dish of boiled grains.

Mutti: German for "mommy, mama."

novice: a new member of a religious community undergoing an apprenticeship of sorts and not yet fully committed by vows.

nunnery: a religious house for nuns; a convent.

oath-helper: a person who pledges their word in support of an accused.

oblate : a child given to a monastery for upbringing.

ordeal: a method of trial by which the accused was given a physical test to determine guilt.

Ordnung: German for "order."

paten: the dish on which the bread of the Eucharist is placed.

pater: Latin for "father."

Pater Noster: Latin referring to the Lord's Prayer.

Pfennig: German for "penny."

plenary indulgence: according to the Roman Church, the remitting of temporal punishment due for sins already forgiven by God.

portcullis: iron grate dropped along vertical grooves to defend a gate.

pound: an accounting measurement of money equaling 20 shillings, or 240 pennies—a pound of silver.

postulant: a candidate for membership in a religious order.

pottage: a brothy soup, usually of vegetables and grains.

prior: the official ranked just below an abbot. Sometimes the superior of a community under the jurisdiction of a distant abbey.

putrid fever: diphtheria.

pyx: the box in which the Eucharist is kept.

quinsey: tonsillitis.

reeve: village chief, usually elected by village elders.

refectory: the dining hall of a monastery.

rod: a measurement equivalent to 6 feet.

routier: mercenary.

scapular: a long smock worn over the front and back of a monk's habit.

scriptorium: the building in a monastery where books were maintained and copied.

scrofulous: skin disease.

scutage: a tax paid by a freeman in lieu of military service obligations to his lord.

See: the seat of ecclesiastical authority, i.e. bishop.

serf: a bound person of little means.

shilling: an accounting measurement of money valued at 12 pennies.

signora: Italian for "lady, Mrs."

signore: Italian for "gentleman, Mr."

Spiritus Sanctus: Latin for "Holy Spirit."

Stube: German for "parlor."

St. Anthony's Fire: skin infection.

St. Vitus's Dance: nervous twitches.

steward: chief overseer of a manor, typically including legal and financial matters.

tithing: a unit of ten persons.

tonsure: the shaving of the crown of the head to signify Christ's crown of thorns received as part of religious vows.

trebuchet: a catapult.

trencher: flat board used as a plate.

tunic: garment worn as an overshirt, typically hooded, sleeved, and belted outside the leggings.

vassal: a freeman who held land from a lord in exchange for his oath of fealty, usually obligated to perform military service.

Vati/Vater: German for "daddy/father."

vattene: Italian for "hurry along, leave."

vellein: a bound person of some means owing labor to his lord and subject to certain taxes.

venial sin: according to the Roman Church, a sin that interferes with a Christian's fellowship with God, though not serious enough to violate the state of grace.

vielen dank: German for "many thanks."

virgate: One-fourth of a hide. Considered the minimum amount of land necessary to support one peasant family for one year.

Volk: German for "people."

wattle-and-daub: construction material consisting of woven sticks and clay.

whitlow: boils.

winter fever: pneumonia.

wunderbar: German for "wonderful."

woodward: manorial overseer of the lord's woodland.

yeoman: a free farmer of modest means.

The Word at Work Around the World

A vital part of Cook Communications Ministries is our international outreach, Cook Communications Ministries International (CCMI). Your purchase of this book, and of other books and Christian-growth products from Cook, enables CCMI to provide Bibles and Christian literature to people in more than 150 languages in 65 countries.

Cook Communications Ministries is a not-for-profit, self-supporting organization. Revenues from sales of our books, Bible curricula, and other church and home products not only fund our U.S. ministry, but also fund our CCMI ministry around the world. One hundred percent of donations to CCMI go to our international literature programs.

CCMI reaches out internationally in three ways:

· Our premier International Christian Publishing Institute (ICPI) trains leaders from nationally led publishing houses around the world.

· We provide literature for pastors, evangelists, and Christian workers in their national language.

· We reach people at risk—refugees, AIDS victims, street children, and famine victims—with God's Word.

Word Power, God's Power

Faith Kidz, RiverOak, Honor, Life Journey, Victor, NexGen — every time you purchase a book produced by Cook Communications Ministries, you not only meet a vital personal need in your life or in the life of someone you love, but you're also a part of ministering to José in Colombia, Humberto in Chile, Gousa in India, or Lidiane in Brazil. You help make it possible for a pastor in China, a child in Peru, or a mother in West Africa to enjoy a life-changing book. And because you helped, children and adults around the world are learning God's Word and walking in his ways.

Thank you for your partnership in helping to disciple the world. May God bless you with the power of his Word in your life.

For more information about our international ministries, visit www.ccmi.org.

Additional copies of *QUEST OF HOPE*
and other RiverOak titles are available
from your local bookseller.

How it began:
CRUSADE OF TEARS

If you have enjoyed this book,
or if it has had an impact on your life,
we would like to hear from you.

Please contact us at:

RIVEROAK BOOKS
Cook Communications Ministries, Dept. 201
4050 Lee Vance View
Colorado Springs, CO 80918
Or visit our Web site: www.cookministries.com

RIVEROAK®
Good News in Fiction